Tell me how long the train's been gone

by James Baldwin

A DELL BOOK

ACKNOWLEDGMENTS

"*In the prison of his days* . . ." by W. H. Auden: Reprinted from *The Collected Poetry of W. H. Auden.* © Copyright 1966 by W. H. Auden and used by permission of Random House, Inc.

"*Ain't misbehavin'* " by Andy Rezaf, Fats Waller & Harry Brooks: © Copyright 1929 by Mills Music, Inc. © renewed 1957. Used by permission.

"*Mad About Him, Sad About Him, How Can I Be Glad Without Him Blues*" by Dick Charles and Larry Markes: © Copyright 1941. 1945 by MCA Music, a division of MCA, Inc. All rights reserved. Reprinted by permission.

Waiting for Lefty by Clifford Odets: All rights reserved. Copyright © 1935 by Clifford Odets. Copyright renewed 1963 by Clifford Odets. Reprinted by the permission of the Estate of Clifford Odets.

"*Stormy Weather*": © Copyright 1933 by Mills Music, Inc. © Copyright renewed and assigned to Arko Music Corporation, 31 West 54th Street, New York, N.Y. Used by permission.

"*Dark As a Dungeon*" by Merle Travis: Copyright © 1947 and 1961 by American Music, Inc., Elvis Presley Music, Inc. and Noma Music, Inc. Used by permission.

"*River, Stay 'Way From My Door*" by Mort Dixon and Harry Woods: Copyright 1931 by Shapiro, Bernstein & Co., Inc., N.Y. Copyright renewed. Used by permission.

Never seen the like since I been born,
The people keep a-coming,
    and the train's done gone.

—TRADITIONAL

Tell me
how long
the train's
been gone

BOOK ONE:

The House Nigger

In the prison of his days,
Teach the free man how to praise.
— W. H. AUDEN

THE HEART ATTACK was strange—fear is strange. I knew I had been working too hard. I had been warned. But I have always worked too hard. I came offstage at the end of the second act. I felt hot and I was having trouble catching my breath. But I knew that I was tired. I went to my dressing room and poured myself a drink and put my feet up. Then I felt better. I knew I had about twenty-five minutes before I was due onstage. I felt very bitterly nauseous and I went to the bathroom but nothing happened. Then I began to be afraid, rather, to sit or lie down again and I poured myself another drink and left my dressing room to stand in the wings. I had begun to sweat and I was freezing cold. The nausea came back, making me feel that my belly was about to rise to the roof of my head. The stage manager looked at me just as I heard my cue. I carried his face onstage with me. It had looked white and horrified and disembodied in the eerie backstage light. I wondered what had frightened him. Then I realized that I was having trouble finding my positions and having trouble hearing lines. Barbara delivered her lines. I knew the lines, I knew what she was saying, but I did not know how to relate to it, and it took an eternity before I could reply. Then I began to be frightened and this, of course, created and compounded the nightmare, made me realize that I was in the middle of a nightmare. I moved about that stage, I don't know how, dragging my lines up from the crypt of memory, praying that my moves were right—for I had lost any sense of depth or distance—feeling that I was sinking deeper and deeper into some icy void. "Shall we ring down the curtain?" Barbara whispered, and "No!" I shouted or whispered back. At one point in the scene I was called upon to laugh and when I laughed I began to cough. I was afraid the cough would never stop, some horrible-tasting stuff came up, which I was forced to swallow, and then, suddenly, everything passed, everything became as clear and still and luminous as day. I got through a few more lines, and I thought, *Hell, it's over, I'm all right,* and then something hit me in the chest, tore through my chest to my backbone and almost knocked me down. I couldn't catch my breath to deliver my lines. They covered for me. I knew we were approaching the end of the act. I prayed that I could stand up that long. I made a few more moves, I delivered a few more lines. I heard the penultimate line, Barbara's, "So you've come home to stay?" and I answered, "I think, dear lady—but I do not wish to grieve you—that I may have come home to die." The line seemed terribly funny to me at that moment. The curtain came down. I heard the crash of applause, like the roar of a cataract far away, and for the first time I heard the sound of my own breathing, it was louder than the cataract. I took a step and fell to my knees, then I was on the floor, then I was being carried, then I was in my dressing room. I was trying to speak, but I couldn't speak. It was Barbara's face above me that told me how ill I was. Her brown hair fell over her face, half hiding it, and her storm-colored eyes stared into mine with the intention of communicating something which I had to know, but did not know. "Be still," she said, "don't move. Don't speak."

But I wanted to ask her to forgive me for so many errors, so many fears. She took my hand. "Be still," she said, "be still." And this hand held on to me. All my weight, the weight which scales measure, and the weight no scale can measure, seemed pulling downward against that hand. I seemed to be hanging in the middle of the hostile air, ready for the mortal fall, with only the frail white hand of a frail white woman holding me up. It seemed very funny. I wanted to laugh. Perhaps I did laugh, I don't know, everything hurt so much. Barbara's face did not change, her grip never relaxed. My eyes did not leave her face, which now seemed suspended in the middle of the light which filled my dressing room, which fell down on me from everywhere. Behind her face were other faces, shapes, sounds, movements, but they had nothing to do with me. I saw the face of Pete, my dresser, dark, vaguely Oriental, staring at me with the same concentration I have known him to exhibit when watching

a light cue being changed or a move being modified. It
was a look which asked, *If they go about solving the problem this way, how many more problems will they have
created?* I like Pete very much, he's a very good man,
we've worked together for years and I wanted to tell him
not to worry. But, still, his face seemed very funny.
Oddly enough—or maybe it isn't odd at all, I don't know
—I wasn't frightened; or perhaps I simply didn't know
that I was frightened. I thought, *My God, this is no way
to play a death scene, the audience would never be able
to see me.* Then I decided that it was a death scene being
played not onstage but on camera and pretended that the
camera was placed in the ceiling, just above my head—a
huge, long close-up, with lights, and, eventually, music,
to heighten my ineffable, dying speech. But I could think
of nothing to say, though I turned to Barbara with my
mouth wide open. The pressure of her hand increased
very slightly. I felt tears roll out of my eyes and into my
ears and onto my neck. I heard my breathing again,
scratchy and loud, as though each attempt at breathing
were creating a sandstorm. There was a movement far
from me, a movement all around me, all the faces except
Barbara's disappeared, and a strange face, utterly isolated
in the light, stood above me. It was a broad face, with
brown hair and blue eyes, a big, aggressive nose, and
fleshy lips. I recognized him immediately as the doctor.
He reminded me—or, rather, his nose reminded me—of
a Harlem barber who had sometimes cut my hair when I
was a kid; this barber had had the biggest hands, the
biggest fingers I had ever seen. One of his fingers, or each
one of them, seemed bigger to me than my penis. I was
only beginning to be terrified of this imperious bit of
flesh, which was only at the beginning of its long career of
blackmail.

The doctor said that I could not be moved; he in-
structed them to put my feet up on pillows; he wanted
the room emptied. All this I heard, or, rather, divined—
from far away. Everyone left but Barbara. She stood just
behind the doctor. She had let go my hand and now the
doctor took it, loosened my belt, looked at me as though
to say, *It's pretty bad, but don't worry.* I couldn't speak,
but the ham in me wanted to prove that I was no crybaby,
that I was not afraid, and so I smiled. I watched him

prepare the needle; then I sought Barbara's face. She was standing very straight and still, far from me; I realized that she had neither removed her makeup, nor changed into street clothes; I wanted to reprimand her for that. My eye returned to the needle. I knew that there was no point in asking what was in it. I thought of Harlem and all the needles I had seen there. "Make a fist," said the doctor, as who should say, *Come on, now, be a man.* I thought of all the boys I had seen making fists. I made a fist. He swabbed my arm and plunged the needle in. The needle remained in my arm for a long time. Abruptly, he pulled it out, put cotton on the vein, and forced my fist up against my chest. "There, now," he said, "don't move." He said to Barbara, "He must not move for at least half an hour. Then we will see." He had a foreign accent. "I will call my hospital. Can you stay with him?" Barbara nodded. "Remember," said the doctor, "don't let him move. He must not move at all." Barbara nodded again. She sat down and took my hand, the hand against my chest, again. The doctor went out.

Now, for the first time, I began to be aware of my heart, the heart itself: and with this awareness, conscious terror came. I realized that I knew nothing whatever about the way we are put together; and I realized that what I did not know might be in the process of killing me. My heart—*if* it was my heart—seemed to be rising and sinking within me; seemed like a swimmer betrayed by an element in which, by an unanswerable tide, it was being carried far out, by an unanswerable pull, being carried far down; and yet struggled, struggled upward, yet one more time. But the sea is stronger than the swimmer. How many more times could I hope to hear it labor up again?—that labor which caused such a roaring in my breath. And how many more times could it fall far from me, far beneath me, so that I breathed harder than ever, and in an awful panic, to coax it up again? The sound of my breathing was the only sound there was. My own panic, at once stifling like a cloak, and distant like the wind, made me realize how frightened Barbara was, and how gallant. I would not have liked to change places with her. We had known each other for many years; starved together, worked together, loved each other, suffered each other, made love; and yet the most tremendous consummation of our love was occurring now, as she patiently, in love and terror, held my hand. I wondered what she was thinking. But I think she was not thinking, not at all. She was concentrated. She was determined not to let me die.

"Barbara—"

"Be quiet, Leo. There'll be time for talking later. Don't try to talk now."

"I have something to say."

"Later, my dear. Later."

I went down again. My heart and I went down again. I was aware of her hand. I was aware of my breathing. I could no longer see it, but I was aware of her face.

"Barbara. My dear Barbara."

"My dearest Leo. Please be still."

And she's right, I thought. There is nothing more to be said. All we can do now is just hold on. That was why she held my hand. I recognized this as love—recognized it very quietly and, for the first time, without fear. My life, that desperately treacherous labyrinth, seemed for a moment to be opening out behind me; a light seemed to fall where there had been no light before. I began to see myself in others. I began for a moment to apprehend how Christopher must sometimes have felt. Everyone wishes to be loved, but, in the event, nearly no one can bear it. Everyone desires love but also finds it impossible to believe that he deserves it. However great the private disasters to which love may lead, love itself is strikingly and mysteriously impersonal; it is a reality which is not altered by anything one does. Therefore, one does many things, turns the key in the lock over and over again, hoping to be locked out. Once locked out, one will never again be forced to encounter in the eyes of a stranger who loves him the impenetrable truth concerning the stranger, oneself, who is loved. And yet—one would prefer, after all, not to be locked out. One would prefer, merely, that the key unlocked a less stunningly unusual door.

The door to my maturity. This phrase floated to the top of my mind. The light that fell backward on that life of mine revealed a very frightened man—a very frightened boy. The light did not fall on me, on me where I lay now. I was left in darkness, my face could not be seen. In that darkness I encountered a scene from another nightmare, a nightmare I had had as a child. In this nightmare there is a book—a great, heavy book with an illustrated cover. The cover shows a dark, squalid alley, all garbage cans and dying cats, and windows like empty eyesockets. The beam of a flashlight shines down the alley, at the end of which I am fleeing, clutching something. The title of the book in my nightmare is, *We Must Not Find Him, For He Is Lost.*

When Caleb, my older brother, was taken from me and sent to prison, I watched, from the fire escape of our East Harlem tenement, the walls of an old and massive building, far, far away and set on a hill, and with green vines running up and down the walls, and with windows flashing like signals in the sunlight, I watched that building, I say, with a child's helpless and stricken attention, waiting for my brother to come out of there. I did not know how to get to the building. If I had I would have slept in the shadow of those walls, and I told no one of my vigil or of my certain knowledge that my brother was imprisoned in that place. I watched that building for many years. Sometimes, when the sunlight flashed on the windows, I was certain that my brother was signaling to me and I waved back. When we moved from that particular tenement (into another one) I screamed and cried because I was certain that now my brother would no longer be able to find me. Alas, he was not there; the building turned out to be City College; my brother was on a prison farm in the Deep South, working in the fields.

I felt my hand being released. The doctor was back. He tapped, pushed, prodded, a complex hunk of meat. He flashed a light into my eyeballs, a light into my throat, a light into my nostrils. I hoped that they were clean. I remembered my mother's insistence that I always wear clean underwear because I might get knocked down by a car on the way to or from school and I and the family would be disgraced even beyond the grave, presumably, if my underwear was dirty. And I began to worry, in fact, as the doctor sniffed and prodded, about the state of the shorts I was wearing. This made me want to laugh. But I could not breathe.

I must have blacked out for a moment. When the light came on again the doctor had one hand under my back, holding me up, and held a small glass of brandy to my lips.

"Drink it," he said. "Slowly."

He held the glass for me and I tried to get it down. Two men in white were in the room, looking like executioners, and beyond them, Pete, and next to Pete, Barbara. The men in white frightened me terribly. The doctor realized this.

"Slowly," he repeated. "Slowly." Then, "We are taking you to the hospital, where you can rest. You need rest very badly."

In panic I looked around the dressing room, my only home. I was still in costume, my street clothes were hanging against the wall. I had not showered, I had not removed my makeup, I had not got my own face back. The face I was wearing itched and burned, I wanted to take it off. My hair was still full of the cream I used to make it gray. I wanted to cry and I looked for help to Pete and Barbara, but they were dumb. What ruin, what relic, were these men in white ripping from its base, and how could Pete and Barbara bear to see me so heartlessly demolished? I looked at the lights above the long mirror, the tubes, the jars, the sticks, the Kleenex, the empty glasses, the whiskey bottle, the ashtray, the half-empty package of cigarettes. No one would recognize me where I was going! I would be lost. "Oh, Pete," I muttered, I moaned, and I could not keep the tears from falling. "Please wash my face."

Without a word, Pete moved to the long dressing table and picked up the Kleenex and cold cream and came to where I lay. He covered my face with cream, he carefully wiped away the lines and distortions which I had so carefully painted in three or four hours before. "Hold still, now," he said. He threw the dirty Kleenex into the wastebasket, he carefully replaced the box of Kleenex and the jar of cold cream on the long table, he went into the bathroom and returned with a wet face-towel and a dry towel. He ran the wet face-towel and then the dry towel over my face and hair. He said, "That's the best I can do right now, old buddy." He took both my hands and stared into my eyes. "You ready now?"

"Yes," I said. "Thank you."

He smiled. "Anytime. I'll be proud to wash your face

any old time." He held my shoulder a moment. "Don't panic. You'll be all right. But we've got to get you out of here, so the man can lock up his theater."

He stood up. The two men in white brought the stretcher next to the bed. Pete, probably in order to remain where I could see him, held me from the waist down, the doctor from the waist up, and they moved me to the stretcher. I was covered with a blanket. The pain in my chest increased. I almost cried out. We began to move. I kept sinking down and rising up, blacking out and coming back. I felt the cold air. For a moment, I saw the stars. Then I felt myself being lifted into a dark place. Then I saw nothing but Barbara's face and the doctor's face. I heard the siren and felt lights flashing, felt the wheels beneath me begin to turn, realized that we were descending a steep hill at a dangerous speed, felt the ambulance braking, felt the turn—and Barbara caught my hand and held it—and knew that we were rushing through the streets of San Francisco because no one could be certain that the life of Leo Proudhammer, actor, might not now be measured by the second-hand on the clock.

And something strange happened to me, deep in me. I thought of Africa. I remembered that Africans believed that death was a return to one's ancestors, a reunion with those one loved. They had hurled themselves off slave ships, grateful to the enveloping water and even grateful to the teeth of sharks for making the journey home so swift. And I thought of a very great and very beautiful man whom I had known and loved, a black man shot down within hearing of his wife and children in the streets of a miserable Deep South town. There are deaths and deaths: there are deaths for which it is impossible and even ignoble to forgive the world, there are deaths to which one never becomes reconciled. But, now, for a moment, I was reconciled, for I thought, *Well, I'll see him. And we'll sit around and bullshit about everything and get drunk, like we planned*. And this thought made me fantastically, inexpressibly happy. I saw my friend's face and felt his smile and heard his voice. Then I thought, *But I won't see Caleb*, and all my pain came back, my chest felt as though all the weight of the pyramids lay on it, and the sound of my breathing roared and resounded through the narrow car.

Caleb was seventeen when I was ten. In that year he

went to prison. We were very good friends. In fact, he was my best friend and for a very long time, my only friend.

I do not mean to say that he was always nice to me. I got on his nerves a lot and he resented having to carry me around with him and being responsible for me when there were so many other things he wanted to be doing. Therefore, his hand was often up against the side of my head, and my tears caused him to be punished many times. But I knew, somehow, anyway, that when he was being punished for my tears he was not being punished for anything he had done to me; he was being punished because that was the way we lived; and his punishment, oddly, helped to unite us. More oddly still, even as his great hand caused my head to stammer and dropped a flame-colored curtain before my eyes, I understood that he was not striking *me*. His hand leaped out because he could not help it and I received the blow because I was there. And it happened, sometimes, before I could even catch my breath to howl, that the hand which had struck me grabbed me and and held me, and it was difficult indeed to know which of us was weeping. He was striking, striking out, striking out, striking out; the hand asked me to forgive him. I felt his bewilderment through the membrane of my own. I also felt that he was trying to teach me something. And I had, God knows, no other teachers.

For our father—how shall I describe our father?—was a ruined Barbados peasant, exiled in a Harlem which he loathed, where he never saw the sun or the sky he remembered, where life took place neither indoors nor without, and where there was no joy. By which I mean, no joy that he remembered. Had it been otherwise, had he been able to bring with him into the prison where he perished any of the joy he had felt on that far-off island, then the air of the sea and the impulse to dancing would sometimes have transfigured our dreadful rooms. Our lives might have been very different. But, no, he brought with him from Barbados only black rum and a blacker pride, and magic incantations which neither healed nor saved. He did not understand the people among whom he found himself, for him they had no coherence, no stature and no pride. He came from a race which had been flourishing at the very dawn of the world—a race greater and nobler than Rome or Judea, mightier than Egypt—he came from a race of kings, kings who had never been taken in battle, kings who had never been slaves. He spoke to us of tribes and empires, battles, victories, and monarchs of whom we had never heard—they were not mentioned in our schoolbooks—and invested us with glories in which we felt more awkward than in the secondhand shoes we wore. In the stifling room of his pretensions and expectations, we stumbled wretchedly about, stubbing our toes, as it were, on rubies, scraping our shins on golden caskets, bringing down, with a childish cry, the splendid purple tapestry on which, in pounding gold and scarlet, our destinies and our inheritance were figured. It could scarcely have been otherwise, since a child's major attention has to be concentrated on how to fit into a world which, with every passing hour, reveals itself as merciless. If our father was of royal blood and we were royal children, our father was certainly the only person in the world who knew it. The landlord did not know it and we observed that our father never mentioned royal blood to *him*. Not at all. When we were late with our rent, which was often, the landlord threatened, in terms no commoner had ever used before a king, to put us in the streets. He complained that our shiftlessness, which he did not hesitate to consider an attribute of the race, had forced him, himself, an old man with a weak heart, to climb all these stairs to plead with us to give him the money that we owed him. And this was the last time— he wanted to make sure that we understood that this was the last time. The next time our ass would be on the sidewalk. Our father was younger than Mr. Rabinowitz, leaner, stronger, and bigger. With one blow into that monstrous gut, he could have turned Rabinowitz purple, brought him to his knees, he could have hurled him down the stairs. And we knew how much he hated Rabinowitz. For days on end, in the wintertime, we huddled around the gas stove in the kitchen because Rabinowitz gave us no heat; and when the gas was turned off, we sat around the kerosene stove. When windows were broken, Rabinowitz took his time about fixing them; the wind made the cardboard we stuffed in the window rattle all night long, and when snow came the weight of the snow forced the cardboard inward and onto the floor. Neither

Rabinowitz nor the city was alert about collecting garbage or shoveling away snow; whenever the apartment received a fresh coat of paint, we bought the paint and painted the apartment ourselves; we caught and killed the rats; a great chunk of the kitchen ceiling fell one winter, narrowly missing our mother. We all hated Rabinowitz with a perfectly exquisite hatred; great, gross, abject liar of a Jew—and this word in our father's mouth was terrible, as dripping with venom as a mango is with juice—and we would have been happy to see our proud father kill him. We would have been glad to help. But our father did nothing of the sort. He stood before Rabinowitz, scarcely looking at him, swaying before the spittle and the tirade, sweating—looking unutterably weary. He made excuses. He apologized. He swore that it would never happen again. (We knew that it *would* happen again.) He begged for time. Rabinowitz would finally go down the steps, letting us, and all the neighbors, know how good-hearted he was being, and our father would walk into the kitchen and pour himself a glass of rum. But we knew that our father would never have allowed any black man to speak to him as Rabinowitz did, as policemen did, as storekeepers and pawnbrokers and welfare workers did. No, not for a moment—he would have thrown them out of the house; he would certainly have made a black man know that he was not the descendant of slaves! He had made them know it so often that he had almost no friends among them, and if we had followed his impossible lead, we would have had no friends, either. It was scarcely worthwhile being the descendant of kings if the kings were black and no one had ever heard of them, and especially, furthermore, if royal status could not fill the empty stomach and could not prevent Rabinowitz from putting, as he eventually did, our collective ass, and all our belongings, on the city streets. It was then, and I don't remember how, that we moved into the tenement from which Caleb was arrested.

And it was because of our father, perhaps, that Caleb and I clung to each other, in spite of the great difference in our ages; or, in another way, it may have been precisely the difference in our ages which made the clinging possible. I don't know. It is really not the kind of thing which anyone can ever know. I think it may be easier to love the really helpless younger brother because he cannot enter into competition with one on one's own ground, or on any ground at all, and can never question one's role, or jeopardize one's authority. In my own case, certainly, it did not occur to me—or did not occur to me until much later—to compete with Caleb and I could not have questioned his role or his authority because I needed both. He was my touchstone, my model, and my only guide. But there is always, on the other hand, something in the younger brother which eventually comes to resent this. The day comes when he is willing to destroy his older brother simply because he has depended on him so long. The day comes when he recognizes what a combination of helplessness and hard-hearted calculation go into the creation of a role, and to what extent authority is a delicate, difficult, deadly game of chance.

Anyway, our father, dreaming bitterly of Barbados, betrayed by Garvey, who did not succeed in getting us back to Africa, despised and mocked by his neighbors and all but ignored by his sons, held down his unspeakable factory job, spread his black gospel in bars on the weekends, and drank his rum. I do not know if he loved our mother. I think he did. They had had five children—only Caleb and I, the first and the last, were left. We were both dark, like our father, but two of the three dead girls had been fair, like our mother. She came from New Orleans. Her hair was not like ours. It was black, but softer and finer and very long. The color of her skin reminded me of the color of bananas. Her skin was as bright as that, and contained that kind of promise and she had tiny freckles around her nose and a small black mole just above her upper lip. It was the mole, I don't know why, which made her beautiful. Without it, her face might have been merely sweet, merely pretty. But the mole was funny. It had the effect of making one realize that our mother liked funny things, liked to laugh. The mole made one look at her eyes —large, extraordinary, dark eyes, eyes which seemed always to be amused by something, eyes which looked straight out, seeming to see everything, seeming to be afraid of nothing. She was a soft, round, plump woman. She liked nice clothes and dangling jewelry, which she mostly didn't have, and she liked to cook for large numbers of people, and she loved our father. She knew him—knew

him through and through. I am not being coy or colloquial,
but bluntly and sadly matter of fact when I say that I will
now never know what she saw in him. What she saw was
certainly not for many eyes; what she saw got him through
his working week and his Sunday rest; what she saw saved
him. She saw that he was a man. For her, perhaps, he was
a great man. I think, though, that, for our mother, any
man was great who aspired to become a man: this meant
that our father was very rare and precious. I used to
wonder how she took it, how she bore it—his rages, his
tears, his cowardice. On Saturday nights he was almost
always evil, drunk, and maudlin. He would have come
home from work in the early afternoon and given our
mother some money. It was never enough—of course;
but he always kept enough to go out and get drunk; she
never protested, at least not as far as I know. Then she
would go out shopping. I would usually go with her, for
Caleb would almost always be out somewhere and our
mother didn't like the idea of leaving me alone in the
house. She was afraid the house would burn down while
she was out—fires were common enough in our neighborhood, God knows. So, while our father stood sternly
and gloomily in a bar not far away, getting drunk on
rum, and Caleb and his friends were in somebody's
cellar, getting drunk off cheap wine, we took on the
Harlem streets. And this was probably, after all, the best
possible arrangement. People who disliked our father
were sure (for that very reason) to like our mother; and
people who felt that Caleb was growing to be too much
like his father could feel that I, after all, might turn out
like my mother. Besides, it is not, as a general rule, easy
to hate a small child. One runs the risk of looking ridiculous, especially if the child is with his mother.

And especially if that mother is Mrs. Proudhammer.
Mrs. Proudhammer knew very well what people thought
of Mr. Proudhammer. She knew, too, exactly how much
she owed in each store she entered, how much she was
going to be able to pay, and what she had to buy. She
entered with a smile, ready—she attacked:

"Evening, Mr. Shapiro. Let me have some of them
red beans there."

"Evening. You know, you folks been running up quite
a little bill here."

"I'm going to give you something on it right now. I need some cornmeal and flour and some rice."

"You know, I got my bills to meet, too, Mrs. Proudhammer."

"Didn't I just tell you I was going to pay? I don't know why you don't listen, you must be getting old. I want some cornflakes, too, and some milk."

Such merchandise as she could reach she had already placed on the counter. Sad Mr. Shapiro looked at me and sighed.

"When do you think you're going to be able to pay this bill? All of it, I mean."

"Mr. Shapiro, you been knowing me for years. You know I'm going to pay it just as soon as I can. It won't be long. I ain't going to move."

Sometimes, when she said this, she had the dispossess notice in her pocketbook. Mr. Shapiro looked into my face from time to time as though my face would reveal my mother's secrets. (But it never did.) Sometimes he looked at my mother as though he were wondering how such a handsome, almost white woman had got herself trapped in such a place.

"How much does it all come to? Give me that end you got there of that chocolate cake."

The chocolate cake was for Caleb and me.

"Well, now you put this against the bill." Imperiously, as though it were the most natural thing in the world, she put two or three dollars on the counter.

"You're lucky I'm soft-hearted, Mrs. Proudhammer."

"Things sure don't cost this much downtown—you think I don't know it? Here." And she paid him for what she had bought. "Thank you, Mr. Shapiro. You been mighty kind."

And we left the store. I often felt that in order to help her, I should have filled my pockets with merchandise while she was talking to the storekeeper. But I never did, not only because the store was often crowded or because I was afraid of being caught by the storekeeper but because I was afraid of humiliating her. When I began to steal, not very much later, I stole in stores which were not in our neighborhood, where we were not known.

Not all the storekeepers were as easy to get around as sad Mr. Shapiro. The butcher, for example, was a very different man, not sad at all, and he appeared to detest all children; still, our mother managed him most of the time, though with an effort considerably more acrid and explicit. But there were times when she did not feel up to it and then we would not even pass his store. We would cut off the avenue at 133rd Street and walk the long blocks west to Eighth Avenue and then walk down to the big butcher shop on 125th Street. Because this shop was so much bigger it could sometimes be a little bit cheaper and yet we did not break our necks to go there because most of the people who served you were so unpleasant. There was something intolerable about being robbed and insulted at the same time, and yet, I suppose, our mother reconciled herself, while stonily and silently making her purchases, by remembering that it was only, after all, a matter of degree.

When we had to do "heavy" shopping, we went shopping under the bridge at Park Avenue, Caleb, our mother, and I; and sometimes, but rarely, our father came with us. The most usual reason for heavy shopping was that some relatives of our mother's, or old friends of both our mother and our father were coming to visit. We were certainly not going to let them go away hungry—not even if it meant, as it often did mean, spending more than we had. Caleb and I loved to hear that visitors were coming, for it meant that there was going to be a banquet at our house. There were always visitors, of course, at Thanksgiving or Christmas, visitors bringing their hams and chickens and pies to add to ours; but people also showed up for birthdays and anniversaries or for no reason at all, simply because the spirit had so moved them. In spite of what I have been suggesting about our father's temperament, and no matter how difficult he may sometimes have been with us, he was much too proud to have any desire to offend any guest of his. On the contrary, his impulse was to make them feel that his home was theirs; and besides, he was lonely, lonely for his past, lonely for those faces which had borne witness to that past. Therefore, he would sometimes pretend that our mother did not know how to shop and he would come with us, under the bridge, in order to teach her. There he would be, then, uncharacteristically, in shirt-sleeves, which made him look rather boyish; and, as our mother showed no desire to take shopping lessons from him, he turned his attention to Caleb and me. "Look at that woman," he would say, pointing out a woman who was having something weighed, "can't she see that that Jew's hand is all over that scale? You see that?" We agreed that we had seen it, whether we had or not. He said bleakly, "You got to watch them all the time. But our people ain't never going to learn. I don't know what's wrong with our people. We need a prophet to straighten out our minds and lead us out of this hell." He would pick up a fish, opening the gills and holding it close to his nose. "You see that? That fish looks fresh, don't it? Well, that fish ain't as fresh as I am, and I *been* out of the water. They done doctored that fish. Come on." And we would walk away, leaving the fish-stand owner staring; a little embarrassed, but, on the whole, rather pleased that our father was so smart. Meantime, our mother was getting the marketing done. She was very happy on days like this because our father was happy. He was happy, odd as his expression of it may sound, to be out with his wife and his two sons. If we had been on the island which had been witness to his birth instead of the unspeakable island of Manhattan, he felt, and I also eventually began to feel, that it would not have been so hard for us all to trust and love each other. He sensed, and I think he was right, that on that other, never to be recovered island, his sons would have looked on him very differently and he would have looked very differently on his sons. Life would have been hard there, too—he knew that—which was why he had left and also why he felt so betrayed, so self-betrayed; we would have fought there, too, and more or less blindly suffered and more or less blindly died. But we would not have been (or so it was to seem to all of us forever) so wickedly menaced by the mere fact of our relationship, would not have been so frightened of entering into the central, most beautiful and valuable facts of our lives. We would have been laughing and cursing and tussling in the water instead of stammering under the bridge: we would have known less about vanished African kingdoms and more about each other. Or, not at all impossibly, more about both.

If it was summer, then, we bought a watermelon, which either Caleb or our father carried, fighting with each other for this privilege. And it was marvelous to see them fighting this way, the one accusing the other of being too old, and the ancient of days insisting that if his son carried a watermelon for another block that way all the girls in the neighborhood would live to regret it. "For the sake of the family name, man," he said, "so the family name won't die out, let me carry that melon, Caleb. You going to bust your string." "Little Leo'll see to it that we carry on," Caleb said, sometimes; sometimes he hinted broadly that he was carrying on the blood even if he wasn't yet in a position to carry on the name. This some-times led to a short footrace between them to the steps of our tenement. Our father usually won it, since Caleb was usually handicapped by the weight and the shape of the melon. They both looked very much like each other on those days—both big, both black, both laughing. Caleb always looked absolutely helpless when he laughed. He laughed with all his body, perhaps touching his shoulder against yours, or putting his head on your chest for a moment, and then careening off you, halfway across the room, or down the block. I will always hear his laughter. He was always happy on such days, too. If our father needed his son, Caleb certainly needed his father. Such days, however, were rare—one of the reasons, probably, that I remember them now. And our father's laugh was like Caleb's laugh, except that he stood still, and watched. Eventually, we all climbed the stairs into that hovel which, at such moments, was our castle. One very nearly felt the drawbridge rising behind us as our father locked the door.

The bathtub could not yet be filled with cold water and the melon placed in the tub because this was Saturday, and, come evening, we all had to bathe. The melon was covered with a blanket and placed on the fire escape. Then we unloaded what we had bought, rather impressed by our opulence, though our father was always, by this time, appalled by the money we had spent and the quality of what we had bought. I was always sadly aware that there would be nothing left of all this once tomorrow had come and gone and that most of it, after all, was not for us, but for others. How come we could do all this for others and not for ourselves? But I knew better than to give tongue to this question. Our mother was calculating the pennies she would need all week—carfare for our father and for

Caleb, who went to a high school out of our neighborhood, downtown; money for the life insurance, money for milk for me at school, money for cod-liver oil, money for light and gas, money put away—if possible—toward the rent. She knew just about what our father had left in *his* pockets and was counting on him to give me the money I would shortly be demanding to go to the movies. Caleb had a part-time job after school and already had his movie money. Anyway, unless he was in a very good mood, or needed me for something, he would not be anxious to go to the movies with me.

Our mother never insisted that Caleb tell her where he was going, nor did she question him as to how he spent what money he made. She was afraid of hearing him lie and she did not want to risk forcing him to lie. She was operating on the assumption that he was sensible and had been raised to be honorable and that he, now more than ever, needed his privacy. But she was very firm with him, nevertheless.

"I do not want to see you rolling in here at three in the morning, Caleb. I want you here in time to eat and you know you got to take your bath."

"Yes, indeed, ma'am. Why can't I take my bath in the morning?"

"Don't you start being funny. You know you ain't going to get up in time to take no bath in the morning."

"Don't nobody want you messing around in that bathroom all morning long, man," said our father. "You just get your butt back in the house like your mama's telling you."

"Besides," I said, "you never wash out the tub."

Caleb looked at me in mock surprise and from a great height, allowing his chin and his lids simultaneously to drop and swiveling his head away from me. "I see," he said, "that everyone in this family is ganging up on me. All right, Leo. I was planning to take you to the show with me, but now I've changed my mind."

This suggestion always had exactly the effect he desired. Our parents were relieved, not only because, as they supposed, I would now operate as a check on Caleb and not only because Caleb would be protection for me— this dulling the uneasy, incipient guilt they felt about my

being in the streets at all; they were above all relieved that
they might now, without worrying, be truly alone for a little
while, friendly and vertical, in the broad daylight. I was
repentant and overjoyed.

"I'm sorry," I said quickly, "I take it back."

"You take *what* back?"

"What I said—about you not washing out the tub."

"Ain't no need to take it back," our father said stubbornly, "it's true. A man don't take back nothing that's
true."

"So *you* say," said Caleb lightly, quickly, with a hint of
a sneer. But before anyone could possibly react to this, he
picked me up, scowling into my face, which he held just
above his own. "You take it back?"

"Leo ain't going to take it back," our father said.

Now I was in trouble. Caleb watched me, a small grin
on his face. "You take it back?"

"Stop teasing that child and put him down," said our
mother. "The trouble ain't that Caleb don't wash out the
tub—he just don't wash it out very *clean.*"

"I never knew him to wash it out," said our father,
"unless I was standing behind him."

"Well, ain't neither one of you much good around
the house," said our mother with finality, "and that's the
truth."

Caleb laughed and set me down. "You didn't take it
back," he said.

I said nothing.

"I guess I'm just going to have to go on without you."

Still, I said nothing.

"You going to have that child to crying in a minute,"
our mother said. "If you going to take him, go on and
take him. Don't do him like that."

Caleb laughed again. "I'm going to take him. The
way he got them eyes all ready to water, I'd better take
him somewhere." We walked toward the door. "But you
got to make up *your* mind," he said to me, "to say what
you think is right."

"What movie," asked our father, "you fixing to take
him to see?"

"I don't know," said Caleb. "We'll see what's playing
at the Lincoln."

"I don't want his mind all messed up—you know that."

"He ain't going to get his mind messed up—not by going to the movies."

"You don't know the Jew like I know him."

"Let them go on," said our mother, "so they can get back here in time for supper."

"It's the Jew makes them movies, man, in order to mess up our minds. That's why I don't never go to see them."

"You don't never go to see them," said our mother, "because you too lazy and too old. And can't nobody tear you away from that rum. Let these children go on—"

"You'll see," he said, grimly, "you're going to see one of these days just what I'm talking about. And you ain't going to like what you see at *all*."

"Hush," she said, "I ain't afraid of what I'm going to see. I know what I've seen already."

I grabbed Caleb's hand, the signal for the descent of the drawbridge. She watched us cheerfully as we walked out, he watched us balefully. Yet, there was a certain humor in his face, too, and a kind of pride. "Dig you later," Caleb said, and the door closed behind us.

The hall was dark, smelling of cooking, of boiling diapers, of men and boys pissing there late at night, of stale wine, of rotting garbage. The walls were full of an information which I could scarcely read and did not know how to use. We dropped down the stairs, Caleb going two at a time, pausing at each landing, briefly, to glance back up at me. I dropped down behind him as fast as I could. Sometimes Caleb was in a bad mood and then everything I did was wrong. But when Caleb was in a good mood, it didn't matter that everything I did was wrong. When I reached the street level, Caleb was already on the stoop, joking with some of his friends, who were standing in the doorway—who seemed always to be in the doorway, no matter what hour one passed through. I didn't like Caleb's friends because I was afraid of them. I knew the only reason they didn't try to make life hell for me the way they made life hell for a lot of the other kids was because they were afraid of Caleb. I came through the door, passing between my brother and his friends, down to the sidewalk, feeling, as they looked briefly at me and then continued joking with Caleb, what

they felt: that here was Caleb's round-eyed, frail and useless sissy of a little brother. They pitied Caleb for having
to take me out. On the other hand, they also wanted to go
to the show, but didn't have the money. Therefore, in
silence, I could crow over them even as they despised me.
But this was always a terribly risky, touch-and-go business,
for Caleb might always, at any moment, and with no
warning, change his mind and drive me away, and, effectively, take their side against me. I always stood, those
Saturday afternoons, in fear and trembling, holding on to
the small shield of my bravado, while waiting for Caleb
to come down the steps of the stoop, to come down the
steps, away from his friends, to me. I prepared myself, always, for the moment when he would turn to me, saying,
"Okay, kid. You run along. I'll see you later."

This meant that I would have to go to the movies by
myself and hang around in front of the box office, waiting
for some grown-up to take me in. I could not go back
upstairs, for this would be informing my mother and father
that Caleb had gone off somewhere—after promising to
take me to the movies. Neither could I simply hang around
the block, playing with the kids on the block. For one thing,
my demeanor, as I came out of the house, those Saturdays,
very clearly indicated that I had better things to do than
play with *them;* for another, they were not terribly anxious
to play with *me;* and, finally, my remaining on the block
would have had exactly the same effect as my going upstairs. Someone would surely inform my father and mother,
or they might simply look out of the window, or one of
them would come downstairs to buy something they had
forgotten while shopping, or my father would pass down
the block on his way to the bar. In short, to remain on the
block after Caleb's dismissal was to put myself at the mercy
of the block and to put Caleb at the mercy of our parents.

So I prepared myself, those Saturdays, to respond with
a cool, "Okay. See you later," and prepared myself then
to turn indifferently away, and walk. This was surely the
most terrible moment. The moment I turned away I was
committed, I was trapped, and I then had miles to walk, so
it seemed to me, before I would be out of sight, before the
block ended and I could turn onto the avenue. I wanted to
run out of that block, but I never did. I never looked back.
I forced myself to walk very slowly, looking neither right

nor left, trying to look neither up nor down—striving to seem at once distracted and offhand; concentrating on the cracks in the sidewalk, and stumbling over them, trying to whistle, feeling every muscle in my body, from my pigeon toes to my jiggling behind, to my burning neck; feeling that all the block was watching me, and feeling— which was odd—that I deserved it. And then I reached the avenue, and turned, still not looking back, and was released from those eyes at least, but now faced other eyes, eyes coming toward me. These eyes were the eyes of children stronger than me, who would steal my movie money; these eyes were the eyes of white cops, whom I feared, whom I hated with a literally murderous hatred; these eyes were the eyes of old folks who also thought I was a sissy and who might wonder what I was doing on this avenue by myself. And these eyes were the eyes of men and women going in and out of bars, or standing on the corners, who certainly had no eyes for me, but who occu- pied the center of my bewildered attention because they seemed, at once, so abject and so free.

And then I got to the show. Sometimes, someone would take me in right away and sometimes I would have to wait. I looked at the posters which seemed magical indeed to me in those days. I was very struck, not altogether agreeably, by the colors. The faces of the movie stars were in red, in green, in blue, in purple, not at all like the colors of real faces and yet they looked more real than real. Or, rather, they looked like faces far from me, faces which I would never be able to decipher, faces which could be seen but never changed or touched, faces which existed only behind these doors. I don't know what I thought. Some great assault, certainly, was being made on my imagination, on my sense of reality. Caleb could draw, he was teaching me to draw, and I wondered if he could teach me to draw faces like these. I looked at the stills from the show, seeing people in attitudes of danger, in attitudes of love, in at- titudes of sorrow and loss. They were not like any people I had ever seen and this made them, irrevocably, better. With one part of my mind, of course, I knew that here was James Cagney—holding his gun like a prize; and here was Clark Gable, all dimples, teeth, and eyes, the eyes filled with a smoky, taunting recollection of his invincible virility; here was Joan Crawford, gleaming with astonish-

ment, and here was proud, quivering Katharine Hepburn,
who could never be astonished, and here was poor, down-
trodden Sylvia Sidney, weeping in the clutches of yet another gangster. But only the faces and the attitudes were
real, more real than the lives we led, more real than our
days and nights, and the names were merely brand-names,
like Campbell's Baked Beans or Kellogg's Corn Flakes. We
went to see James Cagney because we had grown accustomed to that taste, we knew that we would like it.

But, then, I would have to turn my attention from
the faces and the stills and watch the faces coming to the
box office. And this was not easy, since I didn't, after all,
want everyone in the neighborhood to know that I was
loitering outside the moviehouse waiting for someone to
take me in, exactly like an orphan. If it came to our father's
attention, he would kill both Caleb and me. Eventually, I
would see a face which looked susceptible and which I did
not know. I would rush up beside him or her—but it was
usually a man, for they were less likely to be disapproving
—and whisper, "Take me in," and give him my dime.
Sometimes the man simply took the dime and disappeared
into the movies, sometimes he gave my dime back to me
and took me in, anyway. Sometimes I ended up wandering
around the streets—but I couldn't wander into a strange
neighborhood because I would be beaten up if I did—until
I figured the show was out. It was dangerous to get home
too early and, of course, it was practically lethal to arrive
too late. If all went well, I could cover for Caleb, saying
that I had left him with some boys on the stoop. Then, if *he*
came in too late and got a dressing down for it, it could not
be considered my fault.

But if wandering around this way was not without its
dangers, neither was it without its discoveries and de-
lights. I discovered subways—I discovered, that is, that I
could ride on subways by myself, and, furthermore, that I
could usually ride for nothing. Sometimes, when I ducked
under the turnstile, I was caught and cuffed and turned
back, and sometimes great black ladies seized on me as a
pretext for long, very loud, ineffably moral lectures
about wayward children breaking their parents' hearts; as
to this, however, the ladies very often and very loudly
disagreed among themselves, insisting that wayward children were produced by wayward parents, and calling

down on the heads of my parents the most vivid penalties
that heaven could devise. And heaven would have had to
go some to have surpassed their imaginations. Sometimes,
doing everything in my power not to attract their attention, I endeavored to look as though I were the charge of
a respectable-looking man or woman, entering the subway in their shadow, and sitting very still beside them. It
was best to try to sit *between* two such people, for, then,
each would automatically assume that I was with the
other. There I would sit, then, in a precarious anonymity,
watching the people, listening to the roar, watching the
lights and the cables and the lights of other stations flash
by. It seemed to me that nothing was faster than a subway
train and I loved the speed because the speed was dangerous. For a time, during these expeditions, I simply sat
and watched the people. Lots of people would be dressed
up, for this was Saturday night. The women's hair would
be all straightened and curled and the lipstick on their full
lips looked purple and make-believe against the dark skins
of their faces. They wore very fancy capes or coats, in
wonderful colors, and long dresses, and sometimes they
had jewels in their hair and sometimes they wore flowers
on their dresses. They were almost as beautiful as movie
stars. And so the men with them seemed to think. The
hair of the men was slick and wavy, brushed up into
pompadours; or they wore very sharp hats, brim flicked
down dangerously over one eye, with perhaps one flower
in the lapel of their many-colored suits and a tiepin
shining in the center of their bright ties. Their hands were
large and very clean, with rings on their heavy fingers, and
their nails glowed. They laughed and talked with their
girls, but quietly, for there were white people in the car.
The white people would scarcely ever be dressed up, and
never as brilliantly as the colored people. They wore just
ordinary suits and hats and coats and did not speak to
each other at all—only read their papers and stared at the
advertisements. But they fascinated me more than the
colored people did because I knew nothing at all about
them and could not imagine what they were like. Their
faces were as strange to me as the faces on the movie
posters and the stills, but far less attractive, because,
mysteriously, menacing, and, under the ruthless subway
light, they were revealed literally, in their true colors, which

were not green, red, blue, or purple, but a mere, steady, unnerving, pinkish reddish yellow. I wondered why people called them white—they certainly were not white. Black people were not black either—my father was wrong. Underground, I received my first apprehension of New York neighborhoods, and, underground, first felt what may be called a civic terror. I very soon realized that after the train had passed a certain point, going uptown or down-town, all the colored people disappeared. The first time I realized this, I panicked and got lost. I rushed off the train, terrified of what these white people might do to me with no colored person around to protect me—even to scold me, even to beat me, at least their touch was familiar, and I knew that they did not, after all, intend to kill me; and got on another train only because I saw a black man on it. But almost everyone else was white. The train did not stop at any of the stops I remembered. I became more and more frightened, frightened of getting off the train and frightened of staying on it, frightened of saying anything to the man and frightened that he would get off the train before I *could* say anything to him. He was my salvation and he stood there in the unapproachable and frightening form that salvation so often takes. At each stop, I watched him with despair. To make matters worse, I suddenly realized that I had to pee. Once I realized it, this need became a torment; the horror of wetting my pants in front of all these people made the torment greater. Finally, I tugged at the man's sleeve. He looked down at me with a gruff, amused concern—he had been staring out of the dark window, far away with his own thoughts; then, react-ing, no doubt, to the desperation in my face, he bent closer. I asked him if there was a bathroom on the train. He laughed.

"No," he said, "but there's a bathroom in the station." He looked at me again. "Where're you going?"

I told him that I was going home. But the pressure on my bladder made it hard for me to speak. The train looked like it was never going to stop.

"And where's home?"

I told him. This time he did not laugh.

"Do you know where you are?"

I shook my head. At that moment the train came into the station and after several hours it rolled to a stop. After

a slightly longer time than that, the jammed doors opened
and the man led me to the bathroom. I ran in, and I hurried
because I was afraid he would disappear. But I was glad he
had not come in with me.

When I came out, he stood waiting for me. "Now," he
said, "you in Brooklyn—you ever hear of Brooklyn?
What you doing out here by yourself?"

"I got lost," I said.

"I *know* you got lost. What I want to know is how
come you got lost? Where's your mama? Where's your
daddy?"

I almost said that I didn't have any because I liked his
face and his voice and was half hoping to hear him say
that *he* didn't have any little boy and would just as soon
take a chance on me. But I told him that my mama and
daddy were at home.

"And do they know where *you* are?"

I said No. There was a pause.

"Well, I know they going to make your tail hot when
they see you." He took my hand. "Come on."

And he led me along the platform and then down
some steps and along a narrow passage and then up some
steps onto the opposite platform. I was very impressed by
this maneuver, for, in order to accomplish the same purpose, I had always left the subway station and gone up
into the streets. Now that the emergency was over (and I
knew that I would not be late getting home) I was in no
great hurry to leave my savior; but I didn't know how to
say this, the more particularly as he seemed to be alter-
nating between amusement and irritation. I asked him if
he had a little boy.

"Yes," he said, "and if you was *my* little boy, I'd pad-
dle your behind so you couldn't sit down for a week."

I asked him how old was his little boy and what was
his name and if his little boy was at home?

"He *better* be at home!" He looked at me and laughed.
"His name is Jonathan. He ain't but five years old." His
gaze refocused, sharpened. "How old are you?"

I told him that I was ten, going on eleven.

"You a pretty bad little fellow," he said, then.

I tried to look repentant, but I would not have dreamed
of denying it.

"Now, look here," he said, "this here's the uptown side—can you read or don't you never go to school?" I assured him that I could read. "Now, to get where you going, you got to change trains." He told me where. "Here, I'll write it down for you." He found some paper in his pockets, but no pencil. We heard the train coming. He looked about him in helpless annoyance, looked at his watch, looked at me. "It's all right. I'll tell the conductor."

But the conductor, standing between the two cars, had rather a mean pink face and my savior looked at him dubiously. "He *might* be all right. But we better not take no chances." He pushed me ahead of him into the train. "You know you right lucky that *I* got a little boy? If I didn't, I swear I'd just let you go on and *be* lost. You don't know the kind of trouble you going to get me in at home. My wife ain't *never* going to believe *this* story."

I told him to give me his name and address and that I would write a letter to his wife and to his little boy, too. This caused him to laugh harder than ever. "You only say that because you know I ain't got no pencil. You are one *hell* of a shrewd little boy."

I told him that then maybe we should get off the train and that I would go back home with him. This made him grave.

"What does your father do?" This question made me uneasy. I stared at him for a long time before I answered. "He works in a"—I could not pronounce the word—"he has a job."

He nodded. "I see. Is he home now?"

I really did not know and I said I did not know.

"And what does your mother do?"

"She stays home. But she goes out to work—sometimes." Again he nodded. "You got any brothers or sisters?" I told him No.

"I see. What's your name?"

"Leo."

"Leo what?"

"Leo Proudhammer."

He saw something in my face.

"What do you want to be when you grow up, Leo?"

"I want to be"—and I had never said this before—"I want to be a—a movie actor. I want to be a—actor."

"You pretty skinny for that," he said.

But I certainly had, now, all of his attention.

"That's all right," I told him. "Caleb's going to teach me to swim. That's how you get big."

"Who's Caleb?"

I opened my mouth, I stared at him, I started to speak, I checked myself—as the train roared into a station. He glanced out of the window, but did not move. "He swims," I said.

"Oh," he said, after a very long pause, during which the doors slammed and the train began to move. "Is he a good swimmer?"

I said that Caleb was the best swimmer in the world.

"Okay," my savior said, "okay," and put his hand on my head again, and smiled at me. I asked him what his name was. "Charles," he said, "Charles Williams. But you better call me *Uncle* Charles, you little devil, because you have certainly ruined my Saturday night."

I told him (for I knew it) that it was still early.

"It ain't going to be early," he said, "by the time I get back home." The train came into the station. "Here's where we change," he said.

We got out of the train and crossed the platform and waited.

"Now," he said, "this train stops exactly where you going. Tell me where you going."

I stared at him.

"I want you," he said, "to tell me exactly where you *going*. I can't be fooling with you all night."

I told him.

"You sure that's right?"

I told him I was sure.

"I got a very good memory," he said. "Give me your address. Just say it, I'll remember it."

So I said it, staring into his face as the train came roaring in.

"If you don't go straight home," he said, "I'm going to come and see your daddy and when we find you, you'll be mighty sorry." He pushed me into the train and put one shoulder against the door. "Go on, now," he said, loud enough for all the car to hear, "your mama'll meet you at the station where I told you to get off." He re-

peated my subway stop, pushed the angry door with his
shoulder, and then said gently, "Sit down, Leo." And he
remained in the door until I sat down. "So long, Leo," he
said, then, and stepped backward, out. The doors closed.
He grinned at me and waved and the train began to move.
I waved back. Then he was gone, the station was gone, and
I was on my way back home.

I never saw that man again but I made up stories in
my head about him, I dreamed about him, I even wrote a
letter to him and his wife and his little boy, but I never
mailed it. I had a feeling that he would not like my father
and that my father would not like him. And since Caleb
never liked anyone *I* liked, I never mentioned him to
Caleb.

But I never told Caleb anything about my solitary
expeditions. I don't know why. I think that he might
have liked to know about them; or perhaps I am only
reacting to his own, later, guilty feeling that he *should*
have known about them; but, I suppose, finally, at bottom, I said nothing because my expeditions belonged to
me. It scarcely seems possible that I could have been as
silent and solitary and dangerously self-contained as the
melancholy evidence indicates me to have been. For certainly I cried and howled and stormed. Certainly I must
have chattered, as children do. Such playmates as I had,
in spite of my size and strangeness, my helpless am-
biguity, I eventually dominated—without quite knowing
how this had come about; I was able to do it, that was all,
and, therefore, condemned to do it. I know that, as I grew
older, I became tyrannical. I had no choice, my life was in
the balance. Whoever went under, it was not going to be
me—and I seem to have been very clear about this from
the very beginning of my life. To run meant to turn my
back—on lions; to run meant the flying tackle which
would bring me down; and, anyway, run where? Certainly not to my father and mother, certainly not to Caleb.
Therefore, I had to stand. To stand meant that I had to
be insane. People who imagine themselves to be, as they
put it, in their "right" minds, have no desire to tangle with
the insane. They stay far from them, or they ingratiate
them. It took me almost no time to realize this. I used
what I knew. I knew that what was sport for others was

life or death for me. Therefore, I had to make it a matter of life or death for them. Not many are prepared to go so far, at least not without the sanction of a uniform. But this absolutely single-minded and terrified ruthlessness was masked by my obvious vulnerability, my paradoxical and very real helplessness, and it covered my terrible need to lie down, to breathe deep, to weep long and loud, to be held in human arms, almost any human arms, to hide my face in any human breast, to tell it all, to let it out, to be brought into the world, and, out of human affection, to be born again. What a dream: is it a dream? I don't know. I know only what happened—if, indeed, I can claim to know that. My pride became my affliction. I found myself imprisoned in the stronghold I had built. The day came when I wished to break my silence and found that I could not speak: the actor could no longer be distinguished from his role.

Another time, it was raining and it was still too early for me to go home. I felt very, very low that day. It was one of the times that my tongue and my body refused to obey me—this happened often; when I was prey to my fantasies, or overwhelmed by my real condition; and I had not been able to work up the courage to ask anyone to take me into the show. I stood there, watching people go in, watching people come out. Every once in a while, when the doors opened, I caught a glimpse of the screen —huge, black and silver, moving all the time. The ticket-taker was watching me, or so I thought, with a hostile suspicion, as though he were thinking, You just *try* to get somebody to take you in, I dare you! It'll be your ass. Actually, it's very unlikely he was thinking at all, and certainly not of me. But I walked away from the show because I could no longer bear his eyes, or anybody's eyes.

I walked the long block east from the moviehouse. The street was empty, black, and glittering. The globes of the streetlamps, with the water slanting both behind them and before, told me how hard the rain was falling. The water soaked through my coat at the shoulders and water dripped down my neck from my cap. I began to be afraid. I could not stay out here in the rain because then my father and mother would know I had been wandering the streets. I would get a beating, and, though Caleb was

too old to get a beating, he and my father would have a
terrible fight and Caleb would blame it all on me and
would not speak to me for days. I began to hate Caleb. I
wondered where he was. If I had known where to find
him, I would have gone to where he was and forced him,
by screaming and crying even, to take me home or to take
me wherever he was going. And I wouldn't have cared if
he hit me, or even if he called me a sissy. Then it occurred to me that he might be in the same trouble as
myself, since if I couldn't go home without *him,* he, even
more surely, couldn't go home without *me.* Perhaps he
was also wandering around in the rain. If he was, then, I
thought, it served him right; it would serve him right if
he caught pneumonia and died; and I dwelt pleasantly
on this possibility for the length of the block. But at the
end of the block I realized that he was probably *not*
wandering around in the rain—*I* was; and I, too, might
catch pneumonia and die. I started in the direction of our
house only because I did not know what else to do. Perhaps Caleb would be waiting for me on the stoop.

The avenue, too, was very long and silent. Somehow,
it seemed old, like a picture in a book. It stretched
straight before me, endless, and the streetlights did not so
much illuminate it as prove how dark it was. The familiar buildings were now merely dark, silent shapes, great
masses of wet rock; men stood against the walls or on the
stoops, made faceless by the light in the hallway behind
them. The rain was falling harder. Cars sloshed by,
sending up sheets of water and bobbing like boats; from
the bars I heard music faintly, and many voices. Straight
ahead of me a woman walked, very fast, head down,
carrying a shopping bag. I reached my corner and crossed
the wide avenue. There was no one on my stoop.

Now, I was not even certain what time it was; and
everything was so abnormally, wretchedly still that there
was no way of guessing. But I knew it wasn't time yet for
the show to be over. I walked into my hallway and wrung
out my cap. I was sorry that I had not made someone take
me into the show because now I did not know what to do.
I *could* go upstairs and say that we had not liked the
movie and had left early and that Caleb was with some
boys on the stoop. But this would sound strange—I had

never been known to dislike a movie; and if our father was home, he might come downstairs to look for Caleb; who would not know what story I had told and who would, therefore, in any case, be greatly handicapped when he arrived. As far as Caleb knew, I was safely in the movies. That was our bargain, from which not even the rain released me. My nerve had failed me, but Caleb had no way of knowing that. I could not stay in my hallway because my father might not be at home and might come in. I could not go into the hallway of another building because if any of the kids who lived in the building found me they would have the right to beat me up. I could not go back out into the rain. I stood next to the big, cold radiator and I began to cry. But crying wasn't going to do me any good, either, especially as there was no one to hear me.

So I stepped out on my stoop again and looked carefully up and down the block. There was not a soul to be seen. Even the Holy Roller church across the street was silent. The rain fell as hard as ever, with a whispering sound—like monstrous old gossips whispering together. The sky could not be seen. It was black. I stood there for a long time, wondering what to do. Then I thought of a condemned house, around the corner from us. We played there sometimes, though we were not supposed to, and it was dangerous. The front door had been boarded up but the boards had been pried loose; and the basement windows had been broken and boys congregated in the basement and wandered through the rotting house. What possessed me to go there now I don't know, except that I could not think of another dry place in the whole world. I thought that I would just sit there, out of the rain, until I figured it was safe to come home. And I started running east, down our block. I turned two corners and I came to the house, with its black window sockets and garbage piled high around it and the rain moaning and whistling, clanging against the metal and drumming on the glass. The house stood by itself, for the house next to it had already been torn down. The house was completely dark. I had forgotten how afraid I was of the dark, but the rain was drenching me. I ran down the cellar steps and clambered into the house. I squatted there in a still, dry

dread, in misery, not daring to look into the house but
staring outward at the bright black area railing and the
tempest beyond. I was holding my breath. I heard an
endless scurrying in the darkness, a perpetual busy-ness,
and I thought of rats, of their teeth and ferocity and fearful size and I began to cry again. If someone had come up
then to murder me, I don't believe I could have moved
or made any other sound.

I don't know how long I squatted there this way, or
what was in my mind—I think there was nothing in my
mind, I was as blank as a toothache. I listened to the rain
and the rats. Then I was aware of another sound, I had
been hearing it for a while without realizing it. This was
a moaning sound, a sighing sound, a sound of strangling,
which mingled with the sound of the rain and with a
muttering, cursing, human voice. The sounds came from
the door which led to the backyard. I wanted to stand,
but I crouched lower; wanted to run, but could not
move. Sometimes the sounds seemed to come closer and I
knew that this meant my death; sometimes diminished or
ceased altogether and then I knew that my assailant was
looking for me. Oh, how I hated Caleb for bringing my
life to an end so soon! How I wished I knew where to find
him! I looked toward the backyard door and I seemed
to see, silhouetted against the driving rain, a figure, half
bent, moaning, leaning against the wall, in indescribable
torment; then there seemed to be two figures, sighing and
grappling, moving so quickly that it was impossible to tell
which was which—if this had been a movie, and I had
been holding a gun, I would have been afraid to shoot,
for fear of shooting the wrong person; two creatures, each
in a dreadful, absolute, silent single-mindedness, attempting to strangle the other! I watched, crouching low. A
very powerful and curious excitement mingled itself
with my terror and made the terror greater. I could not
move. I did not dare to move. The figures were quieter
now. It seemed to me that one of them was a woman and
she seemed to be crying—pleading for her life. But her
sobbing was answered only by a growling sound. The
muttered, joyous curses began again, the murderous
ferocity began again, more bitterly than ever, and I trembled with fear and joy. The sobbing began to rise in

pitch, like a song. The movement sounded like so many dull blows. Then everything was still, all movements ceased—my ears trembled. Then the blows began again and the cursing became a growling, moaning, stretched-out sigh. Then I heard only the rain and the scurrying of the rats. It was over—one of them, or both of them, lay stretched out, dead or dying, in this filthy place. It happened in Harlem every Saturday night. I could not catch my breath to scream. Then I heard a laugh, a low, happy, wicked laugh, and the figure turned in my direction and seemed to start toward me. Then I screamed and stood straight up, bumping my head on the window frame and losing my cap, and scrambled up the cellar steps, into the rain. I ran head down, like a bull, away from that house and out of that block and it was my great good luck that no person and no vehicle were in my path. I ran up the steps of my stoop and bumped into Caleb.

"Where the hell have you been? Hey! what's the matter with you?"

For I had jumped up on him, almost knocking him down, trembling and sobbing.

"You're *soaked*. Leo, what's the matter with you? Where's your cap?"

But I could not say anything. I held him around the neck with all my might, and I could not stop shaking.

"Come on, Leo," Caleb said, in a different tone, "tell me what's the matter. Don't carry on like this." He pried my arms loose and held me away from him so that he could look into my face. "Oh, little Leo. Little Leo. What's the matter, baby?" He looked as though he were about to cry himself and this made me cry harder than ever. He took out his handkerchief and wiped my face and made me blow my nose. My sobs began to lessen, but I could not stop trembling. He thought that I was trembling from cold and he rubbed his hands roughly up and down my back and rubbed my hands between his. "What's the matter?"

I did not know how to tell him.

"Somebody try to beat you up?"

I shook my head. "No."

"What movie did you see?"

"I didn't go. I couldn't find nobody to take me in."

"And you just been wandering around in the rain all night?"

I shook my head. "Yes."

He looked at me and sat down on the hallway steps. "Oh, Leo." Then, "You mad at me?"

I said, "No. I was scared."

He nodded. "I reckon you were, man," he said. "I reckon you were." He wiped my face again. "You ready to go upstairs? It's getting late."

"Okay."

"How'd you lose your cap?"

"I went in a hallway to wring it out—and—I put it on the radiator and I heard some people coming—and—I ran away and I forgot it."

"We'll say you forgot it in the movies."

"Okay."

We started up the stairs.

"Leo," he said, "I'm sorry about tonight. I'm really sorry. I won't let it happen again. You believe me?"

"Sure. I believe you."

"Give us a smile, then."

I smiled up at him. He squatted down.

"Give us a kiss."

I kissed him.

"Okay. Climb up. I'll give you a ride—hold on, now."

He carried me piggyback up the stairs.

Thereafter, we evolved a system which did not, in fact, work too badly. When things went wrong and he could not be found, I was to leave a message for him at a certain store on the avenue. This store had a bad reputation—more than candy and hot dogs and soda pop were sold there; Caleb himself had told me this and told me not to hang out there. But he said that he would see to it that they treated me all right. I did not know exactly what this meant then, but I was to find out. I had to wait for him in that store many nights; and for years I was to wish that I had never seen it, never heard of it; and for years I was to avoid the store's alumni, who also had their reasons for not wishing to face me.

But this store was not the only place I sometimes waited for, or met, Caleb. I went in the store one Saturday night, and one of the boys who was always there, a boy about Caleb's age, looked up and smiled and said, "You looking for your brother? Come on, I'll take you to him."

This was not the agreed-on formula. I was to be *taken* to Caleb only in cases of real emergency, which was not the case this night. I was there because the show had turned loose a little earlier than usual; and so Caleb was not really late yet, and since it was only about a quarter past eleven, I figured I had about half an hour to wait. But I also knew that the boss, a very dour, silent, black man—he spoke only to curse—was made very nervous by my presence in the store, especially at the hours I would be there, and he sometimes sat me alone in the back room. Otherwise, I must say, they were, in their elegantly philosophical fashion (I was simply another element to be dealt with) very nice to me. They didn't say much to me, since they didn't consider that there could be very much in the way of common ground between us—or, insofar as a common ground existed, it was far safer not to attempt to describe it—but they bought me Hershey bars, sometimes, and malted milks, and soda pop. They themselves drank wine and gin and beer, and, very rarely, whiskey.

This particular Saturday night, when the boy made his invitation, I assumed it was because of some prearrangement with the boss—who looked at me from behind his counter, munching on a toothpick, and said nothing. There were only a couple of boys in the store, silently playing cards.

I said, "Okay," and the boy, whose name was Arthur, said, "Come on, sonny. I'm going to take you to a party." He grinned down in my face as he said this, and then waved, more or less at random, to the store: "Be seeing you!" We walked out. He took my hand and led me across the avenue and into a long, dark block. We walked the length of the block in silence, crossed another avenue, Arthur holding tightly to my hand, and passed two white cops, who looked at us sharply. Arthur muttered under his breath, "You white cock-suckers. I wish all of you were dead." We slowed our pace a little; I had the feeling, I don't know why, that this was because of the cops; then Arthur said, "Come on, sonny," and we walked into a big house in the middle of the block. We were in a big vestibule with four locked apartment doors staring away from each other. It was not really clean, but it was fairly clean. We climbed three flights of stairs. Arthur knocked on the door, a very funny knock, not loud. After a moment, I heard a scraping sound, then the sound of a chain rattling and a bolt being pulled back. The door opened. A lady, very black and rather fat, wearing a blue dress which was very open around the breasts, held the door for us. She said, "Come on in—now, what you doing here with this child?"

"Had to do it. It's all right. It's Caleb's brother."

We started down a long, dark hall, with closed rooms on either side, toward the living room. One of the rooms was the kitchen. A smell of barbecue came out and made me realize that I was hungry. The living room was really two living rooms, one following the other. The farthest one looked out on the street. There were about six or seven people in the room, women and men. They looked exactly like the men and women who frightened me when I saw them standing on the corners, laughing and joking in front of the bars. But they did not seem frightening here. A record player was going, not very loud. They had drinks in their hands and there were empty plates and half-empty plates of food around the room. Caleb was sitting on the sofa with his arm around a girl in a yellow dress. "Here's your little brother," said the fat black lady in blue.

Caleb looked at me and then, immediately, to Arthur. Arthur said, "It was just better for him not to have to wait there tonight. You know." To the lady in blue, he said, "The train is in the station, everything's okay. I'm going to get myself a taste."

Caleb smiled at me. I was tremendously relieved that he was not angry. I was delighted by this party, even though it made me shy. I wished I had come sooner.

"How you doing?" Caleb said. "Come on over here." I went to the sofa. "This is my kid brother," Caleb said. "His name is Leo. Leo, this is Dolores. Say hello to Dolores."

Dolores smiled at me—I thought she was very pretty; she had a big mouth and blue gums and a lot of shining hair—and shook my hand and said, "I'm very happy to meet you, Leo. How've you been?"

"Just fine," I said.

"Don't you want to know how *she's* been?" Caleb grinned.

"No," said the fat black lady, and laughed, "I'm sure he don't want to know that." She had a very loud, good-natured laugh and Caleb and Dolores laughed with her. "They're not being very nice to me, are they, Leo?" Dolores asked. "I don't think you ought to let them laugh at me this way."

I did not know what to say. I just stared at her red lips and her shining eyes and her shining hair. She had a bright, round, red pin at the center of her dress, where her breasts met. I could not keep my eyes away from it; and Arthur and Caleb laughed. Dolores said to Caleb, "I guess you come by it naturally, honey. I guess it runs in the family," and Caleb said, "Lord. Let me get him out of here before he steals my girl."

The lady in blue came to my rescue. "Don't just go rushing him off like that. I bet he's hungry. You been stuffing yourself all night, Caleb, let me give him a little bit of my barbecue and a glass of ginger ale."

She already had one hand on my back and was beginning to propel me out of the room. I looked at Caleb. Caleb said, "Just remember we ain't got all night. Leo, this is Miss Mildred. She cooked everything, and she's a mighty good friend of mine. What do you say to Miss Mildred, Leo?"

"Dig Caleb being the big brother," Arthur muttered, and laughed.

"Thank you, Miss Mildred," I said.

"Come on in the kitchen," she said, "and let me try to put some flesh on them bones. Caleb, you ought to be ashamed with your great, big, fat self, and letting your brother be so puny." She walked me into the kitchen. "Now, you sit right over there," she said. "Won't take me but a minute to warm this up." She sat me at the kitchen table and gave me a napkin and poured the ginger ale. "What grade you in at school, Leo?" I told her. "You must be a right smart boy, then," she said with a pleased smile. "Do you like school, Leo?"

I told her what I liked best was Spanish and History and English Composition. This caused her to look more pleased than ever. "What do you want to be when you grow up?"

Somehow, I could not tell her what I had told the man—=my friend—on the train. I said I wasn't sure, that maybe I would be a schoolteacher.

"That's just what I wanted to be," she said proudly, "and I studied right hard for it, too, and I believe I would have made it, but then I had to go and get myself mixed up with some no-count nigger. I didn't have no sense. I didn't have no better sense but to marry him. Can you beat that?" and she laughed and set my plate in front of me. "Go on, now, eat. Foolish me. You know I had a little boy like you? And I don't know where he's gone to. He had the same big eyes like you and a dimple right here" —she touched the corner of her lip—"when he smiled. But I give him to my sister, she lives in Philadelphia, because I couldn't raise him by myself, and my sister she was married to a undertaker and they was right well off— of course my sister and I never did get along too well, she was too dicty for me, you know how some folks are—and they said they'd raise him just like their own. And I reckon they tried. But he walked off from them one day —I reckon he was about sixteen—and don't nobody know where he went. I keep expecting him to come through this door. Now, your brother," she said suddenly, "he's a right fine boy. He wants to make something of himself. He's got ambition. That's what I like—*ambition*. Don't you let him be foolish. Like me. You like my barbecue?"

"Yes ma'am," I said. "It's good."

"But I bet you like your mama's better," she said.

I said, "My mama's barbecue is different. But I like yours, too."

"Let me give you some more ginger ale," she said, and poured it. I was beginning to be full. But I didn't want to go, although I knew that, now, it was really beginning to be late. While Miss Mildred talked and moved about the kitchen, I listened to the voices coming from the other rooms, the voices and the music. They were playing a kind of purple lazy dance music, a music which was already in my bones, along with the wilder music from which the purple music sprang. The voices were not like the music, though they corroborated it. I listened to a girl's voice, gravelly and low, indignant, and full of laughter. The room was full of laughter. It exploded, at intervals, and rolled through the living room and hammered at the walls of the kitchen. But it traveled no further. No doubt, lying in bed, in one of the rooms off the hall, one would have heard it, but heard it dimly, from very far away, and with a certain anger—anger that the laughter could not travel down the hall and could not enter one's dark, solitary room. Every once in a while, I heard Caleb, booming like a trumpet, drowning out the music, and I could almost see him, bouncing his head off Dolores' shoulder, rising like a spring from the sofa and jack-knifing himself across the room. Now, someone was telling a story: it concerned some fool he worked with in the post office. Only this voice and the music were heard. The voice began to be hoarse with anticipation and liquid with exuberance. Then his laugh rang out, and all the others laughed, rocking. "He said—he said—I don't know what's the matter with you niggers. You ain't got good sense. I'm *working for my pension*. And Shorty say, he say, Yeah, baby, and that pension's going to buy you enough beans for you to fart your life away! Ho-ho! Ho-ho! Ha-ha!" Then, by and by, the voices sputtered out, the voices dropped, and the music took over again. I wondered how often Caleb came here and how he had met these people who were so different, at least as it seemed to me, from any of the people who ever came to our house.

Then Caleb's hand was on my neck. Dolores stood in the doorway, smiling. "You stuffed yourself enough, little brother? Because we got to get out of here now." I stood up. "Wipe your mouth," said Caleb, "you ain't civilized at all."

"Don't you pay him no mind," said Miss Mildred. "He's just evil because Dolores thinks you got prettier eyes than him."

"That's the truth," said Dolores. "I was just thinking what a pity I didn't see your little brother first."

I knew that she was teasing me, but I fell in love with her anyway.

"Keep on talking," said Caleb, "and I'll give him to you. Ain't neither one of you noticed how much he can eat. Come on, Leo, put on your coat. One of these mad chicks is liable to kidnap you and then I don't know what I'll say to your mama."

We walked slowly down the hall, Miss Mildred, Dolores, and Caleb and me. I wanted to say good-night to all the others but I knew I couldn't suggest this. We reached the door, which had a metal pole built into it in such a way as to prevent its being opened from the outside, and a heavy piece of chain around the top of the three locks. Miss Mildred began, patiently, to open the door. "Leo," she said, "don't you be no stranger. You make your brother bring you back to see me, you hear?" She got the pole out of the way, then she undid the chain. She had not turned on the hall light; I wondered how she could see. To Caleb she said, "Bring him by some afternoon. I ain't got nothing to do. I'll be glad to look after him—let your mama and daddy have a day off, go to the movies or something." I thought this was a splendid suggestion and wondered how I could persuade Caleb of this. There was no question of ever being able to persuade our parents. The last lock yielded and Miss Mildred opened the door. We were facing the bright hall lights; no, the building was not very clean. "Good-night, Leo," Miss Mildred said, and then she said good-night to Dolores and Caleb. She closed the door. I heard the scraping sound again, and we walked down the stairs. "She's nice," I said, and Caleb said, yawning, "Yeah, she's a very nice lady." Then he said, "Now, I don't want you telling nobody at home about this, you hear?" I swore I wouldn't tell. "It's our secret," Caleb said.

It was colder in the streets than it had been before and there were not many people.

Caleb took Dolores' arm. "Let's get you to your subway," he said. We started walking up the wide, dark avenue. We reached the brightly lit kiosk which came up out of the sidewalk like some unbelievably malevolent awning or the suction apparatus of a monstrous vacuum cleaner. "Bye-bye," said Caleb, and kissed Dolores on the nose, "I got to run. See you Monday, after school."

"Bye-bye," said Dolores. She bent down and kissed me quickly on the cheek. "Bye-bye, Leo. Be good." She hurried down the steps.

Caleb and I began walking very fast, down the avenue, toward our block. The subway station was near the moviehouse and the moviehouse was dark. But we knew we were late—we did not think that we were *very* late.

"It was a *very* long show," Caleb said, "wasn't it?"

"Yes," I said.

"What did we see?"

I told him.

"What were they about? Tell me about *both* pictures. Just in case."

I told him as well and as fully as I could as we hurried down the avenue. He held me by the hand and he was walking much too fast for me and so my breath was short. But Caleb had great powers of concentration and could figure out enough from what I said to know what to say if the necessity arose. But our troubles, that night, came from a very different source than our parents. I had just reached the point in my breathless narration where the good girl is murdered by the Indians and the hero vows revenge, we were hurrying down the long block which led east to our house, when we heard the brakes of a car and were blinded by bright lights and were pushed up against a wall.

"Turn around," said a voice. "And keep your hands in the air."

It may seem funny, I don't know, but I felt, at once, as though Caleb and I had conjured up a movie; that if I had not been describing a movie to him, we would not have suddenly found ourselves in the middle of one. Or was it the end? For I had never been so frightened in my life before.

We did as we were told. I felt the grainy brick beneath my fingers. A hand patted me all over my body, front and back, every touch humiliating, every touch obscene. Beside me, I heard Caleb catch his breath.

"Turn around," the voices said.

The great lights of the police car had gone out; I could see the car at the curb, the doors open. I thought I could see, across the street, a colored man, in the shadows, staring, but I could not be sure. I did not dare to look at Caleb, for I felt that this would, somehow, be used against us. I stared at the two policemen, young, white, tight-lipped, and self-important. They turned a flashlight first on Caleb, then on me.

"Where you boys going?"

"Home," Caleb said. I could hear his breathing. "We live in the next block," and he gave the address.

The flashlight had gone out and I could see their faces. I memorized their faces.

"Where've you been?"

I trembled. I did not know of whom the question had been asked. I did not know what to answer.

Now I heard the effort Caleb was making not to surrender either to rage or panic. "We just took my girl to the subway station. We were at the movies," And then, forced out of him, weary, dry, and bitter, "This here's my brother. I got to get him home. He ain't but ten years old."

"What movie did you see?"

And Caleb told them. I marveled at his memory. But I also knew that the show had let out about an hour or so before. I feared that the policemen might also know this. But they didn't, of course, know: such knowledge is beneath them.

"You got any identification?"

"My brother doesn't. I do."

"Let's see it."

Caleb took out his wallet and handed it over. I could see that his hands were trembling. I watched the white faces. I memorized each mole, scar, pimple, nostril hair; I memorized the eyes, the contemptuous eyes. I wished that I were God. And then I hated God.

They looked at his wallet, looked at us, handed it back. "Get on home," one of them said, the one with the mole. They got into their car and drove off.

"Thanks," Caleb said. "Thanks, you white cock-sucking dog-shit miserable white mother-fuckers. Thanks, all you scum-bag Christians." His accent was now as irredeemably of the islands as was the accent of our father. I had never heard this sound in his voice before. He raised his face to the sky. "Thanks, good Jesus Christ. Thanks for letting us go home. I mean, I know you didn't have to do it. You *could* have let us just get our brains beat out. Remind me, O lord, to put a extra large nickel in the plate next Sunday." And then, suddenly, he looked down at me and laughed and hugged me. "Come on, let's get home before the bastard changes his mind. Little Leo. Were you scared?"

"Yes," I said. "Were you?"

"Damn right, I was scared. But—*goddamn!*—they must have seen that *you* weren't but ten years old."

"You didn't *act* scared," I said.

And this was the truth. But I also felt, I don't know how, nor do I really know why, that I couldn't let him feel, even for a moment, that I did not adore him, that I did not respect him, love him and admire him.

We were in our own block, approaching our stoop. "Well. We certainly have a good excuse for being late," he said. He grinned. Then he said, "Leo, I'll tell you something. I'm glad this happened. It had to happen one day and I'm glad it happened now. I'm glad it happened while I was with you—of course, I'm glad you were with *me*, too, dig, because if it hadn't been for you, they'd have pulled my ass in and given me a licking just as sure as shit—"

"What for?"

"Because I'm black," Caleb said. "That's what for. Because I'm black and they *paid* to beat on black asses. But, with a kid your size, they just *might* get into trouble. So they let us go. *They* knew you weren't nothing but a kid. They knew it. But they didn't care. All black people are shit to them. You remember that. You black like me and they going to hate you as long as you live just because you're black. There's something wrong with them. They got some kind of disease. I hope to God it kills them soon." We started up the steps to our house. "But it's liable to kill us before it kills them."

I said nothing. I said nothing because what he said was true, and I knew it. It seemed, now, that I had always known it, though I had never been able to say it. But I did not understand it. I was filled with an awful wonder, it hurt my chest and paralyzed my tongue. *Because you're black*. I tried to think, but I couldn't. I only saw the policemen, those murderous eyes again, those hands, with a touch like the touch of vermin. Were they people?

"Caleb," I asked, "are white people people?"

"What are you talking about, Leo?"

"I mean—are white people—*people?* People like us?"

He looked down at me. His face was very strange and sad. It was a face I had never seen before. We climbed a few more stairs, very slowly. Then, "All I can tell you, Leo, is—well, *they* don't think they are."

I thought of Mr. Rabinowitz and Mr. Shapiro. Then I thought of my schoolteacher, a lady named Mrs. Nelson. I liked her very much. I thought she was very pretty. She had long, yellow hair, like someone I had seen in the movies, and a nice laugh, and we all liked her, all the kids I knew. The kids who were not in her class wished they were. I liked to write compositions for her because she seemed really interested and always asked questions. But she was white. Would she hate me all my life because I was black? It didn't seem possible. She didn't hate me now; I was pretty sure of that. And yet, what Caleb had said was true.

"Caleb," I asked, "are all white people the same?"

"What do you mean, the same?"

"I mean—you know—are they all the *same?*"

And Caleb said, "I never met a good one."

I asked, "Not even when you were little? in school?"

Caleb said, "Maybe. I don't remember." He smiled at me. "I never met a good one, Leo. But that's not saying that *you* won't. Don't look so frightened."

We were in front of our door. Caleb raised his hand to knock. I held his hand.

"Caleb," I whispered, "what about Mama?"

"What do you mean, what about Mama?"

"Well, Mama"—I stared at him; he watched me very gravely. "Mama—Mama's almost white—"

"Almost don't get it," Caleb said.

I stared at him.

"Our mama is *almost* white," Caleb said, "but that don't make her white. You got to be *all* white to be white." He laughed; inside, we heard our father cough. "Poor Leo. Don't feel bad. I know you don't understand it now. I'll try to explain it to you, little by little." He paused. "But our mama is a colored woman. You can tell she's a colored woman because she's married to a colored *man,* and she's got two colored *children.* Now, you know ain't no white lady going to do a thing like that." He watched me, smiling. "You understand that?" I nodded. "Well, you going to keep me here all night with your questions or can we go on in the house now?"

I told him to knock, and he did, and our mother opened the door.

"About time," she said dryly—she was chewing on a

porkchop bone, and had her hair piled in a knot on the top of her head. I liked her hair that way. "You must have sat through that movie four or five times. You're going to ruin your eyes and that'll just be too bad for you because you know we ain't got no money to be buying you no glasses. Leo, you go inside and get ready to take your bath."

"Let him come over here a minute," said our father. He was sitting in the one easy chair, near the window. He was drunk, but not as drunk as I had seen him, and this was a good mood drunk. In this mood, he would not talk about his job, or the white workers on the job, or his foreman, or about white people, or about African kings. In this mood, he talked about the islands, his mother and father and kinfolk and friends, the feast days, the singing, the dancing, and the sea.

I approached him, and he pulled me to him, smiling and held me between his thighs. "How's my big man?" he asked, smiling, and rubbing his hand gently, and with wonder, over my hair. "Did you have a good time tonight?"

Caleb sat on a straight chair near him, leaning forward. "Let Leo tell you why we so late. Tell them what happened, Leo."

"We were coming down the block," I began—and I watched my father's face. Suddenly, I did not want to tell him. Something in Caleb's tone had alerted him, and he watched me with a stern and frightened apprehension. My mother came and stood beside him, one hand on his shoulder. I looked at Caleb. "Maybe you could tell it better," I said.

"Go on, start. I'll fill in."

"We were coming down the block," I said—and I told him which block—"coming from the movies"—I looked at Caleb.

"It's not the way we usually come," said Caleb.

My father and I stared at each other. There was, suddenly, between us an overwhelming sorrow. It had come from nowhere. "We got stopped by the cops," I said. Then I could not continue. I looked helplessly at Caleb and Caleb told the story. As Caleb spoke, I watched my father's face. I don't know how to describe what I saw. I felt the one arm he had around me tighten, tighten; his

lips became bitter and his eyes grew dull. It was as
though, after indescribable, nearly mortal effort, after
grim years of fasting and prayer, after the loss of all he
had, and after having been promised by the Almighty
that he had paid the price and no more would be demanded of his soul, which was harbored now; it was as
though in the midst of his joyful feasting and dancing,
crowned and robed, a messenger arrived to tell him that a
great error had been made, and that it was all to be done
again. Before his eyes, then, the banquet and the banquet
wines and the banquet guests departed, the robe and
crown were lifted, and he was alone then, frozen out of
his dream, with all that before him which he had thought
was behind him. My father looked as stunned and still
and as close to madness as that, and his encircling arm
began to hurt me, but I did not complain. I put my hand
on his face, and he turned to me, his face changed, he
smiled—he was very beautiful then!—and he put his
great hand on top of mine. He turned to Caleb.

"That's all that happened? You didn't say nothing?"

"What could I say? It might have been different, had
I been by myself. But I had Leo with me, and I was afraid
of what they might do to Leo. You know those bastards.
You *can't* get no lower than those bastards until they
lower you six feet under."

"No, you did right, man, I got no fault to find. You
didn't take their badge number?"

Caleb snickered. "What for? You know a friendly
judge? We got money for a lawyer? Somebody they going
to *listen* to? You know as well as me they beating on black
ass all the time, all the time, man, they get us in that
precinct house and make us confess to all kinds of things
and sometimes even kill us and don't nobody give a
damn. Don't nobody care what happens to a black man.
If they didn't need us for work, they'd have killed us all
off a long time ago. They did it to the Indians."

"That's the truth," said our mother. "I wish I could
say different, but it's the truth." She stroked our father's
shoulder. "We just thank the Lord it wasn't no worse."

"*You* can thank the Lord," said our father. "I ain't
got nothing to thank him for. I wish he was a man like
me!"

"Well, you right," said our mother. "It was just an expression. But let's don't sit here brooding about it. We just got to say: well, the boys got home safe tonight. Because that's the way it is."

I asked, "Daddy, how come they do us like they do?"

My father looked at me for a long time. Finally, he said, "Leo, if I could tell you that, maybe I'd be able to make them stop. But don't let them make you afraid. You hear?"

I said, "Yes sir." But I knew that I was already afraid.

"Let's not talk about it no more," our mother said. "No more *tonight*. If you two is hungry, I got some pork-chops back there."

Caleb grinned at me. "Little Leo might be hungry. He stuffs himself like a pig. But I ain't hungry. Hey, old man"—he nudged my father's shoulder; nothing would be refused us tonight—"why don't we have a taste of your rum? All right?"

Our mother laughed. "I'll go get it," she said. She started out of the room.

"Reckon we can give Leo a little bit, too?" our father asked. He pulled me onto his lap.

"In a big glass of water," said our mother, laughing. She took one last look at us before she went into the kitchen. "My!" she said, "I sure am surrounded by some pretty men! My, my, my!"

I awoke suddenly, rising up abruptly from darkness, and flowers faced me on a table far away, great, blatant, triumphal blooms, reminding me of Barbara's dressing room on opening nights. The table was placed before a large, high window, hung with yellow drapes. The drapes were slightly parted, and I could see the sun outside. The rest of the room was white—white walls, a white closed door. My blue dressing gown hung against the wall nearest my bed. I tried to raise myself up to see the rest of the room and then discovered that I had no strength at all. I felt as light and as hollow and as dry as a bleached bone in the sand. My skin seemed flaking. The hair on my head felt like an affliction. A woolly trap, it felt so heavy that I might have been in the grave for days. Then I wondered what day it was, and how long I had been here. All was silent—silent and white. I tried to guess from the sun what time it would be, and I decided it would probably be about eleven. But nothing mattered—except my heavy load of hair; I didn't care if the silence never ended; I didn't care if the room remained empty of people forever. I stretched my legs. They did not feel like mine, they had no weight at all. I felt a great peacefulness—such as I had never felt before. I turned my shell of a body into the white sheets and closed my eyes.

In no time, it seemed, I opened them, but now the sun was in another place and I supposed it must be about four. The nurse was in the room. "Hi, there, sleepy-head!" she cried cheerfully—with that really unnerving cheerfulness of nurses; one dare not speculate on what awful knowledge the cheerfulness hides—"You certainly got a good rest. How do you feel?"

She was young, very pretty, with a clean, scrubbed face, and with short red hair under her starched cap.

"I feel pretty exhausted," I said. I did. And I suddenly felt very depressed.

"That's only natural," she said. "Please—may I?" And she extended the thermometer toward me.

"How long have I been here?"

"Just a day and a night—well, a night and a day and a night. Does it feel longer?"

"I don't know," I said. "It feels like my hair's been growing for a month."

She laughed. "Well, I think we can fix that," she said, "in a couple of days." She extended the thermometer again, purposefully, and stuck it under my tongue. She looked at my chart, she pulled the curtains, she watered the flowers. She worked in silence, with short, childish movements. I watched her pleasing rump and her round arms and her aggressive, and at the same time helpless, breasts. I had the feeling that she hadn't long since lost her baby fat. She opened the door and came back with an enormous basket of fruit, which she placed on the table next to the bed. "Some of your friends wanted to send over a case of champagne," she said, "but we didn't think we could allow that. Much as I wanted to. Oh! and aren't some of the girls just *sick with jealousy!* Of me! Because *I'm* nursing Leo Proudhammer! They can hardly eat their lunch for asking me questions. I just tell them, Well, he's sleeping. There's not much difference between one man and another when they're asleep."

"Well," I said, as she took the thermometer from my mouth and stared at it gravely, "now you can tell them that I'm awake. And I'm still not different."

"Oh, but you are," she said. "Yes, you are." She carefully noted my temperature on my chart, and replaced the thermometer in its glass jar. "The doctor will be in to see you later," she said. "We're going to be running some tests on you. But right now," she said firmly, "I will require a urine specimen, please." She handed me the medieval jar, which was covered with a towel, and placed the screen in front of my bed. "I'll be right back," she said, and I heard the door close behind her.

I laughed as I prepared to obey her. How had she ever learned to say it that way? So impeccably firm and impersonal. But there obviously wasn't any other way to say it, except, perhaps, between lovers, or parents and children. *We will require a mucus specimen, please.* But we said, *Blow your nose. Harder. That's better.* The troubling, tyrannical, inconvenient flesh. The sacred flesh. I filled up the jar. The color seemed all right; there wasn't any odor. But I was suddenly trembling, and cold with sweat. I might have been running for an hour. My body suddenly began to reassert its claims over me, plaintively proclaiming itself as exhausted, petulantly demanding that I *do* something. I had barely strength enough to wrap the towel around the bottle and place it on the lower shelf of the table. I just lay there. The basket of fruit was at my head, I wanted to know who had sent it, but it was too much trouble to lift my hand and look at the card. I began to realize that I was helpless—a big, grown, stinking man, and as helpless as a child. Perhaps, even more than most people, it is a state I cannot endure. It is terrible to depend on others, on another, for the execution of the simplest functions, terrible to see the book one wants at the other end of the room and be unable to get there. It causes one to begin to hate oneself. And, indeed, this vile, creepy, slimy, self-loathing came back as I lay there and realized that I had to go to the bathroom. I would have to use the bedpan; but I would never be able to sit up, unsupported. And I wanted to die—to drop my black carcass someplace and never be humiliated by it any more. I thought I had left this feeling far behind me, but here it was, now, as strong as ever—stronger; as I pictured the clean, apple-faced nurse supporting my back while I strained and sweated and my heavy stink filled the room. I put my hands to my woolly hair, that vile plantation, as though I would tear it from my skull. And I knew that I had felt this, in some way, all my life. But I had buried it; and made a point, certainly, of never being helpless. But if I had always felt this, then, certainly, I must have shown it, and shown it most, perhaps, when I was least aware of it. My body, after all—I told myself—was no more vile than others; my stink was not original, it had no greater resonance; the rats and the worms would find me as tasty as another. "Ah, Leo," I said, "what a child you are." This reflection did not mitigate my distress. The nurse came back. She picked up the bottle. There was no help for it. I said, "Nurse, I have to go to the bathroom."

She said, "I can't let you move. Wait just a moment." Then she smiled a real smile. "I *know* it's awful. But *please* don't let it worry you. Please don't." She disappeared, then returned with the grim utensil. Her words hardly helped and yet I guess they helped a little. Anyway, we were still friends when it was over. I lay back. I wondered why humiliation seemed, after all, at bottom, to be my natural condition.

The doctor came in, the little nurse beside him. He was very cheerful, too, seeming to bring into the room with him the stinging air of the bay. His face was ruddy and he was immaculate, from his smooth, gleaming brown hair to his gleaming brown shoes. "You have decided," he said, "to return to us. I thought you would, just as soon as you got a little rest. You know, I have never seen a man so tired as you. And that is very unwise." He sat down and took my pulse. The nurse showed him my chart. He looked at it for awhile, looked at me. "Ah, yes," he said. "How do you feel today? Any pain?" He watched me very carefully.

"No. I just feel as weak as a newborn kitten."

"Naturally. You had quite a battle to fight. But we will get you on your legs again." He took out his stethoscope and forced me to breathe this way and that way, he prodded me and tapped me and flipped me over once or twice, like a baby or a flapjack. He took my blood pressure. "We will be running some tests on you," he said, "for a few days—blood, the liver—oh, a million sordid elements but I will not bore you with the details. At least not yet. This," he said, preparing a needle, "*may* be a little unpleasant."

When he was through, the nurse gathered up the needles and trays and towels and went out. The doctor pulled his chair closer to the bed. "Now," he said, "listen. I do not know exactly all that I should know—I expect to discover more in a few days—perhaps everything." He laughed. "Who knows? You have had a fairly serious heart attack. Not *very* serious—but fairly serious. It has been brought about by nervous exhaustion and overwork. Now, there is nothing wrong with your heart—yet—as, oddly enough, as far as I can tell now, there is nothing wrong with your liver. But you are thirty-nine years old, Proudhammer—you are not a boy. And you will not, from this time onward in your life, recover like a boy. If you make, as I think you say in show business, a change of pace, you will live a long time and I will be able to go and see you play many, many times more. I think you are a marvelous artist, by the way, and my wife and my daughter become speechless when your name is mentioned—so there is some selfishness in what I say. It would be a great pity to lose you. I mean that, that is true. But, you see, if you do not make a change of pace—drink less, smoke *much* less, and arrange your working schedule so that you have time to rest —and by rest I do not mean five minutes in the dressing room—then you will have another attack, and then another, and by then you will be seriously damaged, and then"—he grimaced—"it will be too late and one of your attacks will carry you away. And that would be too bad, a terrible waste, it is not necessary. You understand me?"

"Yes," I said. "I understand you."

"You do not need to push yourself so hard," he said. "You have enough money. Oh! I know we never have enough money." He laughed. Then he said, in a different tone, "But it is not really money with you, anyway. It is an impertinent question—but what is it? I simply would like to know. You have been extraordinarily successful for more than a decade—you see, I know, I did not hear of you yesterday. I should guess that the odds against you were fantastic. So—indulge me, if you please? I should like to know."

I did not know how to answer. I had never put the question to myself—at least not in that way. I said, "I don't know if I know. I'm an actor—I think I'm a pretty good actor"—I was listening to myself and I sounded very lame and defensive—"I've always tried not to repeat myself. I mean—I've always tried to do things I wasn't sure I could do. If I knew I could do it, then there didn't seem much point in doing it. And then you just do the same thing over and over again and pretty soon you're not an actor, you're just a kind of highly paid—man-nequin." I coughed. "Manipulated." And then I said, surprised, rather, at the vehemence with which, in spite of myself, it came out, "And in my own case, after all, it's been both easier and harder. When I say easier I guess I mean that I'm not at all—*likely*—so when I *get* on a stage, people notice me. But I'm what's known as a hard type to cast—and a hard type to cast has got to be better, about thirty-seven thousand times better, than anybody else around—just to *get* on a stage. And then, when you start getting jobs—when they start *casting* you"—I sub-sided—"well, you've got a certain kind of advantage. But you can't afford to lose it."

"I see." He smiled. "You are what a friend of mine would call—an obsessional type." His face suggested, and I also felt, weakly, that there was more to it than anything I had said. But I did not know how to say more; I felt, inexplicably, on the brink of tears; and I decided that this was due to my weariness.

But I forced myself to smile, I forced myself to be together. "Is there anything wrong, doctor—with being an obsessional type?"

"Most artists," he said discreetly, "are obsessional types. There is nothing to be done about that. I will leave you now and I will see you in the morning. But you must think about what I have said."

"I promise that I will. Thank you. Good-night."

"Good-night, Proudhammer."

He went out. But he returned almost at once. "Your friend and coworker, Miss King, has been here every day and has called every night. She will be here this evening. But I have told her that she cannot stay with you very long."

"Thank you, doctor."

"Good-night."

"Good-night."

Now, the room was beginning to fill with twilight. I discovered a lamp near my bed, and I turned it on. I looked at the basket of fruit and picked up the card. It was not really a card, but a telegram. It read, *Stop jiving the people and get yourself back here. You know you can't get sick.* And it was signed, *Love, Christopher.* It was very moving, though in an oddly remote way—but everything seemed remote—for Christopher and his friends had no money. It must have demanded some ingenuity, from New York, to make certain that a basket of fruit would be in my hospital room in California. Not very long ago, such ingenuity on Christopher's part would have filled me with joy—not now; I put the telegram, folded, on the table and wondered if I would ever feel anything again, for anyone. Black Christopher: because he was black in so many ways—black in color, black in pride, black in rage. *No wonder I had a heart attack,* I thought. And then I thought of what the doctor had said. *Leo,* Barbara had sometimes said, *you also have the right to live. You have the right. You haven't got to prove it.*

I thought of the years I had first met Barbara, in the Village—the grimy, frightening, untidy years. I had not imagined that I could ever feel nostalgia for those years, or that I would ever, abruptly, bleakly, see in them, and in myself, a vanished, a blasphemed beauty, a beauty which I had never recognized and which I had, myself, destroyed. None of it had seemed beautiful then, myself least of all. There we were, filthier than gypsies, more abject than beggars, our mouths open obscenely for the worm, the morsel, the crumb, which the world never dropped—but the world dropped other things, we gagged and vomited, we feared that we were poisoned!—with our stolen books, our "borrowed" records, our frail pretensions, our ignorance, our stolen food. For a time, four or five of us—or, indeed, to tell the truth, whoever would—shared two floors in a falling-down tenement on the East Side. It was hidden, for decency's sake, from the street; one entered it through a gate, finding oneself in a courtyard where two buildings leaned crazily toward each other; a third building, at the end of the courtyard, seemed leaning upon these two —three drunken, lunatic friends, all about to go down together. We called this place Paradise Alley—odd it is, to reflect now that in some way we loved it. Nothing locked, we soon gave up any such attempt, and formed the habit of climbing in and out of each other's windows, walking through each other's doors. Nothing belonged to anybody, so that whatever there was (or whoever there was) could be found, and possibly collected, anywhere in the building. It was here that Barbara had become pregnant for the first time—by a hometown, childhood sweetheart, who had joined the Marines and come to visit her, emphatically to let her know what he thought of girls who ran away from respectable homes and lost their morals. She had had to have an abortion, I helped her raise the money—by waiting on tables, by hustling—and after that she became very sick and we became much closer. We went "shopping" at dawn, following a long and circuitous route. Bananas had been delivered outside the A&P. We put these in our shopping bag. (We took turns "shopping": we couldn't all get arrested at once.) We picked up the bread and milk and vegetables which had been delivered to the stores along Bleecker Street—sometimes we even got eggs. We were home before six, and ready for breakfast. Meat was our only problem, but we had a friend who worked in a big hot dog stand on 14th Street; to this day, I have no affection for hot dogs. We drank beer in the bars in the Village, shamelessly flattering the uptown strangers, who drank whiskey, who ordered whiskey for us, who might buy us a meal, who might, indeed—why not? it happened from time to time—buy us several; who might, in return for being allowed to lean at the candle of our ardor and our youth, in return for holding us (who desperately wanted to be held) between darkness and dawn on Saturday nights, see to it that we ate meat. What in the world had I been like in those years? But I remembered Barbara. For a time, we had both been artists' models at the Art Students' League on 57th Street. Barbara lasted much longer than I. She was rather more round-faced then, with very high color, and with very long, brown, curly hair, which she wore in bangs and pigtails. She had a marvelous laugh—she looked very much like what she was, a refugee schoolgirl from Kentucky. She had a very boyish figure, small breasts and not much of a behind—she was still in her teens—and wonderful long legs. She almost always wore pants, which got her in some trouble in some quarters, sometimes, but every once in a while she would put up her hair and put on lipstick and wear a dress. And it was astonishing what a difference this made. She became extraordinarily pretty, vulnerable, glowing. Then she looked like the rather proud daughter of proud Kentucky landowners. I was always delighted and secretly intimidated when she dressed, for I could not meet her on that ground at all. It made me wonder what she, really, in her secret heart, thought of me, what she thought of us all. The world in which we lived threatened, every hour, to close on the rest of us forever. We had no equipment with which to break out—and I, least of all. But she could walk out of it at any instant that she chose.

I remember going with Barbara to an uptown party one summer night. It turned out, in fact, to be my first theatrical party. I was not supposed to go. A friend of ours, Jerry, who also lived in Paradise Alley, was supposed to take her. But when the time came, he was nowhere to be found. I had been sitting in my—quarters, I suppose I must call them—for the last hour, reading, and listening to Barbara, in the room across the hall, humming, and slamming drawers. I heard her call up the steps:

"Jerry!"

She had a big voice for such a little girl, too. There was no answer. She called again. This time the voice of the old Russian lady sculptress who lived on the top floor answered:

"Barbara, he is not up here. There is no one up here but me."

"Thanks, Sonia." Then, "Damn!" She knocked on my door, simultaneously opening it, and leaned there, glowering at me. "Have you seen Jerry?" She was wearing a light blue dress, and high heels.

"I haven't seen him all day. Where're you going?"

"To a party. To an *uptown* party. Jerry was supposed to come with me."

"Well—maybe he's with Charlie."

Loosely speaking, we operated in pairs. One became a pair by sharing the same quarters—in my case, a mattress on the floor, and a victrola—and the half that was out was technically supposed to remember that the half at home was certainly hungry. Which I was. But Charlie hadn't been seen since the day before.

"I don't think so. Jerry's probably gone to see his mother. He can't seem to stay away from her, although he keeps me up all night, every night, telling me how much he hates her."

"We both seem to have been abandoned. But you're in luck. You're going to a party. Will they feed you?"

"There'll be lots of food. Come with me."

"I *can't* come with you!"

"Why not? I've got enough money for a taxi, Leo, honest. And I can borrow some money up there. Really. Come on. You're not doing anything down here. And you'd be doing me a favor."

She mentioned the taxi because we had had terrible trouble, many times, trying to get through the streets of my hometown together, black and white. Nothing would ever induce us to take a subway again together, for example. But I admired Barbara for her unsentimental clarity. Lots of other girls I had known before her had been very sentimental indeed, and had almost got me killed.

"Just put on a clean shirt, and tie. And your dark jacket."

"What about these pants?"

"They're all right. They're not torn, or anything. They just need to be pressed. Keep smiling, because you've got a wonderful smile, you know, and don't stand too long in one place and nobody will notice anything. Now, hurry up, we're supposed to be there right now."

She sat down on my mattress, not that there was anyplace else she could have sat, and leafed through my book.

"Leo, why are you suddenly reading *Swinburne?*"

I said defensively, "Because I never read him before, that's why." I was very ashamed of my lack of education and, in those days, I was reading everything I could get my hands on.

"Well. I think he's pretty silly. Eliot's the only great poet. Leo, your hair looks perfectly all right. Leave it *alone* and put on your *shirt*."

"I was only brushing it. And I need a haircut."

"Why, oh why," crooned Barbara philosophically, "do we never like ourselves as we are? I love your hair, it goes with your face. But you probably wish you had silly stringy hair like mine."

"Shut up." I put on my shirt. "Who's giving this party?"

"Well, one of the instructors at the League used to do set designs years ago, for the people who're giving the party. Nothing big—summer theater, little things, you know —and, well, he knows I want to be an actress and he thought that they might give me some ideas about how to get started—especially where to study, *that's* my problem. Oh. You see, his friends went on to become part of The Actors' Means Workshop. So—it might be interesting."

"For you. He doesn't know I'm coming."

"He knows a friend is coming. If they're shocked, well, *you* can take it, and the hell with them. They're so god-damn liberal, anyway, they make me want to puke. God, give me back my old Kentucky home, where a spade" —she began to laugh, and I laughed with her—"is called a spade!"

We walked down the stairs and crossed the quiet yard and walked out through our gate, into the streets. I always had to force myself to walk through the gate, especially if I was with Barbara. But, today, there were not many people in the streets—mainly the elderly, in windows, or on stoops. They seemed not to notice us. Avenue A was completely deserted, and we walked up to 14th Street before we found a cab. It was about seven in the evening, a marvelous summer evening. Barbara gave the driver the address. I leaned back, with my hand in hers.

"I think I should break up with Jerry," she said.

I took my hand away, and watched the streets go by. "I wasn't sure you were really *with* Jerry," I said.

"Well, why do you think you've been seeing him all the time, coming in and out of my door, for the last six weeks?"

"I wasn't *in* your room, sweetheart. And he's been coming in and out of my door, too."

"That sounds like Jerry. I'm beginning to think he's not very particular about his doors."

"But *you* are," I said. "Or you certainly should be." I looked at her. I looked out of the window again. "Hell. *I* don't know."

She bit her lip. We were approaching the park at 23rd Street and Fifth Avenue. "D'you know anybody who lives on Gramercy Park?" she asked. "Because *I* do. Gramercy Park South."

"Good for you, princess. Do you want to stop and pay them a visit?"

"God, no. They're just friends of my family, they're here for a couple of weeks. My mother wrote me about them, and asked me to go and see them."

"Suppose they come to see *you?*" I sat straight up.

"Well," she said, "I don't think they *can*. I *think* they still think I'm at the Y. I always write them on Y stationery."

"What about when they write *you?*"

"Yes. That's happened. But, then, I explain that I'm at another branch. And now I've told them to write me at the Art Students' League."

"I think it might be simpler, after all," I said, "just to give them your address."

"But, then," she said, "they'd just keep sending these people up to see me all the time. And that would be awful."

"They'd have a fit."

"Yes. And I'm just so tired of fighting with them."

"And they wouldn't like Jerry. Or Charlie. Or me."

"That's true. But they don't like *me*."

The taxi kept rolling. I said nothing.

"Do you get along with *your* family?" she asked.

I said, "No." Then, "But I don't really *have* any family. Not like you do."

She sighed. "Poor Leo. Poor Barbara. What's the matter with us all?" She looked out of her side of the cab and suddenly started laughing. The cab driver chuckled, too. "Oh, Leo. You didn't see it. This old, *old* lady in the middle of the street—and the bus was practically on *top* of her—she had no business out there—and she just put up her hand like this"—and she raised her hand in a gesture that looked like the Hitler salute—"and the bus just *stopped*. What brakes, boy. Or what a hand. You should have seen it. Sunday in New York. Wow. Kentucky was never like this."

We got to the party, which, as I remember, was somewhere in the Eighties, west of the Park. I remember an enormous foyer, artificial brown brick, lights flush with the ceiling, mirrors, and fake Greek columns. Levels, so that you had to watch where you were going, or you'd break your neck. A doorman stared at us, or, rather, at me; and we stood next to him while he called upstairs. Even then, he wasn't satisfied but left his post and came upstairs with us. The door was open and there were many people in the room. But the doorman rang the bell and stood there. Barbara had been amused. Now she was getting angry, and this, as always, made me cool. He kept looking from Barbara to me, and looking over the heads of the people, waiting for the host to appear. I kept staring at him; but—cowards all!—he refused to meet any eye. Barbara said, "The Führer is proud of you. You have done your duty like a good little soldier, and tomorrow you will be promoted to the latrine detail. Come on, Leo." She took my arm; the doorman danced as though he had to pee; the host, thank God, appeared. "But why are you standing out here?" he cried. "Come on in!"

"Your man didn't seem to want to let us in," I said.

"I just wanted to make sure it was all right, Mr. Frank," said the doorman. "You understand."

"What? Sure it's all right. What are you talking about? Kids!" He opened his arms wide. "Come on in."

Mr. Frank was smiling, but Barbara was dry. "This is Mr. Frank," she said. "Mr. Frank, this is my friend, Mr. Proudhammer."

"Pleased to meet you," we said, and our handshakes and our smiles meshed perfectly together. We went on in.

I look back on that party now—I see it through the veil of years—in an indefensibly romantic way. In the light of all that came after, it has the weight of the portentous, the dreadful value of the crucial turning. There we were, Barbara bright in blue, I dull in dark. Young, young, terribly young, and with scarcely any weapons save our youth and what time was to reveal as our character—by which I mean our real preoccupations. Time was

to tell us what we really cared about. Then, we really did
not know. I see us moving into the room, piloted by the
rather desperately smiling Mr. Frank—who had a mus-
tache, an open, boyish face, much graying hair, perhaps
too deliberately unkempt, and long eyes, placed very
close together. He was the Art League instructor, and
Barbara's friend; I do not know what it was in his smile
which made me feel how often—three times a week, at
least—he had seen Barbara naked. And this was revealed
in Barbara, too, in an attitude at once shrinking and
haughty. Barbara had been imprecise—she was forever to
remain so. It was not Mr. Frank's friends who were giving the party, but Mr. Frank himself. His friends were
the guests of honor. But it took a while before we met
these friends, who were to have such an effect on our
lives. There were, I am sure, hundreds of people there,
and both Barbara and I, in our bright blue, dull dark
fashions, were intimidated by them all. They glittered,
they flashed, they resounded; they had that air, inimita-
ble absolutely, of those who have succeeded. We recognized many of them, for many of them were famous. I
think Sylvia Sidney was there, she was doing a play in
New York then; and Franchot Tone; and Bette Davis.
And many playwrights and many directors. I was amazed
that I recognized so many. Yes, we were dazzled, dazzled
indeed. In the long, high room, this elegant room—elegant
if one bears in mind that elegance is scarcely permissible
in America—they seemed different, both younger and older
—for one saw the faces, off-guard, in life—and certainly
smaller than they appeared on stage or screen. One saw
that so-and-so's teeth, for example, were a little crooked;
and this one had bowlegs; this one was very drunk and
was clearly intending to become drunker. One very famous
actress struck me as having very narrowly missed being a
dwarf: but she had seemed very tall, in her regal robes,
when I had seen her on the stage as the queen of all the
Russias. It may have been that night that I really decided
to attempt to become an actor—really became committed
to this impossibility; it is certain that this night brought into
my mind, in an astounding way, the great question of where
the boundaries of reality were truly to be found. If a dwarf
could be a queen and make me believe that she was six
feet tall, then why was it not possible that I, brief, wiry,

dull dark me, could become an emperor—*The Emperor Jones,* say, why not? And I then watched everybody with this cruel intention in my mind.

Barbara, meanwhile, was being very much the heiress of all Kentucky. She was armed with her beauty, and she knew it, and her intentions were no less cruel than mine. If the other guests flashed, glittered, resounded, she more than confronted this display with her own unanswerable radiance, an innocence more presumed on their part than assumed on hers—but she was certainly no more above using their presumptions against them than I was—and a trick she had, which was to make her fortune later, of dropping her voice. She sometimes sounded as though she suffered from laryngitis, and one had to listen very carefully to hear what she said. She knew, however, that she had the power to make one listen very carefully, she knew very well that she was not at all what she seemed to be, and, furthermore, she knew how to make the company know that, though they had fame, she had youth, and time was on her side. The trick with her voice was something she had picked up from Margaret Sullavan, an actress she admired very much. But it always astonished me that no one ever recognized this. Perhaps it was because she had mastered the trick and made it her own. It was no longer a trick, but a fact.

The room had a fireplace and a mantelpiece. Rather unpleasant objects were placed on the mantelpiece, curios meant to remind one of Africa and of Rome. The room contained the necessary elements of Picasso and Matisse and Rouault, and, hanging from the center of the ceiling, was an extremely depressing and sibilant mobile. Just as the room was grim with splendor, it was also very heavily freighted with liquor and with food on two immense tables, near the open windows. Barbara saw that I had found my feet, knew what to do—that girl always trusted me—and, as we were operating, in any case, in tandem, she went on to her job in the perfect assurance that I would do mine. Her job was mainly to be charming, thus divesting the company of their spiritual valuables. My job was to be surly—my surliness being, precisely, my charm. At this point in our lives, Barbara and I had never slept together, but we had also, by now, been forced to discover how extremely unattractive and indeed offensive most people considered the truth to be. We no longer dreamed of telling the truth. Thus, Barbara knew herself to be branded, merely by the fact of my presence, with a letter far more dreadful than the scarlet one—and far more attractive, therefore she dropped her voice, forcing everyone to lean in to listen, and used her teeth and eyes to such moving effect that everyone wished they were me—and I was invested, by *her* presence, with an aura of dangerous recklessness and power. Nothing could have been further from the truth, but we were, as Pirandello puts it, in the process of living our play and playing our lives.

Preparing myself for my role—I was to live with this inane concept for many years—I went to the tables and heaped food on a plate. Then I poured a very genteel glass of red wine. Since Barbara was now being so very delicate and Southern—she was pretending to be Scarlett O'Hara, was being extremely girlish and completely untruthful concerning the family "domains—but I reckon y'all say real estate, don't you?"—I carried the immense plate of food and the genteel glass of wine to her. I even remembered to drape a napkin over my arm.

"Why, my darling Leo," she said, in her highest voice and with her richest accent, "How sweet of you! But how in the world"—she turned, glowing indeed, to the couple she had been so brutally seducing—"am I to manage it?"

"I'll hold the glass," I said.

"Not at all. He's completely impossible," she now informed the fascinated couple—"really! I will find a seat and sit *down*. And you will find yourself something to eat, and a drink—he drinks far too much," she said to the couple, "but I've given up fighting him about it, it's simply a waste of time. Do come with me," she said to the couple, who were now regarding me with a very definite awe, "and, Leo," she said imperiously, "do come immediately back and I will introduce you to the guests of honor. I don't dare do it now because you're not in the least amenable until you've got something in your stomach." She smiled at the couple. "He's really a very sweet boy."

I said, "Thank you, princess. Them's the kindest words I've heard from you all week." Then, precisely on cue, I gave the couple my most irresistible grin. "I'll be right back," I said. I went to the tables and got down a lot of chicken livers in a hurry and loaded up a plate and poured myself an enormous Scotch.

They were sitting on a sofa near the fireplace. Barbara had a very definite eye on all the other actresses in the room and was selecting and discarding various details of their dress and manner. She was also attempting, with a success far from complete, some of the worldliness of Tallulah Bankhead. Her audience, though, which was probably amused, was also very firmly held. Barbara was talking about *Miss Julie*. "Leo and I love that play," she said. "We're convinced that poor, mad Strindberg wrote it with us in mind."

"But, my dear," said the female of the couple, "the preoccupations of *Miss Julie*—we wouldn't go far wrong, I think, in saying the *obsessions* of that remarkable play —and I believe my husband feels as I do—are so very *Northern*. Surely. You are not like that at all. You are— *tropical*. Truly. You give off heat." She smiled, and batted her enormous blue eyes. "I feel it. All the way over here." Her husband was sitting between them, and I was sitting on the other side of Barbara, practically in her lap. I ate with a silent, surly ferocity and, from time to time, I smacked my lips. I took great swallows of the Scotch. But I was also concentrating, for I had never read *Miss Julie*, and I now had to figure out, from what they— or, more particularly, Barbara—said, just what the devil our favorite play was about. The blue-eyed lady, however, had sunk the subject of *Miss Julie* without a trace. She said, "My dear Miss King, you haven't introduced us to your silent, hungry, and very attractive friend." Whereas, before, she had looked very steadily at Barbara in order to avoid looking at me, she now looked very steadily at me in order to avoid looking at Barbara. "So I will intro- duce myself. Lola San-Marquand is my name and this is my husband, Saul." She extended her hand and I care- fully wiped mine on my napkin before taking it. We shook hands. I liked her at once. I liked her enormously. I do not know what it was in her which made me feel, immediately, and with great force, that she was a sad woman, a lost and ruined woman, and, even, a gallant one. Her details were preposterous, but I read these de- tails as the very signal of her bewilderment and sorrow. She was enormous, not fat in a hard way, fat in a soft way:

one felt that she had become fat out of despair. Yet, she
covered this despair with a stylish, loose, black sack. Her
hair, which was very beautiful, very blond, and very long,
was severely, impeccably even, perhaps masochistically,
pulled back from a rather stunning brow and ferociously
knotted at the back of her head. And over this glory she
wore a black chiffon scarf, knotted beneath her—chins,
perhaps accuracy compels me to say, but the original chin
was a firm one. This was the uniform of Lola San-Marquand. I never knew her to dress in any other way. She
must have had hundreds of black dresses and scarves—
though, in fact, a black and impetuous toque sometimes
did duty for the scarf. This, however, was mainly on
opening nights. She impressed me—she impresses me still
—as one of the most curious, most loving, devious, ruthless, and single-minded people I have met in all my life.
She was brilliantly and brutally manufactured: she had
not grown into her present shape, but had been hammered into it, or perhaps, as in some unspeakable vat,
been lowered. Her hands were white and pudgy and soft.
Yet, they were not without power, and the fingers were
elegant. One felt that the pudginess of the hands was no
more inevitable than the rings they bore—rather awful
rings; that, trapped within Lola San-Marquand, was a
beautiful, dying girl. But, alas, fatally, overwhelmingly at
last, one became aware of the odor of that corruption.

Barbara said, "You're very right, Mrs. San-Marquand,
and I'm terribly sorry"—but I felt that she did not, now,
quite know how to carry on. My reaction to Lola—for
Barbara was swift—had disarmed her; had caused the top
she had been maliciously spinning to fall, with a perceptible
thunder, uselessly and tamely down. She looked at me
briefly, wondering if I thought she should be ashamed of
herself, then concentrated on her plate, having made it
very clear that she now waited to take her cue from me.

Saul San-Marquand had also shaken my hand. His hand
was wet and white, I felt nothing when I took his hand
except a deep aversion. I disliked him at once, and as
profoundly as one man can dislike another—from the
very bottom of my balls. His lips were thin, his eyes were
vague, his nearly snow-white head seemed far too heavy
for his neck. He impressed me as a Jeremiah who had
never had any convictions. Perhaps I disliked him be-

cause I liked Lola—*he* seemed, certainly, the most pre-posterous and deadly of all her preposterous details—or perhaps it was because I knew that Barbara admired him very much. Women liked Saul. No doubt it is due to some fatal lack in me that I never understood this at all.

But perhaps I disliked him because he was one of the very few men I've ever met, if not the only one, who seemed really to dislike men. I am probably being unjust here, and, if I'm to be honest, I must confess to a certain bewilderment and to a very definite awareness that my attitude cannot be defended by logic. For I get along with women who dislike women very well. Perhaps the male ego finds the female antipathy flattering and per-haps it also flatters itself that it is able to understand this antipathy. Barbara, God knows, can't bear women and has only had, in all the time we've known each other, a single close female friend—who can't bear women, either, and who can't even, in fact, bear the theater, and who has lately taken a post in a hospital in Hong Kong. But my own instinct, as to the male relation, is that men, who are far more helpless than women—because far less single-minded —need each other as comrades, need each other for cor-rection, need each other for tears and ribaldry, need each other as models, need each other indeed, in sum, in order to be able to love women. Women liked Saul, but I never felt that Saul liked women. I felt that he used them, collected them, huddled like an infant between their breasts, and used their furnace to diminish his chill. If his chill could be— barely—diminished, it could certainly not be conquered. It eventually began to seem to me that the women clung to Saul in the hope of being able to get back some of the heat he had stolen. Perhaps some of them managed to do so, but his wife was not to be numbered among that im-probable few. For warmth she had substituted a deft imi-tation, a most definite style, which was bizarre and bewil-dering precisely to the degree that one sensed beneath it a genuine impulse, perpetually, and not without bitterness, held in check.

"We know that Miss King is from Kentucky," said Lola San-Marquand, "but she has not told us where *you* are from. And, while I'm aware that the most unlikely things happen every day—that's the very lesson, the *charm*, the *discipline* of the theater—yet, I must say, that the script which would have the two of you meeting in Kentucky would"—and she laughed elaborately, a high, clear, rather girlish sound—"impress me as lacking *verisimilitude*. Now, I'm sure that you'll shatter all my preconceptions and tell me that you both grew up in Kentucky in the same house."

"Well," I said, "that's happened more than once, though —friendship—wasn't the usual result. But I've never even seen Kentucky. I rather hope that I never do. I was born in New York. In Harlem."

For reasons securely hidden from me, the mention of Harlem created in Lola's husband a comparative vigor, a stunning hint of life. "We lived there long ago," he said. He looked at nothing and no one as he said this, and I concluded that he was seeing the streets of Harlem. "Oh," I said, quickly, "where?"

"It was a long time ago," he said. He then lapsed, as it were, out of our sight, and then again was shaken with a brief convulsion. This one reached his lips and caused the corners—nearly—to turn up. "Did you know Ethel Waters?" he asked.

"No," I said, "but, of course, I know who she is." I didn't like Saul, but he had the power—how the years were to prove it!—of bewildering me, of throwing me off-guard, of distracting my attention to *him* when it should have been on the terrain. "She's a wonderful singer," I said inanely, and felt, at once, with a sharp and furious resentment, that this nerveless, wormy little man had somehow carried me beyond my depth. I stared at him. I felt Barbara concentrating on her plate in order the more deliberately and totally to concentrate on me. And I also felt—and this, too, I resented, feared—that my immediate affection for Lola and my unshakable love for Barbara— for it was love—had created, with the speed of flame, a deep, speechless communication between them. And this communication had to do with Saul and me—they were exchanging signals over our heads, quite as though my quality, far from nerveless, and my value, were to be equated with that of this unspeakable refugee from the garment center. I had worked in the garment center, pushing trucks, and indeed I was to work there many times again, and Saul San-Marquand was the very distillation of my foremen and my bosses. I choked on my food, which now seemed, as, in a way it was, stolen, and my Scotch burned me. But of course I was going to be cool, and, in any case, I needed time to calculate, and so I used my sputter and my cough to make my statement impeccably ingenuous and juvenile: "I hear she's a marvelous actress, too, but I've never seen her."

"But, my dear boy," cried Lola, leaning forward, and with something very genuine in her face now—perhaps it was a genuine affection—"how could you possibly have seen her? You're far too young. *I* am old enough to be your mother, and *I* have seen her very seldom—Saul, my dear"—leaning forward again, beautifully interrupting herself, and moving a compassionately nerveless hand toward her magnificent brow—"she never acted, did she, at the Lafayette Theater—which is before *your* time, my dear youth," turning now to me, "though it's in your territory. I *don't*," she said portentously, leaning back, "*think* that she did. But your memory is so much better than my own."

Saul's obsessive perusal of the streets of Harlem elicited, "No. We saw Rose McClendon there. Before we met."

"Of course! *Wasn't* she superb. What was the play? Oh. My memory. I do not know what I would do without Saul. And he does me the honor of pretending not to know what he would do without *me*. Do you remember the name of the play, my dear?"

"Ethel Waters," Barbara interrupted, "couldn't possibly have acted in the Lafayette Theater. I don't think. She wasn't considered an actress then, she was only, as Leo says, known as a singer. Isn't the first thing she did as an actress"—she leaned into Lola San-Marquand's quite incredible breasts—"the play called *Mamba's Daughters?* Which *I* didn't see. I was still doing penance in Kentucky then."

Lola threw back her head and laughed—that oddly genuine, girlish sound. "My dear. If you *had* seen it, I assure you that your penance in Kentucky would have been perhaps more painful, but certainly more brief. I assure you—"

"The play in which we saw Rose McClendon," said Saul, with what I was now beginning to recognize as the unanswerable firmness of the totally infirm, "was a play by Paul Green—you remember Paul Green—it was called *In Abraham's Bosom.*"

"Of course!" said Lola. "About the schoolteacher. Neither of you, of course, could possibly have seen—"

"But I read it," I said. I was beginning to find my feet again. "I'm not sure I really liked it."

"If you were older," said Lola San-Marquand, with assurance, "it would be a very good role for you. Miss King has confided in us that she wished—aspired—to become an actress. Are you also tempted toward the sacred flame? I must tell you—and Saul will tell you that I am *never* wrong about these things—these *elements*— he likes to pretend that I was really born to be a medium" —and now she laughed again, not as long as it seemed, not as loud as it sounded, with her marvelous head thrown back—"and, truly, I never *am* wrong. In *these* matters." She looked at her husband roguishly; he had not yet looked at her. "And I must tell you—my beamish boy—that, whether or not you are tempted toward the sacred flame, the *flame*"—she raised her hand, she spread her fingers wide; the lights flashed, like flame, like flame, on her abjectly jeweled fingers: it was as though, with the same gesture, she were warding off and abjectly awaiting the mortal blow—"the flame has very definite intentions toward *you*. The flame demands you. The flame will have you. You are not handsome. You are not, really, even, very good-looking. But you are—*haunting.* If you are capable of discipline—and I *know* that you are, it shows in the way you carry yourself, it shows in ways that you do not see—which you will never see—my dear, you will go far. Much further than you imagine. I know. I am gifted in these matters. In fact," and now she leaned toward Barbara; they had been continually exchanging signals—over our heads; now Lola hurled her deadliest, most crucial flare, which was also her vow, to Barbara, of fidelity. "Miss King will also go very far—very far indeed. Her fame will be greater than yours, and it will certainly come sooner. But she will not have had to cross your deserts. And she will have to pay for that. And so will you." And then she leaned back, mighty, exhausted.

Barbara said, much to my surprise, "I hear you. I hear

you. I think you're right. I'm very glad you've said it. I've never known how."

I was amazed. I was flattered. I was frightened. I looked at the two women, who looked neither at each other nor at either of us. Barbara leaned back and put her empty plate behind the sofa, on the floor. "I still don't like," I said, with a certain, very deliberate obstinacy—deliberate, but far from calculated—"*In Abraham's Bosom*. I'd like—if you think I can act—to try *The Emperor Jones*—"

"You're much too thin for that," said Lola, with finality, "and, frankly—I hope you aren't *inordinately* sensitive—much too young—"

"Leo," said Barbara—she looked at Lola—"*I think the play we should try to do is All God's Chillun Got Wings.*"

Lola clapped her hands. "Of course," she said. She smiled at Saul. "And Rags could direct it. Rags would *love* to do it."

"We are," said Saul, sounding far more definite than he had sounded all night, "the artistic directors of The Actors' Means Workshop."

"Rags—Rags Roland—was once, I believe, a good friend of the actress who did that play in London. With great success." Lola spoke now with a bright, matronly vagueness which impressed me as being a way of stalling for time. "You've heard of Rags Roland? You know who she is?"

"Oh, of course," said Barbara, "she's a very successful producer."

Lola leaned back, raising one finger, closing both eyes. "She is not only *that*, my dear. She is also a *most* interesting director. *Most* interesting. The world does not yet know it, but *we* do—and many of the actors she has worked with are very aware of who *really* directed them in some of their greatest performances—oh, there is far more to Rags Roland than her mere function as *producer*. She is part of our staff at the Workshop. She is one of our oldest friends. And *invaluable*."

"Is there really any hope of our being allowed to study at the Workshop?" Barbara now asked. She asked this of Saul. Lola, continuing to smile, now looked very steadily at Barbara in order, I felt, not to look too directly at her husband, on whom Barbara's effect was now, critically, practically, to be tested. "I've heard marvelous things about it, but, of course, we both also know that it's virtually impossible to be accepted there."

Barbara had decided that she *wished* to be accepted, had decided, indeed, that she was *going* to be accepted, on terms, whatever these might prove to be, which she would simply have to prepare herself to meet. I was undecided. Events seemed to be moving rather faster than I liked. But I struggled to be ready with my answer when the moment for my answer would be ripe.

"Well, of course," said Saul, and he looked very briefly at me—he liked me no more than I liked him—"we would be derelict in our duty, in our responsibility to the theatrical community at large and to the American theater in particular, if we didn't insist that those who wish to work with us meet the very highest standards. Many people feel that our standards are ridiculously high, I have even heard us accused, in some quarters, of cruelty. This has never dismayed us for a second, we have steadfastly gone on with our work, and we have achieved what we consider, and not only we, if we may say so, some exceedingly fine results. Our harvest has not been negligible, we are very much encouraged, and we intend to continue in the great light which our long experience has permitted us to achieve." He paused. I watched him; I think my mouth was open. "Now, you," he said, "and your friend, Mister—?"

"Proudhammer," I said.

"Yes. You are both very interesting young people. You impress us very much. Your own quality," and he favored Barbara with a meek, shy smile, "is something like a—stormy petrel, so to say. We don't yet have, honestly, as clear an impression of your—uh—*friend*. Proudhammer. As we do of you. But this is not to say that we find him less interesting," and he attempted a smile in my direction which failed, quite, to reach me. "But our methods at the Workshop are extremely severe and not everyone can bring to the Workshop the necessary background, the background which will enable them to achieve the necessary *discipline*. We have a responsibility, as we have said, not only to the theatrical community at large, but to all those who work with us and who try

to learn from us." I was silent, for Barbara's sake. I finished my drink and, only for Barbara's sake, did not immediately leave the sofa to pour myself another. But I
leaned forward, with my empty glass in my hand, deliberately in the attitude of imminent departure. "You are
an exceedingly attractive young lady, but what makes
you feel that you are qualified to become an actress?"

"You have asked me that question," Barbara said,
very coolly and distinctly, "only to set a trap for me. Or
to give me a kind of test. I refuse to fall into your trap
and so you'll have to give me good marks for passing my
first test. I am an actress because *I* know it, and I intend
to prove it, and I *shall* prove it. I'll prove it, yet, to you.
To *you*, I may prove it late or early, but, actually, that's
your option—that's for you to decide."

"That's my girl," I said. Saul looked slightly stunned,
but not displeased. Lola now watched Barbara with
something in her enormous, her brilliantly blue and candid
eyes, which made them seem hooded, which darkened the
blue with what I could only read as patience. I rose. Saul
looked up at me.

"And what," he asked me, "do you consider *your*
qualifications to be?"

I said, "I think you're looking at them." Then I smiled.
"I need another drink. But I'm sure you realize already
that I can't be as definite as Miss King because of the great
difference in our backgrounds."

"My," said Lola, mildly, "you *are* young. But spirit
you have."

"That's how darkies were born," I said, and walked back
to the whiskey bottle.

I was bitter, I was twisted out of shape with rage; and
I raged at myself for being enraged. I dropped ice recklessly into my glass, recklessly poured Scotch over the
rocks, took too large and swift a swallow, and, trying to
bring myself to some reasonable, fixed place, to turn off
the motor which was running away with me, I lit a cigarette and turned my back on the company to stare out of
the window. I knew that I was being childish, and, in the
eyes of the company, perhaps definitely and inexcusably
rude; but I could not trust myself, for that moment, to
encounter a human eye or respond to a human voice. It
did not help, and it could not have, to recognize that I

really did not know—assuming that I aspired to walk in
the light of clarity and honor—what had triggered this
rage. I refused to believe that it could truly have been
Saul San-Marquand: how could it have been if it was
really true that I held him in such low esteem? But the
measure of my esteem had, fatally, to reveal itself in the
quantity of my indifference—which quantity was small
and shameful indeed. Here I stood at the Manhattan
window, seething—to no purpose whatever, which was
bad enough: but it was worse to be forced to ask myself,
abjectly, now, for my reasons and find that I did not have
any. Or, which, really, I think, caused the cup of my
humiliation to overflow, to find that I had no reasons
which my reason—by which, of course, I also mean that
esteem in which I hoped to earn the right to hold myself
—did not immediately and contemptuously reject. I was
not—was I?—stupidly and servilely to do the world's
dirty work for it and permit its tangled, blind, and merciless reaction to the fact of my color also to become my
own. How could I hope for, how could I deserve, my
liberation, if I became my own jailer and myself turned
the key which locked the mighty doors? But my rage was
there, it was there, it pretended to sleep but it never
slept, the merest touch of a feather was enough to bring it
howling, roaring out. It had no sight, no measure, no
precision, and no justice: and it was my master still. I
drank my Scotch, I stared at the stars, I watched the park,
which, in the darkness, was made shapeless and grandi-
ose, which spoke of peace and space and cooling, healing
water—which seemed to speak of possibilities for the
bruised, despairing spirit which might remain forever,
for me, far away, a dark dream veiled in darkness. A faint
breeze struck, but did not cool my Ethiopian brow.
Ethiopia's hands: to what god indeed, out of this despairing place, was I to stretch these hands? But I also felt,
incorrigible, hoping to be reconciled, and yet unable to
accept the terms of any conceivable reconciliation, that
any god daring to presume that I would stretch out my
hands to him would be struck by these hands with all my
puny, despairing power; would be forced to confront, in
these, my hands, the monstrous blood-guiltiness of God.
No. I had had quite enough of God—more than enough,
more than enough, the horror filled my nostrils, I gagged

on the blood-drenched name; and yet was forced to see that this horror, precisely, accomplished His reality and undid my unbelief.

I was beginning to apprehend the unutterable dimensions of the universal trap. I was human, too. And my race was revealed as my pain—my pain—and my rage could have no reason, nor submit to my domination, until my pain was assessed; until my pain became invested with a coherence and an authority which only I, alone, could provide. And this possibility, the possibility of creating my language out of my pain, of using my pain to create myself, while cruelly locked in the depths of me, like the beginning of life and the beginning of death, yet seemed, for an instant, to be on the very tip of my tongue. My pain was the horse that I must learn to ride. I flicked my cigarette out of the window and watched it drop and die. I thought of throwing myself after it. I was no rider and pain was no horse.

I was standing near a piano. A strange girl, with real eyes in a real face, was watching me with a smile. "You've been very far away," she said.

"Yes," I said. Somehow, she cheered me; my heart lifted up; we smiled at each other. "Yes. But I'm back now."

"Welcome," she said. "Welcome!"

I felt like a boy. I wanted to please her. I touched the piano keyboard lightly. "Would you like me to try to play something for you? Would you like that?"

"I'd love that," she said.

I sat down. She took my glass and set it on top of the piano for me. She leaned there, smiling on me like the sun. I felt free. "I don't play very well," I said, "and I don't sing very well any more—my voice changed, you know, when I got to be a big boy"—and she threw back her head, like a very young horse in a sun-filled meadow, and laughed, and I laughed—"but I like to try it from time to time. It—helps—to—keep me in touch with myself." I stared at her. She nodded. I struck the keys. "I'll try to sing a blues for you," I said, "and, after that, even if I'm asked to leave, if you've liked it, I won't mind my exile at all."

"You won't," she said, "be exiled. And I'm sure you know it."

"All *right*," I said. "Well, all *right*, then," and I
jumped into a song which I remembered Caleb singing,
which Caleb had loved, and when I reached the lines,
*Blues, you're driving me crazy, what am I to do? Blues,
you're driving me crazy, what am I to do? I ain't got
nobody to tell my troubles to,* I looked up and found
that the entire room had gathered around the piano. I
looked into Barbara's face—she was smiling. She was
proud of me. I looked at the nice girl, the girl who had
said, "Welcome!" She was smiling, too. Then I looked at
Saul and I struck the keys again. "What," I asked Barbara, "do you think of my qualifications now, princess?"

"We are still," said Lola, "looking at them. And you
can't stop now."

"If I were you," said Barbara, "I'd just keep on keeping on."

"Well, then, all *right*," I said, and I sang some more.
We all got drunk. Barbara borrowed some money from
Mr. Frank, and also extorted from him an unopened bottle of Scotch. He was too drunk to care—or, rather, too
drunk to help himself, for he certainly cared about his
money and his liquor. Saul and Lola, and Barbara and I,
were the last to leave the party; and Barbara and I had
sufficient genuine elegance and enough borrowed money
to drop the San-Marquands, in style, at their stylish Park
Avenue apartment. It had been decided that we would
work at the Workshop, that summer, in New Jersey, in
effect, as student handymen. Barbara and I were to prepare, for Saul's inspection, one or two improvisations, the
nature of which he would dictate, and one or two scenes,
which we were to choose ourselves. And, depending on
what the summer revealed of our qualifications, we
would be accepted into the Workshop. We were very
confident and we were very happy. The sky was purple
and the sun stood ready, behind this curtain, waiting for
her cue, as we reached falling-down Paradise Alley. I had
held Barbara in my arms all the way home, and I think
that we would surely have slept together that night—or
that morning—but Jerry was asleep in Barbara's quarters, and Charlie was snoring in mine. So we woke them
up, and opened the whiskey, and told them of our triumphs. And that summer, in fact, for one night, Barbara

and I both appeared in *Of Mice and Men*. Barbara played Curley's wife, and I played Crooks.

And now, Barbara, as though conjured up by the twilight, as silently as a reverie, entered my hospital room, "Hi, my love," she said, and came to the bed and kissed me. "How nice to have you back."

"It was worth the journey," I said, "just to have you say that."

She looked at me. "I trust," she said, "that one day soon you'll find less drastic ways of being reassured." Then she smiled. "But I haven't come to lecture you. Dr. Evin has promised to take over that department from me. He's a very nice man, don't you think?"

"Very nice. Have you told him a lot about me?"

"No more than I had to. And *much* less than I know." I laughed. She walked to the window and touched my flowers. "I hope the nurse knows that these must be taken out of here at night. She doesn't seem to know much, I must say. Would you like me to read some of your telegrams to you? These silent messengers seem to be merely piling up dust over here. I must speak to that nurse."

"Leave her alone. She's a nice kid."

"She is far too easily dazzled by fame. She looks on me as a combination of Queen Victoria and Madame X. And the good Lord knows *what* delicious nightmares *you* are evoking in those covered-wagon breasts. So naturally she can't do her work properly." She picked up the telegrams and came back to the bed.

Time had not done much for Barbara's figure, though she no longer, as one of her directors had put it, promised only a bony ride. Time had thinned her face and dimmed its color; the theater had put her hair through so many changes that the color which it had now adopted—due to the demands of her present role—was probably as close to the original as she would ever again be able to get; and, though there were no silver locks in it yet, there were, perceptibly, silver strands. Her elegance was swinging and it was also archaic; perhaps elegance is always archaic. She was rather splendidly dressed, in something dark, with a dull, heavy brooch at the neck; her hair was piled very tightly up, in the fashion in which she wore it in the play. She caused one to think, I don't know why, of sorrow and fragility: she caused one to think of time. Her splendor seemed extorted, ruthlessly, from time, and she wore her splendor in that knowledge, and with that respect, and also with that scarcely perceptible trembling. One wondered how such a fragility bore such a ruthless weight. This wonder contributed to her force as an actress. Barbara had become a very good actress—one of the best on a scene which she knew, however, to be barren. Since she knew the scene to be barren, she was not much impressed by her eminence. She tried to work with as little show, and, she hoped, to as decent an effect, as any honorable cook or carpenter—though she knew very well that there were not many of these left, either. This lonely effort had stripped her of her affectations. Of course, on the other hand, the authority with which this effort had invested her caused many to insist that her affectations had all been disastrously confirmed, and constituted, furthermore, her entire dramatic arsenal. Barbara went on her swinging way. She seemed to listen to life as though life were the most cunning and charming of confidence men: knowing perfectly well that she was being conned, she, nevertheless, again and again, gave the man the money for the Brooklyn Bridge. She never gained possession of the bridge, of course, but she certainly learned how to laugh. And the tiny lines in her face had been produced as much by laughter as by loss. If life had endlessly cheated her, she had resolved not only never to complain, but to take life's performance as an object lesson and never to cheat on life.

"How's the show going?"

"Oh, the show's okay. Your understudy is still going through his all-white-men-to-the-sword-and-all-white-women-to-my-bed bullshit—but—oh, well, you *can* hear him across the Hudson River and he doesn't bump into the furniture. Anymore. He's the only person who doesn't miss you. Naturally." She opened one telegram. "Do you know anybody named Joan Nelson?"

"No."

"Well, she knows you and she wants you to get well." She opened another telegram. "So does someone named Bradley Timkins. Do you know *him?*"

"No."

"You impress me as being a somewhat solitary type. Not that it's any wonder, as heartless as you are." She opened another. "Oh. This is from Marlon—you *do* know *him?*"

"Oh, yes. The friend of my youth."

"I think that he really *does* want you to get well. He wants *everyone* to get well."

"So do I."

"Yes. Well, we haven't got a prayer, sweetheart."

"How goes the nation?"

"The nation goes abominably. And it's no subject for a sick man to discuss—or a well one, either." She smiled. "Oh. Here's one from Lola. Show business!"

"Christopher sent the basket of fruit," I said.

She looked up. The light in the room seemed to change; or, a more tremendous light than the twilight entered it. Perhaps it was Barbara's face at that moment which finally reconciled me to life. "Did he? Oh, let me see." And I handed her Christopher's telegram. She read it and she laughed. "Oh. That black mother. He'll never change. Christopher." And then she was far from me. I watched her face. Although I knew her face so well, I did not know it now at all. It was incredibly trusting and triumphant; it existed in another realm, which spoke another language; there is truly something frightening in a woman's face. And yet—how can I say it?—the mystery that I saw there contained a help for me, and promised me my health. "Dear Christopher." Then she looked down at me. "Leo, I think we have done something very rare." She smiled. But I cannot describe that smile. It was neither sorrowful nor joyful, neither was it both: it spoke of journeys. I cannot describe it because I could not read it. Then she spoke, very carefully, testing, as it were, each word. "I think we have managed to redeem something. I think it's our love that we redeemed. Who could have guessed such a thing? Black Christopher!" She walked back to my flowers. "And I was afraid it was too late—that it had all been for nothing —that we'd betrayed and discarded all the best of us—for —what anyone with five dollars can buy at the box office." She laughed and turned and looked at me again. "Well. Thank you, Leo. We made it one time."

"What," I asked, a little frightened, and at the same time amused and moved, "are you talking about, Barbara?"

"I'm talking about our journey through hell. I'm

talking about Christopher. *You* know what I'm talking about."

"Maybe," I said, "you're making too much of it."

"That's possible. But you're making too little. You always do." She laughed softly again, looking, against the yellow blinds and in the dimming, changing light, exactly like the Barbara of Paradise Alley—and yet not, that laugh had cost her everything—and then became grave again. "We have come a long way together, you and I," she said. *"Des kilomètres."* She looked out of the window for a second, then closed the blinds. She looked briefly at her watch. The room was dark. She switched on the light. "Well. I must get to the theater. The show must go on."

"Those days with Christopher must have been very hard on you," I said.

She looked at me. "Oh. They were brutal. But why do anything easy? Those days were very hard on you, too."

"But I always felt," I said, smiling, "that you'd done nothing to deserve it."

"But *you* had. Of course!" She laughed again. "Dear Leo!"

"I have the feeling that you're making fun of me. But I don't know why."

"Because you're funny," she said.

"Bon. Bravo pour le clown."

"Well. It's true. When you were at your funniest, I didn't laugh. I'm sorry for all the things I didn't see. And for all the things *you* didn't see. What you didn't see, I saw, it seemed to me, very clearly. Leo, you always want people to forgive *you*. But we, we others, we need forgiveness, too. We sometimes need it, my dear"—she smiled—"even from so wretched a man as you." And she watched me very steadily, with that steady smile.

I said, after a moment, with difficulty, "True enough, dear lady. True enough. But I wonder why I feel so depressed."

"I should think," she said, dryly, "that the state of your health might have something to do with that. And I've stayed longer than I promised Dr. Evin I would." She leaned down and kissed me on the lips. "Bye-bye. Is there anything you want me to bring you tomorrow?"

"Only the heads," I said, "on pikes, of many politicians."

"Now you sound like Christopher."

"He'd be proud of me."

"He was always proud of you. He couldn't understand why you couldn't understand that. Christopher had a rough time, too."

"How have *you*," I asked suddenly, "managed to put up with me for all these years?"

"I love you," she said, "and so I can't really claim to have had much choice in the matter." She looked at her watch again. "Leo, now I really must run. If the heads of politicians prove to be scarce tomorrow, is there anything else you want?"

"Surprise me."

"I'm honored. I'm one of the few people left in the world who can still do that. To you. Throw everything out of your mind, Leo, eat your supper, read a little, sleep. The world will still be here when you wake up, and there'll still be everything left to do. Good-night."

"Good-night."

She left, closing the door carefully and softly behind her.

But she had left me, as our much loved Bessie Smith would have been prompt to inform her, with everything on my mind. Christopher had always wished to see Africa; we became friends partly because I had. I told him once that he was certainly black enough to be an African, and even told him that the structure of his face reminded me of faces I had seen in Dakar. This enchanted him: which meant, fatally, that he then invested me with the power of enchantment. I did not want this power. It frightened me. But my fright frightened him, and it made him cruel: for to whom was he to turn, in all this world, if not to an elder brother who was black like him? And I began to see, though I did not want to see it, the validity of Christopher's claim. If it is true, as I suspect, that people turn to each other in the hope of being created by each other then it is absolutely true that the uncreated young turn, to be created, toward their elders. Thus, whoever has been invested with the power of enchantment is guilty of something more base than treachery whenever he fails to exercise the power on which the yet-to-be-created, as helplessly as newborn birds, depend. Well, yes, I saw at last what was demanded of me. I would have to build a nest out of materials I would simply have to find, and be prepared to guard it with my life; and feed this creature and keep it clean, and keep the nest clean; and watch for the moment when the creature could fly and force those frightened wings to take the air.

On the other hand, any threat to their enchanter, which is simply a threat to life itself, is answered by the young with the implacable intention to kill.

I first realized this—through Christopher—at a monster rally in downtown New York. Thousands of people were gathered in a park near City Hall. We were there to protest the outrages taking place in the city (and also in the nation) against those who, already poor and defenseless, were rendered even more so by the apathy and corruption of the municipality, and by the facts of their ancestry, or color. The rally was guarded by the police, whom we were, in fact, attacking. They were there to make certain that none of the damage which we asserted was being done to the city's morals would so far transform itself as to become damage to the city's property.

I was one of the speakers at this rally. I would have been there anyway, but not as a speaker, as one of the oppressed: but I was seated on the wooden platform because my name can draw crowds. Having never been quite able to consider my name my own, this fact meant something else for Christopher, and also for the crowds, than it could have meant to me: but opportunity and duty are sometimes born together. There I sat on the platform, then, uneasy and indignant, and not altogether at my ease with the other luminaries, who were certainly not at their ease with me. Our common situation, the fact of my color, had brought us together here; and here we were to speak as one. But our intensities, our apprehensions, were very different. In many ways, perhaps in nearly all ways, they disapproved of me, and I knew it; and they knew that in many ways I disapproved of them. But we were responsible, commonly, for something greater than our differences. These differences, anyway, could be blamed on no one and could never have risen to the pressure of a private quarrel had it not been for the nature of our public roles. Our differences were reducible to one: I was an artist. This is a very curious condition, and only people who never can become artists have ever imagined themselves as desiring it. It cannot be desired, it can only—with difficulty—be supported, and one of the elements to be supported (along with one's own unspeakable terrors) is the envy, rage, and wonder of the world. Yes, we on the platform were united in our social indignation, united in our affliction, united in our responsibility, united in our necessity to change—well, if not the world, at least the condition of some people in the world: but how different were our visions of the world! I had never been at home in the world and had become incapable of imagining that I ever would be. I did not want others to endure my estrangement, that was why I was on the platform; yet was it not, at the least, paradoxical that it was only my estrangement which had placed me there? And I could not flatten out this paradox, I could not hammer it into any usable shape. Everyone else desired to be at home in the world, and so did I—or so *had* I; and they were right in this desire, and so had I been; it was our privilege, to say nothing of our hope, to attempt to make the world a human dwellingplace for us all; and yet—yet—was it not possible that the mighty gentlemen, my honorable and invaluable confreres, by being unable to imagine such a journey as my own, were leaving something of the utmost importance out of their aspirations? I could not know. I watched Christopher's face. He trusted none of the people with whom I was sitting. Most of them were from five to ten years older than I, and from twenty to thirty years older than Christopher. And nothing we had done, or left undone, had been able to save him.

There was a little black girl on the platform, she was part of a junior choir from a Brooklyn church. They were singing. I knew that when the choir finished singing, I would be on, and this is usually a very difficult moment for me, but the little girl's voice pushed my stage fright far to the side of my mind. They were singing a song about deliverance; she had a heavy, black, huge voice. She was the leader of the song, and her voice, in all that open air, rang against the sky and the trees and the stone walls of office buildings and the faces of the open-mouthed people and the closed faces of the cops, as though she were singing in a cave. *Deliverance will come,* she sang, *I know it will come, He said it would come.* And, again, *Deliverance will come. He said it would come. I know it will come.* I watched her face as she sang, a plain, black, stocky girl, who was, nevertheless, very beautiful. Deliverance will come. I wondered how old she was, and what songs she would be singing, and in what company, a few years from now. Deliverance will come. Would it? We on the platform certainly had no patent on deliverance—it was only because deliverance had *not* come that we sat there in all our uneasy rage and splendor. Deliverance will come: it had not come for my mother and father, it had not come for Caleb, it had not come for me, it had not come for Christopher, it had not come for this nameless little girl, and it had not come for all these thousands who were listening to her song. I watched the little girl's face, but I saw my father's face, and Caleb's, and Christopher's. Christopher did not believe that deliverance would ever come—he was going to drag it down from heaven or raise it up from hell—for Christopher, the party, that banquet at which we had been being poisoned for so long, was over. Yet, he watched the little girl, and listened to her, with delight. And all my speculations began to paralyze me again, and again I wondered what I could say when I rose. I wanted deliverance—for others even more than for myself: *my* party, *my* banquet, in ways which Christopher could not possibly imagine, was over, too. But I wondered if it was possible, and not only for me, to live without the song. No song could possibly be worth the trap in which so many thousands, undelivered, perished every day. No song could be worth what this singing little girl had already paid for it, and was paying, and would continue to pay. And yet—without a song? Was Christopher's manner of deliverance worth the voices it would silence? Or would new songs come? How could I tell? for the question engaged my life and my responsibilities and perhaps even my love, but it no longer engaged my possibilities. I was defined. I was relieved to recognize that I was not cast down by this quite sufficiently weighty fact, only troubled by the question of how not to fail this little girl, and Christopher. Whatever had happened to me could have no meaning unless it could help to deliver them. But the price for this deliverance, this most ambitious of transactions, could only be found in a wallet which I had always claimed was not mine. I began to sweat. The little girl's voice rang out. Caleb's face hung steadily in the center of my mind. *Deliverance will come.* Well, if she believed it, then it had to be made possible; though only she, after all, plain, stocky, beautiful, black girl, could really make it true.

I watched Christopher's face as the song ended, watched his big white teeth in his big black face and watched him clap his big black hands. Then, as silence descended, and his face changed, and the master of ceremonies rose, I suddenly realized, with a violent nausea, that it was *my* turn now. Every single orifice in my body first threatened, shamefully, to open, then closed, despairingly, forever, and I began to drip with sweat. Christopher's face was very calm and proud—I was *his* big brother, *his* boy, or my *man!* as we say in Harlem; and my little girl looked very tranquil, too, as though she had just been seated at a fried chicken dinner. But I knew, as I stood up and walked to the dangerous promontory, that she hadn't tasted it yet. Deliverance will come.

There is a truth in the theater and there is a truth in life—they meet, but they are not the same, for life, God help us, *is* the truth. And those disguises which an artist wears are his means, not of fleeing from the truth, but of attempting to approach it. Who, after all, could believe a word spoken by Prince Hamlet or Ophelia should one encounter this unhappy couple at a cocktail party? Yet, the reason that one would certainly never make the error of inviting them back again is that their story is true—and not only for the Prince and his mad lady; is true, is true, unbearable, unanswerable: and one's disguises are designed to make the truth a quantity with which one can live—or from which one can hope, by the effort of living, to be delivered. But on that afternoon I was facing the people with no recognizable disguise—though perhaps by this time my disguises were indistinguishable from myself—and I was very frightened. I don't know what I said. I tried to be truthful. I tried to talk to the little girl, and to Christopher, and from time to time, I peeked, so to speak, from the promontory of my despair at their faces. Their faces were very bright. The little girl seemed to be enjoying her fried chicken dinner. Then I wondered if I was right to give her a fried chicken dinner which she could enjoy. Maybe I should have given her a dinner which would cause her to overthrow the table and burn down the house. But I did not want her to vomit or to burn: I wanted her to live. Deliverance, however, was not in my hands. Christopher looked like a black sun when I finished and opened his big black face and clapped his big black hands. The little girl ran over to me with her green autograph book held out. She reminded me of everything I hoped never to forget. I took the autograph book and signed it and I wrote above my name, *Deliverance will come*. It was folly, for I was immediately surrounded and trapped on the platform which the policemen wanted me to leave. I wanted to come down, but I did not know how. I did not see the friends who had driven me to the rally. I could no longer see Christopher. I did not know how to get to the car. Then I saw Christopher's furious and terrified face, struggling to break through the crowd to get to me and in a flash, an awful one, I saw what he saw: the Leo who certainly did not belong to himself and who belonged to the people only on condition that the people were kept away from him, surrounded by the uncontrollable public madness, and in the very heart of danger. For it was the time of assassins. Christopher could not know, nor, abruptly, could I, who, in the crowd pressing around me, desired my death nor who was willing to execute it. I felt myself being pushed off the platform by the police: it was like being pushed off a cliff. Then Christopher leaped— but it really seemed rather more like flying—onto the platform, placing his body in front of mine, his arms stretched wide on either side; and evidently he had already given a signal to five others of his age and history, who joined him and joined hands, forming a human barricade, and led me to the car—which, however, was also, now, surrounded. Christopher used his shoulders and his elbows ruthlessly, and his voice, and got the car door open, got in first and pulled me in after him. Then two of his friends piled in and slammed the door—so that I was protected on all sides. The driver of this car, and his companion, were both white, and so Christopher had to take out his wrath on me instead of on all the white devils. But he managed to suggest, in that language he had mastered, that not even the white people in the front seat were above wishing that I were dead. What was most vivid to me was how deeply *he* desired that I should live. I was not flattered by this, but frightened; for this was a passion impersonal indeed, and it proved how little I belonged to myself. Not a soul in that crowd mattered for Christopher, nor would a soul have been safe from him as long as that crowd menaced—as he later put it: "my only hope."

The nurse now entered with a tray, on which she bore my supper and a threatening black object which turned out to be a transistor radio. "Miss King brought the radio," she said, "but since you only woke up today, we forgot about it." I understood, from her chastened and bewildered air, that Barbara had been rather hard on her. She was bewildered because this had revealed—or, rather, had failed to reveal—a Barbara King and a Leo Proudhammer whose names were not in lights. She did not know her idols, therefore she did not know herself, and she was full of a resentment which she masked by her attention to details. In a chill silence, in which, nevertheless, she kept smiling, she raised the head-rest, arranged the pillows, imprisoned me with the tray. She said, with her firm, girlish impeccability, "You must try to eat it all." Then she picked up some of the flowers. "These must all be taken out at night," she said. "I'll be back when you've finished your supper. Then the night nurse takes over. The bell is next to your bed." She left the room, a poor little girl with her feelings hurt. I resolved to make Barbara do something on the morrow to cheer up my little nurse.

I looked at my supper, which did not interest me, but I forced down my soup and a little salad. Then I lay back, wide awake—it wasn't even show time yet—and wondered what I would do with the night. But either my keepers or my body had foreseen this, for, while I was wondering, I fell asleep:

Barbara and I were painting signs in a wooden shed, the toolshed in New Jersey. Barbara was very clumsy and kept laughing at her clumsiness. Every time I got my sign nearly painted, she came over with her bucket and her brush and spoiled it. Every time she came near me, she seemed to envelop me; she seemed deeper than water, as inescapable as air; I felt myself suffocating in the foul,

sticky web she was spinning with her laughter. I began to
be angry. I said, Stop that, now, you stop it! She kept on
laughing. She spilled red paint all over my sign. I said,
Barbara, you do that again, and I'll—You'll what? she
asked, and danced very close to me. *What* will you do,
Leo? And she sounded pleading. I was overcome with
fear. I'll kill you, I said. Honest. But I also sounded
pleading. We lay down together in the scarlet paint.
Then something happened, and we were running. Caleb
was chasing us. His voice came over the mountains: What
are you doing with that white girl? *What are you doing?*
Caleb grabbed me, and with the great wooden Bible in
his hand, he struck me. Nothing. Caleb. Nothing. Caleb
struck me again. I began to cry, and I fell to my knees.
Caleb struck me on the back of my head. I cried out and
I started trying to crawl away from him. I crawled through
dirty water which became deeper and deeper, and suddenly I was staring at the bottom of the sea. The filthy
water filled my nostrils, filled my mouth. I kicked to keep
from drowning. I turned to look for Caleb. I could see him
through the veil of water, he stood watching me, and now
he was stark naked, black and naked. I reached out my
hand, but he would not take it. I screamed and started
going down. I woke up.

The nurse stood with the tray, watching me. "I was
about to wake you up," she said. "You seemed to be having a bad dream."

It took a second before I could bring her into focus.
"I guess I was."

"Do you have them often?"

"Not very often. Only when I've done something bad
—like in those plays by Shakespeare."

She smiled. "I'll bring you a sleeping pill," she said,
and left again.

I turned on my radio. I listened to the news for awhile,
but Barbara had been right—it was not for a sick man,
or a well man, either. I turned the dial and found Ray
Charles. And he was playing my story for me.

The winter came, and we were evicted, and ended up
in two rooms on the top floor of a defeated building on
the edge of the Harlem River. The music Ray was playing
reminded me of this house. I have lived long enough to
see my language stolen—I was about to say betrayed; but

it has certainly been pressed into a most peculiar service. "Beat," in those days, meant something very different from what it has since come to mean: for example, our poor father was "beat to his socks," which meant that his hope was gone. And no one, in those days, desired to be "funky": funk was a bad smell, it was the invincible odor which filled our house, the very odor of battle, the battle waged by the living in the midst of death. In those two rooms we acted out our last days as a family. Our father had been laid off from his job, which is why we had been evicted; all he found were odd jobs for a day or two, helping to tear up the city's streets, or shoveling away the snow downtown—I never saw any snow being shoveled away in Harlem! And Caleb quit school—to my father's wrath and despair—but he scarcely fared any better than our father. Our mother began working as a maid in the Bronx, and brought home odds and ends from Miss Anne's kitchen. Our father would not eat the food that she brought home—he said it would have choked him, and I believe it would have. It was hard enough for him to accept the fact that without the money she made, we would probably all have starved to death. I became a shoeshine boy, downtown, after school, and on the weekends I sold shopping bags in front of the department stores and the five and dimes on 14th Street. And we went on relief—not for the first time; for the last time. Our father no longer drank rum, but a pale, sticky, sweet white wine.

We were cold and frightened, and we were hungry, but, except for our father, we were not in despair. Our mother was holding on—grim, silent, watchful, but not cheerless; she was determined to bring us to the daylight. But she had a lot to watch, a lot to carry. She was watching our father, praying that the daylight would come before his spirit should be forever broken; she was watching Caleb, praying that the daylight would come before his hope, which was his youth, should be forever destroyed; and she was watching me, wondering what I was learning, and what I would be like when the daylight came. The daylight may always come, but it does not come for everybody and it does not come on time.

My shoeshine box, my shopping bags, were the emblems of my maturity; and I now began to learn less from my elders than from my peers; and from the mysterious

downtown strangers whose touch on my head made me
recoil, whose eyes were as remote as snowcapped mountain peaks. They had no rhythm which struck any chords
in me. The wonder with which I watched them, and the
distaste which I somehow sensed in their distance, needed
but a touch to be transformed forever into enmity. I was
trying to discover what principle united so peculiarly
bloodless a people. I suspected that the principle was
cruelty, but I was not sure. My white peers did not really
baffle me, not even when they called me names—I could
call names, too. We fought all the time and sometimes I
won and sometimes I lost—usually, I guess, I lost; but I
was lucky in that we usually fought fair, and so defeat did
not bring about a poisonous rancor. In any case, at least
from time to time, we had to band together against the
cops—and I had long ago dismissed the cops from all
human consideration. But the others, the men and women,
young and old, sometimes smiling, sometimes harsh, always distant—if I fell into their hands, would they treat
me like the cops? I was not certain: but I feared the worst.
And my black peers thought that my wonder was foolish,
that it proved me soft in the head. And I learned a new
folklore, by which I did not dare to admit that I was
frightened, manfully laughing with them at their pictures
of Popeye with a hard-on, screwing Olive Oil, giving respectful attention to their accounts of their sexual discoveries, wondering what was wrong with *me*, for I had
certainly never done any of those things. I could not really
imagine them. But I never said so. I never said much, for
I was afraid of revealing my ignorance. But, without quite
knowing it, I began to look at everyone around me in another way. Did everybody do it? It was impossible to believe.

I had fallen into the habit of going to see Miss Mildred
every once in a while. If it was raining or snowing and my
shopping bags could not be sold, or my shoeshine box
could not be used; when I was frightened, when I was sad,
I would go to see Miss Mildred, for perhaps no one would
be home at my house; and I very often met Caleb there.
Sometimes, when I got there, it would be a long time
before Caleb and Dolores came out of one of the rooms off
the hall. And this made me wonder. But I loved Caleb too
much to wonder long. One day I would ask him if what I

was told was true: and I knew that he would tell me the truth. When I look back—now—it seems to me that the air knew that we were to be parted; and so the air informed us; for Caleb and I clung to each other as we never had before. He teased me, as before, of course, but this did not make me feel ashamed. On the contrary, it made me feel proud. I felt that he was beginning to treat me like a man, that he expected great things from me. And I did everything I could to live up to his expectations: not to be a crybaby, to fight back, no matter how big the adversary was (and then to give Caleb his name and address), to wash myself, even in the coldest weather, to be respectful to old folks (if they were colored), to do my schoolwork right so that our father and mother would be proud of me. And he said that he would try to send me to college—"because you're smarter than I am, little brother"—and he was teaching me to box, and, when summer came, he was going to teach me to swim. Sometimes, he and Dolores took me to the movies with them. And, at night, when we lay in bed, Caleb would sometimes give me a stolen Milky Way, and talk to me for hours. I don't remember what we talked about. I just remember the sound of his voice in the darkness, the breathing of our parents in the other room, the ferocious industry of the rats which we heard in the kitchen, in the walls, which sometimes took place beneath our bed, the music coming from another apartment, the frost on the windows, so thick sometimes that one could not see out, the blunt, black shape of the kerosene stove which had now been extinguished, for safety and for thrift, and Caleb's arm around me, his smell, and the taste of chocolate, and the electrical sound of the paper. "You ain't sleepy yet?" he might ask, and I would shake my head, No. "Well, little brother," he would say, with a yawn, "*I* am, and you *better* be." Then he would rub his hand over my head, a trick of our father's, and say, "Goodnight, little Leo." Then he would turn on his side, saying, "Snuggle up tight, now. You all right?" I put one arm around him and nodded my chin against his back, and we fell asleep.

One day—one day—I came down the avenue on my way downtown to buy and sell my shopping bags, and I noticed that the store where Caleb and I always met was closed, was padlocked. There was no one in the store and none of the people who were usually hanging around the store were in the streets. This seemed very odd, especially since this day was a Saturday. But I couldn't wonder about it too much; I had to get downtown. And nothing that happened during all that long day, that cold, bright day, warned me of what was coming. The sun shone all day long—a cold sun; nobody bothered me, neither my peers, nor the police; people tipped me nicely, that day, and I sold all my shopping bags. I was tremendously proud of myself when I got on the subway to go home. I didn't think of stopping by Miss Mildred's because I had to give my mother the money I had made.

But when I started up the steps to our house something whispered to me, something whispered, *trouble*. It was in the darkness of the hall—the lights had gone out— it came out from the walls, it came out—I suddenly realized it—from the silence. These steps, these landings, had never been so silent before. I ran faster up the stairs. I pushed on our door, and it opened at once. But it was usually locked. I stared at my father and mother, who stood in the center of the room, staring at me.

"You seen your brother?" my mother asked.

"No," I said. "I just come from downtown." I took the money out of my pockets. "Here." But she didn't see the money, she didn't take it. I just held it. It got heavier and heavier. My mother sat down, crying. I had never seen her cry before. I looked at my father. He stood above my mother, holding her tightly by the shoulder.

I asked, "What's the matter, Mama?"

My father asked, "You know any of your brother's friends?"

I said, No, because I wanted to hear what he would say.

"They done robbed a store, whoever they is, and stabbed a man half to death. They say Caleb was with them."

"A boy named Arthur—Arthur something-or-other," said my mother, "he the one say Caleb was there."

"Do you know him?" my father asked.

I shook my head, No: for a different reason this time.

"They used to steal things—they used to steal things," said my mother, "look like they was a regular gang, and the cops say—the cops say—they used that store for a hiding place."

"The cops say!" said my father.

I had seen the cops in the store many times; they had always been perfectly friendly with the owner. "The store is closed," I said. I went over to my mother. "Mama—Mama—what they going to do if they find Caleb?" My mind had stopped, stuck, screaming, on the faces of white cops.

"They going to take him away," she said.

I looked at my father. "But Caleb don't steal! Caleb never stole nothing in his whole life!" My father said nothing. We heard footsteps on the stairs. Not one of us moved. But the steps stopped just below our landing. Then I realized that I would have to find Caleb and tell him not to come home. I stuffed my money in my pockets —maybe he would need it. I said, "I'll be right back," and I ran out of the house and down the stairs. I ran down those stairs faster than Caleb ever had, and into the startling wind of the street. Everything was new, everything was evil, every house was dangerous. The people all were strangers. I do not think I saw them. And yet, something cautioned me not to run too fast; something cautioned me to dissemble my distress; something cautioned me to look, to look about me, before I moved. I stood on my stoop and I looked toward the dreadful river. Only small boys were playing there. Across the street, there were ladies in windows and men on stoops; and up the street, more men and boys and ladies, and no cops. I touched the money in my pockets—I don't know why; perhaps I wanted everyone to believe that I had been sent to the store. And then I started walking, out of the block, toward Miss Mildred's house. But I did not go down the avenue because I was afraid to pass the store. I went straight west until I came to Miss Mildred's avenue. I passed cops on my way, but they did not stop me, or seem to look at me. I reached Miss Mildred's building and I ran up the steps. I tried to give the funny knock I had heard Arthur give, but, then, I broke, I pounded on the door with all my might, and I screamed, "Miss Mildred! Miss Mildred! It's Leo. It's *Leo!* Let me in!" Then I heard the pole being moved out of the way, and the rattle of the chain, and the locks unlocking. She stood before me, and I knew she knew.

"Miss Mildred? Is my brother here?"

She pulled me inside, with one hand, saying nothing.

In the hall stood Dolores. I was led down the long hall to
the two big rooms. Caleb sat on the sofa, dressed in his
black lumberjacket. He had his arms wrapped around
himself, as though he were cold. He looked over at me.
His face looked dry, as though he had never sweated. He
said, "Hello, little Leo. Don't look so frightened." I
started to cry, and I walked over to him. He pulled me
onto his lap.

"Caleb didn't do it, Leo," Dolores said. "*We* know he
didn't do it, and we'll go to court and say so." Caleb
continued rubbing his hand over my head. He sighed, a
great sigh, my head moved with it, and he pulled my
head back and looked into my face. "Don't be afraid,
Leo," he said. "Please don't be afraid. Will you do that?
For me?" I nodded. Then he said, "I didn't do it. I just
want you to hear it from me. All right?"

I said, "All right." Then I said, "But I don't care if
you did!"

He laughed. He cried, too. He said, "I know that,
Leo." He laughed again.

"Caleb—are you going to run away?" He stared at
me. "The cops have been at the house," I said.

"Did you see them?"

"No. Mama and Daddy told me."

The three of them looked at each other. "That Arthur,"
said Miss Mildred, "that Arthur."

"If I run," said Caleb, "I won't get far. And then they'll
fix my ass for sure."

"I got some money," I said. But he didn't hear me. He
was listening to something in the street. Dolores walked
to the window and looked out. She turned back into the
room. "Here they come," she said. I had never seen a face
so bitter. And she did not seem to be able to move. Then
she looked at Caleb, and she smiled. She tried to say something. Caleb suddenly rose and ran to her, and grabbed her.

"I hear you," said Miss Mildred, for there was a
pounding at the door. She started down the hall. "I *hear*
you," she cried again, "ain't no *need* for all that." I heard
her opening the door. Dolores stood with Caleb; now it
was I who could not move. "Do you people *have* to make
such a racket?" I heard Miss Mildred ask. "Don't you
people have good sense? Don't you *push* past me this way!

This is *my* house! Ain't you people able to *ask* for what you want?"

They came down the hall, three of them, white; one of them had his gun drawn. Still, I could not move.

"We're looking for Caleb Proudhammer," one of them said.

"What for?" asked Dolores.

"That's none of your business," one of them said.

"Yes, it *is* my business," Dolores said, "to ask you what you're arresting him for. And it's your business to tell me."

"Listen to the nigger bitch," one of them said.

"I'm Caleb Proudhammer," Caleb said. "You don't need those guns. I've never shot nobody in my life."

"Come on over here. We're taking you down to the station."

"What for?"

"You're a very inquisitive bunch of niggers. Here's what for," and he suddenly grabbed Caleb and smashed the pistol butt against the side of his head. The blood ran down—my brother's blood. I jumped up, howling, from the sofa, trying to get to Caleb, but they knocked me back. I couldn't catch my breath; they were pulling him down the hall. I called his name. I tried to crawl down the hall. Miss Mildred was trying to hold me back, Dolores was screaming. I punched Miss Mildred, I bit her hand. They were carrying him down the steps. I screamed his name again. I butted one cop in the behind, with all my might I dragged on one of his legs. "Get that kid out of here," one of them said, and somebody tried to grab me, but I kicked and bit again. I tumbled headlong down the steps and grabbed the policeman's leg again. I held on, I held on, he dragged me down. I called Caleb's name again. We were in the downstairs hall. They were carrying him into the streets. Now, the cop kicked me, and I tasted blood. I crawled down the hall, screaming my brother's name. We were in the cold air; there were many people. I picked myself up, and I ran to the car, crying, Please. Please. That's my brother. I tried to crawl into the car, but I was pushed out of it; then I tried to get in front of it, to push it back, but someone lifted me high in the air. I called his name again. I heard the car doors slam, and I cried, Please. *Please.* I heard the

motor start, and I cried, *Please. Please.* I fought my way
to the sidewalk, I punched and kicked myself free, I ran
after the red lights of the car. Oh Caleb Caleb Caleb
Caleb Caleb. Oh Caleb. Caleb. The lights of the car disappeared, I stumbled and fell on my face on the sidewalk,
I cried, I cried. They picked me up, they took me upstairs, they washed me, they took me home. My father
tried to stroke my head. I pushed his hand away. My
mother offered me a bowl of soup. I knocked the bowl
from her hand. I hate you, I said, I hate you, and I buried
myself in the pillow which still held Caleb's smell.

BOOK TWO:

Is There Anybody There?
said the traveler

Ain't misbehaving.
Saving myself for you.
—FATS WALLER

BARBARA AND JERRY were in front of the toolshed painting signs which read, THE ACTORS' MEANS WORKSHOP PRESENTS THE CELEBRATED PLAY BY GEORGE BERNARD SHAW, *Arms and the Man*. Barbara wore a scarlet, two-piece bathing suit, her hair was tied up with a string; she was on her knees, being very meticulous with the small *a* in "play." Jerry, standing, in black trunks, was being very swift, and far from meticulous, with "Bernard." The sweat glistened on his brown back, and he kept throwing his hair back from his eyes. Jerry and Barbara had nearly as much paint on their bodies as they had managed to get onto the signs. I had just driven the Workshop jalopy from The Green Barn where one set of actors was rehearsing *Arms and the Man,* and where it would soon open to play for six performances. The drawing card was not Shaw, but an aging, rather pompously dipsomaniacal actor, who was no longer in much demand in Hollywood. From what I had seen of him in rehearsal, this present venture wasn't going to help him any. Now I was on my way to town to get hamburgers and coffee and Coke for another group of actors, who, in Lola San-Marquand's living room, were rehearsing a play by Ben Hecht, called *To Quito and Back*. This play, which was to follow the Shaw, had no drawing card, merely some fairly well-established professionals and a few kids like ourselves; and since it was political in subject, we felt that we were being very brave. Then I was to come back to Bull Dog Road and collect the signs, and Barbara and Jerry and I were to drive into town to hang them up. But, at the rate Barbara and Jerry were making it, I would have to pitch in and help them.

They were at a distance from the road. I stopped the car and I yelled, "Jesus! Are you two still fucking around?"

Jerry turned, and gestured with his paintbrush, managing to splash paint on his hairy chest. I laughed. He shouted, "Up yours, buddy! I don't see *you* doing any work."

Barbara stood up. "Leo! You have been driving around like an overseer all *day!* Where are you going *now?*"

"To town, baby! To town!"

"What are you going to do in *town?*"

"I'm going to drink me a couple of mint juleps while you all finish painting them signs. *We* have been placed in a supervisory position—and we expect *you* to have them signs ready when *we* return!"

They both looked for something to throw at me. I yodeled, "Oh, I wish I was in the land of cotton!" and roared down the road, away.

Jerry had come out at our insistence, and also because he really had nothing else to do. He was a big, cheerful, open-hearted Italian boy, a very gentle creature. He was not at the Workshop, he was working as an artists' model in town; but he hung out with us and he helped us out. I had been evicted from my quarters in Paradise Alley. This made the idea of working at the Workshop not only more attractive, but imperative, for it meant that I would be certain to eat all summer long and that I would spend the summer in the open air. The money was nominal—so nominal that both Barbara and I were also working as artists' models, and Jerry and I mowed lawns. But we were happy, or nearly so. We worked hard all week, sometimes we got drunk in town at night, on Sundays we went rowing or fishing. My Paradise Alley roommate, Charlie, had gone hitchhiking back to Iowa—to find an old girl-friend, he said, though this quest, this possibility, did not appear to cheer him. Barbara had padlocked her door in Paradise Alley, and her things and Jerry's things and mine were there.

It was early July, and the sun was a busy and persistent sun. I had turned darker, with a lot of red in my skin and hair; while Barbara had turned mulatto and her hair had turned blond on her forehead and on the curly sides and edges. Jerry was browner than Arabs, and we called ourselves, when we journeyed through town, "the Negro color problem." We were just outside a small town on a bluff above a river. The Indian Magua, in *The Last of the Mohicans,* had forced the British maiden, for whom honor was more important than life, over this bluff, into this river—so, at least, Fenimore Cooper and his Hollywood descendants had informed me; it was not hard to imagine Indian braves catapulting down this river, and one heard the fury of their arrows through the leaves of trees. In the hope of catching some whisper of the past, we sometimes wandered through the graveyard in town— a dreadful town, built and ruined by financiers, but saved by a war. Though the graveyard failed to give us any sense of our past, the town gave us all too vivid a sense of our actual condition. The town had been moribund a long time, but factories and government contracts and army installations and eventually soldiers with their pay came to the town and saved it. The people in the town were, therefore, happily making money and the nature and the degree of their happiness made them haltingly friendly and quickly cruel. Although it was recognized that our presence in the town conferred on the town a peculiar prestige and was even good for business, we certainly were not liked. The San-Marquands had rented a big, white wooden house in town, and it was a tremendous sign of status to be invited to one of their parties. It was suspected that the San-Marquands were Jewish, and people said terrible things about them behind their backs; but, on the other hand, they were friends with the stars of stage and screen, and some of these stars would, in fact, be appearing under the Workshop banner. The gentry came to the San-Marquand parties, dazzled, supercilious, and drunk; and we, the Workshop kids, who were often there, serving canapés and drinks, sometimes picked up an odd job or two—or vice versa; but, whatever the use they might occasionally make of us, the combination of our youth and our aims was distressingly and sharply distasteful to them. Everyone was certain that the San-Marquands were exotically, unimaginably, erotically corrupt, and so were the movie stars, their friends. They had gotten away with it, and, thus, were obviously a bad example for us; obviously, kids in such fast company were bound to be depraved. They did not want to know why, when we could have been doing other things, we painted signs and mowed lawns and posed naked. They disliked Jerry because he was Italian, they disliked Barbara because she was not, and, therefore, had no excuse, and they disliked me be-

cause I did not appear to realize that both Barbara and
Jerry were white. I did not, in fact, appear to know that I
was colored and this filled them with such a baleful exasperation, such an exasperated wonder, that the waitress'
hand, when I stopped in the diner, actually trembled as
she poured my coffee, and people moved away from me,
staring as though I were possessed by evil spirits. Naturally, I despised them. They didn't even have the courage
of their sick convictions, for, if they had, they would have
tarred me and feathered me and ridden me out of town.
But they didn't dare do this because of my connection
with the Workshop. Naturally, they brought out the worst
in all three of us. Their minds were like dirty window-
panes; and so we obligingly acted out their fantasies for
them. When Jerry and I walked through town together,
for example, everyone assumed we were queer—there
couldn't be any other reason for our walking together;
and so we sometimes walked with our arms around each
other. If Jerry had not been so big and I had not been so
bold, we would have paid—more often than we did—a
bloody price for this. But Jerry's size intimidated and bewildered them—he certainly didn't *act* queer—and so did
my boldness, which seemed to contradict my color; on
the whole, we were rather *too* queer to be easily molested.
Of course, when Barbara and Jerry walked through town,
Barbara had only to put her head on Jerry's shoulder for
them both to become, at once, a pair of lewd and abandoned
lovers; while for the three of us, walking together and
holding hands, they had no words at all. Nevertheless,
they endured us because the San-Marquands gave parties at
which they might meet movie stars.

The Workshop kids—there were about fifteen of us—
lived along a mile or two of roads, about three miles
outside of town, in wooden shacks. These shacks had
been built in the twenties; the place was known as Bull
Dog Road; it had been a celebrated artists' colony. But
all the artists had eventually left it, either upon becoming
successful or upon realizing that success was impossible.
The Actors' Means Workshop, aided by the gentry, had
taken over this celebrated road. It cost almost nothing to
live there, except energy; but it took rather a lot of that.
Barbara and Jerry and I shared a two-story shack, for
which we paid, I think, about twelve dollars a month.

We thought it was a fine place. Downstairs, where Barbara and Jerry stayed, there was a small, dark kitchen with old, battered pots and pans and chipped dishes and heavy stone mugs; Jerry had strung it with his Italian spices, and it stank of gorgonzola cheese. We loved it—luckily, since Jerry was the only one of us who really knew how to cook. The bathroom was very old and primitive, with a metal tub which took hours to fill and hours to empty; Jerry and I put up a shower of sorts in the yard—really no more than an ingenious way of being enabled to dump a couple of pails of water over oneself. Their big room had an enormous double bed, big enough for six people, and a fireplace, and two rocking chairs. We screened all the windows and doors and then left them open all the time. At night, we put the rocking chairs on the porch and sat there, talking, and wondering, silently, what it would be like to be old. My room was smaller than theirs, but it had two big windows and outside of one window leaned an old tree, taller than our house, and the other window faced the far-off mountains. We had whitewashed the entire house, inside and out, and the moonlight did strange things to the walls of my room at night. I sat there many nights, all alone, after Barbara and Jerry had gone to bed, sometimes simply staring out at the night and sometimes strumming the guitar I had bought.

Though we had been at the Workshop for three weeks, neither Barbara nor I had yet presented Saul with a scene or an improvisation. The kind of workers we had become would more probably have been appreciated in a mill or on a farm; at least insofar as this work could reveal any of our qualifications for the theater. We began to mind this, but we had not minded it in the beginning. We were too excited by the hard preparation necessary tó get the Workshop set up, and to get its first summer production on the stage. Our first week, we did a great deal of demolishing—of walls, doors, panels—and a great deal of carting and burning; we became relatively efficient with the hammer and the nail and the saw, and also fairly swift with first aid; and then we plastered and painted. We made an inventory of the props, which were piled helter-skelter, and covered with dust, in the attic of the theater, and built shelves and compartments for the bells, knives, samovars, lamps, and telephones, and classified them according to a system worked out by Barbara and Lola which I found peculiarly pretentious. PERIOD, TOLSTOIAN, for example, took care of the samovars and ikons, of which there were a great many, the San-Marquands being partial to the Russian drama; MODERN, NORTH AMERICA, took care of all the phones but one, which stood arrogantly alone on a shelf labeled, CONTEMPORARY, VIENNA. "Contemporary, my ass," Jerry snarled. "When was the last time anybody around here saw Vienna?" Nor was it likely that anyone would be seeing it soon. We examined every costume, no matter how old, faded, or torn, and salvaged as many as possible. The costumes gave me a strange, sad thrill: these uniforms of Czarist generals, of Civil War soldiers, the shawls and dresses of Lorca heroines, the patched jackets of Steinbeck peasants, of Odets insurgents, these buckles, shoes, boots, pumps, bonnets, rugged shirts and ruffled shirts, tight breeches and baggy pants, cowls, capes, helmets, swords, shields, spears, drums, harps, horns, so deeply drenched in human salt that sometimes they shredded at a touch, so icily trapped in time's indifference that they chilled the hand, spoke of the reality, operating relentlessly every hour, which would one day overtake me and all my styles and poses and all my uniforms. These garments had been worn—by real people; real music had been played for them, and they had moved in a genuine light; they had put their hands on their hearts and delivered their vows, and the curtain had come down. These costumes were like their dispersed, indifferent bones, and the attic always reminded me of Ezekiel's valley, and Ezekiel's question: Oh, Lord, can these bones live?

I had never been on a real stage before, and the first time I stepped on the stage of The Green Barn, one stormy summer afternoon when the sky was wailing as though heaven had gone mad, sending down water in merciless, blinding sheets, and drumming on the roof like all of Africa, I looked up before I looked out, and was astonished to realize how high a stage could be. I looked up and up, into dust and darkness, scaffolds and ropes. It would be terrible to fall from there. I was all alone that afternoon. I had been sent on some kind of errand—I was always being sent on errands. But I had to wait for the summer storm to end, and, in the meantime,

no one was very likely to be able to get to me. I looked
out at the dark, spooky theater—very spooky now, with
the rain roaring—and wondered if my destiny could be
involved in such a place. But destinies, as I was beginning
to discover, are strange—and must be, being so mysteriously hung up with desire. For I desired, I realized one
day—if these bones could live—to stand here before those
living with whom I would fill this dusty void, and hear
them bearing witness as I now heard the sound of the rain.
I had never before thought of my desire as a reality in-
volving others; neither had I thought of others as needing
my desire; but I, now, for the first time, in that dusty
barn, suspected that this coupling defined one's destiny,
and that on this coupling depended the mysterious life of
the world. I was young. Perhaps it is hard, now, to credit,
still less to sound, the depth of my bewilderment. I merely
suspected in the chilling height, the dusty, roaring darkness,
the presence of others, each of whom was myself. But
these others could not know it, and neither could I, unless
I was able, being filled by them, to fill this theater with our
lives. This was, perhaps, my highest possibility of the act
of love. But I did not say it that way to myself that afternoon. I merely walked up and down the stage. I measured
its length, breadth, and depth, and threw my voice to the
topmost balcony. In that empty space, I thought, in spite of
the rain, that I heard it echo back; and I wished that I had
brought my guitar with me.

In spite of all our manual labor—which included hanging drapes for the San-Marquands—we, by which I mean
principally Barbara and I, read and studied and argued.
Saul had explicitly informed us that our improvisations
were to be solo, that we were not to work together on them,
or even to discuss them—which we couldn't, anyway,
have done since he hadn't given either of us a theme. We
were to choose our scenes and we were free to do them
solo or not, as we liked; but we didn't know if Saul wanted
to see the scenes before he saw the improvisations or wanted
to see the improvisations before he saw the scenes. We
were aware that our improvisations might disqualify us
for any scenes, and this made us rather edgy with each
other sometimes—we both dreaded our first test, especially
as it had come about so improbably and promised to be so
definitive. I had refused to consider doing anything from

All God's Chillun Got Wings; Barbara, when the chips were down, conceded that we would probably disgracefully disappear beneath the quicksand of *Miss Julie*—which I had read by now; and we had compromised, I guess, on the scene between the young hack and his girl in *Waiting for Lefty.* It was a scene which we felt we could play. Then, when we began to work on it, the scene began to be, in a wordless way, a terrifying challenge. I soon began to wish that we had chosen some other scene, the scene between the gangster and his girl-friend turned whore, in *Dead End,* for example, but once we had begun work, my pride wouldn't let me back down. We had felt ourselves very bold to choose this scene, and had also felt that our doing it would put the liberal San-Marquands to a crucial test— we hadn't realized that it would also put *us* to a crucial test. It was a scene which gave us both a chance to show off a little; we had to dance with each other and I got a chance to whistle and do a short tap dance routine. The young hack, Sid, and his girl, Florrie, can't marry because it's the depression and they don't have any money and this is the scene in which they give each other up. We couldn't make it and we couldn't let it go—I had not known make-believe could be so painful, and, indeed, I now began to learn something about make-believe. At one point in the scene, after remembering their furtive lovemaking in parks and hallways, the girl offers to go with Sid to a room somewhere. But he refuses; he says there is no future for them. There is great tension in the scene, which connected with an unspoken tension in us, and we began to be appalled. For it is also the most crucial of love scenes, the moment of loss and failure: perhaps a great deal of superstition was mixed with our recoil. I don't, in detail, remember the scene very well anymore, but perhaps I'll never forget how it choked me, made me stammer, how it caused me, sometimes, almost to hate Barbara. This I saw in her bewilderment and slowly divining eyes: which both helped the scene and hurt it. Anyway, this scene was very much on my mind the first time, that rainy afternoon, when I paced the stage of The Green Barn and threw my voice to the balcony. For, by this time, I had become impatient with all my hard labor and wanted to be tested. Though I tried to be gallant, I was nevertheless watchful, and I knew that there was something ambiguous, at best, about the uses, the errand boy uses, to which I was permitting myself to be put. I realized how unlikely it was that I would ever work on a stage, and I also realized that my future did not really matter to the San-Marquands at all. My future mattered, really, only to me. That was why I had bought my guitar. I didn't expect much of the summer, it was a stop-gap: but I had to be ready for the winter.

I stopped the car in front of the diner. I was wearing an old T-shirt and some old pants and sneakers—this was one of my uniforms; the other was a devastating blue serge suit, with which, however, I was careful never to wear a white shirt. The diner was in the shape of a Pull-man car, booths on one side, counter on the other. It was late in the afternoon, and there were only about half a dozen people there, all of them older than I, and all of them evil, and all of them, as they supposed, white. They looked at me as I came in, and turned away. I smiled at the waitress, whose eyes were as fixed as varnished brown buttons, and who rose slowly, as though pulled up by the hair, as I and my smile—or my smile and I—walked over to the counter.

"Hello," I said—my smile was loud, but my voice was low—"can you fill this order for me, please?" And I handed her the list. She looked at it as though it were a chemical formula. I looked pleasantly around me, and sat down at the counter. "You've got great weather in this town. Could I have a beer while I'm waiting, please?" I knew she wouldn't refuse me because the one time she'd dared to ask my age, I'd been with Jerry who had told her *his* age and sworn that I was his older brother. She handed my order over into the short-order cook's domain—who peeped out of his cage at me—and then, slowly, frowning as over a knotty theological question, produced a bottle of beer, placed it before me, and slowly opened it. Then she walked away and got a glass and placed it on the counter before me.

"Thank you," I said. I poured myself a beer. I began to hum: *"Sinner man, where you going to run to?"* I lit a cigarette. I heard the hamburgers begin sizzling over yonder.

"I don't care," one of them said, "right is *right*."

"Don't get yourself upset, Bill," one of them said.

"It ain't worth it," one of them said.

They were talking to each other. I continued to hum. The waitress, whose name was Sally, began putting coffee in the cardboard containers.

"Did you ever hear the story about a nigger fucking a elephant?" one of them said.

They looked sideways at me. I continued to hum. They whispered, they laughed; then they shouted. "That was the end of *that* elephant!" I had heard the story before. "Sally," I asked, in my mildest voice, "could I please have another beer?"

She looked at me with something very like hatred in her button eyes—but hatred makes one servile. "Your hamburgers is almost ready. You might not have enough time to finish it. Before they get cold, I mean."

"I'll manage." I finished, nearly gagging, my tasteless beer—but pride can control one's reflexes, though I also suspect that one's reflexes *are*, sometimes, what one takes to be one's pride—and set my glass down. "There. Okay?"

"Come on, Bill," said one of them. They took him out. The diner was empty. She stared after them. Then, in a genuine, bewildered sorrow, she looked at me, found a bottle of beer, opened it, set it before me, and started picking up the hamburgers.

"I hope you have a box for all this," I said. "I don't. Mrs. San-Marquand said that she was sure you would."

"I'll see," she said—after a considerable pause.

"Good," I said. "Thank you." And I drank my beer.

The short-order cook produced the box. I let her put everything in the box herself. I finished my beer. Then I wanted to piss, but I calculated where I could piss on the road. I paid her. She rang up the money. "I must have a receipt," I said.

"All *right*," she said, "just a minute. I *know* the people you work for always want a receipt." And she gave me one. She had won. But I went down smiling. "Bye-bye, Sally. See you tomorrow, God willing." And I picked up the box and carried it out to the jalopy. I placed it on the front seat next to me. This was sometimes the trickiest moment of all my days, for, since I couldn't spill the coffee or the Coke, couldn't fail to feed the hungry, I couldn't let my fury release itself on the road.

I drove up the San-Marquand driveway. They had rented a pretty house, big and rambling—much too big for the two of them, but, then, on the other hand, they were never alone. Their house was always full of people, and Rags Roland was spending the summer with them. Rags was very impressive; big, and so ugly that she was positively splendid. In fact, a woman who looked like Rags had scarcely any choice but to become splendid if she were to achieve any bearable human quality at all. She was bigger than most men, with a face as square and as expressive as a block of granite—a block of granite veined with fine red lines. She had been given, in belated and incongruous compensation, a great deal of very bright, curling hair which was red by the time I met her. She wore it as though it were a helmet, not, I must say, that she could have worn it in any other way. Her clothes all seemed, on her, to be made of metal—relentless two-piece tweed suits, sometimes somber but sometimes star-tlingly plaid, which gave way, come summer, to equally relentless, sacklike prints. They boomed like trumpets, they hurt the eye. She was incredibly energetic, one of the people whose relentless good-nature at length becomes rather frightening. She was always smoking and joking; one wondered if she could ever be still. She had told me once, sitting on the San-Marquand porch, in a large, ornate double swing made of South American straw, that she could not get through a single day without listening to music. I wondered when. I wondered how she could ever turn off all the noise she lived with long enough to hear anything: I should have thought that her spiritual eardrums had long ago been broken. But photographs of herself and the San-Marquands, taken years before when they had just begun the Workshop, showed another Rags, a Rags unreconciled. These photographs were on the walls of The Green Barn office, and in Saul's study at home. The photographs showed them sitting around under trees, reading scripts, or in rehearsal. Saul looked very different, his hair had not been white then; in one of the photographs he was without his glasses and he looked like a startled boy. Lola had been round but not shapeless, her hair had been long, and her face very ear-nest and girlish. And Rags—Rags had worn her hair very long then, and braided into a crown. The big face, the big mouth, the great square mass of her, seemed, some-how, vulnerable. And she was wearing something which looked gray in the photographs, long and soft and full. She had been trying to be an actress in those days, and she wrote poetry. "Wretched poetry," she said, "but I've never had the heart to burn it. It'll turn up in my private papers after I'm dead. Don't let the world laugh at me too much." This was when she was drunk, at one of the San-Marquand parties.

I had arrived during a break. The cast was on the lawn and when they saw the car toiling toward the house, they sent up a great cheer. Rags was standing on the porch.

"Boy," she said, "that's by far the most exciting business we've got out of them all day. I wonder what makes *you* so popular. Could it be the grub?"

"It could be," I said, "but, then, again, it might be my pretty brown eyes."

"Come on, Leo. Your eyes can't begin to compete with those hamburgers."

"Are you going to sit here on all this—*food*—all afternoon?" asked Madeleine, the company's leading lady, "or are you going to get up off it and give us some?" She winked at me. "And I know you know what I mean, honey. How are you? I hope you're not forgetting your red-hot mama?"

"How *could* I forget you? Sugar, you know I got to give you some."

"Promises, promises. And I've been so *ravenous* for so long." We laughed together. Madeleine and I always carried on like this, but I didn't know to what extent it was for real and I didn't know how to make the first move. She was about thirty, which was intimidating, blonde, rather hefty, but very nice. She was a respected minor actress, who had never been a leading lady before, divorced, with an eight-year-old daughter. The daughter was in the city, with Madeleine's parents.

The other kids came over and took away the boxes of food and drink and put them under a tree. They picked up their Cokes and hamburgers and dispersed. I got out of the car, and stretched, and sat down on the bottom step of the porch.

"Aren't you hungry?" Rags asked me.

"No," I said. "I ate a big breakfast." I looked up at her. "Aren't you?"

"God, no," she said. "I'm directing this shambles. I can't eat until they've all gone home. Actors take away my appetite."

I smiled. "You're always with them," I said. "You must eat an awful lot after they've gone home."

"I think you're being impertinent," Rags said, and laughed, and ground out her cigarette in the grass. She sat down on the porch step beside me.

"*Is* it a shambles?" I asked her. "I thought Lola said that it was going very well."

"Lola daren't say anything else. It's her job to keep up everybody's morale—poor Lola. She's been walking around here these last few days like the white angel—the lady with the lamp." She lit another cigarette and offered one to me, and lit it for me. "But it's *got* to be a shambles, boy, if you're dealing, on the same stage, with a group of untried amateurs and a group of aging, uncertain professionals. You spend half the time keeping them from each other's throats. And the play, just between you and me, is not exactly *Hamlet*. Oh, well."

"Then why are you doing it?" I asked.

"Well—we think the play has something important to say. And why not try to jolt this town a little bit? Besides, it's a play they've *heard* of—it was done on Broadway. *With* Sylvia Sidney."

Lola came over and sat down in the grass before us, like a girl.

"How'd you like that cheer you got?" Lola asked. "Wasn't that something? We rehearsed it all morning."

"We might as well have," Rags said grimly.

"Rags," Lola said, "it didn't go badly. Really."

"Madeleine will never learn how to hold that letter," Rags murmured. "What's the matter with her? Doesn't she ever get any mail?"

"In my class this morning," Lola said, "I told her to hold the letter as though the letter were her final divorce papers—Madeleine's divorced, you know," she said to me—"and to realize that now that she *is* divorced, she doesn't really want to be. I thought it began to make a difference in the way she held the letter. I really did."

"Maybe," Rags said, gloomily. "I *still* think she looks as though she were holding a raw pork chop."

"Oh. You are such a perfectionist," Lola said.

I ground out my cigarette and stood up. "I have to go," I said.

"I hope we have those signs all over town," said Lola.

"We don't yet," I said, "but we will."

"But they should have been up by now!"

"The kids are just getting finished. I'm going to collect them now. They'll be all over town in a couple of hours. Don't worry."

"Oh! I'm not complaining about *you*," said Lola. "You are really an exemplary model of industry and devotion. It's just—"

"Opening night nerves," said Rags, and laughed grimly.

"Well. I think it will prove to be a very exciting theater experience."

"Especially," said Rags, "if he's sober."

"How *is* it going over there today?" Lola asked me.

"He's sober today," I said. I got into the car.

"And the others? How are they?"

"Like they've always been. No better. No worse." I started the motor. "But, you know, I don't really have much time to watch rehearsals."

"Leo! You are the rock on which we all depend. I trust that you are not *also* about to have an attack of temperament. You know that as soon as this *grueling* week is over, we will begin serious *work*. You have my word for that. And *Saul's* word."

"Yes, ma'am," I said. "I'm glad. Because I sure am tired of being a rock."

I turned the car around.

"Boy," Rags said, "you don't seem to realize that you're getting a college education in the theater."

"I'd feel better about being in college," I said, "if somebody would give me a test."

"All right," Lola said, "you shall have your test. Now, off with you. Good-bye."

"Good-night, ladies," I said, and I drove away.

When I drove past the toolshed this time, Barbara and Jerry were nowhere to be seen. I drove up Bull Dog Road and collected the signs from the other kids, and then drove to our shack. Barbara was in the shower and Jerry was on the porch, scrubbing himself with turpentine. He looked as though he were in makeup to play a wounded soldier. "You're a mess," I told him, and came up the porch steps and sat down in one of the rocking chairs.

"You're a mess, too," he said mildly. "What's the matter, native son? The theater getting you down?"

"The theater, shit," I said. "It's all this fucking running around."

"Do not despair," said Jerry. "You will make your mark. I think I got paint on my shoulder. You want to rub it out for me?"

I got up and took the rag and scrubbed his left shoulder blade. "Christ, you stink," I said.

"Sometimes I can't stand myself." Jerry grinned. He took the rag from me and walked into the kitchen. "You want a beer?"

"Yeah. You coming to town to help me with those signs?"

"Hold your horses. I'll be ready just as soon as Barbara comes out of the shower and I can wash this stink off me." He came out with a bottle of beer and two glasses. "Here." He poured beer into my glass and then into his own, and he sat down. "That's better. First time I've sat down this whole fucking day."

"Yeah. We might as well be working for the railroad."

"Well. You asked for it," Jerry said.

"It must be nice to be philosophical."

"It is. You ought to try it."

He lit two cigarettes and gave one to me. We listened to Barbara singing.

"Do you want another pail of water?" Jerry yelled.

"I've got those mad about him, sad about him, Lord I can't be glad without him—what?"

"I asked you if you wanted another pail of water?"

"No, thank you! I'll be right out." And she went on singing: *"I'm not the first on his list, I'd never be missed, I wish I had a dime for every girl he's kissed, I swear, I'd be a millionaire*—"

Jerry and I looked at each other and smiled. "She's quite a girl," said Jerry. Then he blushed. "I don't think I'm good enough for her."

"Oh. You're out of your fucking mind."

"You really think so?"

He asked it so very humbly that I looked over at him as though it were the first time I'd ever seen him.

"Of course I think so. What are you worrying yourself about? She's happy. Listen to her sing."

"I don't think she's singing because of me," Jerry said. "She just likes to sing." He paused. "She says singing will help her in her career."

"He's just an ornery sort of guy and yet I'll love him till I die, poor me!" We heard the water splashing over her. "Jerry! Towel!"

"Coming, princess!" He picked up a bath towel from the porch rail and handed it in to Barbara. He came back and sat down in the rocking chair, and, in a moment, she appeared, covered with the towel. She ran up the porch steps.

"Ah!" she cried, seeing me, "the overseer is back. I'll be ready in a minute. Jerry, take your shower!"

"Yes, princess," Jerry said. He winked at me. "You want to fill the bucket for me? Or maybe you want to take a shower first?"

"No. Go ahead. After you. I told you how you stink." He hesitated. "Go on, idiot. I'll fill the buckets. Then you can fill them for me."

"Okay," he said, "I'll start soaping myself. I won't be long," and he stepped out of his shorts and stepped into the wooden cubicle. I detached the two buckets from their platform at the top of the cubicle and filled one with fairly hot water and one with fairly cold water and replaced them. "You're on," I told him, and went back to the porch.

I heard him yell and heard the water splashing and heard Barbara singing in the room. I lit a cigarette and drank my beer. As soon as the signs were up, our working day would be over and it was not yet five o'clock. "Hey!" I yelled, "why don't we have dinner in town?"

"I don't think we have enough money," Barbara said. She shouted to Jerry, "Jerry, do you have any money? Besides—Leo—we were supposed to work on our scene tonight. You remember?"

"The hell with it. I think we ought to take a night off from that scene. Really. I've got six dollars."

"I think I've got about ten dollars," Jerry shouted. "Look in my pants pockets. How much do you have, princess?"

"I've only got five," she informed him, singing it out

like an aria, and arrived at the door, scrubbed and tom-
boyish, in an old white shirt of Jerry's and some blue
pants of her own. "May I have a cigarette, sir?" she asked,
and came over and leaned on my rocking chair.

"Certainly, princess." I lit one for her and gave it to
her. "There you go."

"Princess is something Jerry picked up from you and
now I think you've picked it up from Jerry. I don't really
like it. Why do you call me princess?"

"It's in tribute to your birth." She blew a great cloud
of smoke into my face. "Why don't you like it?"

"I think you're making fun of me."

"I'm not making fun of you. Jerry's not making fun
of you—God knows. Don't think like that." I watched
her. "We're just teasing you a little bit." Then I said,
"It's only because we love you."

"Ah!" She moved away and sat down in the other
rocking chair. "Can I have a sip of your beer, please?"

I gave her my glass. I asked, "Shall we have dinner in
town?"

"Okay. I don't think Jerry feels like cooking tonight
—and I can't cook at all—and you're not much better."
She sipped my beer. "But I want to get back here early, so
I can get up early."

"Okay. I've got to get up, too."

"Hey!" Jerry yelled, "throw me a towel!"

"Just a minute," Barbara said, and gave me back my
beer and rushed into their room. In a moment she reap-
peared, laughing helplessly, leaning against the door. She
waved a small face towel in front of her. I began to laugh.
"Jerry," Barbara called, "we only have one towel left.
And it's—Jerry—it's pretty small."

"Will you two stop fucking around and bring me a
towel? Leo, you got a towel upstairs? I'm *wet!*"

"I'll get you a towel. But you can come on out now.
Barbara won't look." I got out of the chair and started up
the stairs. "I'll bring it to you inside." I ran up the stairs
to my room. I heard the cubicle door open and slam and
I heard Jerry yell, *"Geronimo!"* as he ran up the porch
steps. I came back down the stairs with two towels, and
tossed one towel into their room where they both were,
Barbara still laughing. I cried, "Hurry up! I need a couple
of pails of water." And, to show that I meant business, I

took off my T-shirt. "We've still got to hang up those signs, children."

"Okay," Jerry yelled, "okay. Go on in, I'll fill up the buckets." And he threw a towel around him and went into the kitchen. I heard him running water and I took off my shoes and socks, took off my pants and walked into the cubicle. I took off my shorts and hung them on the nail and hung my towel on the nail and picked up the soap. "You're on," yelled Jerry, and then I was alone with the water and the soap and my body.

We drove into town at exactly six o'clock—so the courthouse clock informed us—and by seven we had placed our last sign in the window of the pizza joint which we had virtually taken over. The people who ran this joint weren't natives of the town—thank God; in fact, they weren't natives of the country. They came from Sicily, I think, they hadn't been in America long, and they were beginning to be gravely confused. They—the old mother and father, the sons and daughters and in-laws—still considered, in their barbaric, possessive, and affectionate fashion, that they were responsible for each other, that what happened to one affected all. This showed in their manner with each other and this manner marked them as foreign. This meant, of course, that they were disreputable and so we naturally gravitated there— it was our oasis. Neither had this Sicilian family yet arrived at anything resembling a perfect comprehension of what color meant in America, and so it was the only place in town where Negroes sometimes ate and drank, or, rather, it was the only place in town where Negroes and whites sometimes ate and drank together. Only the younger members of the family, and of these mainly the women, were beginning to suspect what this meant for their status and might mean for the material future of their children. One sensed this in their worried frowns, in their occasional hesitations, above all in their steadily developing realization that the respectable people never ate their pizzas at the brightly colored tables, but always took them out. They were not yet materially menaced, for soldiers came, and sailors, and frequent travelers, and laborers; and these all had money to spend. But the soldiers and the sailors often brought their girls—rather dubious, rather dangerous girls—and so did the travelers, and the laborers were loud. It was inevitable that some of the town Negroes would also appear, inevitable that the Sicilians would not have the sense to turn them away—it was against the law to turn them away, though this was not their reason—and inevitable, immediately thereafter, that the guardians of the law should descend to deepen the Sicilian confusion. They began to stare at the Negro laborers, who, after all, were often there with white laborers, eating and drinking and laughing and cursing, exactly like the laborers they still remembered, with the definite and desperate intention of discovering what was wrong with them. It began to occur to the women that there might be something wrong with being a laborer, since it meant, apparently—they were indeed confused— that one had to be friends with Negroes. They had seen where the Negroes lived by now, and how they lived. But they had yet to ascend high enough in the American scale to become reconciled to the American confusion; they had not yet learned to despise Negroes, because they were still bemused by life. They liked Barbara and Jerry and me. They didn't know how to hide it. They didn't yet know that there was any reason to hide it. Or course, they particularly liked Jerry because they could speak Italian with him, and they gave each other tremendous joy because Jerry could put them down for being Sicilian and they could put Jerry down because his family came from Naples. I didn't speak a word of Italian in those days, but I used to love to watch them and to listen. For Jerry's relationship with these Sicilians was very unlike my relationship with the Negroes in the town. I envied Jerry. Perhaps I hated him a little bit, too.

Also, in the pizza joint, since we were in the theater, we were special, we were gentry. It didn't seem at all odd to them that I should be in the theater—it was not only logical, it was, so to speak, my inheritance, my destiny. The only Negroes they had ever heard of had been in the theater, or in the ring. They were in awe of Paul Robeson —I must say that they really were. They loved Joe Louis. They loved Marian Anderson. They loved Josephine Baker. They made me tell them everything I knew about Father Divine. He had helped to feed the hungry, I told them, and they agreed with me that this meant that he was a good man; even though, as I later realized, their nods and

thoughtful frowns referred not to Father Divine, but to
Mussolini; who had also, perhaps, helped to feed the
hungry, but who had turned out, after all, not to be a good
man.

Angelo, the youngest son, seventeen or so, much
taken and bewildered by Barbara, had helped us place
our sign in the window, just so; long before this opera-
tion was concluded, his entire family had become involved in it, coming out on the sidewalk to judge the
effect, and leaving customers waiting for their dinner.
When it was finally judged an artistic success—which
meant rearranging the window—Angelo returned to his
function as dishwasher, the others returned to their functions, and we sat down at our table. We had decided that
we needed a drink, but before we could order anything,
Giuliano, the second son, brought us three dry martinis.

"For us," he said, and smiled and winked. "I hope
your play will be a success."

"We aren't *in* the play," said Barbara.

"Oh, but you will be in another play," he said. He
looked at Jerry and laughed. "Of course you know," he
said, "this one is of no use. He will *never* be in a play."

Jerry said something in Italian and they both laughed
again. "I hope you do not understand Italian," Giuliano
said to Barbara, "he is a pig, your friend here."

Jerry said something else in Italian, and they both, as
it were, vanished in a hurricane of laughter, into Italy.
Barbara and I helplessly laughed, too. She lifted her glass.
I lifted mine. We turned toward Jerry and Giuliano.
Jerry lifted his glass.

"Cheers," I said. "And thank you, Giuliano."

He smiled and bowed. "It's a little pleasure." He
looked at Barbara, then at Jerry. "Do you want a menu,
or do you want a pizza?"

"We want a pizza," Barbara said. "The biggest you
have, with everything on it."

They very nearly, in their brief glance at each other,
vanished into Italy again, but Giuliano restrained himself while Jerry choked slightly on his martini. "Very
well," said Giuliano, "a pleasure," and he inclined his
head slightly and walked away.

"What were you two laughing about?" Barbara asked.

"Family jokes," said Jerry. He put one arm around

her. They were together on one side of the booth, I was
alone on the other. He lit a cigarette for her, and kissed
her lightly on her restless forehead. "And family jokes
can't be translated."

She looked at him, but said nothing. I sipped my martini, and I said, "This drink is on the house, isn't it? Well,
that means that we can have another one. I mean, we
were going to have a drink, anyway."

"That means you want to get drunk," Barbara said.
"Leo—we really should try to work tonight."

"Barbara, I'm tired of working in the dark. I know
that goddamn scene ass-backward. I dream about it. And
I don't know if I know what I'm doing and you don't,
either. It's like—jerking off."

"I didn't know acting was *that* much fun," said Jerry,
and grinned. Barbara hit him lightly on the head.

"Maybe I'll try it." Barbara raised her hand again, but he
caught it and held it.

"Have you said any more to Saul," she asked me,
"about when he's going to start working with us?"

"No. But I talked to Lola this afternoon."

"And what did her Highness say?"

"She said that as soon as this *grueling* week was over,
we would begin serious *work*. She said we had *her* word
for that, and *Saul's* word." I stared at Barbara. "If she
breaks her word, I'm going back to the city." At that
moment, I really meant it. "It's not going to be any good,
hanging around here all summer, if I'm not learning anything."

Barbara opened her mouth, but Jerry spoke first.
"You wouldn't just go away and leave us? We'd miss you,
baby."

"Well—you two have each other." I said this a little
awkwardly.

"Oh, Leo," Barbara said. "Really!" Wrathfully, she
put out her cigarette. Then she looked up at me with a
smile. I could never resist her, never, when she looked
at me that way, she could make me do anything. "Nothing
would be the same without you, Leo. Really not." She
put her hand, gently, on mine. "Let's wait out the week.
They'll keep their word. You have *my* word for that."
And she nodded her head firmly, humorously pulling
down the corners of her lips, and took her hand away.

"If you're lonely," Jerry said, winking, "there are a couple of girls in the Life class who are very hot for your fine brown frame." He laughed and told Barbara, "They sit there drooling all over their sketch pads. They're supposed to be working in charcoal but they're really doing water colors, believe me." He looked at me. "How about it? Just to while away the long summer evenings?"

"Those fat old bags? You must be out of your mind."

"They're not so old. They're at the right age, baby." The earnest, quizzical expression on his face made me laugh. "They're not worried about having babies anymore, you see, so—well, you know. Anything goes."

"Jerry," Barbara said, "those women are awful. Especially Mrs. Jenkins. She must weigh more than two hundred pounds—just in the *behind.*"

"But Leo likes that," Jerry said. "Little men always like big women."

"Jesus," I said, "I wish you'd keep your cotton picking hands off my sex life."

"Hey, I'm glad you put it that way," Jerry said. "A couple of the guys in the class are pretty hot for you, too, and they told me—" I dipped my paper napkin in my water glass and wadded it up and threw it at him. It hit him on the shoulder; he dropped it on the floor. "Gosh, Leo. I was only trying to help."

"Shit. I'm going to have another drink." I grinned at Barbara. "Sex-starved actor takes to drink."

"But I really feel for you, baby, sometimes, when I know you're going to be up there on that stand," Jerry said. "In front of those harpies. Christ. They make my skin crinkle. You know what I mean?"

"Hell, yes." The patriarch of the tribe, Salvatore, came across my line of vision, and I signaled for more drinks. "I know what you mean, all right."

The Life class was pretty depressing. It was made up mainly of aging, idle women, and not one of them, as far as I could judge, had the remotest hint of talent. They usually placed me somewhere in Africa and I was often invested with a spear. But their concept of the African savage was fatally indebted to, and entangled with, their concept of the American Indian; the results on paper were stunning indeed. I found it disquieting that anyone could look at me and see what they saw; it was not less disquieting to realize that their bland, dumpling exteriors concealed so much of fantasy, helpless, lonely, and vindictive. These ladies gave me my first glimpse of a species of psychology which I eventually summed up—or dismissed—as the fig leaf complex; they were all working members of the fig leaf division. It did indeed, as Jerry said, cause my skin to "crinkle" when I stood before them naked. At first, I was most intimidated by my color—all of me naked seemed a vast quantity of color to bear; but it was not long before I began to be intimidated, far more grievously, by the fact of my sex. I wore the regulation jockstrap, though this seemed silly to me. Female models wore nothing at all. But then I began to feel that the jockstrap actually functioned—and perhaps was meant to function—as a kind of incitement, both for them and for me. I began to resent the jockstrap, for it seemed a kind of insult to my body. I couldn't help but become terribly conscious of what the jockstrap concealed and this made my penis nervous. I was always frightened of having an erection: all of me could be seen except that most private and definitive part of me, which was on no account to announce its presence. Well, it was agony. With all of my anxiety centered below my waist, I always, inexorably, felt the vengeful organ begin to stretch and swell—with anxiety, I suppose, certainly not with lust—pulling the jockstrap down. But I kept my eyes straight ahead of me, and held my pose, expecting at any moment to hear the women scream and faint, while sweat poured from my armpits and over my pubic hair and down my legs. Holding a five-minute pose before my ladies was harder than working in the mines. But the ladies worked steadily with their pads and pencils and brushes, sometimes holding a pencil up before them to dissect me, while I felt my rebellious black prick pounding against the walls of its dungeon, and threatening, as it seemed to my unhappy imagination, to destroy it. When it was over and I stepped down, they had achieved a noble savage who was carrying a spear and adorned with a loincloth as bland and as shapeless as their faces—a harmless savage, suitable for a pet, and one who could certainly never have any children.

Salvatore himself brought our fresh round of drinks and began setting up our table. He was a very sturdy, peaceful man, built rather like a short tree, incontestably and effortlessly the ruler of his house. Though he liked Barbara, as a patriarch he was also slightly disapproving of her; but the fact that Jerry was Italian reassured him, for he knew that Jerry would surely regulate their situation and then they could begin to have babies. Salvatore did not take any other human possibility very seriously.

There was something very wonderful which Salvatore brought to the fore in Jerry. Jerry showed a side of himself to Salvatore which he showed to no one else. I think if I had never seen Jerry with Salvatore, I would never have known what pain and love were in the boy, could not have guessed how much he had lost already, and why it was possible for Barbara really to care about him. Salvatore treated Jerry like a son; and this brought forward the man in Jerry. It brought forward in him elements of delicacy and courtesy which Jerry, in most of his daily life, disguised by rough speech and rough play. The lost and loving boy Jerry was attempting—helplessly—to divorce and deny was the only creature Salvatore saw, and it did not even occur to him to doubt the value of this creature. Salvatore could not know it, but he thus reached directly into the heart of Jerry's loneliness, and also foreshadowed his hard and lonely life. When I watched Salvatore and Jerry together, I was happy for Jerry but I was sad for me. For the old, sturdy man recognized Jerry, he had seen him before. He found the key to Jerry in the life he himself had lived. But he had no key for me: my life, in effect, had not yet happened in anybody's consciousness. And I did not know why. Sometimes, alone, I fled to the Negro part of town. Sometimes I got drunk there, and a couple of times I got laid there. But my connections all were broken.

Salvatore and Jerry were conversing in Italian, Jerry looking up at him with a child's huge, limpid eyes, when Madeleine came in. And perhaps because I wished to be protected from my thoughts—or from Barbara and Jerry, who were my thoughts made flesh—I was irrationally glad to see her. She had that polished look women have when they come back from the hairdresser and she was wearing a bright orange dress—of which Barbara, I realized, as she gave a small, theatrical shudder, completely disapproved.

"Well," said Madeleine, with her big, good-natured grin, "are you all having a conference, or can I join you?"

"The conference ended," I said, "when we hung up the last sign. So you can come on in the house."

"Good." She sat down and beamed at Barbara. "How are you, sugar? I think they've been running the ass off you kids this week, haven't they?"

Salvatore did not approve of Madeleine at all. He abruptly ended his conversation with Jerry, glanced quickly at Madeleine, and walked away. And I realized that Jerry was a little embarrassed. "Hi," he said, with a crooked smile, "how're things going?"

"It seems to me that they work *everybody* like slaves," Barbara said. "You must be weary, too. But at least *you're* doing a play."

"*Am* I?" asked Madeleine, with her eyes big, and her hands in the air. "Is *that* what I'm doing? I'm glad somebody told me—*I* need a drink."

"What's wrong?" asked Barbara. "Isn't it going all right?"

"Look. I know I'm not a big Hollywood star, like that broken-down lost weekend you've got over at The Green Barn now—and is *that* going to be a mess, my God!—but I'm a *good* actress and I've worked hard and, after all, they hired me for this damn thing—and I won't tell you what they're paying me because I'm too ashamed—for *them*—and I just don't think artists should be treated like shit. Baby, if I survive this mistake, you can *have* The Actors' Means Workshop, *believe* me. Especially that old dyke who calls herself a director, who couldn't direct a kid on rollerskates across the yard." She paused. She subsided. She looked at us and laughed. "Well. I had to tell somebody before I burst." Giuliano came and she smiled up at him and ordered a double bourbon.

"You've got a rehearsal tomorrow morning," Barbara said. "You'd better be careful tonight."

"*Fuck* them," said Madeleine. "Maybe I'll get there and maybe I won't. Maybe I'll walk out on them. And let them *try* to find somebody else *now*."

"What happened?" I asked.

"Oh," she said wearily, and looked at Barbara, "what happened? They don't know what they're doing, that's what happened. That's what's been happening ever since

I joined this bullshit outfit." Giuliano brought her her drink and she smiled at him again. She sipped it. "Let's not talk about it—at least not until I've finished my drink and had something to eat." She looked at me and smiled her really quite disarming smile. "One of these days, baby," she said to me, "you'll maybe wish you'd stayed in the post office."

I smiled. "Or the church. But they both threw me out."

"And how'd that happen?" Jerry asked, grinning.

"He just couldn't deliver the messages," Barbara said, and she looked at me and we all laughed.

Giuliano now returned to ask us, most politely, if the lady were going to eat, and, if she were, if we wished to wait for her or begin before her.

"What do you want to eat, Madeleine?" Barbara asked. *"We've* just ordered the biggest pizza in the house."

"Well, may I share your pizza?" Madeleine asked. "I need company much more than I need food." She looked quickly from Jerry to Barbara, and then leaned forward to Barbara. "Sugar—I know they pay me more than they pay you—and I've crashed your party—so please let me pick up the tab." She looked at Jerry and then at me. "If you won't let me do it, then I'll have to go. And I don't want to go."

Giuliano stood listening to this with a face as closed as a wall. Jerry was aware of Giuliano and Barbara was aware of Jerry. Therefore, she leaned forward and grabbed both of Madeleine's hands, and said, "Actually, we were just waiting for someone like you to come along, Madeleine. We haven't got a dime between us." After a second, Madeleine threw back her head and laughed, and Barbara laughed. Giuliano smiled, and Jerry informed him, in Italian, that the pizza was now to be divided among four instead of among three. Giuliano gave Madeleine a look very different from that which his father had given her, and bowed, and walked away. But he had also thrown a look at me, a look of adolescent envy. He was sure that Madeleine was my girl—or, rather, my woman; and he was sure that such a woman, though, of course, one could never marry her, must be wonderful to sleep with. Jerry, following a different route, had arrived at essentially the same point of view.

"Here's hoping your prayers will be answered," he said, and raised his glass and winked at me.

"Is Leo still saying his prayers?" Madeleine asked. She turned to me. "I thought you were emancipated."

"I am," I said, "but Jerry isn't. He's been burning candles for me."

"Is there something," asked Madeleine, "that you need that you don't have?" We all laughed. "Until I met Leo," Madeleine said to Barbara, "I never knew that a colored person could blush. But look at Leo!"

"Oh, Leo can blush," Barbara said gravely, "but he hates anybody to notice it. He thinks that if you know he can blush—just like white folks—you'll think he's just ordinary."

I protested, "I never said anything like that, and you know it."

"Leo also thinks," said Barbara, still speaking to Madeleine, "that unless he tells you, you can't tell."

"Poor Leo!" Jerry said. "Barbara's been on his ass all afternoon."

"She's mad at me," I said, "about that goddamn scene. But I swear I don't see any point in working on it tonight. I *meant* what I said. I've got to find out what I'm *doing*." She said nothing. She watched me. "All right," I said, "all right. Maybe we'll work on it after supper. Okay, princess?" And she dropped her eyes.

"What scene are you two working on?" Madeleine asked.

I told her. "We've been working on it for a long time. But Saul's supposed to look at it and he hasn't looked at it yet—and—well, you know, I just feel like we're going round and round in a circle. Somebody's *got* to tell me something."

"Well, Saul can tell you *some* things," said Madeleine. She paused and sipped her drink. "I don't know. I used to think much more of him than I *think* I think right now." She looked at Barbara, then at me. "I'm not sure he can tell you the most important things."

"Well, can *any* director do that?" Barbara asked.

"In the first place," said Madeleine, "let's face it, Saul is *not* a director. He's a teacher. That's a mighty funny breed of cat, especially in the theater. Some people think he's a great teacher. Some people think he's a lousy teacher." She paused. "I don't want to say anything to discourage either of you two lambs—let's put it this way: So-and-so may be a great director for *you* and a lousy director for me. If a director can reach you, if you trust him, then he can probably direct you, and maybe get things out of you which nobody knew were there—which *you* didn't know were there." She looked at me again; I knew she was not saying all she meant; I began to suspect that I knew what she meant. "Look. Let's leave actors out of it for the moment. How many directors can direct Chekhov, for example? For that matter, not many can direct Ibsen or Shaw or Shakespeare, and of that few"— she laughed, and took another swallow of her drink— "*none* are to be found at The Actors' Means Workshop."

"But we don't, mainly," Barbara said, "*play* Ibsen or Shaw or Shakespeare in this country."

"Well," said Madeleine, and threw up her hands again, "that's why directors direct what they direct, isn't it? It's not their fault. But I wouldn't expect too much from any of them, if I were you. But I'm talking too much."

"No," said Barbara, "I see your point." She looked astonishingly grave, even weary; then, after a moment, "Can't we change that?" she asked. She looked very hard at Madeleine, as though, with that look, she intended to convey to Madeleine a question beneath her question.

"*Can* we?" asked Madeleine. She leaned forward. "Look. I've got a daughter and she's got to eat. You don't think I think I'm doing a masterpiece, do you? No, sugar. I needed a job. It's the lead, and I think I can make something out of the part. If I can, I'll get better jobs. I might even appear in a couple of really good productions of really good plays. But, mainly, you take what you can get."

"You take what you can get," Barbara said, "but then, when you've taken it, you can make it do what you want."

"*Can* you?" asked Madeleine.

There was a pause. Barbara finished her drink.

"*I* can," said Barbara.

Giuliano came, with the pizza.

"Let's celebrate," said Madeleine, "and have a bottle of Chianti."

"Baby," I said, "you had *better* be good in this play. You're going to need another job right quick."

"I'm going to be splendid," she said, "in *spite* of Rags Roland. *And* Madame Lola *Sans Gêne*. The hell with it. If I hadn't run into you kids, I'd probably have ended up in that river they've got howling over yonder."

Giuliano began cutting up the pizza, and, while he was doing this, two young Negro laborers came into the place. I say they were young—they were both somewhat older than I; than I was then. One was perhaps about thirty, chunky, dark, and cheerful. And I say laborers, but, actually, the younger, not far into his twenties, impressed me as being a soldier, for I remember that he was dressed in khaki. He was lean, light brown, long, and shy, with a narrow face. I had seen the chunky one before, on the Negro side of town, in a bar, but he had not spoken to me and I had not known how to speak to him. But I had not seen the younger one before, and something in his manner—the particular manner of his diffidence—made me decide that he was a stranger here. I suppose I mean that the older one, the chunky, cheerful one, was accustomed to being uneasy, and sailed into it, smiling, as into the wind of his life, whereas the younger, stiff and silent, was only beginning to be aware of the chill. Here they were, here they came, and the elder, with that ready smile, and with all those lighthouse teeth, piloted the young one to a table—a table three tables from us. Jerry and Barbara were facing Madeleine and me; we certainly looked like a unit. Besides, I was already notorious, because, in complete innocence, like a foreigner outrageously overtipping in a desperate nation, I had disrupted the town's emotional economy. I had not known, after all, and could not have, what it would be like to deal with such a town, and there was absolutely no possibility that I could accept, much less survive, on such terms. But if it was vivid to me that they *had*, it was equally vivid to them that I hadn't—either because I knew more or because I knew less; either because I wouldn't or because I couldn't; either because I despised my color or because I didn't. We desperately wished to get to the root of the matter, but we did not know how to begin. Here I was, sitting with three white people—or, rather, with two white women. I could not leave my table and go to theirs. They could not leave their table and come to ours—or, rather, in this context, mine. We could not do what we wished to do, which was simply to be easy with each other. No: there we sat, under the eyes of the observant and bewildered Sicilians, studiously ignoring each other, the chunky, black, cheerful cat giving the order, the lanky, lean, brown cat looking down, with his hands between his knees. For a moment, I hated all of my companions, for whom, as I supposed, nothing had happened. We were all concentrating on our pizza and our wine.

"Actually," Madeleine said abruptly, "I'm not sure I really go for all this Actors' Means bullshit, anyway. I mean, I'm not sure an actor *can* be taught, or *should* be taught."

"Then how do you learn?" I asked. I had one eye on the laborers; I was making a certain resolution.

"Leo," she said, "I think you'll learn more by going out and falling flat on your ass in front of five hundred people than you'll ever learn from Saul. Believe me."

"But how," asked Barbara, "do you get the *chance* to fall flat on your ass before five hundred people?"

"Oh, well, there I agree," said Madeleine, "the Workshop label helps. That's because everybody else is as full of shit as they are. But, baby, that's just politics—it's a way of getting a job."

Barbara was silent. I watched the laborers. They were drinking rye and water. The darker one was laughing and talking—easily and slowly, even intimately, but absolutely onstage. The light had hit him early—that unspeakable light; he would be onstage until the day he died. And the proof of his authority was that the young one, uneasily, chuckled, with his head down. "Now," the black one was saying, "you can't find a better black broad than my old lady—you see what I mean? She is a champ, baby. I mean, she is a *champ*. But even *she* is started to go for the jive. You see what I mean? She want me to keep working my ass off so she can get to look like Rita Hayworth." And he looked wisely at the young one, who was watching him carefully, his drink held in both hands before his face, and then turned carelessly, laughing, away, showing us all his teeth.

"You make it sound pretty depressing," Barbara said.

"The truth usually is pretty depressing, Barbara," Jerry said. "You know that."

"Yes. I know that." She smiled. "I know a hell of a

lot, really—but I don't seem to understand very much."

I laughed. "Be careful, Madeleine. She's cracking up."

"Stop teasing her." She leaned forward and tapped Barbara lightly on the cheek. "You're very nice."

"I think you're very nice, too," Barbara said.

They were finishing their drinks. I gestured to Giuliano. "Please," I told him, "buy the two colored cats over there a drink for me? Just take it to them."

Giuliano smiled, and nodded, and left. Jerry and Barbara and Madeleine looked at me.

"Oh! Here we *go!*" said Madeleine.

"Pretty reckless," said Barbara, smiling, "pretty reckless." But she seemed pleased. "Do you know them?"

"No. But I thought we might as well get to know each other. Only"—I said to Madeleine—"I might have to borrow a couple of bucks from you till I get paid."

Madeleine slapped me on the thigh. "Don't worry about it," she said. And her hand rested on my thigh for a second.

"What made you do that?" Jerry asked. He looked amused.

"I don't know. I just felt like it."

Giuliano brought the drinks to their table. I concentrated on my pizza. They looked bewildered for a second. Giuliano pointed to our table, and they turned and looked at us. I raised my glass of wine. Barbara and Jerry and Madeleine raised theirs. We were all smiling. Everything, suddenly, had changed. If we had not broken through to each other, at least we had managed to accept each other's presence. The boy was still very shy, but very pleased, and the older man glowed; partly because we had helped to please his boy.

"Hello," I said.

They said, "Hello. Thank you."

"Let's have a drink together," Madeleine said, "after we finish eating?"

The young one said, shyly, after a glance at the older one, "That's fine with me."

"Only, it's got to be on us," said his mentor.

"We'll fight about that later," Jerry said. We all laughed. We raised our glasses again. "Cheers!"

Perhaps my heart shook in my chest like the wings of a small bird, but I was incredibly happy not to have been rejected. I was happy enough, I realized, to be on the point of tears. Barbara and Madeleine began gossiping about the theater. Three tables away, they resumed their talk about women. Giuliano came up to Jerry and they had a quick conversation in Italian. Giuliano went away. Jerry looked at me.

"Baby," he said, "I have a feeling that we're all going to be drunk—and broke—by morning."

"The hell with it," I said. "It's Saturday night."

Bye and bye, it was time for coffee, and our coffee came; and then Giuliano brought up a small table and two chairs. "This is for your friends," he said.

Jerry turned, smiling, and said, "Come and join us!"

The elder, because his hesitation was the greatest, deepest, rose at once, smiling—like a man accustomed to rise quickly if he were to rise at all; while the younger, because of his eagerness, seemed for a moment unwilling to rise. But here they came. Jerry half stood, holding out his hand. "My name is Jerry. This is Barbara"—and Barbara smiled and held out her hand, and they shook hands—"and this is Madeleine"—"Hi, fellows," said Madeleine—"and this is Leo."

We shook hands. "Hello," I said. "Sit down."

"My name," said the older one, "is Fowler. And this is my buddy, Matthew." And they sat down.

"Do you fellows live in this town?" Madeleine asked. She had the invaluable attribute of a friendliness completely uncorrupted by imagination. It meant that she could ask anything—it also meant, probably, that she could not hear whatever was stammered back.

"I do," said Fowler. His smile could be read as the precise barometer of his attention; the more he smiled, the more he was watching, the more he saw.

"I don't," said Matthew. "I come from Philadelphia."

"Are you going to be here long?" Barbara asked.

"A few days."

"And then do you go back to Philadelphia?"

Fowler and Matthew looked at each other with a brief smile. "I'm not sure I know *where* I'm going from here," said Matthew.

"None of us do," I said.

Matthew looked at me. Fowler ceased to smile; I was not a danger. "Where are *you* from?" he asked me.

"I'm from New York," I told him. "I mean, from the city—Harlem."

"Then what are you doing here?" Matthew asked me, with a shy smile.

"I'm studying," I said, "to be an actor." He looked a little blank—not hostile, merely blank. I could not imagine what he was thinking. "We're supposed to do a couple of shows this summer."

"We're working with The Actors' Means Workshop," said Barbara carefully. "I don't know if you've heard of it—"

"No," said Fowler, "I haven't."

"Well, since you live here," said Madeleine, "you've heard of The Green Barn—the theater up Bull Dog Road?"

"Out Bull Dog Road way? Oh, yes," he said, "I've heard of The Green Barn, all right."

"Well," said Barbara, "that's where we are. We have a play opening there tomorrow night."

"And I," said Madeleine, "am opening in a play there five nights from tomorrow night—would you like to come? Just tell me how many tickets you want—"

"And we'll get them for you," said Barbara. "You'd be doing us a favor, really. That way, we'll be sure of having at least *two* people in the audience."

"Thanks, sugar," Madeleine said.

"They mean," I said, "for you to come as our guests."

Fowler and Matthew looked at each other. "Look here," Matthew said to me, "are *you* going to be in this play?"

"Not *this* play," I said.

"We're just students," Barbara said. "We won't be in a play until—oh, about a month from now."

"I'll be gone by then," said Matthew.

"What kind of play you going to be in, boy?" Fowler asked me. He was smiling. There was a shrewd, amused speculation in his eyes.

"I don't know yet," I said. "I've just started."

"What made you decide you wanted to be an actor?"

"I don't know that, either. But I guess it's because I'm crazy."

They laughed at that—they really laughed. Matthew looked at me, and said, "You all right."

He reminded me of Caleb.

"You been over to our side of town yet?" Fowler asked me.

"I've been over at Lucy's Place a couple of times."

"Oh! Lucy's!" and he laughed.

"I saw you there one night," I said.

"And I'm going to tell the missus on you," Matthew said.

"You saw *me* there? Why didn't you say something?"

"Well," I said—lamely—"I didn't want to bother you."

He sucked his teeth. "I'm going to take you to my house one of these days and let my wife put some meat on your bones. You need some good down-home cooking. How much do you weigh?"

I told him. "Oh, boy," he said, "would my wife love to get her hands on you!"

"It appears like," Matthew said to me, "that you miss your mama's home cooking."

"Well," I said, "I've been missing it for awhile."

"Where *is* your mama?" Fowler asked.

"She's in New York—in the city."

"And your papa?"

They were both watching me with an interest which made me uneasy; and Barbara and Jerry and Madeleine were watching, too.

"He's with my mother," I said.

They began to react to my discomfort. They remembered that there were white people at the table. "What are you folks drinking?" Fowler asked.

"*We* invited *you*," said Madeleine.

"Oh, now, don't you start coming on like that," said Fowler. "I asked you what you was drinking."

"I can see you're a hard man to fight," Jerry said. "We'll give you the first round. Madeleine's drinking bourbon. What do you want, Barbara?"

"Oh—I don't know—whiskey. With ginger ale."

"And what's your chaser, ma'am?" Matthew asked Madeleine.

Madeleine opened her eyes very wide, looked resentfully around the table, and then back to Matthew. "I've been called a great many things in my life," she murmured, "but I didn't expect to be called ma'am for yet awhile." Matthew laughed helplessly. "My name," she informed him, "is Madeleine. Have you got that?"

"All right, Madeleine," Matthew said. "I'm sorry. What do you want with your bourbon—water or ginger ale or soda—or—or beer?"

"Beer!" Madeleine said. "First he treats me like a schoolteacher and now he treats me like a lush." We all laughed. She turned to Matthew again. "I'll have a little water, please. You better watch your step, Matthew. I'm an extremely vindictive woman."

Matthew laughed again. "Well, I promise," he said, "to try not to upset you any more." And he looked at her with interest, in rather the way Giuliano had looked at her, in fact. He looked very briefly at me, and then, "Where are *you* from, Madeleine?" he asked.

"I'm from Texas," she said, "a town you never heard of. I'm sure that's what makes me so vindictive."

"Oh, come on," said Matthew, "I don't believe you're vindictive at all. You just like to try and frighten folks."

Madeleine laughed. "I do pretty well at it, too, let me tell you." She turned to Barbara. "I scared the living shit out of Rags Roland this afternoon." She turned to Matthew and Fowler. "Rags Roland is a horrible old woman, built exactly like an army base, and she's the director— God help us all!—of the play I'm in."

"The play," said Barbara, "of which you are the star."

"That's right," said Madeleine. "My first starring role." Matthew nodded appreciatively. "Out here with the corn and the cows." Matthew and Fowler laughed. "Anyway," and Madeleine turned again to Barbara, "Rags was giving me hell this afternoon—in front of the whole company— about that scene near the end when I find out that my lover isn't ever coming back from that half-assed revolution in Ecuador. Part of my trouble with this play is that I've never understood why he went in the first place—but I'm not playing *that* part, thank God. Anyway, I finally blew my top and I asked Rags how the hell *she* knew what a woman felt like when she'd lost her lover forever. And I said a few other choice things about my co-star, who could certainly never be *my* lover, and walked out. I left them all standing there." She nodded. Our drinks came. Fowler and Matthew looked somewhat bewildered, and also looked amused.

"What did Rags say?" Barbara asked.

"She didn't say anything. She just stood there, like—"

"An army base," said Fowler.

Madeleine raised her glass. "Exactly! It was a terrible thing to say. But the old dyke got my goat."

Jerry said, "You shouldn't call her names like that. You don't know if she's a dyke or not. Anyway, it's nobody's business what a person does—"

"That's right," said Matthew, staring at Jerry: he looked rather as though he had stumbled into a seminar. "What a grown person does with his life is that person's business." And he looked at Fowler.

"Especially," I said, "since it's the person who pays for it. For what he does, I mean."

"That's right," said Fowler. He sipped his drink. "Of course, I *do* think that we can use each other's advice from time to time—we human beings." And he looked at Matthew.

"Are you sure," asked Barbara, smiling, "that we *can*—use the advice we get? We get so much advice. You know. I'm not sure that *I* can use—any of the advice *I* get."

I looked at her. "Do you get so much advice?"

"Oh! All the time. By phone, by wire, by pony express. Oh, yes, my dear. Everyone's anxious to give me advice." She looked back to Fowler. "But I can't *use* it."

"She's like me," said Matthew.

"*Why* can't you use it?" Fowler asked.

"Well, it's wonderful advice—for somebody else. And it's well meant. I mean, I know that. But it doesn't"—she stared helplessly at Matthew—"seem to have anything to do with—*me*."

"What do you mean," asked Fowler, "to do with you?"

"Well," Barbara said—there was a silence—"for example, I'm from Kentucky. Well, if I'd taken all the advice I was given, Leo and I couldn't be friends and I wouldn't be able to sit at this table. I'd be just another dried out—or *drying* out—Southern belle, looking for a rich husband." Belatedly, she laughed. "Do you see what I mean?" she asked Fowler.

"Yeah," said Fowler—he was very thoughtful—"I see what you mean, all right."

"That terrible round of parties and bridge," said Barbara. "Really terrible. And the necking in the woods or in the car or on the porch. Really. Awful! And you're really expected to marry one of them. After you've done just about everything that *can* be done, short"—she coughed—"of actually going to bed with"—she laughed—"a kind of muscular bowl of rice pudding. God! Who can take *that* advice?"

"You're quite a girl," Fowler said.

"Oh!" said Barbara. "I just want to live!"

"Tell me," said Matthew quickly, "do you find it hard to live? I mean"—he was very earnest; Fowler watched him with a smile—"really to live? Not just"—he waved his big hands nervously—"to go to the job and come home and go to sleep and get up and eat and go back to the job—but—to *live*." His hands reached out, his fingers clutched the air. His hands fell to the table, flat, palms downward; and he looked, for a moment, at his hands. Then he looked at Barbara. "You know?"

"Yes," she said.

"And it don't have nothing to do, do it," Fowler asked —"pardon me, young lady—but it don't have nothing to do, do it, with being white or black?"

"No," said Barbara. Then, after a moment, "Not really."

Fowler gestured toward Matthew. "You hear her," he said.

"Oh," said Barbara quickly, "I can't speak for *him*. I can barely speak for myself." She stirred her drink, looking down again. "I don't know enough," she said, "about anything."

"Well," said Fowler, "you seem to be learning pretty fast."

"You've got to learn fast," said Matthew, "this day and age, if you going to learn at all."

"Well, that's true," said Fowler. "That's what I been trying to tell you."

Matthew sighed. He looked at me. "Look here," he said, "are you in the Army?"

"No," I said. "They haven't got around to me yet."

"You want to go?"

I finished my drink. "Hell, no. You must be joking. I'd rather drop dead than fight for this miserable country. What have I got to fight for?"

Matthew smiled faintly, though he also looked a little shocked. "You got a point, boy. I can't deny it."

Fowler was indignant. "You both too young to know what you talking about," he said, with finality. "If you'd been around as long as *I've* been around, you'd know what you got to fight for." He turned to Barbara, as though he had decided that she was the most sensible one. "Matthew's got a great opportunity to go in the Army, and they'll send him to school so he can make something of himself when he comes out—but he don't want to go. He wants to join the Merchant Marine instead." He looked at Matthew with a furious exasperation. "Ain't no future in the Merchant Marine."

"Matthew's got to do what Matthew thinks is best," Barbara said gently.

"We all do," I said. And Matthew and I looked at each other a moment, as though we were really brothers.

"I just don't see myself in the Army," Matthew said stubbornly. "Get sent to some damn base in the Deep South—you know I ain't for that. I ain't *about* to take no crap off them rednecks. No, I can't do it."

"I think I know how you feel," said Madeleine.

"I think I do," said Barbara. "I don't think I could stand it if I was a man."

"Young lady," said Fowler—Jerry signaled to Giuliano to bring us another round—"sometimes a man have to stand a whole lot of things he don't want to stand. Take me. I got three children. I ain't in love with my boss, *believe* me, and I ain't crazy about my job. Sometime that man get on my back like white on rice and call me all out of my name, and everything—now, what am I going to do? I got to feed my kids. They don't want to hear nothing about me being a *man.* They want some food in their little stomachs." He looked at Matthew again. "And Matthew, he got a chance to make something of himself so he won't *have* to work on the kind of jobs *I* have to work—and he too dumb to take it. I declare." And he picked up his drink and finished it.

"Look here," Matthew said, "you keep talking about this fine job I'm going to get when I come out the Army. How many—how many colored folks you know got fine jobs, huh? Tell me." He waited.

"Oh, come on," Fowler said, "things is changing, you know that. And the man promised you. I heard him."

"Fowler," said Matthew, "I don't believe the white

man's promises no more, you hear me? I don't believe them." He spoke very quickly and nervously, almost stammering. Then he looked up. "Excuse me, folks. I ain't talking about none of you, you understand. But I'm sure, you being intelligent people and all, you know pretty well what the score is, right?"

"Hell, yes," said Jerry, looking down, looking sad and sullen, "we know the score, all right."

Giuliano arrived with a new round of drinks. We watched him pick up empty glasses and put full ones down, in a sudden, unhappy silence. Madeleine reached for my hand, and held it for a moment.

"Hell," said Barbara suddenly, raising her glass, "let's drink to the glorious land of the free."

"And the former home," I said, "of the brave."

We drank. "You're going to freeze your ass off," Fowler said, "on that North Atlantic."

"Well, I'd a hell of a lot rather do that," said Matthew, "than get it burned off in Georgia."

We laughed. "I'm with you," I said to Matthew.

"And that's all right with me," he said, and grinned.

We had a couple more rounds, and we all exchanged addresses, earnestly scribbling on scraps of paper brought to us by Giuliano. I think we all really wished to see each other again, but I think we also wondered if we really would—wondered, dimly, if there could really be any point to it. Furthermore, I was aware that I had not really given any address. I had no address. Paradise Alley was not my address, Bull Dog Road was not my address, and where my mother and father were living wasn't my address, either, and I hadn't even written it down. I very much doubted whether Fowler's wife, when confronted with the opportunity of putting flesh on my bones, would react with a positive glee. I suspected that Fowler and I might prove to have very little to say to each other. Matthew and I might have been another matter, but Matthew was leaving within the week. As for the others, Barbara, Jerry, and Madeleine, they were white. They really could not hang out with Fowler, and Fowler could not hang out with them. It was not that the price was high. I don't think they thought of the price, though, indeed, the price would have been highest for Fowler: but connections willed into existence can never become organic.

Yet—we all liked each other well enough. We felt dimly lost and baffled as we finally rose to take our leave.

By this time it was nearly midnight, and we were just about the last people in the place. As soon as we left, Salvatore would throw out the unattractive adolescents who were playing the pinball machine, and Salvatore and his tribe would lock up and go to bed. I did not feel like going to bed at all. I scarcely knew what I felt like doing, but I didn't want the night to end. It was a marvelous night, blue-black, with a crescent moon, the air was fine and soft. It was unbelievably silent. There was not a soul on the streets.

"This is one hell of a wide-open town," Matthew said. He was a little drunk.

"Oh, there's a whole lot happening in this town," Fowler said. "You just got to know where to find it."

"Well, if *you* know where to find it," said Matthew, "take *me* there."

I almost suggested that we have a nightcap on the other side of town, but then I hesitated. Only Fowler could make this suggestion, for only Fowler could take us there. I could not say, *Take me, too,* for this would be abandoning the people I was with. It was the presence of Madeleine which was most inhibiting, for I did not know what—if anything—she wanted from me, and I did not know if I really wanted anything at all from her. Fowler and Matthew, Barbara and Jerry, and Madeleine and I, walked in twos together down the slumbering street.

If Madeleine had not been there, I would have driven Barbara and Jerry home, and then driven back to meet Matthew and Fowler on the Negro side of town.

Madeleine held my hand loosely, and we walked very slowly. "A penny for your thoughts," she said.

"Oh. They're not worth a penny. I was just—thinking —of—of some people I used to know."

"So was I." Then, "That Matthew's a nice kid."

"Yes. Very nice."

We walked in silence. I heard Fowler and Jerry laugh.

"But where," asked Madeleine, "do you suppose we're going? Where's the car?"

"Behind us. I guess we're just taking a walk."

"Well. It's a nice night for walking," Madeleine said, and it seemed to me that she held my hand a little tighter.

We reached a kind of lookout point, above the river. Straight before us was a stone wall; between us and the wall, road signs; the road to New York City was on the right, the road to New England was on the left. The road was very wide, and, on the far side of the road was a large space, for motorists who wished to rest, or possibly picnic, or simply look at the river. We crossed the road and stood in silence at the wall, looking down at the river. The river was black, with a thin coating of silver. Tonight it seemed still, yet it was moving. The sound of this movement, which made me think of pebbles being overturned, great boulders being carried, logs crashing against each other, filled all the night air and seemed very far away.

"Did you grow up in this town?" I asked Fowler.

"That's right," he said peacefully, "this is my town."

"Do your folks come from here?"

"No, my folks is from the South." He lit a cigarette, leaning on the wall, and threw the match into the void. "Where your folks from?"

"My daddy's from Barbados," I said.

"And your mama?"

"Louisiana."

We leaned on the wall, looking at the river. Jerry had his arm around Barbara, who was very still. Her profile looked childlike and defenseless under the crescent moon. Madeleine's hand in mine felt wet. I felt a sudden fear, as present as the running of the river, as nameless and as deep.

"Fowler," said Matthew carefully, "look here. If you ain't too tired, don't you reckon we might have a nightcap —somewhere?"

"We might," said Fowler, looking at the water.

"You got any idea where?"

"Yeah. I know where." He turned to Barbara. "You folks tired, or you want to have a drink with us?"

Barbara looked at him. Her eyes were so bright that I thought for a moment that there were tears in her eyes. But she was smiling, and the moonlight made her more beautiful than she had ever seemed to me before. "Of course," she said, "we'd love to have a drink with you. Even though it means"—and she smiled at me—"that we won't get any work done tomorrow."

"Tomorrow's Sunday," Matthew said.

"Not in the theater," Barbara said. She took Jerry's arm, and Fowler's arm. She smiled up at Fowler. "Will you lead the way? Kind sir?"

"I'll be happy, young lady."

And so we turned from the wall and the river and we crossed the road again, Fowler, Barbara, and Jerry arm in arm, and Matthew, Madeleine, and me. The other side of town, at this hour, was only about a five-minute drive away. Fowler insisted, once he had seen our jalopy, that we all go together in his car, which was an enormous Ford station wagon. We were not pleased by this, it seemed impractical for Fowler to drive us back to our car; but we had already gone too far to turn back and we did not dare to speculate on the reasons for Fowler's vehemence. We piled into Fowler's car, Fowler, Jerry, and Barbara in front, Matthew, Madeleine, and I behind, and crossed the sleeping town.

I have crossed many a frontier since then, have had my passport stamped, say, at the French-Swiss border, at the Swiss-Italian border; and I am beginning to believe that a landscape is not a landscape at all, merely a reflection of the sensibility of the people who live in it—certainly this is what one is watching as one crosses their forests and plains, vineyards and mountains, cities, tunnels, towns. French towns are mostly hideous, all French trees are mercilessly cropped, with a view, presumably, to the landscape, the larger vision—in the way French poodles operate as accessories to the wardrobes of their owners. There is absolutely no nonsense about it, whatever does not fit in is out, down to the merest flickering flower, the puniest, struggling branch. I suppose the French impose such a violent topographical order in order to compensate for an extreme untidiness, indeed, disorder, which the nature of their history—their passion—does not allow them to attack in any other way. The man at the frontier has cigarette ashes all up and down his uniform, and a cigarette is established between his lips. He has not the remotest interest in the voyager, or his passport: he forces himself to squint at both. Sometimes he looks at the baggage, sometimes not. Sometimes he stamps the passport; sometimes one has to ask him to stamp it. His office, were it not in France, would remind one of nothing so much as a cell in purgatory; and he and confreres seem to feel that they are serving a sentence which they probably, after all deserve. Within seconds, the time it takes to cross a small backyard, one has left this outpost, the last witness to this indisputably dour and extraordinarily interesting people, and one is facing the apple-faced Swiss. Their quarters are impeccable, as are their uniforms. The Swiss do not smoke their cigarettes, but leave them quietly burning in one of their millions of ashtrays. Their uniforms are ironed every morning and laundered every night; and the man within the uniform would find himself in something much worse than purgatory if he were not laundered and ironed, too. He examines everything very carefully, passport, luggage, voyager; causes one to think of the dirty socks and shorts in one's baggage, one's filthy armpits, and abruptly active intestines; is unspeakably polite, as patient as a ferret, as distrustful as a thief; and when one has escaped the Swiss correctness, one feels that one is being pursued—they are hoping to delude you into leading them to your accomplice. And then, abruptly, one is at the Italian frontier. They seem extremely surprised, but, on the whole, delighted, that you decided to drop by. Between extravagant offers of extravagant dinners, and impassioned questions as to what drove you from your part of the world, they are perfectly willing to glance at your passport and stamp it on any random page. They swear eternal brotherhood, and so you pass out of their offices and out of their lives. The French landscape is cerebral, this being the form that the French passion deludes itself into taking. The Swiss landscape is ordered, nothing could be more remote from passion—people who cannot make love make money—and it is designed to advertise one of the most flagrantly fraudulent Edens in our unhappy history. The Italian landscape is ragged, wild, unpredictable, like the landscape of Spain, the landscape of Africa. And something in me answers to such a landscape. Something in me is caught and held and solaced. I am profoundly repelled by the smug angularities of northern Europe, the cold sky and the spiteful lips of New England. A day may come, but not for me, when the American South will be habitable. Till then—well, I am wandering. But I was about to say that, however dramatic the frontiers

I have mentioned, the most dramatic, the most appalling, remains that invisible frontier which divides American towns, white from black.

We drove through the sleeping town, mostly in silence now, our thoughts more than ever flesh. Barbara's head was on Jerry's shoulder, Madeleine had her hand in mine, Fowler whistled as he drove, Matthew's thigh was against my thigh. Perhaps for the first time, certainly not for the last, I had a sudden, frightening apprehension of the possibilities every human being contains, a sense of life as an arbitrary series of groupings and regroupings, like the figures—if one can call them figures—in a kaleidoscope. I think we all felt this, in our different fashions. Barbara hid her head in Jerry's warm and gentle shadow. Fowler whistled, Matthew hummed, shifting his weight from time to time, Madeleine held my hand. I was very grateful for her hand. As the car rushed through the darkness, I felt myself being hurtled into some crucial confrontation; with Madeleine; or with Matthew; or with my past. We were approaching a bridge which spanned a narrow creek. On the other side of this bridge lived the dark people to whom I belonged. Matthew moved, and touched me, and I wondered what was in his mind. Then I wondered what was in *my* mind. I held on to Madeleine—but I was terribly aware of her color; for the first time, or so, at least, I wished to think. The car rushed forward, and we heard music. People, black, walking and talking, began to populate the landscape. The streets narrowed, the houses clustered, the music became louder. Children erupted, like beautiful, doomed flowers. They were on porches, playing jacks, a light behind their heads, two boys were rolling around in their yard, a couple of boys and girls were singing. I felt myself in the middle of a turning wheel. It felt like that, as one might feel at a circus, with all its shifting, multicolored, terrifying lights, and with all that sound; or as one might feel walking on the tightrope, with all the lights and sounds and people, mortally, hideously, unbelievably beneath; everything depending on what one was able to achieve of balance. Lord, I wondered—wondered: and Matthew, with one great hand, lightly touched the back of my neck, Madeleine's hand tightened, and Jerry lowered his head to Barbara's. The car sped into the impasse created by a bar on the right hand, a closed warehouse on the left, and that terrifying bluff above the terrifying river directly before us. Fowler turned the car around, and we parked before Lucy's Place. We had crossed from death into what certainly sounded like life. And not only did it sound like life, it looked like life; and not only did it look like life, it looked like a particular life, a life which was a particular reproach to me. I saw, with a peculiar shock, the root of the despicable and tenacious American folk-lore concerning the happy, prancing niggers. Some of these people were moving, indeed, and the jukebox was loud; their movements followed the music which their movements had produced; but prancing scarcely fairly described their uses of their vigor. Only someone who no longer had any sense of what constituted happiness could ever have confounded happiness with this rage. Yet, the scene we entered had been tirelessly reproduced, in stale and meticulous, absolutely libelous detail, in countless musical comedies and innumerable pork-chop-in-the-sky films: the nigger, moving in uncanny time to the music, hips, hands, and feet working, all flashing teeth and eyes, without a care in the world. It was my own uneasiness as we entered which afforded me my key to the domestic fantasy. The music was loud and aggressive. If it held the heat of love, it equally held the heat of fury, and it could not be described as friendly. Passion is not friendly. It is arrogant, superbly contemptuous of all that is not itself, and, as the very definition of passion implies the impulse to freedom, it has a mighty, intimidating power. It contains a challenge. It contains an unspeakable hope. It contains a comment on all human beings, and the comment is not flattering. How logical, then, that those who had been saved by those exquisite qualities with which they had invested the fact of their color and the accidents of their history, should, immediately, inevitably, and helplessly, regard the passion of their servitors as proof that their servitors were less than human and deserved the sentence meted out to them by that God whom the saved had purchased. "God, what I wouldn't give to dance like that," Madeleine muttered—but the history which produced one cannot be given away: so I told myself as we entered, as I saw the faces change, heard Fowler's much too hearty, "Brought some friends by to see you," and forced myself not to let go Madeleine's hand.

Some of the women looked at me with a terrible contempt. Some of the men looked at me as though I were a fool, but, just possibly—looking at Madeleine with a cool, speculative, lewd contempt—a lucky fool. Their eyes said they wouldn't mind, maybe, taking my place in Madeleine's bed, oh, maybe, four or five times. I knew that some of them wouldn't scruple to suggest this. If a white woman would sleep with one black man, then, obviously, she had no self-respect, and would sleep with an entire black regiment. I had not yet learned, though time was to teach me, how hideous it is to be always in a false position. I was hurt for Madeleine, and bewildered—and I was glad that I had not come in holding Barbara's hand—but I was hurt for them, too. It seemed to me that their swift estimate of Madeleine revealed their estimate of themselves, and this revealed estimate frightened me as being, perhaps, after all, at bottom, my own. But—they saw what they saw. They saw themselves as others had seen them. They had been formed by the images made of them by those who had had the deepest necessity to despise them. The bitterly contemptuous uses to which they had been put by others was the beginning of their history, the key to their lives, and the very cornerstone of their identities: exactly like those who had first maligned them, they saw what their history had taught them to see. I did not know then, and I do not know now if one ever sees more than that. If one ever does, it can only be because one has learned to read one's history and resolved to step out of the book. Piloted by Fowler, watched ironically by the bartender, threading our way through the dancers, we arrived at a table in the back.

"Well," said Matthew, "look at us!" And he grinned, and I realized that he knew more than I had thought he knew. He was no one to play with—as the dark lady making it over to our table would have been the first to observe.

"Here's Miss Lucy," Fowler said, and Jerry rose at once, and I rose.

"Sit down," said Miss Lucy—she had a voice like a man—and she didn't shake my hand, she rubbed her hand over my head. "Fowler, does this boy's mama know he's out? And out with *you?* Sit down," she said to Jerry, "make yourself at home. Good evening, you young ladies," and she smiled at Barbara and Madeleine. "What brings you by here this time of evening, Fowler? I thought you was a respectable, church-going man. And you know tomorrow's Sunday."

"We're strangers in town, ma'am," Matthew said, "and old Fowler was kind enough to do us a favor and show us that his town wasn't dead, like I was beginning to think. He said all the life in the town was right here."

Miss Lucy laughed. "Fowler's full of the devil. You liable to get yourself in trouble, hanging out with Fowler."

"But it appears like he was right this time, ma'am," Matthew said.

"Oh, this ain't nothing but a little friendly place," said Miss Lucy, proudly. "Everybody's welcome here. All the time."

"These here young ladies," Fowler said, "they both in that theater come to town—"

"The Green Barn," said Madeleine. "We're actresses. We hope."

"And this young man," said Fowler, indicating me, "he's with the theater, too."

"He's an actor," Barbara said.

"I hope," I said.

A brief, uneasy silence fell before Miss Lucy recovered. "Well. The Green Barn. I've *heard* of it—"

"Out Bull Dog Road way," Fowler said.

"Oh, yes! Out Bull Dog Road. *I've* heard of it. My, that's real nice," she said, and smiled again. "You folks going to be with us long?"

"Till the end of the summer," Madeleine said.

"Well, I sure hope you won't let yourselves be no strangers here," said Miss Lucy. "You welcome any time. Where you from?" she asked me.

"I'm from Harlem," I said.

"Oh, you a Harlem boy! I used to go to Harlem a whole lot. But, now, this place keeps me so busy." She sighed. "Where you from in Harlem?"

I told her.

"I used to have folks lived around there." She looked at me with a quick, speculative interest. "But that was before you was born." She turned to Fowler. "Fowler, let me offer you and your friends a round. What you folks drinking?"

"Will you sit with us, Miss Lucy?" Fowler asked.

"Sure," said Miss Lucy, "I'll come back just as soon as I tend to a couple of folks. Let me just send Andy over. He'll take real good care of you. You all have a good time, now," and she smiled again, and left us. I watched her talking to the bartender, who nodded several times, not looking in our direction. Then she was very cheerful and proud with several other people, who glanced in our direction once or twice: it was established that the form our madness took was not malevolent, that we might be distinguished, or, even, not impossibly, charming.

We were there for a long time, and we got quite drunk. Barbara and Jerry danced. Barbara and Matthew danced. Fowler danced with Madeleine. I was afraid to dance. This realization came as a shock, for I had never been afraid to dance before. But I had never danced with a white woman. In that youth, so swiftly receding, vanishing behind me, I had only danced with black girls; and we danced among the dancers and we had, in effect, no audience. But now there was an audience, a black audience watching a black boy dancing with a white woman; and they would know, from the dance, whether the woman was really his or not. I had no woman, I had only had adventures—though I must confess that I have never, in the sexual context, arrived at an understanding of the meaning of this word. They were not adventures at all, at least not if one supposes that adventure suggests risks joyfully taken: they were dry, predictable, and joyless, as laconic as a thermometer. I was very, very frightened, and because I was frightened, I forced myself to stand up and dance with Barbara. I knew that I could never dance with Madeleine. "Bravo," said Matthew. And I led Barbara onto the floor. It was a slow dance, for I did not feel exuberant.

She was very soft and small in my arms. I felt very strange—quite peaceful in one way; quite disturbed in another. Barbara's hand was very light on my back, her hand in mine was warm and dry, she held me with an unexpected, a surprising intensity. I don't know anything about the way we are put together, how long, in what secrecy, a moment prepares itself, or according to what law it suddenly comes into the light, so that one is standing, abruptly, trembling, face to face with the unimaginable. I don't think that I had been particularly aware of Barbara's body before, but I was now, and I felt that she was aware of mine. I thought, at once, guiltily, of Jerry; perhaps Barbara had also been thinking of Jerry; and I had a sudden, bewildering sense of Barbara as being trapped. I turned my mind away from this too bleak confusion. I became dreadfully uncomfortable, thinking of Jerry and Matthew and all the black people watching: it was almost as though we were making love in public. And yet—how can I explain this?—this profound discomfort did not really disturb my peace. I knew I could not move out of Barbara's arms. Then I was horrified to remember that I was wearing no underwear, and my member, with no warning, with uncontrollable speed, raged and thickened against the cloth of my jeans. Barbara had to feel it, but her face gave no sign; and I—poor me!—had no choice but to keep the rude witness hidden against her body. It was horrible. I thought of all the people watching. Involuntarily, without realizing I was doing so, I pressed Barbara closer. Sweat broke out on my forehead, at the hairline. I wanted the dance never to end. I wanted the dance to end at once. How would I ever be able to get across the dance floor? I tried to move as little as possible, but this made matters worse. I cursed myself. Then I maneuvered us closer to our table, and thanked God that the lights were dim. Yet, beneath it all, I felt a curious peace. At last the record ended. In a grave and decorous silence we walked back to our table and I slipped quickly into my seat. We were silent. Something of the greatest importance had happened to us.

Everyone seemed perfectly at ease. Matthew was involved in a joking flirtation with a rather pretty girl at the next table, who was sitting with two couples. He was quite drunk now, but very cheerful, and it seemed to me that he had certainly scored with the pretty girl, who was clearly much taken with him. Fowler was watching him with a kind of amused and lofty affection. Barbara sat down next to Jerry, her face still and closed; I thought there was a certain fear in her face. She said, "Jerry, I really think it's time we started home."

I didn't want to go home to my empty room, with the two of them together downstairs. I grabbed Madeleine's hand again.

"Any time you ready," Fowler said, "I'll be happy to drive you back to your car."

"I think we might as well be going now," Jerry said.

"You folks thinking of leaving now?" Matthew asked. "The evening's just getting started."

"It's just getting started for *you*," said Jerry.

Barbara rose. "It's been a fine night. Thanks for bringing us here."

"Well, it sure was my pleasure," Matthew said, "and we have to do it again sometime."

He rose, and we all shook hands.

"You fixing to stay here?" Fowler asked.

"I'll stay here till you bring the car back, Fowler. You know I can't just tear myself away from this charming young lady just like that." He grinned and winked at me. "Look here," he said, "I'm going to give you a call up at your theater in a couple of days. We'll have us a couple of drinks together before I cut out of here."

"Good luck on the North Atlantic," Madeleine said.

"Thank you—*Madeleine*. You see, I remembered that time." And we laughed.

"Be good," I told him.

"You too. Bye-bye now."

We walked slowly to the door. "Bye-bye," shouted Miss Lucy. "Don't you all be no strangers now, you hear?"

We told her that we wouldn't be strangers, and we stepped outside. We piled into Fowler's car. Madeleine and I sat in the back, and I put my arm around her. And, looking at her very hard, emboldened perhaps by the whiskey and the fear of my white-washed room, I asked her, "Can I come up and have a nightcap at your place?"

She paused for a moment. She said, "All right. That might be nice."

I asked Fowler to make a slight detour, so we could let Madeleine off before going back to our car. When we reached Madeleine's house, Madeleine and I stepped out and I gave Jerry the car keys.

"I'm going to have a drink with Madeleine," I said. "I'll see you all later. Bye-bye, Fowler, and thank you. I'll see you soon. Good-night, Barbara."

She looked slightly stunned, but she smiled and said, "Good-night, Leo. Good-night, Madeleine."

"Good-night, kids. See you all tomorrow."

"I'll fix a night for supper," Fowler said. "One night at my house. Before Matthew goes."

"Okay. Good-night."

"Good-night."

And they drove off down the dark street, leaving everything empty. Now, I was really frightened, though, now it was too late. What would people say if they saw me coming out of Madeleine's house in the morning? We were crazy, both of us. But Madeleine already had keys out, there was no one, anyone, to see us go in. I took the keys and opened the door and we climbed in silence to the third floor. Still in silence we entered Madeleine's apartment and she turned on the light.

"Well!" said Madeleine. She was smiling.

"Do you think we shocked anybody?"

"I think we shocked Fowler."

"Do you think it matters?"

"No. I don't think it matters."

We walked into the living room.

"But we may," she said, "have shocked Barbara even more than we shocked Fowler."

"Oh, no," I said. "Barbara's not like that." I turned from her and walked about the room. "You've got a very nice place here." It was pleasant enough. She had big, curtained windows, the bedroom was on the right, and the john and the kitchen were behind me.

"Oh, it's all right," she said. "But those windows just open on that awful street—but from the kitchen you can see a little bit of the river. Isn't that silly?"

"All these towns have their ass in the river," I said.

"Come look."

I walked into the kitchen and we stood beside the window. And it was true—through the interstices formed by other buildings and mighty poles and wires and the dull gleam of the railroad tracks, one made out the river. It caught the light differently; or it threw back another light. And if one held one's breath, as now, indeed, we did, one could hear it, faint and steady, rolling along.

For a second, I listened to Madeleine's breathing, which was faint, but not very steady. I didn't know what role she wanted me to play with her, and for the moment I was just stalling, being a kind of bebop kid.

"Put something on the record player," she said, "and I'll make that drink."

"Right." I walked back into the living room. "What do you want to *hear?*"

"Anything *you* want to hear. But keep it very low."

"That's right. We certainly don't want the neighbors barging in here tonight."

She laughed. "No. I don't want to be sent back to the convent."

I couldn't guess what she wanted to hear, she didn't have anything I particularly wanted to hear, and so I put on something very easy, maybe it was *Rhapsody in Blue,* very low. I still felt very sure of myself, probably because I was not alone in my room. I sat down on the sofa. On the table next to the sofa, under the lamp, was a picture of a little girl with long hair, standing near a white fence. Her head was up, and she was laughing.

"That's my daughter," Madeleine said. She came in with the drinks and sat down on the sofa beside me. She put the drinks, with coasters and napkins, on the coffee table. "She was only six then."

"She looks like a nice little girl." I put the picture down. "How old is she now?"

"Eight."

"What's her name?"

"Audrey. She's my pride and joy. She makes my life worth living."

I looked at her. "Good for you." I picked up my drink. "Here's to a life worth living."

"That's a good toast." We laughed and drank and listened to the music. I put my glass down. I pulled her blond head onto my shoulder.

"You're not drinking," she said, after a moment.

Some instinct made me do exactly what she wanted me to do. I looked at her, I changed my position, and I put my head in her lap. She looked down at me, smiling. Her breasts seemed very big. I put my hand on one of them, really rather like a kid playing doctor, but also aware that a strange and mighty storm was rising in me. I was aware that the storm had really nothing to do with Madeleine, except that she was in the path.

"You're a strange boy," she said.

"Why? Why am I a strange boy?"

She took, very deliberately, a sip of her drink. My hand stroked one breast. Part of me felt, Leo, you're nothing but a goddamn sex-fiend and you'll never get out of this house, let alone this town, alive. If this broad could read your mind and know what a freak you are, your ass would be in the river, your head would be on a pike, and your cock and balls would be nailed to the court-house door. And I thought, Fuck it. I want to see how much of a freak *she* is. She's come this far, let's see how far she'll go. I began fumbling with the buttons of her blouse. She put her drink down, and, as she leaned over to do this, I put one hand inside her blouse.

"Tell me. Why am I a funny boy? What's funny about me?" She was silent. I said, "Maybe you better tell me later."

Then—we fooled around. I worked with my lips and my tongue and my fingers, she wasn't working much yet, but she would; we fooled around. I can't say what was driving me. Perhaps I had to know—to know—*if* my body could be despised, how *much* it could be despised; perhaps I had to know how much was demanded of my body to make the shameful sentence valid; or to invalidate the sentence. I got her nearly naked on that sofa, shoes and stockings off, dress half on, half off, panties and bra on the floor. I was striding through a meadow, and it certainly felt like mine. She shook and whimpered and caressed me and I did not recognize her anymore. I won-dered if she recognized me, if we mattered now at all to each other. A terrible bafflement began in me. The baffle-ment, causing a drop in my ferocity, raised the level of my need. I did not want to watch her anymore, I was afraid of what I would see; I was afraid of what I had wanted, and still wanted, to see. I did not want to watch myself anymore either. I wanted to be held and cleansed and emptied. I stroked her face and her body, I felt lost and I wanted to cry. And though she was still now, and I was in the dark, our touch had more meaning—at least, our touch was more friendly. Then I opened my eyes and looked at her, her clothes half off, and all the white flesh waiting, and I wondered if she, while I had been tram-pling through a meadow, had been crawling through a jungle, dreading the hot breath and awaiting the great stroke of King Kong. She was nearly naked, but I was still dressed. I pulled my shirt over my head. She opened her eyes.

"Let's take off these clothes," I said, "and go to bed— like civilized people."

She smiled. "*Are* we civilized?"

"Hell, no. But come on and take me to your big brass bed." I watched her. "And give me some head."

She struggled up on one elbow. "Help me get this silly dress off."

I undid some clips and buttons and she stood up and stepped out of her dress. Then she looked at me, quite helplessly, with a smile. I took her hand and led her to the bedroom. She pulled down the covers. I took off my jeans. She said, "Just a moment—I'll be right back." I pulled her into my arms and kissed her. She pressed against me, then she pulled away. "Just a minute," she said, pleading, and she went into the john. I fell into bed and lay on my back, frightened and evil, patiently waiting, immense and heavy and curdled with love.

I woke up suddenly, out of a sleep like drowning. In my sleep, I had traveled back to Harlem, and I was curled up against Caleb, in our narrow bed. Caleb's chest was hot and heavy, I was soaking with his sweat and choking with his odor. Our mother's voice rang over us like the thunder of a church bell: *Boy, do you know what time it is?* I struggled against Caleb's weight. I turned and struggled, turned and struggled. I woke up.

I could not have been sleeping long, for there was no light in the sky. Madeleine's head was on my chest. She snored very lightly, and drooled a little bit. Her weight was intolerable, and I hated it. I was terribly, terribly afraid. I knew that something awful was going to happen. And there was nothing I could do and there was no place to run. Here I was, in this white cunt's bed; here I was, ready for the slaughter; here I was, I, Judas, with a stiffening prick and a windy heart, lost, doomed, terrified, alone. The air whispered, or I whispered, my brother's name. But nothing, now, forever, could rescue my brother, or me.

I moved from beneath Madeleine's weight as gently as I could, and went into the bathroom and took a piss, and then stepped under the shower. I turned on the water as hard as I could. The needles of the water hit me like Saint Sebastian's arrows. I wrapped myself up in one of Madeleine's enormous towels, found a cigarette and lit it, and recovered my stale drink and sat down before the kitchen window. Leo. You are more than nineteen years old. What the fuck do you think you're doing, with your *life?*

I listened to the river; but I saw my mother's face. I sipped my drink. My abandoned mother. My abandoned father. Their lost sons. This was Saturday night. They would be asleep now on the top floor of the tenement, in their bedroom, which was their only room. The rest of their apartment was rented out. The room which would have been Caleb's was occupied by a junkie and his girl-friend. The room which would have been mine was filled with all that was left of an old elevator operator, he, too, abandoned by all his kith and kin. They all shared the kitchen and the bathroom and the living room—and that was all there was to the apartment, which was like Miss Mildred's apartment, except that it was smaller. We moved there while Caleb was away. Caleb had never lived there; and I did not live there long.

My father would have been drunk, but quietly drunk; his rages were ended; he lived only to sleep. His lips were narrower, his face was thinner, the big eyes were dulled with the heat of his life, but all the fire was gone. My father was a porter in the garment center. My mother spent all day sewing in the same neighborhood, but not for the same firm. In any case, their hours were different. My mother left work before my father did, and hurried home to cook for him. To do this, she had, first, every day, to conquer the filth of the kitchen—for a kitchen used by strangers is always filthy—and do what she could to disguise the disorder of the other rooms. She was always weary, and her hair was almost always knotted on the top of her head. But, sometimes, on Saturday nights, she accompanied my father to a bar in the neighborhood and they laughed and gossiped with the people there. This was to prevent my father from becoming melancholy mad. he drowned in his sorrow when he drank alone. And when she went out with him, she always took care to look her best, and she wore her dangling earrings. But she was wondering, as he was wondering, Lord, where can my children be tonight? They were wondering how it had happened that their lives had come to a full stop so soon. They were close to death, and yet it was as though they had never lived.

"It would have been *better* if you'd never lived," said Caleb, "because then I wouldn't be here, neither. I didn't want this life, this hell, this *hell!* Why did you give it to me?"

He was just a little past twenty-one. I was just a little past fourteen. He had been home a week. We were all standing in the kitchen; and Caleb was very drunk. He and our father had got drunk together. But our father was not drunk now. We had all been, like a family, to a Saturday night function at the Renaissance, on Seventh Avenue. And Caleb and our father had spent more and more time at the bar, talking together. Caleb had begun to weep. And then we left.

He was thinner, much thinner, but harder and tougher. He was beautiful, with a very dangerous, cruel, and ruthless beauty. He had been home a week, but he and I had found it hard to talk—he did not want to tell me what his time away had been like. But I knew what it had been like from the way he flinched whenever my breath touched the open wound, from the distance between us, as though he were saying, *Don't come near me. I've got the plague.*

"Caleb," said our mother—she was still in her green evening gown; her earrings caught the light; there were combs in her splendid hair—"don't try to hurt your father. We did the best we could. We love you."

"We didn't ask to come here, neither," our father said.

"We hoped it would be better," said our mother, "for you, than it was for us."

"You were wrong," said Caleb. "It's worse." But then he relented; he had to relent; tears stood in his eyes. "I wasn't trying to hurt my father." He looked down. "I love my father."

"Then tell him so," said our mother.

Caleb looked at our father. "I'm telling you so," he said.

"Don't you love your mother, too?" she asked, smiling.

"Yes. I love my mother."

"And your brother?"

He looked at me and his face changed. He smiled again, and he pulled me to him. "Yes. Oh, yes. I love my brother."

Then: "But I haven't been able to help him much."

"I don't mind," I said. "I'll love you all my life. And I'll help *you*. I swear it. You'll see."

"Old man," said Caleb, holding me by the neck, "let's have a drink—a loving cup." He looked at our mother. "All right?" Then he looked down at me. "Give us a kiss," he said.

I kissed him.

"That's better," said our mother. "You all sit down and I'll pour the drinks."

And she glittered, jangled, swept, out of the room. Caleb, our father, and I uneasily sat down. Caleb put his hand on my neck again. He said, "Daddy, I know it's not your fault. But you don't know what they do to you, baby, once they got you."

"Man," said our father, "they doing it to me."

Caleb looked down at me. "And they doing it to little Leo. Ain't that the truth, Leo?" He stared at me. He turned away. He took his hand away. "Don't tell me. I know."

"They're not," I said, "doing anything to me that I can't take. So, don't worry about me." Then I said, "I hate them. I hate them. I hate them."

"Yeah," said Caleb wearily, "they're doing it to you, all right." Then I was sorry I had spoken. But what I had said was true; and, anyway, whether or not I had said it, Caleb and my father already knew it. They saw, as I could not, of course, what time had done to me. Whatever they had wanted for me was now locked in the country of dreams. It was now never going to happen. No one knew what was going to happen, and no one could control it. In a way, it can be said that I was the ruin of all their hopes. They had not been able to save me—my life would be like theirs. The streets had claimed me because my challenges were there, and everything now depended on what I could learn in the school which was to prepare me for my life. I was very nearly lost because my elders, through no fault of their own, had betrayed me. Perhaps I loved my father, but I did not want to live his life. I did not want to become like him, he was the living example of defeat. He could not correct me. None of my elders could correct me because I was appalled by their lives. I was old enough to understand how their lives had happened, but rage and pity are not love, and the determination to outwit one's situation means that one has no models, only object lessons. I was no longer Caleb's little brother: I was part of Caleb's heavy load. And this was because he realized that he had become a part of mine, forever.

For even Caleb had become, for me, an object lesson. Furtively, I watched him. Covertly, against my will, God knows, I judged him. My brother. My brother. Big, black, beautiful, he should have been a king. But his girl, Dolores, had turned into a barmaid whore. Miss Mildred was bigger and more aimless than ever; the treacherous Arthur was always stoned. And now there was something in Caleb lonely and sad, shrinking and hysterical. It broke my heart to watch him. He had been beaten too hard. I hated the people who had beaten him; by the time I was fourteen, I was certainly ready to kill; there was no reason not to kill—I mean, no moral reason. But there were too many—too many; they were everywhere one turned, the bland, white, happy, stupid faces. I walked the streets, I went to school, I watched them, and I loathed them. My brother. But it is also hard to love the beaten. It means accepting their condition; whereas, precisely, one is asking oneself, *What shall I do to be saved?*

My encounters with Caleb when he came home the first time are blurred. Some moments are very sharply in focus, others are dim, very nearly advancing into the light, then receding into darkness. Other moments are irrecoverable, and I know it, and I have lately begun to know why. I do not subscribe to the superstition that one's understanding of an event alters the event. No, it is the event which does the altering, and the question one faces is how to live with time's brutal alterations.

This evening, however, when our mother reentered the room with the whiskey Caleb had stolen from the dance-hall bar, he endeavored to be cheerful, and we tried, too. After all, it was good to see him. It had been good to see him, before he and our father became lachrymose at the bar, dancing with the girls and jiving them and making them helpless before his grace and charm. But even the girls, I noticed, with that really awful increase of awareness which I owed entirely to Caleb, did not take him seriously: a boy with an unspeakable past was a man with an unendurable future. He was good to look at, good to dance with, probably good to sleep with: but he was no longer good for love. And certainly Caleb felt this, for in his dealings with the girls there was a note of brutality which I had never felt in him before. He was not really teasing, charming, seducing them: he was taunting them. He was saying, I've got what you want, all right, but I'm not about to give it up to none of you black bitches.

Our mother returned and she poured the drinks. I wasn't really permitted to drink, and, luckily, in those days, I didn't like to drink; but this prohibition, like all of my parents' prohibitions, was rendered a dead letter by the fact that my parents knew very well that I did whatever I wished, outside. Now, my mother said, "I'm making yours real weak, Leo," and handed me a glass of ginger ale only very faintly colored by whiskey. "That's just so you can feel part of the family," she said, and handed drinks to my father and Caleb and sat down. Caleb and our father looked at each other, but neither of them smiled. I drank my ginger ale. I thought of a girl I knew. I tried to think of everything but the room I was in, and the people I was with.

"Little Leo sure ain't grown much," Caleb said. "What you been feeding him?"

"Exactly what we fed you," said our mother. "Red beans and rice and cornbread and pork chops and ham hocks and ribs and greens."

"What did they feed you down the way?" our father asked.

"They fed us on what the pigs didn't want," said Caleb. "One thing I'll never eat no more in life is hominy grits nor beans nor molasses." He paused. "They just fed us so we could work, you know—like you feed a mule. And they beat us like that, too." He looked at me. "Yeah," he said, and sipped his drink.

"What you figure on doing now?" our father asked carefully, "now that you out?"

"Do?" asked Caleb, gently. "Do? What do I figure on *doing?* Is that what you asked me? Why—I might find me a rich white lady and take a trip to Palm Beach with her—as her chauffeur, you understand, a lot of them white ladies suffer from black fever—or I might get a job in a bank—or I might take over a life insurance company—or, let me see now, there's a lot of money in real estate, there's a whole *lot* of money in that, I might take over a few blocks of houses—or, then, again, I might become an aviator, I've always liked to fly. That's what I'll do," he said decisively, "I'll fly."

"You've got to walk," said our mother, "before you can fly. What do you intend to do while you're walking?"

He looked at her. "Walk," he said. "Just walk."

"You've got to eat," she said, "while you're walking."

"I can steal," he said. "I can steal. And I'll be stealing a long time before I get back half of what they stole from me."

"Well, if you can't," she said, "steal it back, it don't look like to me there's much point in stealing."

He was silent. And our father was silent.

"You young, Caleb," our mother said. "Don't let this stop you. You just make up your mind that you can do anything you want to do."

"Can I?" he asked. "Is that the truth?"

She refused to falter. "If you make up your mind to it."

"I see." He stared at the ceiling. He rose. "And you think that's true for other black boys, too?"

"When we make up our minds," said our father.

"When we make up our minds," Caleb shouted, "to *what?*"

"When we make up our minds," said our mother, "that we just as good as they is. Just as good, just as good, just as good!"

Caleb laughed. He mimicked her. "Just as good! Just as good as *who*—them people who beat my ass and called me nigger and made me eat *shit* and wallow in the dirt like a dog? Just as good as *them?* Is that what you want for me? I'd like to see every single one of them in their graves—in their graves, Mama, that's *right*. And I wouldn't be a white man for all the coals in hell." He sat down. "I don't know what I'm going to do. I've got to figure it out. Don't worry about me. I won't be a burden on you for long."

"I ain't worried about you being a burden," said our mother, "and you know it, so don't you talk to me that way."

Caleb smiled, and looked at our father. Our father

looked into his glass. "I know," said Caleb, after a very long moment. "I'm sorry."

"I'm sleepy," I said. "I'm going to go to bed now. Good-night."

They watched me as I walked out of the room. "I guess," I heard my mother say, "that that *is* a good idea."

"Leo's got good sense," said Caleb grimly.

I crawled into the bed. I didn't want to cry. I listened to them. They talked for awhile. Then my father went to the bathroom. He was in the bathroom a long time. I began to be afraid that he was sick. Then I heard water flushing, heard water running, heard him come out. My mother went into the kitchen. Our father and Caleb said good-night and then Caleb went into the bathroom. Our mother finished in the kitchen and turned out the kitchen lights and the lights in the living room. Then she joined our father and I heard their door close. Caleb was running water for a bath. I fell asleep.

I woke to the sound of weeping. Somebody was weeping, all alone, holding his breath, shaking the bed. I listened, extended, so to speak, in a terror unlike any terror I had known. How he wept! How he wept. And it was as though I were weeping; but it was much worse than that. I knew I could not bear it. I turned and I touched his wet face and I whispered, "Caleb. Please, Caleb. Please don't cry. Tell me what's the matter. Please tell me what's the matter."

But his chest continued to shake and the tears fell and fell. I did not know what to do. I put my arms around him. I kissed his tears. "Caleb. Please, Caleb"—but I might as well have spoken to a storm.

"Oh, what they did to me. Oh, what they did to me."

I held him as tightly as I could.

"What did they do to you?"

"Oh. Oh. Oh. Little Leo. Go to sleep."

"You go to sleep. Then I'll go to sleep."

He put his arms around me; it was strange to feel that I was *his* big brother now. And he held me so tightly, or, rather, with such an intensity, that I knew, without knowing that I knew it, how empty his arms had been.

"Go to sleep."

"All right, little brother. You all right?"

"Yes. Good-night."

"Good-night."

The face against my shoulder was still wet; slowly, it dried. His breathing slowly became calmer—the storm began to pass. The storm began to pass, that is, out of him; and into me. I could not really see his face in the darkness, but I studied his face in the darkness of my mind. The eyes, the mouth, the nose, the chin, the forehead, the bright, woolly hair; he was much better-looking than I was, he was beautiful; and the world had taken my brother, for no reason at all, and squeezed him like a lemon, taken out his insides and filled him with sawdust, kicked him about as though he were a dirty rag! Never, never, never, I swore it, with Caleb's breath in my face, his tears drying on my neck, my arms around him, would I ever forgive this world. Never. Never. Never. I would find some way to make them pay. I would do something one day to at least one bland, stupid, happy white face which would change that face forever. If they thought that Caleb was black, and if they thought that I was black, I would show them, yes, I would, one day, exactly what blackness was! I swore it. I swore it. I whispered it to Caleb's kinky hair. I cursed God from the bottom of my heart, the very bottom of my balls. I called Him the greatest coward in the universe because He did not dare to show Himself and fight me like a man. I fell into a stormy sleep, and awoke to find myself, like Jacob with the angel, struggling with a very different god, and one yet more tyrannical, the god of the flesh. My brother held me close, and he was terribly excited; his excitement excited me. I was briefly surprised, I was briefly afraid. But there was really nothing very surprising in such an event, and if there was any reason to be afraid, well, then, I hoped that God was watching. He probably was. He never did anything else. I knew, I knew, what my brother wanted, what my brother needed, and I was not at all afraid—more than I could say for God, who took all and gave nothing; and who paid for nothing, though all His creatures paid. I held my brother very close, I kissed him and caressed him and I felt a pain and wonder I had never felt before. My brother's heart was broken; I knew it from his touch. In all the great, vast, dirty world, he trusted the love of one person only, his brother, his brother, who was in my arms. And I thought, Yes. Yes. Yes. I'll love you,

Caleb, I'll love you forever, and in the sight of the Father
and the Son and the fucking Holy Ghost and all their filthy
hosts, and in the sight of all the world, and I'll sing halle-
lujahs to my love for you in hell. I stripped both of us
naked. He held me and he kissed me and he murmured
my name. I was full of attention, I was full of wonder.
My brother had never, for me, had a body before. And,
in truth, I had never had a body before, either, though I
carried it about with me and occasionally experimented
with it. We were doing nothing very adventurous, really,
we were only using our hands and, of course, I had already done this by myself and I had done it with other
boys: but it had not been like this because there had been
no agony in it, I had not been trying to give, I had not
even been trying to take, and I had not felt myself, as I
did now, to be present in the body of the other person,
had not felt his breath as mine, his sighs and moans, his
quivering and shaking as mine, his journeys as mine. More
than anything on earth, that night, I wanted Caleb's joy.
His joy was mine. When his breathing changed and his
tremors began, I trembled, too, with joy, with joy, with joy
and pride, and we came together. Caleb held me for a long
time. Then he whispered, against my ear, "You all right?"

"Yes," I said. "I'm all right. Are you?"

"Yes. Yes." Then, "You still love me? You not mad at
me?"

"Why should I be mad at you?" Then I said, "Yes, I
love you, Caleb, more than anybody in the whole wide
world. You believe me?"

After a moment, he said, "Yes, I believe you."

"Give us a kiss," I said.

He kissed me.

"Now, go to sleep."

He kissed me again. "Good-night, little Leo. I don't
know what I'd do without you."

"But you haven't got to do without me," I said,
"that's just what I just told you. Good-night."

"Good-night."

And we fell asleep.

I suppose we were both utterly worn out, drained dry,
for we did not wake up until the early afternoon. I
peeked out of the window, which faced the wall of the
house next door. It was both sunny and cold. It looked

like a nice day, and it felt like a nice day. The radios were going, a church service here, a jazz band there, and the irrepressible voices, and the sound and smell of cooking. It was familiar, it was safe, and both Caleb and I were reluctant to move.

"It's cold out," I said.

"And how you know that?"

"I looked," I said. "You'll know it, too, you put your butt out of this bed."

"What you want to do today?"

"I don't know. Anything you want to do."

We listened to the voices of our parents in the living room.

"I just feel lazy," Caleb said. He lit a cigarette. "I just feel like turning over and going back to sleep."

"Then you won't be able to sleep tonight. But suit yourself. Can I have a puff off your cigarette?"

He made a brief, astonished movement, then handed me the cigarette, watching me. "You smoking?"

I gave him back the cigarette. "Just sometimes. With the other guys."

"No wonder you don't grow," he said.

"I don't think I'll ever grow very big. But if you don't want me to smoke, I'll stop."

"Well, I don't think smoking will do you any good."

"All right."

Caleb smoked in silence for awhile. I watched his profile and I watched the smoke. I put my head, so to speak, under his wing, and he held me. Then he put out his cigarette, and moved, slapping me on the behind. "Come on. Let's get up. I'll take you to the show." And he found his shorts, and mine, and put his on, and walked into the bathroom. When he came out, he pulled the covers off me and we fought over the covers, holding our breath, and laughing. We wrestled each other around the room, and our mother yelled, "Are you two finally getting out of bed? You ought to be ashamed of your big, black, lazy selves!"

"Big, black, lazy selves," laughed Caleb to himself; I laughed, too. Caleb yelled, "It ain't *me,* Mama. It's Leo. *I'm* up. I *been* up!"

"I'll bet. You two just better make yourselves presentable and come on out here, if you want to eat today."

Since Caleb was tickling me with one hand and sparring with the other, I was forced to my feet, and spun out of the door and down the hall. "He's out of bed, Mama," Caleb cried jubilantly. "I don't know if *he's* hungry, but *I* am."

"Declare," our mother grumbled, "you both too old to be carrying on like this. It's your father you take after, it surely can't be me." She was in the kitchen. "You want a cup of coffee, Caleb? It ain't good to eat just as soon as you get out of bed. And do you know what time it is?"

"I'd like some coffee, Mama, please. What time is it?"

"It's past two o'clock in the afternoon, that's what time it is. Leo, don't you come out of that bathroom until you take your bath."

"Is it two o'clock in the afternoon?" Caleb cried. "My! We sure must have had ourselves a time last night."

"Keep it up," she grunted. "Keep it up."

"Didn't you have a time, old lady?" asked Caleb, in the kitchen now.

"You stop aggravating your mother," our father cried, "and come on out here."

"Why here I am," Caleb said, and I heard him walk into the living room.

"Yes. To aggravate *me* now, I suppose."

"Why, there's just no pleasing nobody in this house this morning," said Caleb pleasantly, and turned on the radio.

By the time I got dressed and joined them, he had found a station which was playing Calypso, and had one arm around our mother and was waltzing her, half laughing, half protesting, across the floor. "Lord," she said, "now why do I have to be the mother of the *one* nigger in the whole world ain't got no sense of rhythm—now, look, Caleb"— and they both broke up, laughing, and they tried it again. Across the floor, a proud, hincty, mocking prance; then they had to turn together and meet each other and then they had to part; and then they had to meet each other again, and come across the floor, again. "Lord, Caleb," and they both laughed; and the number ended, and they both bent double with laughter. Our father laughed, too. "That ain't the way," he said, "we did it in the islands." Another number started.

"Come on," said Caleb, "and show us how you did it in the islands, man."

And he turned our mother toward our father, and she raised him by the hand.

He was growing old, our father, but he was also very young; and when he rose, tall and courtly, one saw how young he was: With his lips pressed together, he was smiling, smiling with, and at, his woman, who was being led by him. It was almost as though Caleb and I were not present, or present only as a possibility. It was a dance which was a wedding of the English and the islands, for it really was, as it began, in the English sense, formal. Then, without becoming less formal, it became on her part more tantalizing, on his more aggressive; and, as both knew it was a game, a ritual, a sacrament, it became bolder and more humorous. Her plump hips moved like the hips of a girl, and her bright, bright face turned toward him and then away from him. His patient, egg-plant color pursued her everywhere, and his hips moved like the hips of a boy. Their feet beat as though they were barefoot in the fields. He held her by one hip, she held him by one shoulder. They were smiling an indescribable smile. They felt the end of the number approaching, they turned once more, and, as the number ended, she curtsied and he bowed. Caleb clapped his hands.

"Hell," said our father, while our mother sat down in his chair and exaggeratedly wiped her brow, and lit a cigarette, "that ain't nothing. You should have seen us when we could *really* do it."

"Is that a fact now?" said Caleb, after a moment, and then he and our father roared. Our mother glared at both of them, then looked at me.

"Both of them," she said, confidentially, "both of them. They are *both* completely insane. This morning. Caleb, your coffee's cold." She rose, and tasted it. "Stone cold." She took it into the kitchen. "You want some coffee, Leo?"

"Yes, Mama. Please."

"Me too," said Caleb.

"I knew it. Well, you just going to have to wait till I make some more."

Now, the news was on, and our father restlessly clicked the dials: the air was full of a false urgency, such news as there might be entirely muffled by the habits and exigencies of salesmen.

"Now, don't you want to know," asked Caleb, "what's happening in the world?"

"No," said our father imperturbably, still clicking dials, "ain't no white boy living can tell me what's happening in the world. Not before they find out what's happening on my job."

"And they ain't never going to do that," said Caleb.

"No," said our father, and clicked off the radio. "There'll be something lively on it by and by," he said.

Our mother brought in fresh coffee, and we sat at the window, watching the streets. Opposite us, other people also sat in windows, watching the streets. I have sometimes thought that there is probably no more vivid rendering of silence and no more definitive image of attention, than that presented by Harlem windows, some Sunday afternoons. Four or five or six stories up or down, the people sit, or lean, as though they had been stationed or planted there: their faces as still as the stone which frames them. At a top floor window, behind the grillwork he has placed there to prevent his children from falling, sits a man wearing a stocking cap, holding his infant child. The child is restless, but cheerfully restless, and he easily meets the child's movements by slightly shifting his weight from time to time. If it were not for these slight movements, one might wonder if he realized that he was holding a child at all. His face is attentive, but utterly closed and unmoving. A cigarette smolders between his heavy lips; his eyes are attentive to the smoke. It is impossible to say what he is watching; or if he is watching at all. Yet, something is happening in him, one can almost hear small hammers beating and small wheels turning. Just so, the lady on the floor below, her hair tied up in a rag, her elbows leaning on the sill, a fist on either side of her chin. Her face is very black and rather heavy, her lips are very soft and sad, and her long, dark eyes do not move. At the window next to hers, sits a very old lady, in profile, with a strong Indian nose, head thrown back, eyes closed; and at the window below this, sits a boy of eight or nine, his chin on the windowsill, his fists covering his ears, his eyes very wide and black. His hair is very short, and gleams with Vaseline. A fairly light woman, with straightened hair, and wearing a black dress, sits at the ground floor window, with her small daughter standing between her knees. It would appear that they are all watching the street. The street is very long and wide. On either side of the street, long, gleaming automobiles are parked. The cars are much cleaner than the street—indeed, one very stocky man in shirt-sleeves is busy polishing his car. Garbage cans, so full that their lids cannot fit, stand before every house, and garbage blows up and down the street and collects in the windy gutters. Cars come through the street, scattering the boys; and even though it is rather cold today, the streets are never empty. Girls, in their finery, walk proudly along, sometimes alone, sometimes with each other, sometimes with the boys, in their fine clothes. Matrons pass, with Bibles; a drunken man comes singing, howling along, his old black overcoat blowing in the wind; only the children appear to notice him, and this merely to make his life more difficult by calling him, and following after him. Everything is happening and nothing is happening, and everything is still, like thunder. One might be in the catacombs, with the first believers, waiting for a sign. And always, the echo of music, the presence of voices, as constant and compelling as the movement of the sea.

At length, our mother, having decided to feed her children—and Caleb growing restless, smoking one cigarette after another, and staring out of the window—rose, and went to the kitchen and heated the biscuits, the yams, the chicken, the ham, the gravy, and the rice. She set up the card table for Caleb and me, and we sat down to eat. They sat near the window, watching us; it was almost as though we were children again.

"You know," said our father carefully, "the place where I work, they looking for a shipping clerk. The one they had been took by the Army."

Caleb looked up, but said nothing.

"He asked me if I knew of anybody," our father said, "and I said I might. It ain't a bad job—just to tide a person over." He looked at our mother.

"You reckon you want to try it, Caleb?" she asked.

"What do they pay?" asked Caleb.

Our father told him. Caleb laughed. "That'll tide me over, all right," he said.

"I think you might do well at it," said our mother.

"Until you find—until you find—something more to your liking." She met his eyes. Then she said, "You got to do something, Caleb—just for your own sake, I mean. You can't just sit around here and go crazy."

"What I'm going to tell them," Caleb asked merrily, "when they ask me where I been so long?"

"Don't worry about that. Your father can explain all that. They think a whole lot of your father."

Caleb poured himself some coffee and lit a cigarette.

"They ain't particular, anyway," our father said. "They can't afford to be so particular now."

"Yeah," said Caleb, "they can use us now. They got a war to fight. I think *I* might as well join the Army. Be quicker."

"Caleb," said our mother, "don't you talk like that. You hear me?"

"I hear you." He rose. "If you ready, little brother, we'll go on to the show."

"I'm ready," I said. I stood up.

There was a silence. Somebody, somewhere, was singing "A Tisket, A Tasket."

"Okay," said Caleb. "What time you leave in the morning?"

"At seven," said our mother.

"Well, all right," said Caleb, "at seven. Leo, get your coat. Get mine, too." I got our coats. When I came back into the room, Caleb was standing at the door. He took his coat without looking at it, and shrugged himself into it. "Like the farmer said to the sweet potato, 'I'll plant you now and dig you later!'"

The door closed behind us. We dropped down the stairs two at a time. Now we seemed to be fleeing from the voices and the odors. We hit the street. Caleb put his hand on my neck, and hurried us down the long block. He did not say anything, and I did not say anything. One of the Holy Roller churches was making even more noise than usual, and Caleb and I danced past it, laughing.

"What movie you want to see?" he asked.

"I don't know."

"We got enough money to go downtown?"

"I don't know. I got four, how much you got?"

"The old man let me have five."

"You want to go downtown?"

"I don't know. Do you?"

We looked at each other. "Oh, hell," Caleb said, "Let's go on downtown."

"Okay. Let's go."

"You want to take the bus or the subway?"

"Let's take the bus."

We stood on the avenue and waited for the bus. We were very shy with each other, suddenly; we were very happy with each other, too. Because we were shy, I watched the people passing, listened to the music coming from a bar behind us, watched the church members going home from church. We, as a family, had never gone to church, for our father could not bear the sight of people on their knees. But I thought, suddenly, for the first time and for no reason, that he must surely have gone to church in the islands, when he was young. I turned to ask Caleb about this, but I was stunned and silenced by his face. The sun was yellow, it was in his eyes, causing him to squint; it fell over his forehead and curled in his hair; his lips stretched upward in a scowl. He was looking at me. He looked worried and thoughtful and happy: no one had ever before looked at me with such a concentrated love. It stunned me, as I say, for he made no effort to hide it. It made me very proud, and it frightened me. The bus came as we stared at one another, and Caleb pushed me on the bus, before him. He got change, and dropped the coins in the box. We sat down. He made me sit next to the window.

"Well, tomorrow," he said, "I'll be a respectable citizen again." He laughed. "I reckon we going to pass through the garment center, ain't we, on our way down?"

"I could show you the block where Daddy works—but it's further downtown."

"I'm not sure I really want to see it." He laughed again, and the bus rolled down the avenue and we were silent for awhile.

"Leo," he said, "what you reckon you want to be? to do? You know?"

I watched the streets and the houses roll by, and I watched the people in the streets. I said, "You'll think I'm crazy if I tell you the truth."

"Well, as I already know you're crazy," he said, "you might as well tell me the truth."

"I'm going to be an actor," I said.

I did not look at him, but I felt him watching me. I watched the streets.

"An actor?"

"Yes."

"In the movies?"

"On the stage," I said. I looked at him and I looked away. "You'll see."

"How you going to go about it, Leo?"

"I don't know yet. But I'll find out. I'll do it."

"You told Mama and Daddy?"

"No." Then, "I haven't told nobody except you."

"Well," he said, after a moment, "you know the odds, little brother? I mean, you know the odds are against you?"

"Hell, yes," I said, "I know the odds are against me. But the odds wouldn't be any less against me if—if I worked for the garment center!"

He said nothing. I wished to take back my last words, but I did not know how. "That's true," he said at last, mildly, and then, in silence, we watched the streets.

"Look, Caleb," I said, "I know I can't be a janitor. You know? I just know it. I know I can't work in—in—the kind of jobs they give us. Maybe I can't be an actor, either. But I have to try it. I know I have to try it."

"Don't get upset," said Caleb. "You didn't hear me say you couldn't do it, did you?"

"No. But I bet that's what you're thinking."

"Well, then," said Caleb, "you're wrong. That's not what I was thinking at all. I was thinking how proud I am of you. Don't look like that. It's the truth I'm telling you."

"Honest?"

He laughed. "Honest." He raised both hands. "I swear. All right?"

I said, "All right."

Caleb laughed again. "Ah, little Leo." He sobered. "But Mama and Daddy ain't going to like this notion a *bit*."

"I'm not going to tell them. You think I'm crazy?"

Now, he was entirely sober and still. "No," he said. "No. You're not the one who's crazy." Then, "Daddy used to always say, 'I wonder what's the matter with our

people.' I've got to wondering, too. But—baby!—they
sure do have us in a mighty tight place."

"They don't want us to do nothing because we might
do it better than them," I said.

"Well, they *do*," said Caleb, "tend to try to beat the
shit out of you before you can get *around* to doing anything. But we going to have to fox them, little brother."
He put his hand on my neck; he looked out of the window,
with tightened lips and darkened eyes. "Yeah. We going to
have to fox them."

The bus rolled on, turned west at 116th Street, rolled
alongside Morningside Park for awhile, turned again on
110th Street, and started rolling out of Harlem. This was
(in those days) a kind of transition neighborhood; white
boys and black boys were in the streets, and white girls
and black girls, some carrying books; and we whirled past
black and white figures sitting on the benches outside of
Central Park, or walking up and down the pathetic green.
Now, the buildings began to be higher and cleaner, canopies
and doormen appeared, and black and white messengers,
on bicycles. More and more white people got on the bus,
in furs and perfumes and hats, carrying newspapers and
expensive-looking packages. Instinctively, Caleb and I sat
closer together. I kept my eyes on the street, in order not to
look at the people on the bus. I wondered how we were ever
going to fox them if we couldn't even bear to look at them.
I looked up, into the eyes of a red-faced, black-haired,
corpulent man, who had, briefly and idly, looked up from
his newspaper. His hair was very well combed, his face was
very well shaven, his nails were manicured, his shoes
gleamed, his suit and his topcoat were expensive, he was
wearing cufflinks, and I could almost smell his toilet
water. I don't know what was in my eyes—base envy, I
think, base hatred, and great wonder—but whatever it was
held his wandering, not altogether hostile nor altogether
amused attention for a second or so. He glanced at my
brother. Then he returned to his newspaper. Then, all of my
ambitions seemed flat and ridiculous. How could we fox
them if we could neither bear to look at them, nor bear it
when they looked at us? And *who* were they, anyway?
which was the really terrible, the boomeranging question.
And one always felt: maybe they're right. Maybe you *are*
nothing but a nigger, and the life you lead, or the life they

make you lead, is the only life you deserve. They say that
God said so—and if God said so, then you mean about as
much to God as you do to this red-faced, black-haired, fat
white man. Fuck God. Fuck you, too, mister. But there
he sat, just the same, impervious, gleaming and redolent
with safety, rustling, as it were, the Scriptures, in which I
appeared only as the object lesson.

We got off the bus near Madison Square Garden. I
think the circus was in town, for the Garden was surrounded by policemen and the streets were full of dazzled men and women and children. The streets were full
of a noise like gaiety. But one realized that it could not be
gaiety when one looked at the thin lips and the flashing
spectacles, the crisply toasted, curled hair of the ladies;
when one listened to the brutal, denigrating, lewd voices
of the men, and watched their stretched lips and bewildered eyes; when one listened to the despairing, cunning,
tyrannical wail of the children, vaguely and vocally dis-
satisfied by the fair; and when one watched the policemen who moved through the crowd, on foot or on horse-
back, as though the crowd were cattle. There were no
movies in this avenue, and so we turned off it, walking
east, moving now with, now against, the current, sometimes separated by it, often stopped, sometimes, in search-
ing for each other, spun around. People looked into store-
windows, and so did we, walked in and out of stores, but
we didn't bother, and they were visible behind the plate-
glass windows of cafeterias, sitting, in my memory, bolt up-
right, or wandering about with trays. The crowd, no doubt,
would have described itself as friendly; a fair observation
would have been that they were in a holiday mood. But their
holidays were, emphatically, not my holidays—I had too
often been the occasion of their fearful celebrations; and I
did not feel any friendliness in the crowd, only a dry, rattling
hysteria, and a mortal danger. I kept my hands in my
pockets (and so did Caleb) so I could not be accused of
molesting any of the women who jostled past, and kept my
eyes carefully expressionless so I could not be accused of
lusting after the women, or desiring the death of the men.
When my countrymen were on holiday, their exuberance
took strange forms. And I was aware—for the first time,
though not for the last—that I was with Caleb, whose
danger, since he was so much more visible, was greater

than mine. It was not here and not now and not among
these people, that he could protect me by his size. On the
contrary, our roles were reversed, and here, now, among
these people, it was *my* size and my presumed innocence
which might operate as protection for him. He was not,
walking beside me, a burly black man prowling the streets
but an attentive older brother taking his little brother
sightseeing through the great, cultured and so enormously
to be envied metropolis of New York. My presence, po-
tentially, at least, proved his innocence and goodwill and
also bore witness to the charity and splendor of the people
to whom I owed so much and from whom I had so much
to learn. We came to Broadway, and the great marquees.
"You going to have your name up there in lights, little
Leo?" Caleb asked with a smile.

"Yes," I said. "I will. You wait and see."

"Little Leo," said Caleb, "on the great white way."

"It won't be so white," I said, "when I get through
with it."

Caleb threw back his head and laughed. People turned
to look at us: but I made my eyes very big as I looked up
at Caleb, and carefully not at them, and they saw what I
had wanted them to see. Some of them smiled, too, happy
that we were enjoying the fair. "All right, little brother.
What movie you want us to see? And I will bow to *your*
judgment, man, because I see you are becoming an *ex*pert."

Well, in fact, I realized, as I scanned the procession of
marquees, there wasn't anything playing that I was really
dying to see. I had outgrown my taste for some movies
without having acquired any real taste for others. But, of
course, I did not know how to say this. I had begun to be
interested in foreign movies, mostly Russian and French,
but I didn't think that Caleb would especially like seeing
a foreign movie. So I said, "Well, let's look. If *you* see
something *you* like before I see something *I* like, why,
we'll go and see that; and if *I* see something *I* like before
you see something *you* like, why, we'll go and see that.
Okay?"

"Okay," he said, amused—seeming, also, to be impressed by my sense of fair play.

And so we wandered through the holiday crowds,
stopping now beneath this marquee and now that, exam-
ining the merchandise so carefully that we might have

been expecting to buy it and take it home and live with it for the rest of our lives and hand it down to our children. We walked carefully down one side of the avenue, stopping and choosing, rather enjoying ourselves now, all the way to 42nd Street; and then up the other side of the avenue, slowly, although it was getting late; but it didn't much matter what time we got home tonight as long as we got home together, and we weren't planning to separate. We forgot about the other people. We began to talk to each other as we hadn't talked since Caleb had come home—as we had never talked before, in fact, for it was only now that Caleb could talk to me without remembering that he was talking to a child. I was determined to make him know that I was no longer a child. I didn't understand everything he was saying, and yet, in another way, I did. I was concentrating on not being a disappointment to him: I wanted him to know that he could lean on me.

Because Caleb liked Ann Sheridan, we ended up in *King's Row*. I *didn't* like Ann Sheridan, I thought she looked like a dumpling, and I didn't like Robert Cummings, who looked like two or three, and I couldn't stand Ronald Reagan, who looked like a pitchfork and had teeth like a ferret; but I *did* like Charles Coburn and Claude Rains and Judith Anderson, and I especially liked Betty Field because she had a niggerish mouth, a mouth like mine. So, Caleb paid for the tickets, and we went on in. We entered, first, into a kind of cathedral— an impression of tapestries, of hanging gold, a vaulted height, a slinging, descending, mightily carpeted floor, great doors before us, Roman couches on either side, on one of which sat a lone young woman, wearing a green cloth hat and holding a thin umbrella, and smoking a cigarette. A bored male attendant, two bored usherettes, who looked sharply at Caleb and me.

"I'm going to go to the bathroom," Caleb said, and vanished behind the door marked MEN.

I waited. I looked at the photographs of the movie stars on the walls. They were white and cheerful and dramatic. I was already arrogant enough to feel that they couldn't, mainly, act their way out of a sieve, but lights and makeup and an innocence as brutal as it was despairing did marvelous things for these sons and daughters of the one and only God, and very nearly reconciled me to Ronald Reagan's teeth. Caleb came back. We left the cathedral and entered the cave.

Dark, dark indeed, sloping, hushed. We were in the balcony, so that Caleb could smoke, and from other worshipers here and there a taper glowed. The movie had been running for some time, it may indeed have been a revival that we saw, I don't remember, and so, although it was a Sunday night, the house was far from full. Caleb and I sat down somewhere in the middle of the balcony, at an angle as steeply tilted as that of a bucking horse or a dying boat, and Caleb lit a cigarette. We had entered during a newsreel.

There was trouble in the world. We saw Roosevelt, we saw Churchill, we saw Stalin: "I hope they all kill each other," Caleb said. We saw our great Marines in the Pacific, destroying the yellow-bellied Japs. And we saw Old Glory. "Well," said Caleb, "I'll be damned." Some people in the audience applauded. Caleb lit another cigarette. Then the cartoon came on. Woody Woodpecker or Mickey Mouse or Little Red Riding Hood or Bugs Bunny or some fucking body got beaten with hammers, strangled with chains, crushed under a tractor, thrown over a cliff, gored by a cornice, and disemboweled, it appeared, by a monstrous, malevolent thorn; and we, along with all the other worshipers, cracked up with laughter. Then the lights came on. We sat, silently, watching the people.

Strange people, sitting, mainly, all alone. There were one or two couples, very, very young; the boy's hair still bright from the water, the girl's hair still bright from the heat; they sat very close together, and as to popcorn, chewing gum, and candy, the boys were attentive indeed, climbing the tilted steps from time to time to call on the usherettes. I was between fourteen and fifteen then, and the boys and girls could not have been much older. But they impressed me as being children, children forever, children not as a biological fact, but as a perpetual condition. I am sure that I was a very disagreeable boy in those days, for I really despised them for their blank, pimpled faces and their bright, haunted eyes. It had not occurred to me—partly, no doubt, indeed, because it had not occurred to *them*—that they had to shit, like I did, and they jerked off sometimes, like I did, and were just as frightened as I. It had not yet occurred to me that the mask of my bravado was very much like theirs, concealed though it was, and most effectively, by the mask of my color, and by the reflexes which this mask occasioned in them and in me. No: I simply despised them because they were not as I was, and because I thought it might have been better for me if I had been like them. The lights went down, and a majestic music was heard. The curtains slowly parted, and the screen was filled with the immense shield saying WB, WARNER BROTHERS PRESENTS. Brothers. I thought of my own brother, and I think I hated the movie before the movie began.

The names of the actors. The music. The makeup man, the light man, the sound man, the decorators, the set designers, James Wong Howe on camera, the composer of the overwhelming music, the director. A town somewhere in the United States.

I am afraid that my memory of this movie is hopelessly distorted by the fact that it cracked Caleb up completely. I very much doubt that a major masterpiece by Charlie Chaplin or W. C. Fields could have caused him to laugh harder. When we finally picked up the story line— so to speak; it was by no means an easy matter—Caleb whispered, "Shit. They acting just like niggers. Only, they ain't got as much sense about it as *we* got." I rather liked Cassandra, who was played by Betty Field, but Caleb thought that she was a living freak, and wondered why no one had ever told her to tie up her hair. When it developed, coyly enough indeed, and with tremendous laments from the mighty music, that her father had been interfering with her, had lain between her thighs, had, in short, been screwing her, thus causing her to become mentally unbalanced—which we both felt, then, was a somewhat curious result—and we watched Robert Cummings' plum-pudding reactions, Caleb hid his face in his hands, which was thoughtful of him, for we would otherwise have been thrown out of the theater. Of course, he adored Ann Sheridan, winsome Irish colleen, and I found her somewhat more probable than I had ever found her to be before; but when Ronald Reagan lost his legs—"*both* of them!"—Caleb cracked up again, and tears were streaming down his face by the time Robert Cummings delivered *Invictus*. "So *that's* why," he gasped, as we walked up the aisle, out of the cave, "they make us come in the back door. I'll be damned." And he was off again, halfway across the cathedral floor, before I could catch up with him.

Into the streets again, dark now, with a light rain falling, and the incredible people everywhere.

Much later, that night, Caleb had a dream so awful that he shook and cried and moaned aloud, and I shook him and shook him to wake him up. He fought me and he continued to fight me even after his eyes were open, and he seemed to be awake; and I got frightened because my brother was very strong, and I started, helplessly, to cry. The terror went out of his face then—his face had been blank and brutal with terror; and his eyes cleared, with a great astonishment, and a terrible sorrow. "Oh, don't cry. Don't cry, Leo. I didn't mean to hurt you, man. I swear I didn't mean to hurt you." His hands were trying to wipe away my tears. "Hit me. Hit me back. I swear I didn't mean to hurt you."

"You didn't hurt me. You scared me."

He took his hand away. He was silent. "I guess so," he said. "Sometimes I scare myself." He lay back on the pillow, looking up at the ceiling. "Oh. I wonder what's going to happen to me."

"I won't let anything happen to you."

He smiled. "The farm I was on, down yonder. They used to beat me. With whips. With rifle butts. It made them feel good to beat us; I can see their faces now. There would always be two or three of them, big motherfuckers. The ring-leader had red hair, his name was Martin Howell. Big, dumb Irishman, sometimes he used to make the colored guys beat each other. And he'd stand there, watching, with his lips dropping, his lips wet, laughing, until the poor guy dropped to the ground. And he'd say, That's just so you all won't forget that you is niggers and niggers ain't worth a shit. And he'd make the colored guys say it. He'd say, You ain't worth shit, are you? And they'd say, No, Mr. Howell, we ain't worth shit. The first time I heard it, saw it, I vomited. But he made me say it, too. It took awhile, but I said it, too, he made me say it, too. That hurt me, hurt me more than his whip, more than his rifle butt, more than his fists. Oh. That hurt me."

Silence, and darkness, and Caleb's breath—they are with me still, they will be with me when I am carried to my grave. And, from the grave, I swear it, my rotting flesh, my useless bones, will yet cry out: I will never forgive this world. Oh, that a day of judgment should come, oh, that it should come, and I could rise from my grave and make my testimony heard! Yes. Everyone who pierced him.

"The first time I saw this red-haired mother-fucker, I was in the field, working. He was on a horse. He come riding up, and stopped, watching me. But I just kept on working. Then he yells out, Hey, Sam! but I just kept on doing what I was doing. He yells out, Don't you hear me calling you? and then I stopped and put down my fork and I said: My name ain't Sam.

"He rode in a little closer, then, and looked down at me. I looked up at him. He said, Who the fuck do you think you are? and I said, My name is Caleb Proudhammer, mister, and I'd appreciate it if you'd let me get on with my work. He laughed. He actually laughed, like it was the best joke he'd heard in a long time. He said, Nigger, if my balls was on your chin, where would my prick be? And I didn't understand him at first, I just looked at him. Then, when I understood it, I don't know why, I picked up the pitchfork. I didn't do nothing, I just picked up the fork. But the horse kind of jumped. And this red-haired mother-fucker, he looked surprised, and he looked scared, and he was having a little trouble holding on to his horse. I knew he didn't want me to see that. I knew it. He knew I knew it. And he rode off across the field, mainly because he didn't know what to do with me and didn't know what to do with his horse, and he yelled, All right, Sam! I'll be seeing you, you hear me? *I will be seeing* you!

"And, you know, it's funny, I realized right then and there, while I was watching him ride off, it wasn't, you know, exactly like what he'd *said*. I mean, shit, you know. I'm a big boy and I know the score. Shit. You know. If it came down on me like that, well, all right, I'd suck a cock, I know it, shit, if I loved the cat, why the fuck not, and whose business is it? Like, shit. You know. Ain't nobody's business. You know, like, man, I'd do anything in the world for you because you're my brother and because you're my baby and I love you and I believe you'd do anything in the world for me. I know you would. So, you know, it ain't that shit that bothered me. No. He made me feel like I was my grandmother in the fields somewhere and this white mother-fucker rides over and decides to throw her down in the fields. Well, shit. You know. I ain't my grandmother. I'm a man. And a man can do anything he wants to do, but can't nobody *make* him do it. I ain't about to be raped. Shit. But I knew this mother-fucker had it in for me. I knew, like he said, I was going to be seeing *him*.

"And, baby, believe me, I saw this mother, oh, yes, I did. The week wasn't out before I saw him. He was going to break my back. I knew it. He was going to make me kneel down. He was going to make me act out his question. I wasn't going to do it. He knew it. And I knew it. And there we were."

Caleb's voice, his breath: darkness and silence.

"They had a place there where they put you when they was displeased. It was a kind of cellar. We was already in jail, you understand, but they had a jail inside the jail. But, at least, you know, if they wasn't displeased with you, if you could kiss enough ass, or if they just plain didn't notice you, well, you was in the open air, and, you know, you could talk to your buddies—we was only put there, like they said, for our own good. They was making us useful members of society. But that cellar, baby, I won't never forget that cellar. You ain't never smelled nothing like that cellar—phew! baby, I thought I'd never get that stink out of me. Never. I was dreaming about it just now. That's what I was dreaming about. Me, and Martin Howell, and he had his whip. Oh, Leo. Wow. I didn't know people could treat each other so. And I don't want you to think that it was just him. It wasn't just him. It was all of them, really, and the black guys, too, them that was called the trusties. Shit, baby, they loved whipping ass and the blacker they was, the harder they hit. But, old Martin, he was ring-leader. Everybody was scared of him. I don't know why. And he had it in for me. And—you know. I didn't know what I was going to do. I don't think that I was scared of *him*, exactly. I believe I could of beat him, had it come to a fair fight. But I was scared. The other guys knew he had it in for me, and they was scared, too, and they moved away from me. And all I'd said to the fire-head cock-sucker was that my name wasn't Sam!

"Your brother was a very lonely man, because I knew wasn't nobody going to help me. Not even if they wanted to. And I thought of you, you know that—my big-eyed little brother? But I was glad you wasn't there. I was mighty glad you wasn't there.

"First, he made it so that I got took off my job. I worked in the fields, I piled the hay and took care of the grass and all that shit. I liked it, you know, because, you know, fuck it, there I was, and I knew I couldn't get out, and although I knew I didn't have no *business* there, I mean I knew I should never have been sent there, I hadn't done nothing to be sent there, but I couldn't afford to think about that too much and so I thought, well, all right, I'll make me some muscles. But he got me taken off that and they put me in the kitchen. I didn't like the kitchen, but he was going with the head cook, a big old white German lady named Mrs. Waldo. I believe her husband was dead, I don't know. But, anyway—they had me—between them, they had me. They could do anything they wanted to do and couldn't nobody do nothing about it. Baby. That woman worked me like I was somebody's mule. Or maybe nobody's mule. Or *her* mule, but a mule she knew she couldn't never sell and so she might as well work him till he dropped. I had to be there at six in the morning and I had to scrub that kitchen and I washed all the dishcloths and hung them out on the line and then I had to chop wood for the fires. Then I washed the dishes and the pots and pans, they kind of threw them at me, you know, and, shit, it was a big farm and I didn't have but one helper and he didn't help me because Mrs. Waldo didn't want him to and she always had him out of the kitchen, doing something else. She had a funny way with her. She used always to talk about my mother. She used to say, I bet your mama's mighty sad whenever she thinks of you. She'd say, Where's your father? Your father home? Has he been home lately? You ever seen your father? And, Leo, I just did not know how to handle it. I tried not to say anything, but then she'd get mad and most likely hit me on the head with whatever she happened to have in her hand. And, I tell you the truth, I was scared to death of that woman. I

was even more scared of her than I was of him because
she had me all day. You know. And he'd come into the
kitchen, Lord, Lord, Lord, and sit there like a king and
she'd feed him and he'd go on about me and my mama and
daddy and my big tool which he wanted me to show
him, so he could cut it off. Well, you know, Leo, flesh and
blood can't stand but so much. And, one day, I'll never
forget it, it was after lunch and I hadn't had *my* lunch
yet, there was just them and me in the kitchen and I could
hear the boys outside leaving the dining hall, and it was the
kind of day that it was today, cold, you know, and it looked
a little like rain, and he said something about my mama and
my daddy and he come up to me and touched me on the
behind—I was at the sink—and when he said whatever he
said and touched me, I picked up the big black heavy pot I
was washing and I threw the water all over him and I beat
him over the head with that pot. As hard as I could. As
hard as I could. Oh, we wrestled in that kitchen, baby, I
mean we had us a waltz. You ain't never seen such waltzing. I was trying to kill him. I mean, I knew I was trying
to kill him and he knew it, too. And she was screaming.
She came at me with a knife and I knocked the knife
out of her hand and I knocked her down. Then, they all
ganged up on me and some of them held me while he
beat me. Then, they threw me in that cellar.

"In that cellar, there wasn't no window, there was just
a door with bars on it and if you sat near the bars, then
light came down on you, a little light, in the daytime. In
the nighttime, there wasn't no light at all. But you could
hear for awhile. Couldn't nobody come near you. They
shoved the food in through the bars. The food was bread
and water. I mean it, man. Stale bread and cold water.
You had to shit and piss in a pail. And you had to empty
the pail and that was the only time you ever got out of
there and then there was two men with you. And, sometimes they made like they was going to spill the pail on
you, they had a lot of fun that way and sometimes these
mother-fuckers was white, baby, and sometimes they was
black. Shit. When they first threw me in there I was in
pretty bad shape and what saved me was the rats. I mean
it. The rats. I was flat on my back, I guess I was half
unconscious, I don't know, and I was thinking of my
home and all and I was hardly breathing. Then, I heard

this sound, this rattling sound and I wondered what it was and I don't know how to explain this but all of a sudden I felt like I was being watched, like there was eyes on me. And I looked toward the bars, but weren't nobody there. My mouth was caked with blood and I wiped my mouth and I heard the sound again. It was near me, it wasn't at the bars. Then, I saw their eyes. I was so sick I didn't know if I could move. But if I didn't move—oh, man—if I didn't move and there was a whole lot of them and I knew if I didn't move—and I screamed and I got to the bars and I heard them scurrying away because, then, they knew I was alive and I hung on the bars all night. I was afraid to lie down again. I'd feel myself dropping off, you know, and I'd hold on the bars and drag myself up again. And they was still there, scurrying here and yonder. And didn't nobody come near me, nobody, all night long.

"I don't know how long I was down there, Leo, I swear to God I don't, I'll never know. But, one morning, here he come, like I'd known he was going to, Old Martin Howell, red-haired mother-fucker with his whip. He said, Don't you want to see your friends upstairs? and I said, I got no friends upstairs. He said, Ain't you tired of bread and water? and I said, I'm getting used to it, thanks. The thing is, I was scared of him and he was scared of me. But I really believe that he was a little more scared of me than I was of him, because I knew, if it really got down to it, I was going to have to kill him. Yes. I really don't want to be no man's murderer, but, for me, he wasn't a man, I don't know what he was, but I knew he wasn't never going to get me on my knees. He had his boys and all, though, I knew it, just upstairs.

"He said, Nigger, you remember that question I asked you? He was smiling. I didn't say nothing. He walked up and down, kind of weighing his whip. He was trying to scare me with that whip. He wanted me to beg him not to beat me. I watched him. I knew what he *didn't* want to do was have to call in nobody. He wanted me all to himself. I didn't give a shit. I was going to get beaten, anyway. So I called him every name I could think of, just to get it started, just to get it over with, and he raised his whip to strike me and I ducked and he raised it again and I grabbed his hand. I battled him to the bars and, you know,

I'm pretty strong but I was weakened by being on bread and water for so long and he cracked me across the back of the head with the whip handle and I fell down to my knees. When I fell, he came at me again, but I managed to roll out of his way and when he came back at me I pulled him down, hard, and I got him by the balls and, believe me, I made that mother scream. Oh, yeah, he screamed that morning. I beat him with the handle of his whip and I made his red hair a little bit redder. I heard them coming and I tried to hold them off with my whip but of course they got me and when they got through with me I was lying against a wall. He was standing over me. He said, Nigger, you ain't worth shit. Ain't that right? And he kicked me. I could hardly see anything, I could hardly see his eyes. I said, *You* ain't worth shit, and he kicked me again. Then, one of the black trusties spit on me and so I said, You right, Mr. Howell. I ain't worth shit. And they left me. And I was alone down there for a long time. On bread and water."

His voice stopped: his silence created a great wound in the universe. There was nothing for me to say: nothing. I held him, held what there was to hold. I held him. Because I could love, I realized I could hate. And I realized that I would feed my hatred, feed it every day and every hour. I would keep it healthy, I would make it strong, and I would find a use for it one day. I listened to Caleb's breathing and I watched him in the slowly growing light of the morning. He picked up a cigarette and lit it and I watched the glow, watched his nose, watched his eyes. Neither did he have anything more to say. We lay there, in silence. I knew that he had to get up soon, to go down to the garment center. He put out his cigarette. I put my arms around him. And so we slept.

Caleb went downtown with our father in the morning, but by noon, he had left the garment center, forever, and he left New York the early morning of the following day. This is one of the encounters with Caleb which is most dim in my memory, one of the moments which inexorably recedes; most dim, because it was to prove so crucial; most dim, because so painful. I was home around midday, I think. I suppose I had been to school, though I have no recollection of having been at school. Our mother was silent, but I knew she had been crying. Caleb was throwing socks in a bag.

"What's the matter?"

I was standing at the door of our room. I hadn't asked my mother anything.

"I'm going."

I sat down on the bed.

"You going? Where?"

"California."

I didn't say anything. I watched him throw some shirts into a bag—a little cardboard bag.

"California?"

"Yes."

He threw some more stuff into the bag.

"Where's Daddy?"

"Daddy," he said, "is at *work*."

"When are you going?"

"I'm taking a bus out of here in the morning."

"You want to take me with you?"

"No."

I sat there. I watched him. I didn't want to cry, and I wasn't going to cry. I didn't cry. He kept on doing what he was doing. I sat on the bed.

"All right," I said. And I walked out of the room. Then I walked out of the house. I had nothing in my mind. I didn't know what I was doing. I didn't know where I was going.

There is a fearful splendor in absolute desolation: I had never seen it before this day. Everything seemed scrubbed, scoured, older than the oldest bones, and cleaner. Everything lay beneath a high, high, immaculate sky, and was washed as clean as it could be. Everything—and everything was still: the stairs down which I walked, the doors I passed, the garbage, the cats, the old wine bottles, the radiators, the drying scum-bag on the steps, the light in the doorway of the vestibule, the boys in the doorway, the white curtains in the window across the street, the blue sedan which briefly cut off the sight of the curtains, the street, long, long, long, the grocery store, the tailor shop, the candystore, the church which faced us when I reached the end of the block, the red lights, the green lights, the long, loaded buses and the people in the

buses, the subway kiosks and the people coming upstairs
and downstairs, the policeman's badge catching the light,
his club swinging, his holster glowing, the vegetable
stand, with greens, with turnips, potatoes, okra, onions,
cabbage, cauliflower, apples, pears, the sign over another
church, saying THE YOU PRAY FOR ME CHURCH OF THE
AIR, the liquor store and all the bottles in the window, the
bar signs, and the women outside the bar, the men standing at the corners, the lampposts, the undertaker parlors, the
grain of the sidewalk pavement, the light in the water
of the gutter, the polish of the asphalt street, the grating
over the sewer's black and fearful depths, the singing of
tires and the crying of brakes, the shape of doorways, the
monotony of steps, the order and age of cornices, the
height of roofs, the unspeaking sky, the tree, the sparrow,
the Public Library, and the plaque there which held the
name, CARNEGIE, the stone wall of the park, the people
scattered about like bones, the hill, the dying flowers, the
height, the sun, all, all, all, were clean as I was not, as I
could never be, and all—all—were as remote from me as
they would have been had I been in my grave and had
drilled a hole through my tombstone to peep out at the
world. I cared no more than that. I sat down somewhere
in the park.

The stars came out. I watched the stars, and I counted
them. I was really surprised to realize that the sky could
be so black, that the sky could be so closed. I looked for
the moon, but it wasn't there. The moon. For no reason
at all, I suddenly missed the moon; and because I missed
the moon so much, I started to cry. But I think that I had
never cried this way before. I did not cry in the hope of
being comforted. I had no hope. I am not even certain
that there was anything at all in my mind—what we call
the mind. I cried because I could not help it, exactly like
the stars were shining; they couldn't help it, either. Perhaps, like me, they couldn't believe that their sentence
had been passed, and that now they were to serve it. I am
sure that there was nothing in my mind, because, otherwise, my mind would have cracked and I would have had
to go mad. I had walked to the very top of the park. Now,
I rose, for no particular reason, and started walking back
down the hill. It had been daylight when I entered the
park, and now it was night; but I did not start walking

uptown toward our house, but downtown, away from it. It may be odd, I don't know, but I didn't think of what was happening at the house, and I was not afraid to walk through the city, though I had always been afraid before. I did not feel, either, even remotely defiant. I don't think I even saw the cops: I simply walked.

I walked down Harlem's Madison Avenue, which in no way resembles the American one. I watched the boys and girls, who, oddly enough, did not challenge me or make any move to menace me, though I walked very slowly and must surely have looked very odd. But, no, they went on with what they were doing and I went my way; and only when I got to the outskirts of Harlem— only when the streets began to be sedate and quiet, and the faces began to turn pale—did I think that, by now, at my house, they must really be worried. I realized that I could not, after all, spend the night walking the streets. So I walked west, and I started back uptown.

But I did not, in fact, get home that night. It may be that, at the very bottom of my mind, I had never intended to go home. Or, that, as home came closer, my nerve deserted me. It may be that I had a tremendous need to hurt Caleb, or it may be that I was afraid of seeing Caleb. But my memory, for reasons which are not at all mysterious, blurs everything here, resists going over the ground again. This was the night that I discovered chaos, or perhaps it was the night that chaos discovered me; but it certainly began the most dreadful time of my life, a time I am astounded to have survived. It was the first of my nights in hell. It was this night, or a night very soon after it, that I first smoked marihuana, in a cellar with some other, older boys, and a very funky girl. I know that it was around this time that I became friends with an older boy, named Francis, who helped to protect me in the streets; I know that the first time I ever smoked marihuana, I was with him and his friends, and I remember the cellar, which was near the Apollo Theater. Francis later turned into a junkie, and, after many attempts to break his habit, went to his room one morning and cut his wrists. But we had traveled the same road together for awhile. And neither of us had had any reason for not doing whatever came to mind. Or, it may have been this night, or a night very soon thereafter, that I was picked up by a Harlem racketeer named Johnnie, big, Spanish-looking, very sharp, and very good-natured—good-natured with *me*, anyway—who took me home and gave me my first drink of brandy, and took me to bed. He frightened me, or his vehemence, once the lights were out, frightened me, and I didn't like it, but I liked *him*. I had to keep him from buying things for me which I couldn't take home; he was an even greater protection than Francis, and it took me a long time to break with him, simply because he was fond of me—he was often the only person to whom I could turn. Eventually, Johnnie and another pimp tangled, and Johnnie was killed. But we, too, had traveled the same road together for a while.

After the beating, the shouting, the tears, when I got home next day, my mother handed me Caleb's note. I took it in the room and lay down on the bed.

> *Little Brother,*
>   *You shouldn't have walked out on me like that. I must have sounded pretty mean, but you should have known I didn't mean it for you. I just couldn't take working on that job. It wasn't so much for me. It was for Daddy. I couldn't stand the way they talked to him, like he was somebody's hired clown. But I didn't say nothing. Just, when the twelve o'clock blew, I walked out. And I decided that I would have to leave this city. I think I'll be better off someplace else and I'm going to work in the shipyard in California. And I couldn't take you with me, Leo, you know that. You got your schooling to finish and you say you want to be an actor, well what kind of life would it be, when you hanging out with me? You've got very good sense, Leo, like I've always said. You're much smarter than I am and so I know you'll see it my way as soon as you cool off.*
>   *But I'm mighty sorry I had to leave without saying good-bye to you like I wanted to do.*
>   *Take care of Mama and Daddy as well as you can and take care of yourself. I'll write you as soon as I get an address and please write to me. Don't be mad at me. When you get older, you'll see that this was the best way. I guess I love you more than anything in this world, Leo, and I want you to grow up to be a happy healthy man. So, no matter how I thought about it, it seemed*

to me that this was the best way for everybody concerned.
And I want you to have some flesh on your bones
when I look in your face again. Please don't forget me.
                                        Your brother,
                                        Caleb

Caleb got into some trouble in California, and he joined the Army. I hit the streets.

I realized I was shivering, and I pulled Madeleine's big towel closer around me. Then I dropped it and left her kitchen and crawled, naked, into bed beside her. I slept. She woke me up. We made, as the saying goes, love. Then, I slept again.

Like in the movies, I woke to the smell of coffee and the sound and smell of bacon. I don't really know how it goes in the movies, but I know that I lay there on my back, apprehensive, drained, empty—drained and empty without having, really, touched, or been touched. Then, as she entered the room, smiling, in a scarlet negligée, and before I had had time to pretend that I was still sleeping, I realized that I had a performance to give. I realized that I rather liked her, and that was certainly a relief. But, mainly, I wanted to get that white flesh in my hands again, I simply wanted to fuck her: and this was not because I liked her.

"You awake?"

My God, she was cheerful. She sat down on the bed.

I made a sound, it was meant to convey, No, and I turned away and then I turned toward her again and I pulled her down on top of me.

"I got breakfast on the stove, sugar."

"*I* got breakfast here." And, after a moment, I said, "All you got to do is reach out your hand."

"Let me turn down the fire under the bacon."

I laughed. "You do that."

She wavered into the kitchen. She came back. I took her hand. "Did you put out the fire? under the bacon?"

"Yes."

"No, you didn't. Put it out now. Right here. Right now." I took off her robe. "I want to watch you do it." I laughed. But Madeleine certainly wasn't anybody's freak.

She claimed it wasn't because she was unwilling. It was because I was too big. Well, all right. And we fooled around, while I became more and more aware of the smell of coffee and more and more, rather, worried about the disappearing bacon, and we ended up doing it like mama and daddy. Well. All right. And she went away again, and I fell asleep again.

When I woke up again, she was dressed, in blue.

"Listen, my love," she said—my *love!*—"everything you need is out there in the kitchen. I've got a rehearsal, and I've got to run. Here's an extra set of keys." She put them on top of my jeans. She looked at me. "So. Will you be here when I get back? Or—?"

"I don't know. What time do you get back?"

She looked at her watch. "Well. It's nearly two now. Not before six or seven."

Slowly, and most reluctantly, my head began to clear. "I might go home. But I think I'll sleep awhile. I think I'll be here when you get back. But, if I'm not going to be here, I'll call you at Lola's."

"All right, sugar. That's a good boy."

I turned my head into the pillows. "Oh, shit. Whatever I am, God knows I'm not a good boy."

"Oh, well. What God knows and what *I* know seem never to coincide."

"Get on to your rehearsal."

"Aren't you going to kiss me? Just for luck?"

She leaned down; I leaned up; I kissed her. "Break a leg."

"Thanks, sugar. See you later." And she left, being very careful and quiet with the door. So there I was. And I went back to sleep.

When I finally persuaded myself to get up, and had showered, it was past six o'clock. I decided that I had better go and see what was happening out on Bull Dog Road. I was just about to pick up the phone and call Madeleine, when the phone rang. I jumped. It sounded very strange and even ominous in the empty place. Then, I wondered if I should answer it. But Madeleine hadn't said anything about *not* answering it; I was pretty sure she didn't have any boyfriends in town. I decided to take a chance—*she* might be calling *me.*

"Hello?" It was Lola's voice.

"Hello."

"Hello? What number is this, please?"

I told her.

"Well—is Miss Madeleine Overstreet there?"

"No. She's at the theater."

"To whom am I speaking, may I ask?"

"To whom am *I* speaking?—may *I* ask?"

"Lola San-Marquand is my name."

"Oh. Why didn't you say so? *My* name is Leo Proud-hammer."

"Leo? Leo! What are you doing at *Madeleine's* house?"

"I'm cleaning up the joint. A boy's got to make a living."

There was a silence, a calculating silence.

"When I came in," said I carefully, "just before she left, she said she was rushing to rehearsal."

"We broke early. Will you leave a message for Madeleine? The call has been changed. We are to work in the theater tonight, *on* The Green Barn stage, from eight-thirty until twelve. She is not to come to *my* home, but to go directly to the theater."

"Okay. I got it. Eight-thirty."

"Will you write that down?"

"How do you spell theater?"

"Oh! Leo, you can be excessively exasperating. Have you seen Barbara King today?"

"No."

"Well, she will inform you of the exact hour tomorrow morning when Saul will watch your scene."

"Oh? Is he watching us tomorrow?"

"He has been watching you for weeks. You simply haven't realized it."

"What happens if I can't find Barbara?"

"Then *you* will simply have to call Saul. I know nothing of these matters. Saul keeps the details of the teaching side of his life far from me. I only see the results. Write down the message for Madeleine. I hope she's coming home. You wouldn't—would you—know where Madeleine would be likely to go in the event that she does *not* come home?"

"I just work here, lady."

"I see. Thank you. Good-bye."

"Good-bye."

I put down the receiver. I felt an unwilling and un-easy excitement. So, he was going to watch us; and that was something. But why the fuck should I care what the old fart thought of me? And that was something else. But I had to get home, so Barbara and I could work tonight. I wrote out the note for Madeleine, saying that I would see her, or call her, after my class—my first class!—tomor-row. The note sounded, perhaps, a bit too jubilant, but I thought, Fuck it, and I left it in the middle of the table, weighted down with a clock.

Madeleine's door faced the steps, and an elderly man and his wife were mounting these steps as I jubilantly bounced out of Madeleine's door, and locked it behind me. They stared at me as though I were a ghost, and they really seemed, for a moment, unable to move. Perhaps their terror, for an instant, terrified me, I don't know; anyway, for less than a second, snake to rabbit, we stood immobilized by each other. Then, I said gently, "You can keep coming up the stairs, you know. I don't bite."

This broke the charm, and they came briskly to the landing. He had now found his voice, and he asked me sternly, "What are you doing in this building, boy?"

"I was looking for a file, so I could sharpen my teeth. Suh. But I couldn't find none." I grinned. "See?" I shrugged. "Some days are like that." Then I crooned, "Oh, dat old man ribber, he sure do keep rolling along! Ain't it de truf! Laws-a-massy, hush my mouf, he he he and yuk yuk yuk!" and I tapdanced down the stairs. At least they now knew that I wasn't a ghost, but it didn't seem to reassure them.

I went straight home, in a taxi, but there was no one there. I looked upstairs and downstairs for a note, but there wasn't any. I supposed that Jerry and Barbara had gone to town again, which seemed a little strange, but, as I had no way of getting to town and no more money, even if I *did* get there, I scrambled myself some eggs and started reading the scene from *Waiting for Lefty*. I hadn't got far, when I heard a car coming. But it wasn't our car, though it stopped in front of the house, and the powerful lights fell over the line I was reading: *Sid: The answer is no—a big electric sign looking down on Broad-way!* I put down my book, and I walked to the porch, which was bathed in light, as I was trapped in light.

"What's the matter? What do you want?" Some reflex, or perhaps some whisper from my ancestors, helped to keep my mortal terror out of my voice. I sounded angry, and I immediately realized that this was, for the moment, anyway, the only tone I could take. "Get that light out of my eyes! What the hell do you want?"

"We want you to put up your hands," said a drawling voice, "and then we'll put out the light."

I put up my hands. There they were, of course, in blue, two of them, of course, white, of course. One stood by the car, while the other came up to me, and frisked me. Cops love frisking black boys, they want to find out if what they've heard is true.

"All right. You're coming down to the station with us."

People become frightened in very different ways—the ways in which they become frightened may sometimes determine how long they live. Here I was, in the country, and on a country road, alone, facing two armed white men who had legal sanction to kill me; and if killing me should prove to be an error, it would not matter very much, it would not, for them, be a serious error. It would not cost them their badges or their pensions, for the only people who would care about my death could certainly never reach them. I knew this. It was more vivid to me than the policeman's hands, his breath, his holster. I knew that I was frightened, and I knew how frightened I was. But I remembered, vaguely, reading somewhere that animals can smell fear, and that when they do, they leap and they devour. I was determined that *these* animals should not smell *my* fear, and this determination deflected, so to speak, my terror from them to myself: my life was in my hands. I had not yet guessed why they had come for me, and I did not know what was going to happen. But I was going to scheme as long as I had breath, and outwit them if I could.

So I did not whimper, *What for? I ain't done nothing,* but asked, as deliberately as I could, and as mockingly as I could, "What is it that you imagine me to have done?"

I was gambling on their reflexes. They were accustomed to black boys whimpering, or, on the other hand, defiant, and it was easy, in either case, for them to know exactly what to do—to amuse themselves with the whimper or the defiance, and beat the shit out of the boy, and sometimes to beat the boy to death. I had to walk a tightrope between groveling and shouting, and had to hope that a faintly mocking amusement would be sufficiently unexpected to confound their reflexes and immobilize their impulses, at least until I got to the station, where I would have to begin to calculate again. Central to my calculations was the terror of finding myself begging for mercy: I hoped I would be able to see that moment coming, and nullify that moment by causing it to come too late.

There I was, in the car, handcuffed, in the back. We moved along the road, fast; it was, I carefully noted, the road to town. So, I dared, "May I ask you—again—what it is you're arresting me for?"

Neither of them said anything, from which I concluded that they either did not know what to say, or were undecided as to what tone to take. I thought, They came to my house, so even *they* must know that I'm a stranger in this town, and am working with people sufficiently celebrated to get them into trouble. But then I thought, If they were really worried about that, then they wouldn't have come at all. I thought, Saul and Lola and Rags don't really care much about me; I can't depend on them. The two or three movie stars who had been drifting in and out of our ken all summer didn't know me from any other shoeshine boy—though I was determined, if I had to, to use their names as a threat. Barbara and Jerry cared, but where were they? And Madeleine cared. *Madeleine*. She gets to the theater at eight-thirty, but maybe they'll let me call her house, and then I thought, *Madeleine*. Then I remembered the elderly man and his wife. Solid citizens, they had done their duty and called the police. It was unbelievably funny: If I had not been handcuffed, I think I might have laughed.

But it was not a laughing matter. We arrived at the station, which looked ominous indeed, and ostentatiously crossed the sidewalk, while people stared at us, and nudged other people, and came up behind us, and began gathering, staring, on the steps. We walked into the station. *A colored boy. They arrested a colored boy.* I became faint, and hot and cold with terror. It was in vain that I told myself, Leo, this isn't the South. I knew better than to place any hope in the accidents of North American geography. This was America, America, America, and those people out there, my countrymen, had been tearing me limb from limb, like dogs, for centuries. I would not be the first. In the bloody event, I would not be the last. I thought, I wonder if Madeleine has charged me with rape? But, no, I thought, don't you have to be caught in the act? Then I thought, No. They just need Miss Ann's word.

But I knew if I allowed myself to think this way, I would lose my nerve completely. The man was behind the desk, and I forced myself to look him in the eye, and I forced myself, nearly fainting, to attack: "Why have I been arrested?"

He looked at me with a curiously impersonal loathing. He was fat, red-faced, Irish, a true believer, a regular fellow. "It's just routine, boy. We'll satisfy your curiosity when we get around to it."

"I'm sorry. But I think the law compels you to tell me what the charges are against me. You have no right to hold me without charges."

His face got redder, and he seemed to swell, and his eyes got darker. We stared at each other—if I had allowed myself to drop my eyes, I would have fallen to the floor.

"Are you trying to tell me my business, boy?"

"I'm only telling you what my rights are, as a citizen of this country."

He and his buddies laughed. I realized that I had made a tactical error. "What's the matter with you, boy? You some kind of nut? Are you a Red?"

I said nothing, only looked at him. Again, he darkened and swelled. He did not know how frightened I was. He was, Allah be praised, far too dense for that: but he knew that I hated him, and would have been happy to see him dead. And this baffled him and angered him—which increased my danger—for *he,* after all, did not hate *me.* I was not real enough for that. I was not as real for him as he, unspeakably, was for me. But I could not drop my eyes. I told myself that there was nothing I could do, now, to minimize the danger. All that I could do was control my fear.

I was not booked, I was not fingerprinted. I was taken into another room, and left alone there for a while—to meditate, I supposed, on my sins, or else to count over my blues. I knew that this probably meant that they were not yet certain to what extent they were to be allowed to vent themselves on me. I took this as a good sign, though I also knew that this might merely mean that I was being saved for their more accomplished sadists. I knew that it was best not to think, not to undermine myself with visions of what was before me. For the moment, there was nothing I could do. There was no way to tell what would happen, who would enter, when the door opened again. And, not altogether consciously, I began to evolve a trick which was to help me, later, in the theater: Leo, I said, you can't know what's going to happen, and, until it happens, you can't know what to do. You're going to be surprised—so *be* surprised. That's the only way you'll be ready.

But when the door opened—so much for the most impeccable theories!—I was *not* surprised. Two plain-clothesmen stood there, with the elderly man and his wife. I stood up, and we looked at each other. How can I explain this? I still thought that they were funny.

"Is that the boy?" one of the detectives asked.

"Yes," said the man; and "That's him," said his wife. They stood as though they were in a jungle, protected by their hunters, but poised to scream and run at the leap of the jungle cat.

"This gentleman," said one of the plainclothesmen, "says he saw you coming out of an apartment a little while ago, where you had no business to be." He raised his eyebrows at me.

Well, they might beat me up when the couple left the room, but they weren't going to beat me while the couple were still in it; and I didn't care, abruptly. I was tired of this vicious comedy, and ashamed of myself for playing any role whatever in it; something turned in me, in an instant, cold and hard—it might have been the abject posture of the old man and his wife.

I said, "The gentleman is a nervous old lady. He doesn't know whether I have any business in the apartment or not." I felt myself beginning to be angry, and I forced myself to take a breath. "The apartment is rented by Miss Madeleine Overstreet. She is an actress, and she is working here in The Green Barn Theater, and I am an actor, and we are friends." I was damned if I was going to cop a plea, and say that I was working for Madeleine, and

I was cleaning up her joint. Fuck the mother-fuckers. "I believe the gentleman will tell you that when he saw me, I was locking the door of the apartment and had the keys in my hand. The gentleman will certainly tell you that, if his eyesight is not failing, and if he is in the habit of telling the truth. Which," I could not resist adding, though I knew it to be foolish, "on both counts, I doubt."

"Do you have the keys on you now?" the plainclothesman asked.

"I refuse to answer any questions until I have been allowed to make a phone call, which is my right by law, or unless my lawyer is present."

Well, it was funny, all right. I saw what they saw—a funky, little black boy, talking about his lawyer. And I didn't give a shit. All you can do is beat my ass. I knew they were too dumb and too scared to know whether I was bluffing or not. So, fuck you, miserable white mother-fuckers. *Fuck* you. I stared at the detective who was asking the questions, and I charged my eyes to say, Baby, if my prick was a broomstick, I'd sure make your tonsils know that you had an ass-hole. Believe me. Oh, yes. Now come on, you fagot, and beat my ass.

But—I had frightened them. They did not know what to make of it. I don't mean at all to suggest that they believed me. They didn't believe me. They thought that I was mad. But they had not intended to tangle with a lunatic: they had merely been ordered to pick up a black boy.

Well, here I was: black, certainly, and not much more than a boy. And there they were. Now, I was dangerous to them. They did not know what might happen—if I were not a lunatic, then my story might be true. And if my story were true—well, then, yes, they might be in trouble, and they might lose their pensions. If I could happen, then anything could happen. I could see this in their eyes.

"What's your name?"

"I have told you that I will not answer any more questions until I am allowed to make a phone call, or until I am advised by my lawyer. You have not booked me, you have not charged me—it is *you* who are acting against the law!"

One of them moved toward me then, but the other one checked him. Thank God, the couple were still in the room. Or thank my ancestors.

"You say you're an actor?" one of them asked, in a friendly, conciliatory tone.

I sat down on my bench, and folded my arms.

"Young man," said the elderly gentleman—at another moment, I might have been sorry for him—"I just thought —I didn't mean to cause you any trouble—"

"You haven't," I said, "caused *me* any trouble at all. But I can make a whole lot of trouble for *you*."

The plainclothesmen and I looked at each other—for what seemed a long time. Then, they all left the room. And I was alone again, a long time, while my anger subsided and my fear returned.

Someone now entered whom I had not seen before, bluff, hearty, red-faced, who called me by my name and slapped me on the back. "So, you're an actor! Why didn't you tell us that in the first place, Leo? You can't blame us for a little misunderstanding. Mistakes *will* happen, won't they?"

I stared at him, and I said nothing. I really did not know what to say.

"I used to have a brother in show business." He choked a little on his monstrous cigar; he sat down next to me. I decided he was probably from Texas. "Of course, that was a long time ago, before you were born." He chuckled, wrapped in the veils of memory. "Yes, he used to do a routine with the great George M. Cohan himself—now, *there* was a trouper! And a *prince*. A prince among men, Leo, I assure you."

I was very young then. I watched him with an amazement which steadily filled with loathing. I really could not move.

"But it's a rough life, show business. Very rough. I know you realize that, Leo, you look like a very intelligent boy." He chuckled again, and nudged me. "But it's got its good side, too, eh, Leo—just between us men? The best broads. I bet the girls love you, don't they, Leo?" He leaned confidentially toward me, and winked. "You know, there's a saying, Big man, little tool, little man, *all* tool! Ha-ha-ha!" He pinched my shoulder, and it hurt. "Oh, you don't want to say it, but I can see it in your eyes. You've

been around a little, young as you are—how old are you,
Leo?" He looked at me. I looked at him. I said nothing.
There was a choked, ugly pause. "All right. Let me guess.
It's hard to tell with your people. Let's see. Seventeen?
Twenty-two?"

He was very, very good at his job, and I think that I
probably would have made some sign if I had been able
to move my head. I simply stared at him, hypnotized,
dumb; and now really frightened, more terribly, more
profoundly, than I had been before.

When he realized that I was not going to answer, he
said, "Leo, like I said before, mistakes *will* happen. All of
us are human, and we all make mistakes. That's why we
invented erasers." He was watching me closely behind
the veil of cigar smoke; but he was bluff and hearty and
he continued to smile. "I hate to say it, Leo, but you know
as well as I do that people in show business, they tend to
be, well, kind of lax—lax in their *morals*. That's the reason my brother finally just *had* to get out. He couldn't
stand the life." He looked at me with great sympathy.
"I'm not saying this for you, you look like a fine, upstand-
ing boy. I bet your mother's proud of you. Where does
your mother live, Leo?"

"In Johannesburg," I said. "She's a missionary."

He did not know what to say to this, and my face did
not help him. I could see him struggling to find a map
somewhere, but it was difficult to ask me for one. "Oh.
Well, then, I'm sure she wouldn't want you mixed up in
bad company. And, Leo, I'm sorry to say this, but a lot of
your friends are mighty bad company for a fine-looking
boy like you. Mighty bad company. That's how this mistake was made. We wasn't looking for *you*—we wasn't
expecting to find no *colored* people in that house. Of
course not. You can see that. No. We've been getting
complaints about—oh, certain parties, and it's our job to
investigate all complaints and we do our job. Now, I'm
old enough to be your father, Leo, so let me give you a
word of advice." He paused. "Show business broke my
brother's heart. That's a fact. He said"—he jabbed me
with his forefinger, and it hurt; I knew he wanted it to
hurt—"*I wish I had stayed with my own people.* That's
what he said." He leaned back triumphantly. "You see
my point, Leo? You stay with *your own people* and

you're sure to stay out of trouble. Why, we *never* have any trouble with the colored people in this town—they're just the nicest bunch of colored people you'd ever want to meet, they work hard and save their money, and go to church. But this crowd you hang out with, Leo, with their wild parties and loose women and smoking mari-huana—they're going to bring you to grief, son. You see, I said, 'son,' it just slipped out before I thought, but I mean it. That's just the way I feel. And I just hope you won't go to no more of those parties, Leo. I'd like you to promise me you won't continue to undermine your health and your morals by—smoking all that marihuana and running with loose white women—"

I stood up. I said, "If I'm under arrest, arrest me. If not, please let me go."

We stared at each other. He might talk about the "bad" company I kept, but it was only the fear of what they might possibly do which prevented him from rising, and bouncing me about that room like a ball. It was in his eyes, it was in the air, it was in the muscle that beat in his forehead. And I doubted, as we stared at each other, that even this fear would control him very long. My luck had run out. I felt my bowels loosen and lock—for fear; and my mouth turned dry. But, anyway, all my words were gone. I'd run my course. Silence, now, was my only hope, for if I could not open my mouth, I could not beg for mercy. The door opened, and one of the plainclothes-men stood there, saying something. I didn't hear what he said, because, when the door opened, I heard Madeleine's voice in the other room. And I simply walked out, in the direction of the voice. She was standing in front of the desk, with Saul and Lola. Saul and Lola looked blandly indignant, but Madeleine was utterly white, and her hands and legs were shaking. She was staring at the man behind the desk with a malevolence which would have done credit to Medea.

"Now, miss," he was saying, "it was just a mistake, and we're very sorry for it. I wouldn't let it get me all upset. See," he said, turning to me as I appeared, "we haven't harmed a hair of his precious head. He's just as good as new."

"A mistake," she said. "A mistake. You dirty, racist bastard, you're goddamn lucky you *didn't* harm a hair of his head. You'd lose that badge so goddamn fast your head would never stop spinning."

"I don't like your language, miss."

"Fuck you," she said. *"Fuck* you. You goddamn Nazi." Then, she started to cry.

"Madeleine," Lola said. She walked to the desk. "Young man. A word of advice. I will try to put it in extremely simple language, so that you can understand it. The people standing before you are more powerful than you. *I* am more powerful than you, and I can break you by making a phone call. *I* am responsible for my theatrical company, and nothing will prevent me from fulfilling that responsibility. With no justification whatever, you have taken Mr. Proudhammer out of his home and brought him here and forced him, and forced *us,* to undergo needless harassment. You will take good care not to molest any of my company in future—else, *you* will have no future, and I am not a woman to make idle threats. You have already, allow me to inform you, rendered yourself liable to suit for false arrest. Come, Leo. Goodnight, my Nazi friends."

"Heil Hitler," said Madeleine, and Lola took my arm and we walked out.

We got into the San-Marquand car. There were still people in the street, and they stared at us.

Saul started the car. "How could you two be so foolish?" he asked us, then.

"We?" said Madeleine. *"We?* What did *we* do?"

"You know what the people in this town are like," Saul said.

"The people in this town," said Madeleine. "The people in this town. I hope the river rises the moment we get out of here, and drowns them all like rats. Like the rats they are. But why are *we* foolish?"

I said nothing. I leaned back in the car, scarcely listening.

"Not foolish, Saul," said Lola, "but, surely, a little *indiscreet."*

"What do you mean," shouted Madeleine, "indiscreet! Leo left my house in broad goddamn Sunday daylight, and went to *his* house—and the cops dragged him to the police station, because he'd been to *my* house. Now, what the fuck are *you* talking about?"

"We've worked in this town every summer for a long time, Madeleine," Saul said. "We know the people and the people know us and we've never had any trouble. You have to realize that this is a small town and the people here are not very sophisticated—they're not bad people. You just have to—understand their limits. That's how you manage to play a character on the stage, by understanding the character's limits. That's the only way you can play *Hedda Gabler,* for instance—by understanding Hedda's *limits.* I don't think that's so unreasonable."

"I'm not Hedda Gabler," Madeleine said, "but if I ever get a chance to play her, I'll certainly pretend that she's living in this town. But what this town could really use is a couple of Negro cooks, named Lady Macbeth and Medea."

"You mean," I said—but I scarcely knew why I was bothering to speak—"you never had any trouble until I came along. Is that what you mean?"

"Leo," said Lola, "don't be touchy."

I looked at her. "Touchy. All right. I won't be touchy. I just asked a question. *Is* that what you mean, Saul?"

"I don't think there's any point in discussing it now," Saul said. "You are upset, understandably upset, we would say. We do not blame you, Leo, but our schedule has been thoroughly disrupted and we must return to the theater. If you are going home, I'll drop you."

"Thanks," I said, after a moment, "let's do that." And I leaned back again. I didn't know what Madeleine was thinking. I didn't care. I was surprised to realize that I didn't care, and a little ashamed. I knew that she was hurt and baffled; and she wanted to reach me, but did not know how, especially with Saul and Lola in the car. We hit the road leading out of town. Nobody said anything. We passed the theater. The lights were on. Our signs were up.

"Maybe," said Madeleine, haltingly, "you'd rather watch rehearsal, Leo? Especially as there's nobody at home in your place."

Saul did not slow down. I said, "No, thanks, Madeleine. I think I'd just like to get on home. Nothing else will happen to me tonight."

And so we stopped before the whitewashed house. I

could see that no one had come home yet, because the light was still burning as I had left it.

I got out of the car. "Thanks for bailing me out," I said to Saul and Lola. Then, I said to Madeleine, "Please, don't you feel badly. Don't *you* feel badly. These things happen."

She smiled. There were still tears on her face. "Do you want me to come by, later, after rehearsal?"

Saul made a sound between a grunt and a cough, looking straight ahead.

I said, "No. I'll see you tomorrow. Good-night, all."

And the car drove away, and I went into the house.

I sat down in my chair, and I picked up my book. The words bounced around the page, and I followed them around in the hope that they would eventually do something which could capture my attention. I wondered where Barbara and Jerry were. *Sid: But that sort of life ain't for the dogs which is us. Christ, baby! I get like thunder in my chest when we're together. If we went off together I could maybe look the world straight in the face, spit in its eye like a man should do. God damn it, it's trying to be a man on the earth. Two in life together.* Sid's ravings meant nothing to me. The lines seemed bombastic and empty and false; I wondered why I had ever wanted to play this scene; I could never deliver those lines. And, anyway—*should* I? *Should* I submit myself to the judgment of a Saul? I put down my book and I turned out the light. I went up the stairs to my room. I suddenly didn't want to talk to anybody or to see anybody, and I sat there in the dark. I looked at the sky. I picked up my guitar and I strummed it a little. Then, I put it down.

The night was very still. I heard the car coming when the car was still a long way off. If they had heard of my adventure, they would want to talk about it. I didn't want to talk. The car stopped in front of our door. Then, the lights went on downstairs. The car door slammed. I moved back from the window. Barbara called my name.

I couldn't sit and hide in the dark; these were my friends. I opened my door and I walked downstairs.

"Hello," I said. "Where've you two been?"

"We've been to the movies," Barbara said, "but we hear *you've* been in jail."

"A slight misunderstanding," I said. I sat down on the porch.

"Did they really come all the way out here to get you?" Jerry asked.

"Oh, yes. They were right here."

"I'll be damned. I swear to God, they got bacon fat where their brains should be. Jesus Christ. Don't they have anything else to do?"

He sounded—and I was very surprised to hear it—as though he were on the verge of tears.

"But what did they want?" Barbara asked. "Why *did* they come here?"

"They saw a black boy leaving a white lady's apartment," I said, "and they had to do their duty. You know how *that* is."

She turned whiter than Madeleine had been, and her lips tightened, and she dropped her eyes.

"Leo," she said, after a moment, "they didn't do anything to you?"

"No. They just scared me." I stood up. "They humiliated me. They made me feel like a dog. They tried to turn me into something worse than they are. They had a wonderful time doing it, now they all feel more like men. And I was very lucky. They were afraid to go too far. They were afraid the Workshop might make a stink." I paused, and I laughed. "So now I owe my life to Saul and Lola."

"But *they* were all right, weren't they?" Jerry asked.

I shrugged. I didn't want to pursue it, because I didn't get any pleasure out of seeing Jerry hurt. "They were all right." But I had to add, "Saul *did* say that he thought we were foolish."

"Yes," said Barbara. "He told us that."

"You saw him?"

"Yes. We thought you might be there, because—well, we knew that Madeleine had a rehearsal."

"Do *you* think I was foolish?"

"Do *I*?" She stared at me. "My God, Leo, how can you ask *me* that?" She shrugged. "*I* might think you're foolish, because I don't think Madeleine's worth your time—"

"Why?"

"Oh, I don't want to talk about that, it's none of my business, and it's got nothing to do with her. I like her well enough. I just don't think she's good enough for

you—but, you know, that doesn't give me any reason to
call the cops. So, you're foolish. So is everybody else.
That's got nothing to do with the cops. Wow. I wish it
had been me. The police chief of this town would be
looking for a job." She looked around at us, and gave a
little laugh. "I mean it. After all, I'm an heiress. I don't
always *like* being an heiress, but that doesn't mean that
I'm not prepared to use it." She came over to me and
kissed me quickly on the forehead. "Poor Leo. I know
you don't want to talk about it anymore."

"Let's have a beer," said Jerry, "and then I'm going
to hit the sack. We are going to have to haul ass real early
in the morning, children, because we have no money at
all." He went into the kitchen. Barbara sat down next to
me on the porch and put her hand in mine.

"Before the summer's over," she said, "remind me that
there are things I've been keeping from you which I really
must tell you."

"Oh? Such as?"

"Oh," she said, "girlish secrets." She paused. "But I
can't carry them around within me very much longer."

Jerry came back, with two bottles and three glasses,
and sat down on the step below us. "Well," I said, "I'll be
happy to hear your confession whenever you're ready."

"I hope you'll be happy," she said.

Jerry poured the beer. "Confession! You know I
haven't been to confession in more than three years? And
you know what that means? That means my soul is in
mortal danger. It's the truth I'm telling you." He handed
a glass to Barbara, then handed a glass to me.

"How does it feel to have your soul in mortal danger?"
I asked.

"Exciting." He grinned, and kissed Barbara. "Wicked."
Barbara took her hand from mine. We lit cigarettes.
"Every time you make love, you think of the confessional
and you say to yourself, Well, I'm just not going to tell
the bastard, that's all. Let him get his *own* kicks." We all
laughed. "I swear, I believe they sit there, jerking off."

"Don't you ever miss it?" I asked.

"What? Going to confession?"

"Well—the church. All of it. You know—the music, the
others. The—the faith. I guess—you know—the safety—"

"Well. Sometimes, maybe. Especially when I see my

mother. She's always weeping about it. And that makes me feel bad and then I remember a couple of priests I used to like and some other people and the music and Holy Communion and the way it felt—you know, it was nice. But, then, I look at my mother and she's not a bad woman but she is a very fucked-up woman and I know that part of what fucked her up is the Church. You know, she believes a whole lot of *shit*, and I've seen her do some very wicked things because she's so goddamn ignorant. Well—I don't want to be like that, that's all. I want to live my own life the way I want to live it. My mother hates Jews and she hates Negroes, and you know, fuck it, I can't be bothered with all that shit. So they can *have* it."

"Did you ever believe it? I mean, you know—the Son of God and heaven and hell and judgment. You know. The whole bit."

"My mother and my father believed it. And everyone around me believed it. So I believed it, too."

"You never believed it, did you, Leo?" Barbara asked. "You never even went to church."

"No. My father didn't believe it. So none of us believed it. Naturally." I stood up. "It's been a rough day. So, you'll forgive me if I just say good-night now."

After a moment they both said, "Good-night, Leo." I carried my beer upstairs. They stayed on the porch awhile, I could hear them murmuring. Then, they went inside and closed their door. Then, everything was still. I remembered that I had forgotten to ask Barbara what time we were due to appear before Saul in the morning. But I knew that she, or Jerry, would wake me up.

The story grows harder to tell. What did I do that night? When did I make my decision? Or had it already been made? Did I dream that night? Or sleep? I know that the sheet was like a rope, wet and strangling. The window was open. At some point, I awoke and, naked, walked to the window and looked out at the shadow of the trees, the shadow of the land. I lit a cigarette, and stood at the window, and wondered who I was. Downstairs, they were not yet asleep. I heard them murmuring, Barbara's voice more than ever laryngitic, Jerry's with all valves open. They sounded sad, it sounded very sad. I put out my cigarette and crawled back into bed, my narrow bed.

I heard the door close downstairs, and then I heard the car door slam, and I heard the car drive away. I opened my eyes. It was very early in the morning. I pushed my fingers through my heavy hair. I sat up. I wondered where the car was going at this hour of the morning. I wondered about the silence below. I looked out of the window. It was true that our car was gone. So I went back to bed. It seemed beyond me to do anything else. I heard cocks crowing, far away.

When I woke, Barbara sat on my bed, holding a pot of coffee and watching me.

"How long have you been here?"

"Not very long. The coffee's not cold yet—so, you see." And she rose from the bed and poured coffee into two cups, which she had placed on the table before my window. She put in milk and sugar and came back to the bed.

"Where's Jerry?"

"I don't know. Driving around."

I watched her.

"Did something happen?" I asked this very carefully. She walked up and down my room. "Yes. I guess something happened."

"Barbara. What's the matter with you this morning? What happened?"

For something *had* happened; that was why she was in my room. I started to get out of bed, but then realized I was naked, and I pulled the sheet around me, and sat up. "Barbara!"

"I hurt Jerry. I hurt him very much." She was trying not to cry. It hurt to watch; I wished she *would* cry. I sipped my coffee and lit a cigarette. She came to the bed, and took the cigarette, and I lit another one. She walked up and down my room, between the window and me, between the light and me; on and off went the light, on and off. A skinny, pale girl, in a big bathrobe, and her hair piled on the top of her head, and falling over her forehead. "I had planned to do it differently, or do it later—I had hoped not to do it at all. But now I have. And he drove away. I hope he comes back. At least to say good-bye. Because I love him, too. Jesus."

"What did you do, Barbara?"

"I told him"—she stopped—"I told him how much I love you."

"But," I said, frightened, sitting straight up, "Jerry *knows* that! What did you tell him *that* for?"

"Because," she said—my God, she was steady, standing there in the morning light—"it's true." Then, she sipped her coffee; and remained standing in the light.

I watched the blue smoke from our cigarettes.

"Barbara," I said.

I don't know what I was going to say. Barbara suddenly crumpled to the floor, spilling her coffee, and ruining her cigarette, and I jumped out of bed, naked as I was, and grabbed her. I had endured female tears before, God knows, young as I was then, but I knew that these tears had nothing to do with blackmail. But if Barbara had been capable of blackmail, then the terms of our love would have had a precedent and would not have been so hard. We were alone, she in the robe, and I in my skin, under the morning light, and with the spilt coffee all over the whitewashed floor.

"Leo. I'm sorry. Oh, Leo. I'm sorry."

"Get up. Get up. This is no time to be sorry."

I pulled her to her feet. But, naked as I was, and holding her against me, I realized that I did not really feel for her what I had felt for Madeleine, whom I knew I did not love, several hours before. I felt a terrible constriction. It felt, I think, like death. I loved Barbara. I knew it then, and I really know it now; but what, I asked myself, was I to do with her? *Love, honor, and protect.* But these were not among my possibilities. And, since they were not, I felt myself, bitterly, and most unwillingly, holding myself outside her sorrow; holding myself, in fact, outside her love; holding myself beyond the reach of my blasted possibilities. One cannot dwell on these things, these echoes of what might, in some other age, and in some other body, have been; one must attempt to deal with what is, or else go under, or go mad. And yet—to deal with what is! Who can do it? I know that I could not. And yet I knew that I had to try. For there was something in it, after all, and I heard it in her sorrow, and I heard it in my heart, and in spite of our hideous condition, which I had to accept, to which I could not say, No. I carried her to the bed.

"Leo. Leo. Leo."

"Barbara."

Perhaps it could only have happened as it happened. I don't know. I had, then, to suspend judgment, and I suspend judgment now. We had no choice. We really had no choice. I had to warm my girl, my freezing girl. I covered her with my body, and I took off her robe. I covered her, I covered her, she held me, and I entered her. And we rejoiced. Sorrow, what have we not known of sorrow! But, that morning, we rejoiced. And yet, it must be said, there was a shrinking in me when it was over. *Love, honor, and protect.*

"Leo," Barbara said. She was running her fingers along my unshaven chin. I was rather too conscious of my unbrushed teeth.

"Yes?"

"I love you."

"Oh. Well. You *have,* you know, had better ideas."

"I know. But I don't care."

"I've had better ideas, too," I said, after a moment.

"I know," she said. "I really *do* know."

I lit two cigarettes, and I put one between her lips.

"Leo?"

"Yeah?"

"Don't worry about me. I know the score. I accept the terms."

I watched her very closely. "You mean, you know it's impossible—that *I'm* impossible?"

"I don't know if you are—no more than I am, anyway. But I know that *it* is—at least, right now. I've thought about it a lot, up here. And I realized something kind of funny. I mean, it's lucky I'm an actress. I mean—nothing comes before that, and I know that. And that helps me, somehow. Do you know what I mean?"

"I think so. I'm not sure. But I think so."

"It means," she said, with the gravity of a child, "that we must be great. That's all we'll have. That's the only way we won't lose each other."

"A person can't just decide to be great, Barbara."

"Some persons can. Some persons must."

"You think I'm one of those persons?"

"I know you are. I've always known it." She paused. "That's how I know, you see—that you don't belong to me." She smiled. "But let's be to each other what we can."

"*While* we can," I said, watching her.

"Yes. While we can." Then, "But if we do it right, you see, we can stretch out our while a very long while and we can make each other better. You see. I know. I've *thought* about it."

I moved from the bed to the window. "What about Jerry?"

"Well, I thought I was being very clever with Jerry. I thought neither of us would get hurt. He was just a very nice boy, and he liked me very much, and I liked him very much. And I was a little afraid—well, I wanted, partly, *not* to get involved with you. I was afraid it would spoil everything, because we got along so well. I was afraid to startle you. I know you don't like to be startled. Then you run. But—Jerry—got more and more serious. And I realized I wasn't going to be able to handle it at all. So—I thought I'd make everything as clear as I could."

"How did he take it?"

After a moment, she said, "He tried to take it well. He tried very hard. But—I wish—oh, how I wish I'd left him alone! He's far too nice a boy for me."

"Is he coming back?"

"Yes. He's coming back."

I turned and looked at her. "Barbara. Do you know what you're doing? We can't play around with people's lives this way."

"I know that. That's why I tried to make it clear. Before I hurt him too much. Before it went too far." She put out her cigarette. "Before I told myself too many lies. And before—before you went too far away from me."

"But you're not much better off now, are you? With me, I mean. I'm spinning like a feather, Barbara. I don't know where I'll land."

"I'm better off," she said, "because at least I'm not lying now."

I sat down on the bed. "Barbara," I said, "there may be a lot you don't know about me."

"There may be," she said, "but I don't think so."

I laughed. "Well. There's a lot I don't know about myself." I watched her. "Do you know I'm bisexual?"

"Yes. At least, I supposed it."

"Why? Does it show?"

She laughed. "I don't know. I guess it shows to some people. It just seemed logical to me." She laughed again. "Normal." She sobered. "You're very gentle. I always wondered, in fact, if you were having an affair with Charlie."

"Charlie? No."

"I think he wanted you to."

"It doesn't bother you?"

She looked at me. "Why should it bother me, Leo? I'm not in your body. I can't live your life. I only want to *share* your life." She sat up, and pulled the robe around her. "Anyway—what difference would it make if I *did* mind? It wouldn't change anything. It would just make you not trust me—I'm *glad* you know you're bisexual. Many men don't."

"How do you know that?"

"The blue grass of Kentucky," she said, "is great for finding out the facts of life. Especially if neither you nor anyone around you has anything else to do. When I went to parties, I used to pretend I was Jane Austen." She laughed again, and grabbed me and kissed me. "In fact, I thought of being a writer before I thought of being an actress." Then she looked at me very soberly. "Well. I hope you like having a sister—a white, incestuous sister. Doesn't that sound like part of the American dream?"

"Well—like Adam said to the Lord, when all this shit was starting—I guess I'll get the hang of it, all right." I put my head on her breast. "But I am a little frightened."

She held me. "I know. But what is it that one's frightened of?"

"I wonder. I don't know. It's just—so many things have happened to me—"

"But not all bad?"

"Oh, no. I don't mean that. I'm not as mad as that." She was playing with my hair, knotting it knottier than it was already, then pulling it—so to speak—straight, then knotting it again. "But good and bad, that's all tied up together. I mean, like, it's bad to be thirsty but it's good to drink—of course," I added, "you get thirsty enough, you drink anything." She was silent. "You see what I mean?"

"I guess it's very bad," she said slowly, "when the

taste of some of what you've drunk comes up and fills your mouth again."

"Yes," I said, "that's very bad."

"Has that happened to you?"

"Yes. That's happened to me."

She was silent for a long time. I began to be worried about Jerry coming back. But we were peaceful; we might not be so peaceful for a long time again; and I didn't want to break it.

"I suppose," she said, "that people invent gods and saints and martyrs and all—well, one of the reasons, anyway—in order to prevent themselves from drinking—well—a lot of what they're offered to drink. It doesn't seem to work out very well—I mean, then, they just seem to poison themselves and never, even, get nauseous—but I'm sure that's one of the reasons." I couldn't see her face, but I felt her chin bob up and down in a kind of mockery of decision. "I've thought about it, you see," she said. "People need a means of being reproached."

"Reproached? *I,*" I said, leaning up a little, "I been 'buked and I been scorned. Did I *need* it?"

"I don't mean that. I don't mean—*that.* I mean—gods and saints and martyrs don't work for me. They just don't. But I *don't* want to be wicked. People have to find ways of not allowing themselves to become wicked."

"And what's the way?"

"Well, for me," she said, "in a way—*you* are. I wouldn't like you to be ashamed of me."

I sat up, and looked at her.

"I hope you wouldn't like me to be ashamed of you, either," she said. "I'd like—to be the way for you." She watched my face, and she smiled. "I think you think I'm being blasphemous. Or maybe you think I'm insane."

"No. No. I'm just fascinated. I'm trying to follow you."

"Well, look—you'll see that I *have* thought about it. I've never thought about anything so hard in my life. Look. I know this situation is impossible. I even know, in a way, that *I'm* being impossible. And everyone I grew up with would think so, and many people think so who will never dare admit it. I don't care about those people. I care about whether or not *I* know what I am doing. You're black. I'm white. Now, that doesn't mean shit, really, and yet it means everything. We're both very young, and you, after all, really are penniless, and I'm really not. I'm really very rich. Maybe I don't use it now, but I know I can always call on it, they're sure that when I come to my senses, I'll come home. It's all there for me and, anyway, after all, they're going to die one day. So." She shivered a little, and paused, and looked away, out of my window, toward the distant mountain. "If we were different people, and very, very lucky, we might beat the first hurdle, the black-white thing. If we weren't who we are, we could always just leave this—*unfriendly*—country, and go somewhere else. But we're as we are. I knew, when I thought about it, that we couldn't beat the two of them together. I don't think you'd care much that your wife was white—but a wife who was both white *and* rich! It would be horrible. We'd soon stop loving each other. And, furthermore—" She stopped. "Would you light me a cigarette, please?"

"Coming, princess." I lit two cigarettes, and gave one to her. She blew smoke in my face, and smiled.

"And, furthermore—well, look at the way I was raised. You're forbidden fruit. Oh, we'll talk about that another day. But, believe me"—she laughed, it was a very melancholy sound—"by the time a Southern girl has had her first period, she's already in trouble. Everybody's always told you that the old black man who mows the lawn and rakes the leaves and chops the kindling and takes care of the fires—you know, well, he's old, and he's nice to you, and you like that old man and everybody likes him. And, naturally, you don't know any better, you like anybody that old man likes and, naturally, you like his son. Or you'd like to like his son. And his son looks like—the old man. He smells like him. He's nice, like he is. And he's just about your age. But there's something wrong with his son. There's something wrong with him, you can't be friends with the son of the nice old man. He's not nice, like his father, and he's not like other men at all. No. He's a rapist. And not only is he a rapist, but he only rapes white women. And not only that, but he's got something in his underwear big and black and *always* hard and it will change you *forever* if it ever touches you. You won't even be white any more. You'll just belong to him. Well, you know, everybody wants to be changed. Especially if you're not loved. If looking like a zebra means somebody might love you, well, okay, I'll look like a zebra and you can go on looking white. Have a ball." She smiled, and subsided. "Anyway, you know, that's the way I saw you the first time I saw you. I even thought, My God, maybe that's the real reason I left home. To find out. But I didn't think I'd better experiment with you. I knew you'd make me pay if I did. And so then I began to think that you mustn't experiment with anybody. So, I tried to get to be your friend. And—here we are."

"Let me kiss you," I said, "like a brother," and I kissed her on the forehead.

Then she kissed me, first like a sister and then on the mouth, and we lay still together for awhile.

"What time are we due at Saul's?" I asked her.

"Yes," she said soberly, "I'd better get downstairs and get dressed." She sat up, and put her feet on the floor. She wasn't wearing any slippers. "We're due at Saul's at ten. It must be about nine now."

"How're we going to get there?"

She looked at me. "I'm feared we'll have to walk, Leo."

I laughed and pulled her to her feet and put my knee in her behind. "Okay. Go on and get dressed. I'll hurry down."

She went to the door. "I think Jerry's already mowing a lawn somewhere by now." She stood at the door, as though she hated to walk out of it. "Can I please have another cigarette?"

I lit one, and carried it to her.

"Thanks. I'll yell up the time. Do you feel ready for Saul?"

"No. But, as you said, we have to be great."

She smiled, and walked down the stairs.

It turned out to be eight forty-five. Jerry made no appearance. Presently, we were walking the road to town. She was wearing a light, brown, summer dress, or "frock," as she called it, cut below her shoulder blades in the back, and with a wide skirt—this was for the moment in our scene when she pirouettes before me. She wore her hair down over her shoulders; her idea, I think, of the disheveled proletariat, though I myself would have read her for Alice in Wonderland. She wore flat shoes, both for the road, and for the scene. We held hands. The road was long, and there was no one and nothing on it, and so we skipped. We laughed a lot, for no particular reason. I picked a red flower, and I put it in Barbara's hair. The sun was bright, it was going to be a hot day. The road was dry and dusty. When we approached The Green Barn, we made sign language to each other to be very circumspect indeed, and we stopped holding hands. Barbara put her flower between her teeth. I took off my shirt and put it on my head, and then I put her book and my book on my head, and I walked respectfully, wearily, and proudly behind her. But, there being no one to witness this epiphany, we soon walked together again, hand in hand.

But, as we neared the town, when we saw the proud signs announcing it, heard a train, heard the river, and saw the diner, which stood a little by itself; do what we would, we felt the human heat of the town rush out to meet us, we waited for the eyes, we waited for the silence, we waited for we knew not what. It was vivid to both of us, suddenly, that we had never before appeared in this town without Jerry. We had not thought of it that way, but Jerry had been proof, at least insofar as this white girl and this white town were concerned, of my impotence. But now! and Barbara carefully replaced the red flower in her hair, I put my shirt on. The grass roots of America was waiting for us, spoiling for us, all the good white people, just beyond this small hill and this small bridge which spanned a narrow creek. I realized abruptly, as we were on the bridge, that the car in which Jerry had driven away—driven where?—was not his property and not my property, but the property of the Workshop. Technically, anyway, Jerry was driving a stolen car. And the car was my responsibility. And there would certainly be many things for me to do this afternoon, for *Arms and the Man* was opening tonight. I looked, as we passed, to see if the car was parked before the diner, but it wasn't. I didn't see any point in saying anything to Barbara about it. The shit would hit the fan soon enough. I was carrying both our books, and I was wondering how these could be used as weapons. For, now, we were concentrating on how to walk just a few blocks through a hostile, staring, gathering town.

It is not an easy thing to do. One's presence is an

incitement, and therefore, one must do all in one's power
not to increase this incitement. But, by the time one has
become an incitement, not very much is left in one's
power. It is not a matter merely of walking straight, eyes
straight ahead. No, one's eyes must be everywhere at once
—without seeming to be, without seeming to move; one
must be ready for the rock, the fist, the sudden movement; one must see every face, and yet make it impossible
for one's eye to be caught, even for a second, by any other
eye. One must move swiftly, and yet not hurry: one must,
in fact, give the crowd no opening, either by seeming to
be too proud or by seeming to be too humble. All such
crowds are combustible, and they always will be. Their
buried, insupportable lives have brought them together
and on the only terms they can come together; their unspeakable despair concerning their lives. These lives are
like old, old rags in the closet of a very old house. The
merest whisper will set them aflame. All such crowds con-
tain, and they will forever, one man, one woman, who—
if only for the moment it takes to hurl the stone, to leap
the barrier, to prepare and spew the spittle, to grab the
throat—if only for the moment, without ever having
acted before, and never to act again—*is* the collective
despair of the crowd, *is* their collective will. Then, the
fire rages, not to spend itself until yet another man done
gone.

It is easier to walk such a gauntlet alone. It is very
hard for two, especially if they care about each other,
especially if one is black and one is white, especially if
one is male and one is female. One's own body has a front
and a back, has a left and a right. Hopefully, one can
maneuver his body in such a way as to prevent its being
destroyed. But, with two, one's reflexes are off, for one is
trying to calculate danger from too many angles, and one
is also attempting a desperate mental telepathy. The
people were silent. There were not, I thought to myself,
very many. Two or three came out of the diner and stood,
leering; three men, not young, I had seen them before.
They moved in order to keep us in sight, laughing among
themselves. Then, they were joined by another man, and
they began to walk behind us, but at a considerable distance. Two men and a woman came out of a house on the
left, another man stood behind them on the porch. Then,

on the right, first one house, then another, they came out
and stood on their lawn. My right was across the street,
my left was Barbara's left. On my left, an old woman
came rushing to her gate and her face was filled with
fury, she was staring toward us, we were coming closer. A
very young man joined her, then a young woman, then a
child. They were closer to Barbara than they were to me.
A car stopped on the other side of the street, there were
three men in it. Then, a car stopped on my side of the
street, with a young boy in it. He said, "Nigger"—his
voice was melodious—"you are a dead man. We going to
get you. And your white whore, too." The old woman
and the young woman and the young man and the child
were coming closer. I did not dare put a hand on Barbara. I whispered, "Come closer to me," and I stepped
nearer the curb, and she moved with me, just as we passed
the old woman, who shouted, "You hussy! You nigger-
lover! You low-down, common, low-class, poor white
slut!" A great, mocking cheer went up behind us. I
dared not take Barbara's hand, or even look at her. Three
white men were coming toward us, on my side of the
sidewalk. I was astounded to realize that neither Barbara
nor I, who, after all, were not without experience, had
given a thought to our walking into town together, and
on *this* morning, until it was too late, until we were already on the bridge. And, even then, we had not thought
of *this*. I cursed Jerry for having taken the car, I cursed
Barbara for her romantic folly—look what was happening
to us, *look!*—and I cursed myself. The three young men
were coming closer. Once we got past them, we had to
bear right, into a short, tree-lined street, and, in the
middle of this street, on the left, was the San-Marquand
driveway. But the driveway was steep. It was relatively
hidden—which might be good, or bad. I held both books,
but I wasn't going to be able to do much with them, and
nothing at all for Barbara. I hoped she would have the
sense to run. *The sense to run.* But it is always a mistake
to run; unless, of course, you can really run away; which,
in no way whatever, could be considered the case here. I
stared into the puppy-dog face, the flecked eyes, regis-
tered the hanging hair, the pug nose, the crooked teeth.
His buddies were on my left. They were abreast of Barbara. He said, "I want your girl-friend to give me and my

friends a blow job. Do she cost much? Or do she only suck big, black nigger cocks?" His buddies were whispering to Barbara. I kept moving. Barbara touched the flower in her hair: I knew she was wishing it were a rose, and she could rake the thorns across their faces. We passed them. The three young men laughed, the street rocked. Just kids, thank you, Jesus, and the daring obscenity was the entire point. We bore right, and crossed the street. We walked in the shade of the trees, and, like soldiers, in perfect unison, turned left, and began toiling up the driveway. They hadn't followed us—only their voices: "Down with niggers! Down with Jews!"

The sun was very hot in the driveway. We didn't speak until we reached the fairly level ground at the top, and were walking toward the house. Then, Barbara looked at me. I looked at her. She was sweating, and she was pale. Her eyes were full of tears. They spilled over, and ran down her face. I brushed them away with my hand.

"Sister Barbara. Sister Barbara."

She tried to smile. She didn't have a handbag, and so she didn't have a handkerchief. I handed her mine.

"It's dirty," I said. Then, "Blow your nose."

She blew her nose in my dirty handkerchief, and handed it back to me.

"Brother Leo."

"You can go straight to the john. Saul won't notice a thing."

"No," she said. "I'm sure of that."

We walked very slowly toward the house, like two reluctant children.

"Let's not talk about it now," I said suddenly. "Let's not talk about it, ever."

"Oh, we'll talk about it sometime. I think we'll have to. But not now."

We both dreaded entering that house. We knew we had to; but we dreaded it.

"Where's Jerry? Goddamnit, he knows I need the car. Where the fuck is he?"

"He'll be back."

"He'll be back *when?* I got a whole lot of shit to do, this afternoon, just as soon as this class is over—this class! Why has he got to be such a fucking baby? And what am I going to tell Saul, when he asks me where the car is? Shit. Do you know Jerry's driving a *stolen* car? He's got no papers for that car."

"Neither do you. And you drive it all the time."

"I'm *supposed* to drive it. And everybody knows it's the Workshop car. And I only drive it in town." We were at the door now, and I put my finger on the buzzer. "Shit. I just wish some people would fucking grow up, that's all I fucking want." The maid, the Negro maid, came to the door, looking as though she were letting us into a funeral chapel. She put her fingers to her lips, and we walked in. Barbara took her book from me, and ran up the stairs.

The maid and I had seen each other before, but we hadn't particularly liked each other, and we certainly didn't like each other now. She gestured me toward the living room, and so I walked over there, and sat down in one of the camp chairs, way in the back.

Saul had a really enormous living room. I guess it just about took up all of the ground floor of his house, and, at one end, there was a raised, curtainless alcove, where students performed, or exposed themselves, ordinarily, and where celebrities, at parties, did likewise—not that the celebrities needed the height. Saul sat alone in the center of this vast, high room, and the students sat around him and behind him. I had never watched a class before, and, in spite of everything, I was immensely curious. In spite of everything, I was anxious to know what would happen to me when I found myself in that curtainless alcove. Someone handed me a mimeographed program, and I saw that Barbara King and Leo Proudhammer were doing a scene from Clifford Odets' *Waiting for Lefty*. There were three scenes being done this morning. We were the third, and last.

The alcove was currently occupied by a swarthy youth, built big in the head and the belly and the buttocks. He was wearing sandals, and a kind of loose garment; and, at the moment he captured my attention, he was leaning forward, toward us, in great pain. His pain was so great that he could neither speak, nor do anything with his arms —which he held on either side of him, like broken plywood wings. He stumbled about in such despair that I supposed I was expected to believe that he had just been blinded, and the sandals made me think of Oedipus. But, as I couldn't hear him—yet—I wasn't sure.

"Nothing," he said, and straightened to his full height, making a tremendous effort at the same time to do something with those arms, "extenuate." He paused, and looked at all of us—for quite some time. "Nor," he added quickly, as though it had just occurred to him, "set down aught in malice." He had by now succeeded in getting his arms somewhere near his torso, and now one hand held his elbow, while the other gently admonished us: "Then must you speak of one that lov'd not *wisely*—but too *well*." He paused again. He opened both arms wide. "Of one not easily jealous, *but*"—now he began to pace —"being wrought"—and once again he fixed us with his eye—"*perplexed*. In the *extreme*." He shook his massive head. "Of one whose hand"—he raised his head and his voice and threw the voice to heaven, or to us—"*like the base Indian,* threw a pearl away richer than all his *tribe!*" The arms now encircled his girth, his head was down, and he was silent for awhile. Not a soul stirred, including me. He pulled himself together, or, rather, he let his arms go again, and faced us. Barbara came and sat down beside me. She looked all right. I handed her the program; this was *Othello,* and we were next.

"Of one," he said, one hand caressing his chin, the other at his waist, "whose subdu'd eyes, albeit unused to the *melting* mood, drops tears as fast as the Arabian *trees* their med'cinable *gum.* Set you down *this,*" he said, both arms reaching toward us now, "and say *besides*—the intensity dropped, he began to pace again—"that in Aleppo once, where a malignant and a turban'd Turk beat a Venetian *and traduc'd the state*"—he paused, and let us have those eyes again—"I"—now he moved toward us, as tall as he could be, one hand at his waist and one hand stretched toward us—"took by th' throat"—the hand stretched toward us violently closed—"the circumcised *dog!*"—how he glared; and then he paused awhile; he looked us all over, all of us—"*And*"—the throat hand rose into the air, the waist hand produced a dagger, both hands now grabbed it—"smote him—*thus!*" The dagger entered the entrails. The swarthy youth choked for awhile —quite a long while—unable to get his hands away from the dagger. And at last he fell, hands buried beneath him, and his backside somewhat higher than his head. The class applauded. There were about twelve or fifteen people there, some of them visitors. I did not look at Barbara, who did not look at me. The swarthy youth rose, someone brought him a chair, and he sat there in the alcove, waiting.

I did not know what he was waiting for. If what I had just seen was acting, well then, clearly, I had stumbled into the wrong joint. But I wasn't sure. No one seemed to share the embarrassment I felt for the swarthy boy. Every-one seemed very cheerful, and there was a brief buzz of cheerful conversation. Then, Saul cleared his throat. And, with this sound, which was not tentative, but peremptory, silence fell.

"Mr. Parker," Saul said, "can you tell us what you were working on in this scene—what you were working for?"

"Well," said the boy—he blushed and smiled; he was nest—" "I was trying to make Othello's grief—grief, for me, always goes to my stomach. And I I could make you feel Othello's *physical* an-n you'd feel his—his other grief—his, well, his e smiled. "I don't know any other way to say it,

"I think you've made yourself quite clear," Saul said. He looked around the room. "Have we all understood Mr. Parker?"

Everyone had understood Mr. Parker.

"Very good," He had apparently been taking notes during the boy's exposure. He glanced at them now. "We feel," he said, "that you have made very nice progress since you have been with us. Your freedom is becoming much—ah—much greater. You are less afraid than you were of letting us see your insides, so to say." The boy smiled, pleased, and there was an appreciative hum from the stu-dents and the visitors. "Yet—we feel that you are not ready for the classics. We admire your courage in pre-paring this scene, but it was, perhaps—but understandably—slightly overambitious. But there is nothing wrong, let us say, with aiming too high. We are here, not to suggest that you aim lower, but to make your aim more accurate. I hope you understand what we are saying?"

"Yes, sir," said the boy. He seemed very pleased in-deed.

"Well, then. Since you have brought us, not your in-terpretation of, but rather, so to say, your reaction to, Othello, we will try to discuss this baffling character for a moment. You mentioned that you wanted to convey Othello's grief. You hoped to make us feel his grief by means of his physical anguish. Why is he in grief, Mr. Parker?"

"Well," said Parker, "he just killed his wife—Desde-mona—the only girl who ever mattered to him. I mean, he loved her and now he's killed her, she's dead, and now he knows that he did wrong—I mean, that he was tricked, Iago tricked him into killing her." He paused. "So, now, he's all alone. In a way, he's killed himself."

"Do you think that his grief would be different if, in fact, he knew Desdemona to have been guilty?"

"Well, yes, sir, I think so. I mean, he'd still be alone, but at least he'd feel that the honorable thing had been done—that he's done the honorable thing. This just feels tricked. And by his buddy."

"Iago—his buddy—is white. Othello is bl Moor. Do you think that this affects Othello's react

"How so, sir?" Parker asked quickly. He seem easy; he looked quickly in my direction. Then, "No, don't see any reason why it should."

"Then, Othello is in pain only because of the crime he has committed?"

"I think so, sir. I don't think he would be thinking of Iago now at all—anyway, it's his fault for believing Iago."

"But we usually believe our friends," Saul said.

"Do we?" said Parker. "I don't." And everybody laughed. Saul laughed, too.

"Why did you feel it necessary, or advisable, to make Othello's pain physical? In some theatrical circles, that might seem—a little strange?"

"Well, Othello's a great play, I guess, but a lot of it seems a little silly—all that handkerchief stuff, and every-thing, I mean"—he was floundering—"if you think about what Othello's doing, well maybe, you'll just think he's dumb. But if you feel it—like a stomach ache—well, then, maybe you'll understand him." And he looked hope-fully, expectantly, at Saul.

"Well," said Saul, after a long pause, "you certainly

seem to have thought about your problems. We do not feel that you have resolved them, but, as we said before, we are not here to make you lower your aim, but to help you hit the target—on the bull's eye, so to say. We admire the *directness* of your approach to your problem— the idea of Othello with, so to say, a bellyache, we do not reject, as others might, no, we find it a very interesting idea. We feel that if your perceptions lead you into these areas, well and good. We wish to help you to explore; we are not afraid of any discovery; we are dedicated to discovery. We only insist that these discoveries be subjected to the proper theatrical discipline so that these discoveries can take their proper place in the vocabulary of the living theater. We are like, oh, Henry Ford, so to say— the theater is like that—we want the use of your inventions so that we can stay in business." The class laughed. "Thank you, Mr. Parker. Your progress is most gratifying."

Mr. Parker left the alcove. "Take ten," said the student who was acting as Saul's assistant that morning, and the maid brought out a pot of coffee, cups, saucers, milk, sugar, and cookies, and set them on the sideboard.

"Do you need any props?" Saul's assistant now asked Barbara.

"A sofa," I said. "Or a chair."

He had turned away; he turned back. "Well, which is it?"

"A sofa would be better," Barbara said. "Oh. And you know where the phonograph and the record are."

"Right," he said, and he went away. Barbara and I walked over to the coffee table, where the others were.

"Are you scared?" one of the girls asked me, smiling.

I grinned. "Yes," I said. And I suddenly realized that I was. I poured coffee for Barbara. "We didn't really need a sofa. I play the whole scene standing up."

"Well, but *I* can use a sofa, don't you see?" Barbara looked at me, and then she laughed. "You can just *do* more sitting on a sofa than you can sitting on a chair."

The assistant, passing, heard this, and he winked. "I can just see who's going to steal this scene," he said. I looked toward the alcove. The sofa and the phonograph were there.

I drank my coffee, and I listened to the chatter. When

the coffee hit my stomach, I realized I was sick, and I put
the coffee down, and barely made it to the bathroom. My
whole body was covered with a cold, light sweat, and I was
nauseous—perhaps Othello with a bellyache was not such
a bad idea. I had never felt this way before. I was sexually
excited, too, but in an eerie way; it was a tension which
contained no possibility of release. I came back to the
coffee table to find that people were sitting down. Barbara
was already in the alcove, and was talking to the assistant.
She seemed quite calm. What the hell, I told myself, it's
going to be over in less than ten minutes. And it doesn't
matter what these people think. But I wished we had
decided to do some other scene, any other scene. I no
longer believed in this one. Barbara had my book with
her, in the alcove. It was on the sofa. I rushed up, and
opened it, because I suddenly couldn't remember my first
lines.

My first line was, *Hello, Florrie*. I couldn't use my
book. I put it back down on the sofa. I hoped I knew the
scene well enough just to be able to go with it. The assistant picked up my book, and opened it. He stood there,
waiting. I looked at him. Then I realized that he was
going to read the short scene which precedes my entrance,
between Florrie and her brother, Irv, who doesn't want
Florrie to marry me.

I smiled, and said, "Sorry," and left the alcove.

"Nerves, nerves," said the assistant, and there was a
little burst of laughter.

They started.

"I got a right to have something out of life," Barbara
said, and she moved, sullenly, restlessly, about the alcove.
"I don't smoke, I don't drink. So if Sid wants to take me
to a dance, I'll go. Maybe if you was in love, you wouldn't
talk so hard."

"I'm saying it," read the assistant flatly, "for your
good."

I knew that Jerry had cued Barbara for this scene
many times, and yet it was odd to see her play it in a
vacuum. I had no idea whether she was any good or not,
and the way the assistant was reading the lines made it
impossible—for me—to believe in the scene at all. Barbara looked far too young, it seemed to me, to be saying

any of the things she was saying; if *I* had been her brother, I would have turned her over my knee. Still, she was sullen, she was upset, she was terribly nervous; only, I couldn't tell whether it was *she* who was nervous, or Florrie. She certainly sounded very close to hysteria by the time she shouted, "Sure, I want romance, love, babies. I want everything in life I can get!" And she didn't seem so young then. She seemed to know what was in store for her.

Here came my cue: ". . . Take the egg off the stove I boiled for Mom." Then she looked up, and insisted on a rather long silence—long enough to make one wonder. The assistant nervously looked at his—or, rather, *my* book. Barbara turned away. "Leave us alone, Irv."

I stepped into the alcove. The assistant and I stared at each other a moment, and then he disappeared—with my book. Then Barbara turned back, and looked at me.

"Hello, Florrie," I said.

"Hello, honey. You're looking tired."

When she said that, I thought of our walk through town.

"Naw," I said. "I just need a shave."

And so we hit it. She looked so young, so helpless, and so fair. Sid wants to keep her looking as she looks now forever; but he has nothing to give her, nothing which won't blast her into some other unimaginable, unbearable condition; he knows this as the scene begins, but must face it as the scene progresses. Barbara, too, was thinking of our walk through town. Finally, she breaks and runs to kiss me. I say, "You look tired, Florrie."

"Naw," said Barbara, holding on to my upper arms, throwing back her head and laughing at me, "I just need a shave." Then she threw her head against my chest, buried her head in my chest, and held me. This was not the way we had played the scene before. I held her, and I said, "You worried about your mother?"

"No," she said. But she had not moved; and I was taking my cue from her.

I said gently, "What's on your mind?"

"The French and Indian War," she said, and I now understood, holding her by the shoulder, that I could move her slightly away from me and look into her face. "What's on your mind?"

"I got us on my mind, Sid." She looked at me. "Night and day, Sid!"

Well, now I was in the scene and so I couldn't know —it didn't matter—whether we were any good or not. I dropped her shoulders, and I walked away, leaving her standing there. I thought of our morning and I thought of our walk when I said, "I smacked a beer truck today . . . Did I get hell! I was driving along thinking of US, too. You don't have to say it—I know what's on your mind. I'm rat poison around here."

"Not," she said helplessly, "to me . . ."

The scene shifts gears around then, it becomes really very propagandistic, and I had always been most worried about this long section, because the boy has most of the speeches, and because it's hard to speak propaganda while relating to love. But, this morning, it seemed to work; maybe I was still thinking about our walk. Sid starts raving about his younger brother, who has joined the Navy, because he doesn't know what else to do: ". . . Don't he come around and say to you this millionaire with a jazz band—listen Sam or Sid or what's-your-name,—you're no good, but here's a chance. The whole world'll know who you are—yes, sir, he said,—get up on that ship and fight those bastards who's making the world a lousy place to live in. The Japs, the Turks, the Greeks.—Take this gun —kill the slobs like a real hero, he says, a real American. Be a hero!"

I have no idea what I sounded like. The scene drops, then, back into the intensity of the boy and girl. Barbara looked very beautiful, I thought, when she said, "Sid, I'll go with you—we'll get a room somewhere."

But he refuses this. He turns on the phonograph, and they dance. Then he says good-bye. She doesn't answer. That's when I get a chance to do my tapdance routine. And I whistle *Rosy O'Grady*. It felt all right. Barbara was staring at me.

"Don't you like it?" I asked her. It was a real question.

She stared at me for a long time; which forced me to stare at her. Then she said, "No," and dropped her face in her hands, with all her hair falling around her fingers. I dropped on my knees in front of her, and put my face in her lap. She held me. And that was the end of the scene.

I lifted my head, and we looked at each other very briefly, while we listened to the applause, and then I rose, and we sat together on the sofa, facing Saul San-Marquand.

Saul cleared his throat.

"As all of you know," he said, "this last scene is really an audition. That is, neither Miss King, nor"—he considered the program—"Mr. Proudhammer—ah—are really working members of The Actors' Means Workshop. We consider them both to be—ah—very gifted young people."

At this, there was scattered, tentative applause. Saul raised his hand.

"As Miss King is the lady here, or"—he coughed—"certainly, so to say, represents the female principle, we will interrogate Miss King first. Miss King"—he straightened, and Barbara straightened—"why did you elect to do this scene?"

"We liked it," Barbara said. She paused. "We felt that it made a connection—between a private love story —and—a—well, between a private sorrow and a public, a *revolutionary* situation." She paused again. Saul watched her. She watched Saul. "The boy and girl are trapped. For reasons that they can't do much about, anything about— and it's not their fault—not their fault, I mean, that they're trapped."

"Then, your motives in doing this particular scene," said Saul, "were personal?" He looked briefly at me.

"One's motives," said Barbara, sitting very still and straight, "are always personal." Then, after a second, "I hope." And she lifted her eyes to Saul again.

"One's motives," he said, "may always be personal. But one's execution, as I believe you have heard us attempt to tell Mr. Parker, can never be personal. One's motives, ah, that is one thing—but one's execution of these motives, if one is attempting to work in the theater—these must be quite something else again."

"I don't," she said flatly, with a certain calculated rudeness, "know what you're talking about." And she watched him. The silence, like water, rose.

"Miss King," he said, "we are suggesting that your

execution of this scene—which is, if we may say so, a very beautiful scene, and we had the distinction of being present the very first time it was ever played, has been somewhat carried away by your motives." He raised his hand again. "Do not misunderstand us. We admire your motives. We were a revolutionary before you were born, Miss King—and the scene you have just attempted to play is a revolutionary scene. Written by a revolutionary. So, we are in sympathy with your motives." He paused. "But we must question your execution. That is what we are here for." He paused. "What were you working for in this scene, Miss King?"

"I was working," she said—I had never seen her so arrogant, and I rather wondered at it—"at the truth in the scene. They are probably never going to see each other again. And they both know it."

She had left him supposing that she was about to say more. But she said nothing.

"Excuse me, Miss King, but do you know the play? Do you know *why*—it is called *Waiting for Lefty?* Do you know, for example, that your boyfriend goes on strike? And that this changes everything—that they do *not* lose each other?"

"I know the play," she said.

The silence rose and rose; and it was going to be my turn next. The silence rose; and Barbara watched Saul. In the silence, Barbara said, "When they're facing each other in this scene, she can't know, neither of them can know, if they're ever going to see each other again. You don't play what the playwright knows. You play what the character knows." And then she paused, and marvelously conceded, with a smile, "Isn't that so?"

"My dear Miss King," said Saul, after a moment, "we certainly do not wish to make you feel that our more than forty years in the theater is more valuable than your time on earth." There was laughter at this, and Saul also smiled.

And Barbara said, "I very much doubt that anything you can say will make me feel that your time on earth is more valuable than mine."

Everyone was now watching Barbara and Saul, as though we were watching a horse race. But Saul, whatever he wasn't, was shrewd; and his pride had never been a burden. "We like your spirit," he said briefly, "but your spirit is perhaps more interesting offstage than it is on—what do you know about the girl in this scene?"

"I know that she has probably just finished washing the dishes, and her hands are probably still a little damp. I know she can't stand the house she lives in—it makes her feel as though she's in jail." She paused. "She's scared —scared that she'll never get out of jail. She's in love with Sid, but sometimes she almost hates him, too, and— well, she's a virgin. That scares her, too. Maybe that scares her more than anything else."

"Pardon me, Miss King. Have you ever lived—as this girl lives?"

"No. But I've never lived the life of Lady Macbeth, either. And no actress has."

Perhaps Saul could live without being burdened by pride; but he could not live without his control over that world he had made. And Barbara was beginning to jeopardize it. The interest in the scene was shifting from him to her. He cleared his throat. We waited.

"Miss King," he said, "when we said that we admired your spirit, we did not mean to suggest that we approved of bad manners. You are far from being able to play anything at all, let alone Lady Macbeth. If you are here to learn, we will endeavor to help you. If you are here, so to say, to show off, then we must tell you that we cannot tolerate such behavior. We have others to consider, Miss King. We cannot waste *their* time."

Barbara backed down, but not without a brief struggle, and remaining, anyway, irreducibly sardonic. "I'm terribly sorry," she said. "I apologize. I wasn't trying to hog the scene."

Saul watched her. "You have not given us enough for us to be able to criticize you. We would like you to enroll in the Speech class, and in the Dance class. In about two weeks, we would like to see an improvisation. But we will discuss that with you later." He turned to me. "Mr.— Proudhammer!" He looked again at Barbara. "You may step down, Miss King."

Barbara left the alcove.

"Mr. Proudhammer," Saul said, "you, too, are an extremely spirited young person, as you have given us occasion, lately, to realize." There was some laughter at this. "Unfortunately, in spite of your—ah—spirit, we would say that your equipment for the theater is extremely meager." He paused, and raised one hand. "This is not said in condemnation. We know of some names in the theater—not many, but some—who seemed to have no promise at all when they first began. If we had seen some very celebrated names at their beginning, we would have declined to teach them. We would have suggested that they were out of place in the theater. We would have been wrong. We do not mind saying so." He paused. "But we must tell you that these—ah—actors that we have in mind had to struggle for many years against—ah—limits—limits for which no one could blame them, which were not their fault, but—ah—limits which were nonetheless extremely severe, and which handicapped them greatly." He paused again. "The actor's instrument, Mr. Proudhammer, is unlike any instrument used in art. A writer's instrument is his pen, a violinist has a violin, a sculptor has stone and a chisel, an architect has a slide rule, and so forth. But an actor's instrument is his body, is himself. Paul Robeson, for example, is an actor who was made to play Othello. The instrument suggests it, the instrument, so to say, demands it. Other actors could never play Othello. The instrument will not carry the illusion." He coughed, and looked around the room. "We do not wish to say that anything is impossible. We know of a great French actor who is—ah—a hunchback. Art, like life, is full of exceptions. But these exceptions—prove the rule." He looked at me again. "You are certainly an exception. Frankly, we find it difficult to know exactly how to proceed with you. There is nothing to indicate—ah—in our opinion—that you have any very striking theatrical ability. Except, perhaps, for that little dance at the very end of the scene. Then you seemed free, and, so to say, joyous and boyish. We found it your very best moment. And if we decide to continue with you—or if you decide to continue with us—it will be in the hope that we can make such moments come more easily to you."

I said nothing with my voice; I hoped I said nothing with my face.

"This is," he said, after a moment, "a somewhat unexpected scene for you and Miss King to present to us. Why did you choose this particular scene?"

"We thought we could play it," I said. He was making me feel foolish. I had to clear my throat, and I hated myself. "We liked it."

"What do you know about—ah—the young hack—Sid—in this scene?"

I said, "He's a poor boy. I'm a poor boy. He's hungry. *I'm* hungry."

"You look fairly well fed to me," said Saul. This elicited a small wave of laughter. I pressed my palms together. "You do not drive a cab," he said.

"I drive the Workshop car," I said. Then, I wished I hadn't said it. I'd forgotten about the goddamn car.

"But you are not, we hope, about to go on strike against the Workshop." This caused more laughter. "You are not trying to unionize your fellow workers. You are paid a living wage. And you are young to be considering marriage." He reconsidered: "Young, certainly, that is, from a *legal* point of view." He watched me. "We do not think that you have entered into the problems of the young taxi driver at all. We do not think you understood them. We doubt, frankly, that you so much as considered them. You were bombastic, hysterical, and self-pitying. You sounded like a schoolboy who has been beaten up at school. We found it hard to imagine that Florrie would wish to marry you. Frankly, our entire sympathy was with her brother."

He had me; he knew it; there was nothing I dared say.

"As we said earlier to Mr. Parker, there is nothing wrong with aiming too high. Frankly, we think it possible that you *must* aim too high. We are not here to discourage. But we must tell you when we feel that you are aiming at a target which it will simply be impossible for you ever to reach." He paused again. "But you are—ah—a spirited young man, and—ah—we will see what we can do. You will enroll in the Speech class. And we will speak with you concerning an improvisation in the next few days." He looked at his watch. "That is all, for the present."

The class applauded. I stepped out of the alcove.

Barbara had been cornered by Saul. The others did not quite know what to say to me. I walked outside. The car stood in the driveway. Jerry sat in the car.

I walked over to him. It may be odd, but I felt that he was just about the only friend I had in the world. But we couldn't be friends, either.

I stood at the car door, and we stared at each other. He looked very tired. His hair was dirty. He hadn't shaved.

"How's it going?" he asked. His voice sounded dry—light, as though the wind were turning it over, playing with it, blowing it about.

"Jerry," I said, "I'm sorry. I just want you to know I'm sorry. I wouldn't have hurt you for anything—anything in the world. I swear it. If I'd known—I swear—I'd have gone away."

He said, "It's not your fault. I know that."

"It isn't anybody's fault," I said, "is it?"

"Not that I know of," he said. He switched the ignition on, then switched it off. "I just mowed a lawn. Now, I've got to get to my Life class." He looked at me. "I figured you'd need the car. I put some gas in her." He patted the dashboard. "So. I'll be getting along."

"You want me to drive you? I'll drive you."

"They'll be needing you here, won't they?"

"They can go fuck themselves," I said. I got in the car. He moved over. "Fuck 'em." I started the car, and we rolled down the driveway. We hit the streets of the town. I said nothing because I did not know what to say. I hurt for Jerry, and I hurt for me. Neither did Jerry say anything. Everything seemed such a waste.

We stopped before the headquarters of the fig-leaf division.

"Well," Jerry said, and opened his door, "I'll be seeing you, kid. Thanks for the ride." Then, with his last words hanging on the air, we stared at each other.

"Jerry," I said—why was I frightened?—"please forgive me. I didn't mean to hurt you. I really didn't mean to hurt you."

"It's not you who hurt me," he said. He slapped me on the neck quickly, and smiled. "I love you, too," he said. He got out of the car, and slammed the door. He started walking away, then turned. He said, "You got any money?"

I said, "No."

He walked back to the car and handed me a dollar. "I'll have more tonight. I guess we'll be changing rooms." He smiled, frowned, and shook his head. "I didn't mean that. I got to be hauling ass out of here. I just don't know." He shook his head again, and his tears spangled the air. He turned away. "So long, Leo."

"So long, Jerry."

I watched him walk into the house and watched the door close behind him. I sat in the car. I lit a cigarette. Automatically, I turned the car around, to go back to the Workshop. Then I thought, Fuck it, and I turned the car around again, and drove out of town and hit the highway for New York.

BOOK THREE:

Black Christopher

Mother, take your daughter,
  father, take your son!
You better run to the city of refuge,
  you better run!

                    —Traditional

THE BOY sat on the bed, watching me. Everything seemed tilted, he and the bed, as though about to slide off a cliff; this was because of my weariness and the angle at which I lay in the bed and the fact that it was so early in the morning.

I was a little frightened for a moment: but the boy smiled.

"Do you always get up so early?—what time is it?"

He laughed. "No. But I got some people to see today. It's about seven."

He was staring at me, making up his mind about something.

"Do you want me to make you some coffee?"

"No. No, stay in bed. You've really had it." He watched me. "You were pretty drunk last night."

"I know."

"You remember everything?"

"Well—I think I do. Why? Did I do something terrible?"

He laughed again. "No. You were fine. You danced a lot and you laughed a lot. I think you were happy."

"I think I was. Were you?"

He looked away, still smiling a little. "Oh, yeah," he said.

I wanted to get back to sleep, but he was beginning to intrigue me, to wake me up. It was his smile. It made his face like a light. And his voice was rough, like a country boy's voice, and he was big, and his manner was rough. But his smile was very shy and gentle.

"I've got to go now. Can I come to see you later?"

"I'll be home all day—until it's time to go to the theater."

"Well, I'll call you later." He stood up. "If I don't make it back before you go, you want me to pick you up after the show?"

"Yes. That'll be good."

"All right. See you." He leaned down and kissed me quickly on the forehead. He started for the bedroom door.

"You got enough money?"

"I'm all right." He smiled again, and disappeared. I heard the front door close behind him.

I wondered what I had got myself into.

I am at last about to leave the hospital. Pete has brought me my clothes. I do not want to see Caleb, but Caleb will be meeting the plane in New York—in spite of everything, or perhaps because of everything, I am still his little brother, and besides I am famous. Barbara cannot come East with me because the show is still running —though not doing very well—and she will be along presently to take me off to her suite, where I will spend what is left of this day and where I will spend the night. In the morning, I fly away.

Presently, some of the cast will be here with champagne; also, some of the press. But Barbara will be here before them. Pete is here already. I am dressed, and standing in the office with Dr. Evin. And since I am dressed and my hair has been cut and I am wearing *my* clothes and standing in my own skin, I feel—in a way— absolutely in control, delivered again to the land of the living. It is not yet and not now that Leo Proudhammer gives up the ghost! Not yet. Not now. Leo is a very tough little mother.

I am ready: dark-blue suit, blue tie, impeccable handkerchief, white shirt, Brazilian cufflinks, black pumps. I am a star again. I look it and I feel it. It is as though I had never been ill.

But Dr. Evin does not agree with me.

"You have been very ill. I counsel you not to forget that fact." He looks at me very hard. "If you do not remember how ill you have been, you may very well become ill again. I tried to warn you at the beginning—do you remember?"

"Yes. Of course, I remember."

He smiles. "I am not absolutely persuaded that you do—but I will not scold you any more. After all, I was very pleased, like the selfish man I am, to make your acquaintance. And I have more respect now than I did for the—stamina—of your tribe. I am not being racist." We both laugh. "I mean the tribe of show business people." Then, his face changed, he stood up. "Ah! Here is Miss King. Miss King, we deliver him back to you—very slightly damaged, but, with care, he should last"—he looks at me speculatively, smiling; I realized that he really had grown to like me—"oh, twenty, thirty years. If you do not try to drive him up the steep slopes."

"*I,*" said Barbara, "will do anything you say, doctor. But you know, by now, what a stubborn child Leo is." She kissed me. "Look at him! Where do you suppose he thinks he's going, Dr. Evin? He's dressed for an opening night. Darling," she said, "you are merely going to walk to an elevator which is just down the hall and then be gently handed into a car which will drive you straight to my house, where you will immediately take off all those clothes and lie about in state."

"I thought," I said, "that I should look my best, in case of the newspapers. So all my fans will know that I'm recovered."

"Oh," said Barbara, and looked at Dr. Evin, "*I* see. You certainly got him well, doctor, and all his fans are grateful." She smiled, very happy, looking like a little girl. "Some of the cast have come by, and they've brought some champagne. Come, join us, doctor—then *you* can go home and have a nice, quiet heart attack."

She laughed and took us both by the arm and we walked down the corridor to my old room.

There they were, the people with whom I'd been in the play so long. Perhaps, for others, it was only a play, but it was more than that for us, it was a part of our lives and this meant that we were now a part of each other. There really is a kind of fellowship among people in the theater and I've never seen it anywhere else, except among jazz musicians. Our relationships are not peaceful and they certainly are not static, but, in a curious way, they're steady. I think it may be partly because we're forced, in spite of the preposterous airs we very often give ourselves, to level with each other. Everybody knows what's going on in the business, everybody has to know and so some lies cannot be told. One's disasters are as public as one's triumphs, and far more numerous; and everybody knows how it feels. And I think it's also because we're forced to depend on each other more than other people are. I shouldn't think, for example, that trapeze artists are in the habit of having bitter fights with each other just before they climb the high ladder, and start somersaulting about in space. If the bar or the hand isn't there when it's supposed to be, well, then, without a net, that's it. And in the theater, one's always operating without a net. Of course, the theater is full of people whom no one can stand, and careers the mere existence of which fill one with wonder; but one becomes philosophical about this, for not even the most outrageous or destructive theatrical career can begin to rival some of the careers taking place in the world. Here was Andy, an Italian character actor who was playing a featured part in the play—we hadn't worked together for years, but when we met again it was as though we'd never parted; and Amy, blonde, young, wispy, from the Bronx, with whom I'd never worked before, but whom I liked very much; and Sylvia, a fine, tough, mannish Negro character actress, whose age would now never be known, because her hometown courthouse had been burned to the ground—by Sylvia, some people said, and it wasn't hard to see her doing it; and my adored, my steady and steadying Pete; and the chief electrician, Sando; and the doorman, John, and his wife; and my understudy, Alvin, whom I'd never liked very much, but liked today—he seemed to like me, too, and it wasn't only because he knew I wasn't coming back to the show; and some others. The room was crowded, very beautifully crowded. There were flowers and records and boxes of candy. Amy, her face very bright beneath a stylish velvet toque, came over to me with an envelope and an oddly shaped package. First, she kissed me ceremoniously, on both sides of my face.

"Everybody couldn't come," she said. "You know—some people take jobs on radio and television and stuff like that—and *those* peasants"—now she held the envelope very distastefully with her thumb and one finger—"have asked me to give you *this*." I took the envelope from her, and opened it. It was a big card, with a caricature of me on the front as the skinniest boxer you ever saw, with the biggest, most frightened eyes, and the most awkward stance. On the outside, it said—because I'd scored a great triumph when I'd played this part in *Cabin in the Sky*—LITTLE JOE! And on the inside, it said,

"We Glad You Win!" It was signed by every member of
the crew and company. It was very nice. We were all
laughing. My little nurse came in, with a tray of glasses.

"And now," said Amy gravely, "you must open this.
This is from all of us."

I took the package, which was surprisingly heavy. I
wondered how Amy had managed to carry it. I sat down
on the bed, to open it. They were all watching me.

I finally got the package open. Inside, there were two
bronze lions, replicas of the lions in Trafalgar Square.
The card said, "For Leo, the lion. Long may he wail."

"You can use them as bookends. Or paperweights,"
said Amy.

"Or in order to get a taxi," said Barbara.

We all broke out laughing, and that saved me from
crying. I grabbed Amy and kissed her and I kissed Sylvia
and Barbara and I hugged all the men and Pete said,
"Here goes," and he opened the champagne. "A toast,"
said Pete, and he raised his glass and looked at me.

Some moments in a life, and they needn't be very
long or seem very important, can make up for so much in
that life; can redeem, justify, that pain, that bewilderment, with which one lives, and invest one with the courage not only to endure it, but to profit from it; some
moments teach one the price of the human connection: if
one can live with one's own pain, then one respects the
pain of others, and so, briefly, but transcendentally, we
can release each other from pain. Something like this
message I seemed to read in Pete's eyes as he raised his
glass and looked at me. His eyes held my journey, and his
own. His eyes held the years of terror, trembling, hatred,
scorn, inhuman isolation; the YMCA, the Mills Hotel,
the winter streets, the subways, the rooftops, the public
baths, the public toilets, the filthy socks, the nights one
wept alone on some vermin-infested bed; the faithless
loves, the lost loves, the hope of love; the many deaths,
and the fear of death; in all of this, some style evolving,
some music endlessly being played, ringing inexorable
changes on the meaning of the blues. His look was
shrewd, ironic, loving. He knew how frightened I had
been. He knew how frightened he had been.

"A toast," he said, "to our baby, little Leo—we're
glad you came back to us, baby, and don't you be making

no more journeys like that in a hurry, do you hear?"

We laughed again. We had to laugh, perhaps I most of all. I said, "May I propose a toast? Let *me* propose a toast."

"Hear, hear!" said Barbara.

And then, for a moment, I did not know what to say; and I looked at them and they looked at me. I met the eyes of Alvin, my understudy. Alvin was a very good-looking black, or, rather, colored cat, a little bit older than I, and bigger than I; and I am not good-looking. I abruptly understood, as though I had just come back from the dead—which was, after all, nearly the literal truth; and a tremor went through me; I saw Barbara's face, and I was incredibly aware of the sun coming through the curtains—that I had been wrong in supposing that Alvin did not like me. It wasn't that. It was just that I fucked up his sense of reality. He did not know why what, as he supposed, had happened to me had not happened to him. According to the order which had created him and in which, for all his stridency, he yet absolutely believed, he had been dealt a much better hand than mine. This meant, for me, that Alvin did not know the ruthless rules of the game, and since he really did not know what had happened to me, did not know what had happened to him. As long as he did not know this, no one and nothing could help him. He would spend his life envying the blood in the shoes of others. I remembered myself trying to say this to Christopher. And I dropped my eyes from Alvin's, thinking of Christopher's response, and thinking of Caleb. I had supposed that Alvin disliked me because I am a better actor than he. And I *am* a better actor. But in that fact, precisely, lies hidden the unspeakable question, the unendurable truth.

"It is not important," I said, "to be an actor. The world is full of actors—most of them don't know that they are acting. And it's not important to be a star—most stars can't act." I stopped. They were still watching me. I had struck a more somber note than I had meant to strike. I looked for Barbara's face, and Pete's face. Their faces reassured me. They knew their boy. It had cost them something: and they would never let me see the bill. "Well," I said, "if those things are not important, let me say that it *is* important—it is beautiful—to know, when you stand on your feet again, that so many people are glad to see you standing. I'm glad to be back." I raised my glass. "But if you hadn't wanted me back, I might very well not be here. Let me drink to you," I said, "and let me thank you for holding on to me. I'll never forget it." I had no more words, and I drained my champagne glass. They stomped their feet lightly on the floor, for their hands were not free. Barbara drained her glass as I drained mine, and set it down and clapped her hands. It was—somehow—the most extraordinary sound.

"We've got to send the prince home in a few minutes," Pete said. "Who wants more champagne? We got one more bottle."

Then, I sat on the bed and I looked at my records, the records they had bought for me: Sam Cooke and Mahalia Jackson and Ray Charles and Miles Davis and Nina Simone and Joe Williams and Joe Tex and Lena Horne; and I thought what a comfort they would be to me, what a ball I would have with them in the south of France, where I would now be going, to sit in a borrowed villa and think over my life and recover my health and eventually read the script and sign the contract which would bring me back to work again. I realized that I was frightened. This would be the first time in more than twenty years that I had not, in one way or another, been working. When a worker is not working, what does a worker do? I knew that I was chilled by the fear of what I might find in myself with all my harness off, my obligations canceled, no lawyers, no agents, no producers, no television appearances, no civil-rights speeches, no reason to be here or there, no lunches at the Plaza, no dinners at Sardi's, no opening nights, no gossip columnists, no predatory reporters, no *Life and Loves of Leo Proudhammer* (in six installments, beginning in this issue!), no need to smile when I did not want to smile, no need, indeed, to do anything but be myself. But who was this self? Had he left forever the house of my endeavor and my fame? Or was he merely having a hard time breathing beneath the rags and the rubble of the closets I had not opened in so long?

Amy sat down on the bed beside me. She said, "I suppose you've heard the rumors?"

"I never listen to rumors," I said, "and if you want to stay alive in this business, you won't, either."

She laughed. She was a very, very attractive girl—not pretty exactly, but, then, I don't like pretty girls; but attractive, really attractive. Her teeth were a little big, and her face was a little too thin—she was very thin altogether, no hips at all, or, rather, the kind of hips that don't exist until you hold them. My body had been functioning all those weeks I'd been in bed, and, abruptly, seriously, I was terribly horny. I shifted a little bit away from her, more astonished than embarrassed. This particular aspect of Lazarus' return had not before occurred to me: but it certainly made sense. To come up from the place where one thought one was dead means that one becomes greedy for life, and life is many things, but it is, above all, the touch of another. The touch of another: no matter how transient, at no matter what price.

Then I remembered that I was nearly forty, and this frenzy, so I had been told, occurred in men of my age. I looked at Amy again. We had one very short, but very crucial scene in the play. We had been face to face for months, but I had never looked at her before. It scarcely seemed possible. I thought, You'll never work again, old buddy, you've had it, you've gone completely to pieces. I was looking at her face, but I was thinking of her cunt, of what it would be like to go down on this skinny little girl, how it would feel to hold her, to go inside her, how we should move together, and how she would be when she came.

She did not seem to know what I was thinking. She said, "Well. The rumor is that they're going to halt production on *Big Deal*—they were just about ready to go, you know—until you're well enough to play the reporter."

"That's quite a rumor," I said. But I was pleased. A kind of chill made me cough. Barbara looked sharply in my direction, and so did Pete. Pete drained his glass, and Barbara picked up her mink. Alvin came over and sat down on the bed.

"I'm glad you're going to be all right, fellow," he said. And he really meant it. He meant it as much as he could mean it.

"Thank you," I said. But I was suddenly very tired. I thought, You've been ill and you're not well yet. I thought, Maybe you'll never really get well again.

"We got to clear this joint now, folks!" Pete cried. "We got to take the patient home!"

"Isn't it a *nice* rumor?" Amy asked. "Especially—you know—to take away with you?"

"What rumor?" asked Alvin.

I put my fist under Amy's chin, and smiled at her. "Rumors, rumors. It's sweet of you to tell me. But I'm afraid it'll be a long time before I'm ready to work again." I looked at Alvin. "I'm going to go away," I said. "I'm going to go back to the Mediterranean and sit there dressed in nothing but those loincloths we used to wear in Africa before the goddamn missionaries got there, and look at the sea and have some sweet girl take care of me and think about my life and walk up and down the beach and read some of the books I've been saying I was going to read and roll in that sea and get burned in that sun and eat and eat"—Lord, how quickly I had got drunk! —"and maybe weep a little and pull myself together. But it won't be the same self. I guarantee you that." I stood up because I didn't want Barbara to be embarrassed by suggesting that I stand up. "After that," I said suddenly, for Barbara's sake, sober again, and smiling, "I might go back to work. Or I might join the church. Except there isn't any church." I was not sober. I was very melancholy.

"There're a whole lot of churches, man," Alvin said.

"Exactly my point," I said, and straightened, really straightened this time, then bent to pick up my card and my records and my lions. "You've got to forgive me. Now, I've got to go."

I bent, and kissed Amy on the cheek. Alvin stood, and we shook hands. Dr. Evin took the records and the card from me and Pete took the lions.

"Let's go, old buddy," he said, and took my arm and we started for the door. But I stopped to kiss my dazzled little nurse on the forehead.

"Be good," I said. "And come to see me soon—soon, I hope."

"You know I will," she said. "You know I will." She looked dazed and radiant and cheerful—this poor little girl who had had to empty my shit and wash my ass and my cock and balls. She would touch, for many days, the spot on her forehead where I had kissed her. Her face taught me, on the instant, something of the male power and the female hope, something of the male and female loneliness, and it deepened, on the instant, my already sufficiently bitter awareness of the bottomless and blasphemous hypocrisy of my country.

Then—as they cheered—we walked out of my room, Dr. Evin, and Barbara, and Pete, and I, down the corridor to the elevator.

"I hope we will meet again," said Dr. Evin. "I know you know I do not mean that the way it may sound." He smiled.

"I would like very much to see you again," I said. "You have been very nice to me."

"Ah! that was very difficult," he said, and smiled again. The elevator came, and he held the door and gave the packages he carried to Pete. "Good-bye," he said to Pete, and "Good-bye," he said to Barbara. There was a pause. Barbara kissed him on the cheek, and Pete, heavy-laden, smiled. "Take care of yourself," said the doctor gravely to me. Then he allowed the elevator doors to close, and we started down.

"There'll be some reporters waiting downstairs," Pete said. "I thought it was better not to have them come up." He grinned. "Reporters and champagne don't mix."

"We're going to be very tyrannical," Barbara said, "and get rid of them in a hurry. Reporters. The most loathsome parasites on earth. If they had any self-respect, they'd find a rock and crawl under it." The elevator landed, the doors opened. She took my arm. Pete preceded us.

There they were, about ten or twelve of them, with notebooks and cameras. There was a television crew in the streets. It's impossible to describe what it feels like to be facing a gang of reporters, to have the camera's lights flashing around your head and in your eyes. It occasions a peculiarly subtle and difficult war within oneself. In a bitter way, the fact that one is half blinded by the staccato lights is a help, for it means that one can't see anything very clearly, especially not the faces of the reporters. If one really looked into those faces, one would certainly blow one's cool. But the war I mentioned is subtle and difficult—and, at bottom, base—because everyone loves

attention, loves to be thought important. Here are all
these people, the innocent ego proudly contends, here to
talk to you, here because of you. You are, literally, then,
one among countless millions. You are news. Whatever
you do is news. But it does not take long to realize, at
least assuming that one wishes to live, that to be news is
really to be nothing; that the attention paid to one's vicis-
situdes is merely the most cunning way yet devised of
making the adventure of one's life a farce. He woke up
this morning, or he didn't—either way, it's a story—and
he brushed his teeth or he didn't, and then he peed, or
didn't, and then he shit, or he couldn't, and then he
fucked his wife or his broad, or he fucked his boy or his
boy fucked him, or they blew each other, or they didn't—
it's a story, either way, any way: it is all, all, there in the
eager faces of the reporters.

"How are you, Mr. Proudhammer! Good to see you
on your feet!"

"Actually," I said, unwisely, "I'm leaning on Miss
King."

Pete took the ball, and carried it. "Mr. Proudhammer,
as you know, has been ill, and we can't have him leaning
on Miss King too long. So, let's get it over with, quick."

"Would you like a chair, Mr. Proudhammer?" somebody asked, and before I could answer somebody brought
me one. I looked briefly at Barbara, who nodded, and I
sat down.

"We hear you're going to do the movie *Big Deal*. Is
that true?"

"I won't be working for awhile. And no one's approached me about it yet."

"What *are* your immediate plans, Mr. Proudhammer?"

"To go away and rest."

"Where will you go?"

"I'll be in France for awhile."

"Why France? Any particular reason?"

"I have friends in France. One of them has a house by
the sea."

"*Big deal!*" somebody said, and they laughed. The
lights flashed and flashed, their faces gaped and grinned.
I don't tire easily; but I was very tired now. My God, I
thought, I must have been goddamn fucking sick.

"How do you feel about that, Mr. Proudhammer?
—about *Big Deal?* I mean, a few years ago, they wouldn't
have dreamed of putting a Negro in that part."

"You must forgive me. I don't know the script."

I thought of Christopher, and I almost said, Who is
this mighty *they,* and *who* and *where* is Negro? but I
thought, Fuck it. What these wide-eyed, gimlet-eyed, bright-
eyed cock-suckers do *not* know is about to kill them. Before
my eyes.

"Well, it's a role which could be played by any actor.
I mean, it's got nothing to do with race."

Don't blow your cool, said Leo to Leo.

"Oh? Then that's a great departure for the industry.
I'm honored that they thought of me."

"Oh, come on, Mr. Proudhammer. You're one of the
biggest stars we have. No Negro's ever made it as big as
you. It must mean a lot to—your people."

Don't blow your cool, baby. Do *not* blow your cool.

I said, "I don't think it helps them to pay the rent."

"Oh," said a lady reporter, some fat bitch from Queens
—I just knew it—"there are much more important things
than just paying the rent, don't you think so, Mr. Proudhammer?"

"No," I said. "Do you?"

Barbara touched me on the shoulder.

They scribbled it all in their notebooks—God knows
what they were scribbling. God knows I didn't care. I
looked at Pete, and I stood up. Pete moved the chair
away, and Barbara took my arm. Pete said, "We've got to
go now, folks. I'm sorry, but it's doctor's orders."

We started moving, and lights started flashing again.

"Miss King! What are *your* plans?"

"Our tour ends next month, in Hollywood. And I
stay on, then, to do a movie, *Jethro's Daughter.*"

They wrote it all down.

"And when will you and Mr. Proudhammer be working
together again?"

"Soon," said Barbara.

"On stage or on screen?"

"Both. And on television."

"Any firm commitments—anything that can be an-
nounced?"

"We're reading scripts."

"Will you be in touch with Mr. Proudhammer while he is abroad?"

"I will, or we'll get a new postmaster."

"Miss King—I know you won't mind my saying this, you surely must have heard it already—it has sometimes been suggested that your—ah—friendship with Mr. Proudhammer has sometimes tended to compromise your career. That is—putting it bluntly—because some sections of the country still hold very backward ideas about race, and you are white and Mr. Proudhammer is a Negro, and you are friends, some roles which might have been offered to you were not offered to you. Is this true?"

"Is it? I have no idea. I was a little girl when they did *Gone With the Wind*, but since then I've been doing just fine, thank you."

We got into the wind, and there was the television crew, and a man thrust a mike at me and Pete grabbed his arm and held it.

"This man has been sick," he said. "Now, if you want to talk to him, you come on gentle, or you can forget it."

"I'm sorry. I didn't mean to be rough."

"One question," said Barbara, "and one question only. And if your crew isn't ready, it's just too bad. Mr. Proudhammer is still under a doctor's care."

He didn't like her tone. He looked at me and he looked at her. And if we had not been Barbara King and Leo Proudhammer, victims of the economy in a way which it was quite beyond his poor power to understand—looking at Barbara in her mink, and me in my very expensive trenchcoat, and seeing the great black limousine waiting at the curb—what he really felt would have come rushing out, and our blood would have been all over the streets. Along with his, I must say. We looked each other in the eye. He held the mike. The cameras rolled in.

"You've put up a very gallant battle against death," he said—Fuck you! I thought—"and all of America, along with Miss King, I'm sure, have been praying that you would live. One question, one question only, Mr. Proudhammer, because we understand that you are still under a doctor's care: how does it feel to know that you mean so much to so many people?"

I thought of Christopher. I thought of Barbara. I said,

"It makes me feel a tremendous obligation to stay well. It makes me know that I did not make myself—I do not belong to me."

He looked tremendously baffled, but he smiled. "Thank you, Mr. Proudhammer."

"Thank *you*," I said. And we got into the car.

Amy passed, talking to Alvin, then Sylvia, talking to Andy. They all waved. The car moved forward, up a hill.

I really can't bear any of the American cities I know, and I know, or at least I've traveled through, most of them. And most of them seem very harsh and hostile, and they are exceedingly ugly. When an American city has any character, any flavor at all, it's apt to be, as in the case, for example, of Chicago, rather like a soup which has everything in it, but which is now old, tepid, and rancid, with all of the ingredients turned sour. All of the American cities seem boiling in a kind of blood pudding, thick, sticky, foul, and pungent, and it can make you very sad to walk through, say, New Orleans and ask yourself just why a city with no unconquerable physical handicaps, after all, should yet be so relentlessly uninhabitable. Some key, I suppose, is afforded by the faces, which also seem uninhabitable—at least by any of the more promising human attributes. They look like people who are, or who would like to be, cops; or else, with a sad emphasis, they look like people who would *not* like to be cops. And I've often thought that if Hitler had had the California police force working for him, he would surely be in business still—not that I am persuaded that he ever retired; the business was his in name only—but, distrustfully, all the same, I like San Francisco because it is on so many hills, one's always looking, walking, up or down, and because you can walk by the water and you can buy crabs by the water and because there are so many faces there of people who do *not* want to be cops. I am probably wrong. I could probably never live in San Francisco. Yet, I'm always glad to see it, and I was very glad, this day, as the car moved up, moved down, as we saw some real houses, houses which looked as if they contained real people and were happy about it, saw the water and the marvelous bridges, under the cold, old sun. It was very beautiful. I leaned back between Barbara and Pete. I closed my eyes and let myself be carried.

They awakened me. It had only taken a few minutes
for me to fall fast asleep. Barbara held my arms as we
climbed the stone stairs of her building. We walked
straight through the lobby, an ornate one, into the elevator. Pete was bringing up my gear.

Barbara had rented a penthouse, and her wide, wide
windows faced the bay. The sun was just going down.
Barbara's place, at least this big room, was off-white, an
off-white which the sun made very vivid, with very heavy,
very dark blue drapes. It was a very nice room. The sun
was very harsh on my face, it felt wonderful. I walked to
the window, and stood there.

Barbara came, and took my coat, and then she was
very busy behind me, at the closet, in the kitchen, in the
bedroom, in the bathroom, and then back again to the
kitchen. The buzzer sounded and I listened to Barbara's
heels in the uncarpeted passageway and I heard Pete
come in. It was about four o'clock in the afternoon and
the winter sun would soon be going down. I had never
watched the sun on the water before, or so it seemed; the
wrinkles in the water, like the tinfoil I'd played with as a
child, and the sun, like the matches on the tinfoil, and
darkening it like that. And it moved the way the tinfoil
had moved beneath my hands. But the sound was different.
There was a wind on the water, and I could hear it
moaning, all the way up here.

Pete came, and stood beside me.

"It's nice," he said.

"Yes. Yes, it is."

Barbara came to the window. "Leo, there are pajamas
and a dressing gown lying on your bed. I suggest that you
change into them—right now. Then you can have one
drink with us, and, by then, your bath should be ready."
She turned me away from the window. "Take him away,
Pete, and make him comfortable, and I'll make the
drinks."

Pete smiled, and turned into the room with me. "We
don't want you to feel that we're running the show,
baby—"

"Certainly not," said Barbara. "But we are."

Well. The only reason people mind being taken care
of is that they are taken care of badly, or that the price is
too high—it comes to the same thing. But Pete and

Barbara loved me. I was very happy to know that. I was happy to know I knew it. For people *had* loved me, after all, when I had simply not dared to know it, and I had hurt them, and myself, very badly. Beneath Pete's tone, beneath Barbara's wry decisiveness, was a very real fear. They had almost lost me, after all. Soon, the continent, and then the ocean, would divide us and then they would not be able to tease me and tyrannize me and take care of me anymore. And I could only show my love for them by submitting to their tyranny, by trying to prove with all my actions that I certainly loved them enough, now, to take care of myself when all they would have would be reports of disasters in the air or on the sea, news of earthquakes here or there, or revolutions here or there, and maps, the sunny or the stormy sky, and the untrustworthy mail. I started toward the bedroom, shedding my jacket and my tie as I went, and Pete helped me to undress and I got into the pajamas and the dressing gown and put on my old slippers.

There was a fire in the fireplace and Barbara had pulled the sofa up close to it, and piled it high with cushions. I sank down into all this, feeling rather like a pasha. Barbara came in, and handed the drinks around. She sat down on a big hassock near the fireplace, and lit a cigarette.

"Look," she said, after a moment, "do you really think it's wise to take off on such a long trip so soon—you know, and alone? Mightn't it be better to stay here just a few more days?"

"Me and Barbara could take care of you," said Pete. "We'll take turns making nourishing little broths for you, and all"—he laughed—"and you can stay in my pad because the papers will just bug you and Barbara to death if they know you're staying here." He watched me. "Because you are still very tired, man. I don't think you realize how tired you are."

"You aren't on any schedule," Barbara said. "You haven't got to be anywhere at any particular time. I'd think of that as a luxury, if I were you, and make the most of it."

I watched the fire. I was trying to find out what I really wanted to do. It was complicated by the fact that, at the moment, I really wanted to do nothing—just sit by the fire like this, with my friends, in safety. I would not be safe once I walked out of here. I would be a target again. I was tired, that was true, tired, above all, perhaps, of being a target; tired of making decisions, tired of being responsible. And for a while, they were saying, and they knew it could only be for a short while, I would not have to do that: they would do for me whatever had to be done, and I could catch my breath, and rest. But I knew that I dreaded seeing Caleb and his wife and his two children, and I dreaded seeing my father, and I dreaded seeing New York. Should I put it all off, or should I get it over with?

Is it necessary, Leo, I asked myself, to think about it in quite such a melodramatic, beleaguered way? Don't sweat it. If you're tired, rest.

"What you say makes sense. I just thought that as long as I was going, I might as well go."

"But you're not running a race," said Barbara. "Get there when you get there—get there in easy stages."

"It doesn't matter when you get to France," Pete said. "You can have the house as long as you want it. And Barry's housekeeper doesn't care when you get there. In fact, the longer you take, the better she'll like it."

"You've got a point there," I said, and smiled and sipped my drink.

"I just don't want you to get too tired," Barbara said. "I wouldn't mind so much maybe if someone were going with you—but—and New York's going to be a terrible strain." She tapped her foot, and looked at Pete. "As a matter of fact, we almost sent for Christopher to come out here and take you back. He's a very good bodyguard, Christopher, almost as good as Pete," and she smiled. "Frankly, I still think that's a good idea."

Pete backed her up at once. "I do, too," he said, "and why don't we do that? Let's say it takes him a couple of days to get out here, well, you can lie around my pad and read and play records, do whatever you want to do, take the car and wander around the city—you know— and then when he comes, he could have a couple of days investigating all the city's dives and making out with all the black broads and sounding out all the black revolutionaries"—he grinned—"be good for him. And then we'd put you both on a plane, and I'd feel a whole lot better,

man, because we don't want you fooling around with
your luggage and all them simple-minded people and Mr.
and Mrs. Ass-kisser on the fucking plane who will already
have worn you *out*, baby, before the plane gets off the
ground good."

"But if Christopher's on that plane," said Barbara,
"the autograph-hunting housewives from Des Moines will
stay far away, believe me."

"They'll think Christopher was sent by the Mau Mau,"
Pete said.

"He certainly looks it—hell," I said, "I think he was,"
and we laughed.

"And you see," said Barbara, "that will give Mr. and
Mrs. Ass-kisser such a thrill that your box office will
climb astronomically. One must think of these things."

I laughed. "You're very persuasive." I leaned back in
the cushions—what is it about a fire which makes one feel
so safe? "And you might be right. Let me think about
it."

"Well," said Pete, "if your brother's meeting you tomorrow, you ain't got too long to be thinking—we have to
let him know."

"And let Christopher know," said Barbara.

I had no practical arguments. Anyway, I was too tired
to argue. I didn't want to leave this fire, or this room, but
I wanted to get out of the country. I had had it among all
these deadly and dangerous people, who made their own
lives, and all the lives they touched, so flat and stale and
joyless. Once, I had thought a day would come when I
would be able to get along with them—and indeed the
day had come: I got along with them by keeping them far
from me. I didn't have anything against them, particularly; or I had so much against them that the bill could
now never be tallied, and so had become irrelevant. My
countrymen impressed me, simply, as being, on the
whole, the emptiest and most unattractive people in the
world. It seemed a great waste of one's only lifetime to be
condemned to their chattering, vicious, pathetic, hysteri-
cally dishonest company. There were other things to do,
other people to see, there was another way to live! I had
seen it, after all, and I knew. But I also knew that what I
had seen, I had seen from a distance, a distance determined by my history. I was part of these people, no mat-

ter how bitterly I judged them. I would never be able to
leave this country. I could only leave it briefly, like a
drowning man coming up for air. I had the choice of
perishing with these doomed people, or of fleeing them,
denying them, and, in that effort, perishing. It was a very
cunning trap, and a very bitter joke. For these people
would not change, they could not, they had no energy for
change: the very word caused their eyes to unfocus, their
lips to loosen or to tighten, and sent them scurrying into
their various bomb-shelters. And, therefore, I was really
rather reluctant to see Christopher, whose destiny was as
tied to this desolation as my own, but who felt that his
options and his possibilities were different. Indeed, they
were, they had to be: but *what* they were was not to be
deciphered by staring into America's great stone face. I
was nearly twenty years older than Christopher, and it
made me ashamed, very often, listening to him, watching
him, understanding the terrible round of his days, that
not all of my endeavor, not all of the endeavor of so many
for so long, had lessened his danger in any degree, or in
any way at all sweetened the bitter cup. And, since I was
so much older than Christopher, I knew far better than
Christopher could how little warrant I had for agreeing
that his options and possibilities were different. I had to
agree because I loved him and valued him. I had to agree
because it is criminal to counsel despair. I had to agree
because it is always possible that if one man can be saved,
a multitude can be saved. But, in fact, it seemed to me
that Christopher's options and possibilities could change
only when the actual framework changed: and the meta-
morphosis of the framework into which we had been
born would almost certainly be so violent as to blow
Christopher, and me, and all of us, away. And then—how
does the Bible put it? Caleb would know—perhaps God
would raise up a people who could understand. But,
God's batting average failing to inspire confidence, I
committed myself to Christopher's possibilities. Perhaps
God would join us later, when He was convinced that we
were on the winning side. Then, heaven would pass a
civil-rights bill and all of the angels would be equal and
all God's children have shoes.

I knew that I was being coy, a little dishonest, more
than a little frightened: "Are you sure," I asked, "that

Christopher would *want* to come all the way out here—just for a couple of days?"

"Shoot," said Pete, sucking his teeth authoritatively, "he'd have been here already, if he'd had any bread."

Barbara nodded, and sipped her drink, watching me. I wondered if I was worried about seeing Barbara and Christopher together again—life can be a bitch sometimes. She knew, I think, that I was wondering this. She waited, and I said, finally, "Well, all right, if you think that's best—you've sort of got me over a barrel."

But I couldn't help smiling as I said it, and Pete and Barbara smiled and bowed to each other and raised their glasses in triumph. Then Barbara came over, and kissed me.

"Now, tell the truth. That wasn't hard, was it? And aren't you—just a little bit—relieved?"

"Maybe," I said. "Just a little bit. But your triumph's going to cost you something, princess. I want another drink."

She took my glass. "All right. But, then, you *will* take your bath, won't you? Because I've ordered dinner to be sent up in about an hour or so—a nice dinner, all the things you like, and it'd be a pity to eat it cold." She went to the bar, and poured my drink.

"You see, Barbara," Pete said. "I *told* you we should just have gone ahead and sent for the cat."

"Oh, but this way, we're sure to have Leo around for at least a couple more days. After all, how do *we* know how long it will take Christopher to get here?" She winked at Pete, and laughed, and came back and put my drink in my hand.

"I wonder if I could have a cigarette?" I asked.

"You can have one cigarette now," said Barbara, "and one cigarette after dinner and that's all. That's serious. And when you go away from here, you really must make an effort about that—you're going to have to watch your drinking, you know that, but cigarettes are really worse." She watched me, both worried and stern. "Really." She lit a cigarette and put it between my lips. "There. Don't say I never give you nothing."

I inhaled the cigarette, which tasted strange, almost as strange as cigarettes had tasted when I was a kid, just learning to smoke. I looked at it, and gave it back to Barbara.

I said, "Maybe I'll try it again after dinner." I sipped my drink, then I put it on the table. I stared into the fire.

It wasn't that I didn't want to talk to them. It wasn't that I had nothing to say. I wanted to talk, I had much to say. But, whereas they might have known what I was going to say, I didn't: and so I stared into the fire. They talked to each other, unconsciously dropping their voices a little: and I stared into the fire. They were talking backstage shoptalk and gossip for awhile, laughing a lot. I was aware of Pete's rather brown teeth in his brown and Oriental face, and of Barbara's very clear laughter sounding the way running water looks, over stones. It was nice to hear them. It made me feel safe. I knew they didn't care whether I talked or not. They were glad—they were proud, even—that I could stare into the fire, that I was free to stare into the fire.

And what did the fire say? Now that I knew that I was going to live, at least for awhile, the fire seemed warmer than it ever had before. I sipped my drink, watching that crumbling, shaking, brilliant universe. The fire towered high, rising straight up, like a tree or tower—a tower made of air, lifting itself ever higher, vain even in its fall, and glorious. Not for two seconds together did the fire remain the same. It could not be content until everything had come under its dominion, had served its lust, and become a part of itself. I thought of martyrs, saints, and witches perishing in the fire, while multitudes looked on and felt that they were, thus, purified by flame. The man who stole the fire had bequeathed us the instrument of our salvation; and we, like the fire, were never the same for two seconds together, and, like the fire, we had never changed. How had they felt, those who had been destined to make our purity inviolate, when brought chained to the place and tied to the stake or the ladder, watching the faces of their brothers as they piled the fire higher, watching those faces until the smoke and the fire and the anguish intervened, until the sinful flesh had paid its penalty and the multitude were once again redeemed? What a tremendous decision had been made, what a mighty law had been passed, so long ago, and with the roar of universal relief and approval: that only the destruction of another could bring peace to the soul and guarantee the order of the universe! The fire said, in Caleb's voice, *Cease ye from man, whose breath is in his nostrils: for wherein is he to be accounted of?* I wondered why it was a virtue, often presented as the highest, to despise oneself and everybody else. What a slimy gang of creeps and cowards those old church fathers must have been; and remained; and what was my brother doing in that company? Where else should a man's breath be, Caleb, I asked, but in his nostrils? Have you forgotten, have you forgotten, the flesh of our fathers which burned in that fire, the bones of our men broken by that wrath, the privacy of our women made foul by that conquest, and our children turned into orphans, into less than dogs, by that universal righteousness? Oh, yes, yes, yes, forgive them, let them rot, let them live or die; but how can you stand in the company of our murderers, how can you kiss that monstrous cross, how can you kiss them with the kiss of love? How can you? I asked of Caleb, who moaned and thundered at me from the fire. I had not talked to Caleb for years, for many years had cultivated an inability to think of him. But, soon I would be seeing him and his wife and his children. Me, but lately ensnared by death, I returned to my brother, I longed for him. I needed him: but the fire raged between us.

I heard Barbara saying, from a long way off, "Well, of course, part of Amy's trouble is that she's really a quite decent little actress—really, one of the best young actresses I've ever worked with. But Bob can't direct her— you know, he never really *did* direct her. So, of course she's never really felt secure and that can make everyone else very nervous. But I don't think Amy's the one to blame. Sylvia's wrong about that."

"Oh, well. Sylvia. She's just afraid that the child messes up that one kind of shitty sentimental scene they have together."

"Amy isn't good in that scene, that's true. But it's be- cause she's afraid of Sylvia. And that's because *Bob* was afraid of Sylvia. He was so afraid she'd curse him out that he just let her have her way. And so what *else* can poor Amy do but just sort of stand there, plotting to get out of that corner where nobody can see her or hear her, where Sylvia *always* traps her?"

Pete laughed. "Well, Sylvia's been playing maids and clowns for about forty-five years, yukking and shucking and bowing mighty low. Now, at least, she's out of the kitchen—so you *know* she's going to make the most of it."

"She doesn't, though. The scene would go much better if she'd get up off of Amy, and let her work. And if the scene went the way it *should* go, then Sylvia would show to much better advantage, too."

"Well—*you* tell that to our black prima donna."

"Oh, no. Not I. She'd never listen to anything coming from me. I've tried to give Amy a few pointers, but it hasn't helped much. Anyway, thank God, the tour's almost over." She looked over at me. "Are you ready for your bath?"

"Aren't you two going to the theater?"

"We're dark tonight. We wouldn't arrange to take you out of the hospital on a night when we're working."

That made sense, and I would certainly have thought of it if I hadn't been off schedule so long and so forgotten what the schedule was.

"Pete," I said, "when I got sick, did my brother start to come out here?"

"Well," Pete said—he looked uncomfortable—"I don't know if I did right, but this is what I did. I knew the wire services had picked it up right away, and so I called New York—luckily, Barbara had his home phone number. So I called his house and I got his wife. He wasn't there, he was at the church. So I told her you was resting easy and out of danger but you had to rest for awhile and we was taking the best possible care of you we could and I told her not to worry. She sounded relieved and she thanked me and she gave me the number of the church and I called the church." He paused.

"Did you talk to him?"

"Yeah. I talked to him. He was busy running some kind of Youth Drive, I never did figure out what he meant by that, but he sounded worried about you and I told him you would be all right. And then he wanted to know if you wanted him to come out here. He had to let me know that it would be a real sacrifice for him and for the church, but he'd do it for you because you were his brother. Well"—Pete grimaced—"I didn't really go for that sacrifice shit too much, and I didn't think you would, either. But you were in no condition for me to be asking you questions and so I told him, No, not now, and I'd be in touch with him and that was that."

The silence in the room was a little loud. Pete watched me with a smile, Barbara poked the fire. "I just realized," I said, "that he hasn't written to me at all. I haven't heard a word from him." I finished my drink, and stood up. "How come he's meeting me at the plane?"

"He called up and asked when you were coming and we thought we had to tell him and then he said he'd meet you at the plane." He watched me, wry, mocking, with a deep, distant sympathy. "That's it, old buddy. Now you know as much as I do."

I looked from Pete to Barbara. "I doubt that," I said.

"He *did* say," said Pete maliciously, "that he was leaving you in the hands of the Lord."

So that's where he left me, I thought. I laughed. "None of you mothers could have done as much. I hope you thanked him."

"I said I was sure you'd be glad to know we heard from him." He grinned. "And that we was *waiting* on the Lord."

I laughed again. "Well, I must go wash." *Whiter than snow!* I thought, and I walked into the bathroom. The bath was full of bubbles, big and blue. I lowered myself into the water. It licked up around me, as hungry as fire, around my private parts, my belly, my nipples, my chest. I leaned back, I put my head under, I came back up. I put my hands to my soaked, woolly head, like a savage newly baptized. Whiter than snow. Wash me, and I shall be whiter than snow. My Jesus is a rock in a weary land, and all my sins are taken away.

"Get away, Jordan. I've got to cross over to see my Lord."

They sang that song at my mother's funeral. That funeral was a great revelation. She died when I was twenty-six. By that time, I *had* worked professionally as an actor and whenever I was working as an actor, I was an actor. But at the time she died, I was a cook in a barbecue joint. She died, worried about me, I know. I wasn't getting along with the family, and I wasn't getting on in the world. She had met Barbara two or three times; once, when I took her to see Barbara backstage; once, when I brought Barbara to the house; one other time, not long after the Paradise Alley days. I had thought that she would like Barbara, that Barbara would somehow prove to her the helpless depth of my ambition. But, whereas my father, without particularly liking or disliking Barbara, worried about the griefs and dangers she could bring me to, and Caleb kept her carefully quarantined in the limbo of unregenerate harlots—unregenerate because she was white, harlot because she was a woman, in limbo because she was both—my mother hated Barbara, hated her helplessly, depthlessly, felt for Barbara a revulsion so deep that she could scarcely bear to look at her. And she attempted to cover this with a New Orleans gentility which we, her family, had never known her to use before, and which was far more devastating than cursing or spittle or a blow. What made it unbearable was that it revealed a fear I had never noticed in my mother before. "Now, you know," she said to me darkly, once, "that is not what I raised you for. That was no part of my calculations, young man, and you might as well know it front as back."

"What are you talking about, Mama?" I knew what she was talking about. She could almost never bring herself to mention Barbara by name, but the tone was unmistakable.

"I mean, I am not going to have no fair-haired, blue-eyed baby crawling around here and calling me Grandmama. *That's* what I mean. You know damn well what I mean."

I sighed. We were sitting alone in the house. Maybe it was a Saturday. I said, "Mama, what are you getting yourself upset about? Have I said I was going to marry the girl?"

"You might. You might—you *just* that foolish. And then what's going to happen to you I don't know—with a common little thing like that?" She laughed, a coarse, sad, unpleasant sound. "Ha! I sure didn't raise you for *that*."

I knew, as I said it, that I was making a mistake. "Mama, what makes you call her common? She comes from a very rich Kentucky family, and she's their only child."

She laughed again. "Is that so? And what does she do with her money? Spend it on you?" She looked me cruelly up and down. I certainly didn't look as though anybody spent money on me. "Yeah. I reckon that's where you got all them fine clothes you're wearing, from Bon*wit* Teller's."

She had hurt me. People can, mothers can. I said, "All right, Mama. Have it your way. Barbara's a whore and I'm her pimp."

"Well, at least," she shouted, then—for now *I* had hurt *her*—"That would make some kind of *sense*. At least she'd be some use to you! And you wouldn't be walking around here in the wintertime, skinny as Job's mule and with that little piece of rag you got the nerve to call a coat and wearing *sneakers*—in the wintertime! What's going to happen to you, you fool? Is that girl addled your brains for fair?" I turned away, and she continued in another tone, a tone harder to bear: "I thought you was going to make something of yourself. We all thought so, Caleb thought so—we used to be so proud of you! And look at you. Just look at you."

"I guess you think Caleb's made something of himself," I said, "and you want me to be like my big brother."

"Caleb is a respected man. A *very* respected man. I used to worry about Caleb—I used to worry about Caleb more than I worried about you. But, yes, Caleb has made something of himself, and he made it out of nothing and you know it was hard for him, it was hard! But look at what he's done—now it won't be too long before he owns his own home—"

"Yeah. With all those nickles and dimes he steals from all these ignorant niggers! You're proud of *that*? You raised me for *that*?"

"Don't you talk about your brother that way! You've got no right to talk! What have *you* got? Tell me that. Huh? You ain't got a goddamn pot to piss in. And where do *you* live, huh? Tell me that. And where do you steal *your* money? Huh? You want to tell me *that*?" She watched me. "Don't you come around here, being all self-righteous and haughty. Your brother's made a man of himself. But don't nobody know what *you* is *yet*."

I picked up the rag I called a coat. "All right. I'm not a man. I'll never be a man. Forget it. I'm getting out of here."

"*Now*, where you think you going? You just got here. Your daddy'll be home in a few minutes—"

"Yeah. And my big brother and his big-assed wife and their two-headed baby. Tell them little Leo's been here and gone."

"Leo! You come back here!"

"I will not come *back here!* I'm going to see my whore!"

"Leo! Oh, Leo. What's happened to you? Why can't you be the Leo you used to be?"

"I will not ever again," I shouted, "be the Leo I used to be! *Fuck* the Leo I used to be. That boy is dead. *Dead*." And out of the door and down the steps I went.

What a pity. What a waste. I knew, when my mother went on like that, when my mother hurt me, that she was not trying to hurt me. I knew that. And yet—I was hurt. I was frightened—perhaps because I then considered that I was too old to be hurt, especially by my mother. I did not know—then—what nerve was unbearably struck in my mother by the conjunction of Barbara and myself. I wish I had known. But one of the reasons I was so vulnerable—in those days, in those ways—was my unspoken and unspeakable shame and fury concerning my career. I had, indeed, appeared on the professional stage, oh, four or five times, and worked with little theaters all up and down the goddamn country. I still choke on the dust of those halls, will never really recover from the stink and chill of those rooms. And, my God, the roles I played! Roles—roles is much to say. I made my first professional stage appearance, inevitably, carrying a tray. I was on for about a minute, and I had to carry the tray over to some fucked-up, broken-down British fagot, who was one of the great lights of the theater. I had to serve this zombie his breakfast about five hundred fucking times, and every single time I went upstage to uncover his eggs and pour his coffee, Britannia came up behind me and lovingly stroked my balls. Nobody could see it, because he had this wide velvet robe stretched out behind him; but if he had done it in sight of the entire audience, I don't think anybody would have noticed it, or cared; people won't see what they can't afford to see. Well, I took it as long as I could—the point is, I took it too long: and I did it, as I kept saying to myself, because I was being exposed— indeed, I was—and it *was* a Broadway show, and it would look good in my résumé. The end between me and the Britannia—and the show—came during a matinée when I reached behind me a second before he reached and pulled on his balls like I was Quasimodo ringing the bells of Notre Dame. The mother couldn't make a move and he was supposed to be downstage to greet Lady Cunt-face who had just fluttered in; and by the time I let him go, and he stumbled downstage, he looked like a teakettle about to whistle. Well. It went on like that, and it got worse, and I don't think I'd have minded if I could have found a role which had some relation to the life I lived, the life I knew, some role which did not traduce entirely my own sense of life, of my own life. But I played waiters, butlers, porters, clowns; since they had never existed in life, there was no conceivable way to play them. And one learned, therefore, and long before one had learned anything else, the most abject reliance on the most shameful tricks, one learned before one learned anything else that contempt for the audience which is death to art. One was imitating an artifact, one might as well have been an icon, and one's performance depended not at all on what one saw—still less, God forbid, on what one felt—but on what the audience had come to see, had been trained to see. In the most sinister possible way, and, at the same time, the most fearful, they needed to know that you were happy in order to be sure that they were happy. The hidden, hopeful weight in the balance could be one thing only, one's charm. By that I do not at all mean the ability to be ingratiating, but the far more difficult ability—or necessity—of somehow thinking oneself and the audience beyond the confines of the expected. One had to change the beat: one had to find a rhythm which arrested the rhythm. And the price for this was a certain ruthless good humor, for the audience had, after all, placed themselves in your hands by lacking the courage to imagine about you what you knew too well about them. The people saw you showing your teeth: it escaped their notice that they were also showing theirs—and showing them, furthermore, on the cue delivered by their Fool.

But if porters, clowns, and butlers were a big fat drag, those more sympathetic efforts made by the American theater were infinitely more demoralizing. I actually did play, for example, *In Abraham's Bosom,* once, in one of those little church theaters, it may have been in Denver, but it could have been Brooklyn or Birmingham. I was far too young for it, and nothing could have made me either right or ready. I gave an awful performance, and I knew it. I couldn't find my way into the character at all, I didn't believe in his sorrows and I didn't believe in his joys and I found absolutely no way to play the scene in which the hero, having struck down a white man, loudly and sincerely repents. He sounded as though he had struck down the son of God. The white man had beaten him with a whip: why was the nigger supposed to moan because he reacted—and, at that, belatedly—as the dueling codes of Europe assume a man should act? Playing this role, for this was a *role,* was harder than carrying the tray. It was the tray transformed into a boulder, and the play was the mountain up which I had to roll it—escaping narrowly indeed with my dignity when the curtain fell. The play was put on as part of an educational drive: was *this* what we were supposed to learn? Father forgive them, Caleb would have said, for they know not what they do. Well, Father could forgive them till times got better. It was too bad they didn't know what they were doing—*I* knew what they were doing, and as long as they were doing it to me, I was going to do my best to give them a bloody instruction. But this made my life very hard, for after all, I had no power, and it destroyed in me forever much that wished to remain warm and sweet and open.

By and by, in little experimental theaters here and there, I played some roles written for white men. And this was a curious kind of revelation, too, and it was very unnerving. I knew, in the first place, after all, that no matter how well I played, say, Tom in *The Glass Menagerie,* or Mio in *Winterset,* I was never going to be *hired* to play these parts. To do them at all was very forcefully to be made to realize the nature of the vacuum in which, helplessly, one was spinning. It was very hard to persist in learning what would almost certainly prove to be a useless language. And yet one had to learn, one had to; for how shameful to be judged unready should the great day of one's opportunity arrive! I liked playing Mio, and I think I was good—after all, I too had a father cruelly wronged—and yet I always felt that there was something in the character that eluded me. I was very young when I played Mio, but playing him made me feel old. It's hard to explain this. I liked the play very much— liked it more then than I do today—and the role was a beautiful challenge. And yet—I always felt that there was something terribly callow about the boy. It was hard for me not to judge him as being something of a whining boy. He seemed surprised by what had happened; he seemed to feel the heavens should have helped him. I envied him his surprise, I wondered at it, but I myself no longer felt it. The heavens he addressed were blind and cold, no healing there and well I knew it, the fate that overtook him, overtook him, as it were, without even noticing him. The wheel rolled and struck him down and plowed him under—that was all. And, as the years went on, I was to be more and more struck by this numb passivity on the part of characters who, after all, were part of the most active and optimistic nation in the world. They were helpless, they were stricken, from the moment the curtain rose. They seemed unable utterly to suspect any connection between their personal fortunes and the fortunes of the state of which they were a part, and rarely indeed was their heroism anything more than physical. It was not pleasant to be forced to reflect that they operated in a vacuum even greater than mine, and knew even less about themselves than I. I was trying to learn how to work in the theater: it was chilling to suspect that there wasn't any. Most of the roles played by white people could only be played by means of tricks, tricks which would never help one to come closer to life, and all of which one would have to discard in order to play even one scene from, say, Ibsen.

I was discovering what some American blacks must discover: that the people who destroyed my history had also destroyed their own.

But all of this was long ago. I could not have said any of this then. I was merely in the process of testing my own sensibilities against the given. I knew something about the life I lived. It was not reflected, it was not respected, anywhere. And, therefore, my early years were perhaps more solitary than most, and certainly more embattled, and I was considered by nearly everyone to be a very difficult person.

Nearly everyone: who did I know in those days? Well, Barbara, of course, above all, Barbara. She was certainly having her troubles. She worked more steadily than I. She was then trapped in precocious teenage roles, which she hated, but she was doggedly learning, as she put it, how to walk. We both remained members of the Workshop, having learned, with no little difficulty, how to use it for our own purposes. We conducted, from time to time, our own experiments, and reacted with less intensity to Saul's judgments; but Barbara, on the whole, saw much more of Saul and Lola than I. Oh, there was a boy named Steve. There was a colored girl, named Sally. She was studying at NYU, and we were very close for awhile. But, at the point at which, in the ordinary way, we should have married, we parted; for I knew I could not marry. I was in a bizarre situation in those days, for there were not a great many Negroes in the world in which I moved—I hadn't planned it that way, God knows, and I didn't want it that way, but that's the way it was—and there were virtually no Negro girls at all. So, I was lonely, in a very particular and a very dangerous way. I might have been different—those years might have been different—if I had not been estranged from my family. But I was, and this was mainly because of Caleb.

For some reason, my first memory of Caleb, after the war was over, connects with another memory, of Barbara and myself; and I find it impossible to tell the one without first telling the other. I don't know why. I did not refuse to join the Army, but outwitted it by a particular species of ruthless cunning. I was—I say now—prepared to go to jail. The Japanese had already been interned. I was not going to fight for the people who had interned them, who had also destroyed the Indians, who were in the process of destroying everyone I loved: I was not going to defend my murderers. Yet, when my moment came, I did not say any of that. I arrived at the Harlem draft-board with several books under my arm. I deliberately arrived a little late. I pretended that I had just come from the library. I said that I was the only support of my aging parents, and, in fact, I had had the foresight to be working in a shipyard, foresight or luck, it's hard to say now, I've held so many jobs for so many reasons. Anyway, I think I gave a great performance before my draft-board. It was composed, as I knew it would be, of round, brown, respectable old men who had long ago given up any hope of being surprised. Round, brown, respectable old men, whose only real desire, insofar as they still dared desire, was to be white. I knew that, and with my books under my arm, with one brother already in the Army, with two aging people at home, with my impeccable shipyard job, with my flaming youth, and what I could not then have named as a deadly single-mindedness—and using precisely the fact that I was physically improbable—persuaded these round, brown, respectable old men that my potential value to my race—to them; my very improbability contained their hope of power, and I knew that—was infinitely more important than my, after all, trivial value to my country. And they deferred me. I had known that they would: that if I pressed the right buttons, they would have no choice but to defer me. And they checked up on me from time to time, but they never bothered me. I had surprised them, and they were grateful, although some of them grew to hate me later, when they suspected how they had goofed. But then it was too late: I was on my height, in my dungeon, had entered, as we say, my bag.

Anyway: during the Workshop summer, just after Jerry went away, Barbara and I took it into our heads to climb the mountain which overlooked Bull Dog Road. We decided to climb it, and spend the night there. One of the reasons, though we didn't say it, was that we were having a hard time in that house, now that Jerry had left it. We hadn't yet begun to have a terrible time with each other, merely—that was to come; with Jerry gone, we were a scandal. Our dirty secret was out. For years to come, Barbara and I were to encounter people who spoke with the most chilling authority concerning our three-way, black-white arrangement on Bull Dog Road. Jerry was considered, of course, to be the victim of our cruel and deliberate perversity, though Jerry himself never said anything of the kind, and I am sure he never felt that. Dealing with the townspeople was very, very hard, and we avoided them as much as possible. Barbara did most of our shopping, for example, usually alone—though sometimes with a couple of the Workshop kids—enduring the muttering, the jibes, the lewd chuckles, the sly nudges, the outright insults. I continued to pose for my ladies, but no other odd jobs were ever offered me, once Jerry had left, and we were having a hard time making ends meet. Some guys jumped me one night when I was coming home from the theater, blacking both eyes, and bloodying my nose. We sometimes sat in our house in the evening as though we were waiting for the mob to come and carry us away. Some nights, the entire town was in the house with us, and we tried to ignore them and concentrate on each other.

I knew, at the very bottom of my heart, that we could not succeed. Of all the fears there are, perhaps the fear of physical pain and destruction is the most devastating. For I had to admit to myself that I was simply, ignobly, and abjectly afraid. I didn't like the taste of my own blood. I didn't want all my teeth knocked out, didn't want my nose smashed, my eyes blinded, didn't want my skull caved in. To drive to town, to walk about, to get through a single day, demanded at least as much energy as would have been demanded for a fifteen-round fight. More: for a fifteen-round fight supposed a winner and a loser, supposed a resolution, and, hence, a release. But there was no release for me, and especially not where it should most certainly have been found, in Barbara's arms, in bed. Fear and love cannot long remain in the same bed together. And how many nights I lay there, while Barbara slept, filled with an indescribable bewilderment; feeling that all that held me to life was being gnawed away, and feeling myself sink, like a weighted corpse, deeper and deeper in the sea of uncertainty. It's hard, after all, for a boy to find out who he is, or what he wants, if he is always afraid and always acting, and especially when this fear invades his most private life. Barbara and I were marooned, alone with our love, and we were discovering that love was not enough—alone, we were doomed. We had only each other, and this fact menaced our relation to each other. We had no relief, we had no one to talk to— far behind us were the days when we had played at being lovers, and laughed at how easily the world was shocked. We were not playing now, and neither was the world. Even in the pizza joint they now reacted to us nervously, and we stopped going there. Matthew had left town, we never saw Fowler again; I did not go to the Negro part of town anymore. Some of the Workshop kids were nice, but bafflement on their part and pride on mine kept a great distance between us. And the Workshop brass were cold. Apart from Rags and Madeleine, they simply ignored our relationship, ignored it with a condescending charity, treating us as though we had contracted some loathsome disease, which we couldn't help. As for Rags, she once volunteered some motherly advice concerning Barbara's destructiveness, and offered to send me to a psychiatrist. Madeleine was hurt and jealous, tried hard to understand, but couldn't avoid realizing that she had been badly used—and she had been. She did not exactly stop speaking to us, but discovered that she had nothing to say, and, after the fiasco of *To Quito and Back*, returned to New York. And I was a little sorry to see her go. I liked her, and we had had fun together. And, while I knew that having fun wasn't enough, I resented Barbara a little for having forced my hand so soon.

We started out a little late the day we climbed the mountain, and the sun began going down when we were a little more than halfway up. I was pushing us hard, not only because of the sun, but because I was terribly afraid that people might realize that we intended to spend the night on the mountain and follow us up and kill us. We hadn't driven through town, but had taken the long back road which led to the foot of the mountain. I had parked the car there, off the road, in a clump of trees. No one had seen us, as far as I could tell, except a couple of the ladies in the old ladies' home. This old ladies' home sat in the clearing at the foot of the mountain, and the old ladies sat on the deeply shaded veranda, flashing their silver spectacles and their silver hair. Two of them had watched Barbara and me, as we disappeared up the trail. But everyone else, hopefully, would suppose us to be at home.

In spite of everything, we were very happy in the August sun, toiling up the trail. I'm small, but Barbara's smaller, and I am very strong. I was leading Barbara by the hand. The sleeping bag was on my back, and Barbara had the knapsack.

"Let's stop a minute. It's *hot*."

"Barbara, there are snakes all over this place. If we stop now, we'll never make it up. Come on, now!"

I was being Spencer Tracy, in *Northwest Passage*.

She was just being Barbara, who was afraid of snakes. "Shit," she murmured, exasperated—but we kept moving upward, toward the retreating, cooling sun, which had nevertheless set everything around us on fire. Except for our breathing, and the breaking of twigs beneath our feet from time to time, it was very silent. Barbara was a good walker; we moved together like two soldiers. On either side of us, as we climbed, were the green, dark woods, hiding everything, hiding the height, hiding the snakes—there really were snakes—and becoming darker, it seemed, with every instant. The path was very narrow, so narrow that we had to walk single file; and very steep; sweat was pouring down my neck and down my back, seeming to soak into the sleeping bag, and making it heavier. A narrow strip of sky was directly over us, ahead of us was only the path, with sunlight splashing down erratically here and there. The path became steeper and then began to level off, the trees became more sparse, and then more individual—they began to look as though they'd had a hard time growing—and then we saw before us, above us, the gothic shape of the abandoned hotel someone had begun building on this mountain long ago. There were many stories about this hotel. Some mad financier had begun it and then lost all his money; the commune had never built a road. And there the hotel stood, a stone structure as gnarled as the trees, with great holes where windows had been. There was a large court-yard with a stone wall and the memory of a driveway and stone steps leading up to the aperture which had been the front door. This led into a high vault which had been intended as a lobby. In this space were stone steps leading up to the unfinished and unsafe second story, and stone steps leading down into the basement. There was a reception counter, the only detail which caused one to think of a hotel. There had, apparently, been other fixtures; but everything that could be moved had been carted away long ago. Some of the townspeople were earnestly discussing the possibility of tearing down the building and turning the stones to profit. But their in-

genuity had not yet defeated the many practical difficulties
this plan entailed.

It did not look hospitable as we approached, with the
light now failing fast, and the night sounds beginning.
"God," said Barbara, "wouldn't it be awful if some other
people had the same idea as we did—of spending the
night here, I mean."

"Oh, I don't know. I wouldn't mind seeing a friendly
face." And, because I, too, was uneasy, I sang out,
"Hello! You got visitors! Is there anybody here?"

My voice echoed and echoed, crashing through the
trees, sounding in the valley, and returning to us.

I said, "Nobody here, I guess." I dropped the sleeping
bag in the middle of the courtyard, and Barbara put down
the knapsack. I took Barbara's hand. "Come on." We
walked into the lobby. I switched on the flashlight, and
there was a scurrying in the darkness. "Rats. I wonder if
they've got bats, too."

"Oh, Leo. You stop that."

I laughed, and trained the flashlight on the steps leading up. "Let's see what's upstairs."

Hand in hand, like children in a fairy tale, we started
up the steps. We walked close to the wall, for there wasn't
any railing—there had been one, of mahogany, but it had
been hijacked. At the top of the steps, there stretched
before us a high, wide space. I turned the flashlight on
the floor, which was wooden. There was a hole in the
floor, to our right. The solid part of the floor was covered
with all kinds of debris—old paper bags, paper cups; and
facing us was a space in the wall which had been a window; and it gave onto a flagged terrace. We tiptoed across
the floor, worried about whether or not it would bear our
weight, and stepped onto the terrace.

The mad financier had not been so very mad, after
all, for when one stepped onto his terrace, one understood his dream. The terrace faced the valley which
dropped before us, straight down to the river. The trees
were blue and brown, purple and black. In the daytime,
the houses and barns were red and white and green
and brown. Now, the sun had turned them all into a
color somewhere between gold and scarlet. We stood on
the terrace, hearing no sound, and making no sound.

The far-off river was as still as a great, polished copper plate.

"If this had been mine," said Barbara, at last, "I would never have dreamed of making a hotel out of it. I'd have kept it to myself."

"Perhaps he was lonely," I said, "and he wanted people to share this with him."

"It really would have made a marvelous hotel," said Barbara, after a moment. "He was right about that. Poor man. He must have spent a fortune. I hope he didn't break his heart."

"I'll go get the whiskey," I said, "and we can have a drink up here."

I turned back into the dark house, and went down the steps and across the vault, into the courtyard, and picked up the knapsack. I came back to Barbara, who was sitting on the terrace, with her chin on her knees.

"And what are you thinking, princess?"

"I was thinking—that—it's nice to be here. With you."

"We're going to make it all right," I said, and I opened the whiskey and I poured some into two paper cups. I gave one to her and I sat down next to her. We touched cups. We sat and watched the sky and the valley change colors. Slowly, and yet not slowly, the sun entirely left the sky—the streaks of fire and gold vanished. The sky turned mother of pearl and then heavy, heavy silver. In the silver, faint stars gleamed, faint and pale, like wanderers arriving; and the pale moon appeared, like a guide or a schoolmistress, to assign the stars their places. The stars grew bolder as the moon rose, and the sky became blue-black. The trees, the houses, the barns were shapes of darkness now. The valley could not be seen. But, far away, beneath us, the river reflected the moon. They were in communion with each other. Barbara put her head on my shoulder. We had another drink. We looked into each other's eyes, briefly, and moved closer together. We listened to the night sounds, wings beating dimly around us, the electrical whirring of insects, the cry of an owl, the barking of a dog. Lights appeared in the valley, here and there. The lights of a single boat glowed on the river. There were no human sounds at all. We were alone, at peace, on high.

"What shall we do when the summer's over, Leo?"

"Why—we'll go back to the city. What were you thinking of doing?"

"Shall we go back to Paradise Alley?"

"God. I don't know. I've got to get some kind of job —you know."

"Yes. So must I."

"I'll probably get a job as a waiter. So I can eat till I get paid."

"Except that those jobs always take away your appetite."

"That's true. It's pretty hard to make your living watching the human race eat."

"Well," she said carefully, "we ought to be able to work it out all right."

"Don't worry about it. We'll work it out fine." Then I kissed her. "Tell me when you're hungry and I'll make a fire."

"In a little while," she said, and she leaned against me again.

I don't know what she was seeing as we looked out over the dark valley; but I did not see any future for us; I did not see any future for myself at all. Barbara was young and talented and pretty, and single-minded. There was nothing to prevent her from scaling the heights. Her eminence was but a matter of time. And what could she then do with her sad, dark lover, a boy trapped in the wrong time, the wrong place, and with the wrong ambitions trapped in the wrong skin? If I stood in her way, she would certainly grow to hate me, and quite rightly. But I had no intention of standing in her way. The most subtle and perhaps the most deadly of alienations is that which is produced by the fear of being alienated. Because I was certain that Barbara could not stay with me, I dared not be committed to Barbara. This fear obscured a great many fears, but it obscured, above all, the question of whether or not I wished to be committed to Barbara, or to anyone else, and it hid the question of whether or not I was capable of commitment. But these questions were hidden from me then, much as the shape of the valley was hidden. I knew that I had to make my way—somehow. No one could help me and I could not call for help. There was no way for me to know if the fear I sometimes felt when with Barbara, a fear which sometimes woke me in the middle of the night, which sometimes made me catch my breath when walking the streets at noon, was a personal fear, produced merely by the convolutions of my own personality, or a public fear, produced by the rage of others. I could not read my symptoms, for I loved her, I knew that, and loved her more than I loved anyone else. We were not always happy, but when I was happy with Barbara I was happier than I had ever been with anyone else. We were at ease with each other, as we were with no one else. And yet, I saw no future for us.

We left the terrace and came downstairs to the courtyard, and I built a fire. Our fire, then, was the only light for miles around. We roasted the yams I had found, and grilled our hamburgers; and we had a small bottle of Chianti. As the night grew darker, we began to feel safer, for no one would attempt that mountain trail at night. Barbara leaned back in my arms, and I sang to her.

> *It takes a worried man*
> *To sing a worried song,*
> *I'm worried now,*
> *But I won't be worried long,*

I sang, and,

> *I just got a cabin,*
> *You don't need my cabin,*
> *River, stay 'way from my door,*

and,

> *I hate to see that evening sun go down.*

"You've got a nice voice," Barbara said. "You ought to work at it. I bet that's how you'll get your break."

"It's just an ordinary voice. What do you mean, that's how I'll get my break?"

"It's not an ordinary voice. It's a very haunting voice. If you started singing professionally, you'd attract a lot of attention. Well, look, that's practically the classic way for a Negro to break into the theater. Look at Paul Robeson."

"You look at Paul Robeson. Robeson was a football
star, he's one of the greatest singers in the world, and one
of the most handsome men in the world, and he's built
like a hero. You think he's a good model for me?"

"Oh, shut up. You know what I mean."

"And, with all that, what's he played? *The Emperor
Jones* and *Othello.*"

"I didn't say that you looked like Paul Robeson. I
said that your voice is an asset, and you ought to use it.
People will hear you, and that means that they'll see you,
and—well, there *are* other roles besides *The Emperor
Jones* and *Othello.*"

"There are? You've really been scouting around."

"And you could start this winter. Really, why don't
you? So we'd both be working—"

"You have a job lined up for this winter already?"

"No. But I've heard of a couple of things. I was going
to go down to the city next week to—to investigate. You
know, this is August. The summer's almost over."

"I know." For no reason at all, I thought of Dinah
Washington, singing "Blowtop Blues."

"And I know you've been practicing the guitar. And
there are places in the Village where you could start out.
Oh, you know, there's that West Indian restaurant. I bet
they'd be glad to have you start out there."

"If they want people to sing West Indian songs, why
would they come to *me?* I'm not West Indian."

"Oh, Leo, you are too. You're *part* West Indian.
You're just putting up objections so I can knock them
down. I know you. It's a damn good idea, and you know
it."

I had thought about it before; I began to think about
it again. "Maybe."

"You could be the singing waiter." She laughed.
"You'd be a tremendous drawing card."

I thought, It's true that I have to start somewhere. I
said, "I'm not ready to start singing in public yet."

"But, Leo, the whole point of starting out in a place
like that is that you haven't got to be *ready.* They'll think
you're doing it just for fun. But that's how you'll *learn.*"

"And I can just see me, twenty years from now, playing my guitar all over the Bowery."

"You will not. You'll use it to get what you want."

"I'm not always sure that I know what I want." I held her a little closer and I stared at our little fire.

"I think—sometimes—when a person says that, he just says it because he's—afraid—that he won't get what he wants."

"Maybe. But you know what *you* want. Don't you?"

"I know that I want some things I'll never get."

"What things?"

She shifted her weight a little. "Oh. You know. The corny things. A husband. A home." She paused. "Kids."

"Why can't you have those things, Barbara?"

"Maybe I don't want them enough," she said. "I don't know. Maybe I'm wrong." I felt her watching me. "It's funny. I haven't turned out to be the kind of girl I thought I'd be. I'm not yet twenty, and I've had, oh, about three affairs and one abortion already. It makes you feel kind of used up. And sometimes I get frightened —oh, well." She sighed, and shrugged, smiling. "Sing me another song."

"After what you've said, I don't know what song to sing. Poor Barbara. I don't make your life any simpler, do I?"

"I'm not complaining. You didn't make the world."

"No," I said, "I didn't." I looked up at the sky. "Sometimes, you know? I still wonder who did. I wonder what whoever it was was thinking about."

"He wasn't," she said, with an unexpected harshness in her voice, "thinking about you and me."

"No. What rotten casting," I said, and we laughed.

"Sing me one more song, please?" she said. "Before we go to sleep."

I sang,

> *I don't know why*
> *There's no sun up in the sky,*
> *Stormy weather!*
> *Since my gal and I ain't together,*
> *It's raining all the time.*

We crawled into our sleeping bag at last, and lay there for awhile, watching the fire drop and disperse and die. The stars were very close, and I saw one fall. I made a wish. I wished that Barbara and I, no matter what hap-

pened, would always love each other and always be able,
without any bitterness, to look each other in the eye. The
familiar and yet rather awful heat and pressure rose in
my chest and descended to my loins; and I lay there,
while the heat wrapped me round, holding Barbara with
one arm and feeling her delicate trembling. The heat
rose and rose, partly against my will, partly to my delight.
For I was beginning to realize that vows were made with
the body as sacred as those made with the tongue. And
these vows were at once harder to keep, and harder to
break. We turned to each other. Everything was still. We
began to make love very slowly, more gently and more
sorrowfully than we ever had before. We did not say a
word. Every caress seemed to drag us up from the depths
of ourselves, revealing another nakedness, a nakedness we
could scarcely bear. Her face, in the starlight, in the faint
light of the embers of our fire, was a face I had never
known. I caressed that face, and held it and kissed it, with
that passion sometimes produced by memory, the passion
of our deepest dreams. I seemed to know, that night, that
we were trapped, trapped no matter what we did: we
would have to learn to live in the trap. But that night it
did not seem impossible. Nothing seemed impossible.
Barbara began to moan. It was a black moan, and it was
as though, trapped within the flesh I held, there was a
black woman moaning, struggling to be free. Perhaps it
was because we were beneath the starlight, naked. I had
unzipped the sleeping bag, and the August night traveled
over my body, as I trembled over Barbara. It was as
though we were not only joined to each other, but to the
night, the stars, the moon, the sleeping valley, the trees,
the earth beneath the stone which was our bed, and the
water beneath the earth. With every touch, movement,
caress, with every thrust, with every moan and gasp, I
came closer to Barbara and closer to myself and closer to
something unnameable. And her thighs locked around
me, sweeter than water. She held me, held me, held me.
And I was very slow. I was very sure. I held it, held it,
held it, held it because I knew it could not long be held.
All this had nothing to do with time. The moment of our
liberation gathered, gathered, crouched, ready to spring,
and Barbara sobbed; the wind burned my body, and I
felt the unmistakable, the unanswerable retreat, contrac-

tion, concentration, the long, poised moment before the
long fall. I murmured, *Barbara,* and seemed to hear her
name, my call, ringing through the valley. And her name
echoed in the valley for a long time. Then the stars began
to grow pale. I zipped the sleeping bag over us. We curled
into each other, and slept. We had not spoken.

It was a bright morning. The sun woke us early, and,
naked, we dared to wash, and splash each other in the cold
stream which trickled near the path. The silver cold water
stung us wide awake, and made us proud of our bodies.
Naked, I built the fire, and boiled our coffee. Naked and
happy, facing each other, we drank it. We became drunk
on the sun and the coffee and our nakedness and touched
each other's bodies with a terrible wonder everywhere
and we had to make love again. Then, we were covered
with sweat, and we washed in the stream again. Then, the
sun was high, warning us that the world might be on the
way, and we got dressed. I rolled up the sleeping bag, and
Barbara packed the knapsack, and we started down. No
one was coming up the trail. It was a bright, clear, still
morning, and birds were making those sounds we call
singing. As we descended, my fear began to return, like
the throb of a remembered toothache before the new
toothache begins.

As we approached the clearing which held the old
ladies' home, just coming off the trail, now, and walking
on level ground, one of the old ladies, silver hair and
silver spectacles flashing, stepped down from the porch
with astonishing speed and came running toward us, waving a newspaper above her head as though it were a
banner. Barbara and I were too astounded even to look at
each other. We were both afraid that the lady would fall,
and we began to run toward her so that she wouldn't
have to run toward us. But she kept running, just the
same. When we reached her, she was out of breath, and
she just sat down on the grass. "Look," she said, "look!"

We were afraid that she was ill, and we simply stared
at her.

"Look," she said again, *"look!"* With one hand, she
pounded the newspaper into the grass. "The war is over.
The war is over."

Then I saw that she had been crying. Some of the
other ladies were standing on the porch. We looked down

at the newspaper. Well, we understood that the war was over; for a long time, that was all that we understood. Hiroshima and Nagasaki, two cities we had never heard of, had been leveled with single, unprecedented bombs. At first, I only wished that I had paid more attention to mathematics and physics when I had been in high school; what did it mean to split the atom? The old lady kept making sounds between tears and jubilation. I kept thinking, *They didn't drop it on the Germans. The Germans are white. They dropped it on the Japanese. They dropped it on the yellow-bellied Japs.* I stared at the old lady. She was still sitting on the grass. She stared up at me, but I knew she wasn't seeing me. "Isn't it wonderful?" she cried. "Isn't it wonderful? This terrible war is over. *Over!*"

We helped her to her feet.

"Yes," said Barbara, terribly pale in the merciless sun, "yes, it's wonderful that the war is over."

"Truly wonderful," I said, parroting Father Divine— I did not know what I was saying.

We began walking the old lady back to the porch. The other old ladies had gathered now, and they, too, were jubilant. But, unlike the first old lady, they were not blind with jubilation. Behind their spectacles, they watched Barbara with a disapproving wonder and they watched me with a profound distrust; they made a sound like dry pebbles on the bed of a vanished stream. Some they loved had died in the war, in this particular war, for they remembered others. Some they loved were coming home. Their hands, their faces, their voices shook, wavered, cracked, climbed. They looked at me from time to time, and they were not unwilling to include me, but they addressed themselves, in the main, to Barbara. Something made them know, somehow, that their day of jubilee might not be mine. And I was base, I must say. I watched them, and I pitied them. I pitied them with a pity not easily distinguished from contempt, which was yet informed by wonder. They were rejoicing. The faith of their fathers—living yet!—had made them victorious over their enemies—had they ever considered me their friend? What was most vague in their consciousness was most precise and alive in mine. But they were old—old ladies rejoicing in the light of the August morning. I felt that they had little enough to rejoice about.

At last we were moving away, waving, smiling to the last. We got into the car. They remained on the porch, and waved as we drove away. Then, Barbara said, with a shudder, "Maybe we better not drive through town. They'll all be in the streets."

And so we drove back the way we had come, but we were not left in peace for long. As night was falling, some of the Workshop kids came over, to carry us to the San-Marquands. They were having a Victory Ball.

Caleb had been wounded in the European theater, and they had shipped him home. And, again, my memory here is vague. I talked with Caleb about it only once. He was wounded in the lung, and he very nearly died. He was in a military hospital for a long time, but I know I didn't see him in the hospital. I can't remember why. I know my mother and father went down to see him. I remember that they wanted me to come, too, but they couldn't find me—something like that. I think that I was simply afraid to see Caleb. He had already written us a couple of letters about having found the Lord. When he came back to New York, I don't know where I was; by the time I saw him, he had already joined The New Dispensation House of God. He told me he was saved. And then I didn't see him.

Barbara and I came back to New York when the summer ended. We made the mistake—though I don't know if one can accurately describe as a mistake what one couldn't help doing—of returning to Paradise Alley. Well, I had a feeling that we should not have gone there: but we had no place else to go. And, at least, we knew Paradise Alley. It was a decrepit slum, and it didn't matter to the landlord *who* lived there. We didn't have the courage to tackle a strange landlord, and I didn't have any money.

Being back in Paradise Alley meant that we were confronted with the debris of our recent past. Jerry's socks and shoes, sweatshirts, jockstrap, blue jeans, ties, notes in his handwriting, a photograph of Jerry and Barbara, a photograph of Jerry and Charlie and me—all of us looking historical. There was all my old shit, my winter clothes—by which I mean, principally, sweaters—and heavy shoes, everything referring to a life we had ceased to live. But all of it menaced the life we hoped to live. Silently, we were sickened by it, silently we were reproached. We put it all in two boxes and hid the boxes in a corner of the room. (For, one day, the owners might arrive.) And we settled down. We tried to settle down. Barbara got a job as a waitress. And I got a job at the West Indian restaurant as a waiter, a waiter who sang. Late some nights, after we had finished serving, I would take down my guitar and sing a few songs. Barbara had been right. They liked it, and it was good for me. That job held Barbara and me together, that winter, longer than we might have stayed together. And the job had an effect, obliquely, on my career. A singing black waiter in the Village in those days was bound to be noticed, and so, without realizing it, I became what I was later able to sell: a personality.

It went this way: my working day began around five or six in the evening, when I unlocked the restaurant. There were about eight or ten tables. At capacity, we could serve about forty people. I was the only waiter. The restaurant was set down about three steps below the sidewalk. I unlocked the door, I swept out the joint. I checked the garbage cans, both inside and outside the restaurant. If I had left pots soaking, I scoured the pots. I set up the kitchen, putting out the cleaver and the chopping board. I chopped up the salad and made the salad dressing. I peeled the potatoes, poured the water off the black-eyed peas we always left soaking overnight, and washed the rice—for our specialty was a black-eyed peas and rice dish, called Hopping John. Then, I paused and had a drink—of black Jamaican rum. Hilda always kept a bottle in the kitchen. And by this time, Hilda, the cook, who was also the nominal owner, a big, black, and, on the whole, rather mysteriously unattached lady from the islands, had arrived, and was in the kitchen, hacking away at the ribs and the chicken. Hilda and I never said a great deal to each other; this meant that Hilda liked me and trusted me. She worked hard, she worked silently. I understood her reasons, although we never discussed them.

I was sure that whatever she had saved from the years of working as a cook in private houses had been invested in this restaurant; and now she was terrified, although she masked this terror very well. She had, after all, taken on something quite formidable. With or without partners— and I didn't know whether she had any partners or not— for a lone Negro woman to open a Negro joint in downtown New York was the kind of challenge that could easily lead to reprisals. For one thing, Hilda's joint, which we called The Island, would certainly bring other Negroes downtown, and the people who ran the Village were not anxious for this to happen. Hilda and I both knew this, but there wasn't much point in discussing it. Of course, our emphasis was very heavily on the islands, mightily exotic— this may have helped; and we anticipated, if we didn't indeed help to create, the Calypso craze that was shortly to sweep the nation. Negro entertainers, working in Village clubs, very often dropped in, and this gave the place a certain "tone," a certain vibrance, and they sometimes, if the spirit so moved them, sang or danced.

And there was something very impressive in Hilda's stolid, silent single-mindedness. I don't think she ever really liked running that restaurant—it was something she had to do. We knew nothing about her life at all. Unattached she certainly appeared to be. She spent very little money on herself. She sent nearly all of it back to Trinidad, without ever telling us who, there, was dependent on her efforts. And this gave her a black dignity, hard to assail. I think she liked me because, in my different way, I was as single-minded as she, as closed, and, in my way, as bold. We were a good team. If we hadn't been, we would never have been able to manage the tremendous amount of work we had to do each evening. I surrendered the kitchen to Hilda, and set up my tables. I always brought a book with me, and, after I had set up my tables, I poured myself another glass of rum and sat down to read until the people arrived.

We ran a rather late joint. My working day never ended before one in the morning, and sometimes not until four. Some very odd people floated through the doors of that restaurant, and I guess I learned a lot there. One of the things I learned, without realizing that I was

learning it, was how to dominate a room. I certainly
dominated that one. If I hadn't, I would have been trampled
to death.

Here they came: a blond girl, say, with very long hair,
svelte, an uptown girl, in snooty black. Her beau, crew-
cutted, gabardined. They are slumming and they more or
less know it, but, nevertheless, they look rather hard at
me. For very dissimilar reasons, I look rather hard at
them. But, as they are now in *my* territory, and my
mother raised me right, I close my book and rise and
smile—I almost said, rise and shine.

"Good evening. Can I help you?"

Hilda avoided the customers as completely as possible, for she couldn't bear them; and at moments like
these, I always seemed to hear the cleaver in the kitchen
coming down particularly hard.

"We thought we might eat something."

She is looking pleased, or looking bored; with some
girls, it's very hard to tell. Anyway, she is certainly looking bright.

"Certainly. Would you like this table?"

They are seated. The menus are before them. She is
still looking bright, but he has decided to be a regular
fellow. The mother doesn't know how much I know
about him. He might not make out with her, but I might
know somebody, or maybe he can make out with me. I'm
black, but I'm friendly, and no doubt I remind him of
someone he knew in college.

"Would you like a drink?"

And *wham!* goes the cleaver, and I go behind the bar
to prepare their martinis. I am also, I forgot to say, the
only bartender. From my position behind the bar, I look
into the kitchen at black and surly Hilda. The first of our
signals are exchanged. *Just the usual fools,* I silently inform her, *no trouble.* I wink at her, and she winks back.
Then she raises the cleaver again. *Wham!*

"You make a pretty good martini."

"Thank you. Do you want to order now, or—well—
have another martini?" And it was on this line I managed
my most artless and dazzling smile.

"Well. We'll see."

"Okay. Just make yourself at home."

Here they came: she middle-aged, fretful, all in green and orange, he balding, harried, in dark blue.

"What's the name of this place?"

"We call it The Island. Good evening."

"Your food any good?"

"Some people like it. *Some* people are addicted to it."

Looking back, I suspect that one of the reasons they looked at me so hard was that I really didn't give a damn if they never ate another meal again, anywhere in the world. I certainly wasn't drumming up trade, and that was the secret behind my carefully open smile.

"Well, I guess we might as well try it. What do you think, Anita?"

They look at the other couple, look at me. I leave them in their valley of decision, and light a few candles. They sit down—at a table very near the door. I give them their menus.

"Would you like a drink?"

"Can you make a Manhattan?"

"I believe I still remember. Two?"

"Yeah. And make it snappy."

Distrustfully, they taste their drinks. The cleaver continues to fall, and the pots are boiling, Hilda rings the bell which informs me that the first couple's meal is ready. I serve it. He smiles at me, and winks. I smile. Then, back to my other couple.

"Would you like to order now?"

"Yeah. We'll try the chicken. We don't like no spices."

"Very good. Thank you."

Here they came: two boys, certainly under age, certainly from the Bronx, in the Village for the first time.

"Hi. Can we eat?"

"If you can't, you won't live long. How about this table?"

I light their candles.

"Are the ribs good?"

"I like them."

"You the cook?"

"No. I'm the waiter. The cook is in the kitchen."

"What's your name?"

"My name is Leo."

"Can we have a couple of beers?"

They are probably under age, but, on the other hand,

so am I. I don't know what Hilda is paying for protection, but I know it's a lot.

"Okay. And two ribs?"

"Right."

"Thank you."

Here they came: four Southern sailors, a little drunk. This can be very tricky, but Hilda and I have this set of signals, and I always maneuver myself at such moments so that I am near the poker in the fireplace.

"Good evening. Would you like to eat?"

"Yeah. We're hungry."

"You've come to the right place, then. This table suit you?"

"Yeah. Can we get a drink?"

This is also rather tricky, for one doesn't want sailors getting drunk in the joint. But I can't really claim that they are too drunk to be served.

"What would you like?"

They would like boiler-makers, all around.

"Hey, where you from? You from around here?"

"I'm from New York."

"You know where we can find some pussy?"

"All over the street. I guess."

"Man, we been looking and we ain't found nothing. This town is full of fagots."

"Cheer up. It's early. What do you want to eat?"

Looking back, I have to recognize that most of the Southerners who came into that joint surprised me. It was the Northerners who were dangerous.

"Might have me some pigs' feet. They *smell* like pussy."

"Man, they look just like a prick."

"Now, where did you ever come across a prick with claws?"

Laughter.

Here they came: the nice blond girl from Minneapolis, who lived in the Village with her black musician husband. Eventually, he went mad and she turned into a lush. I don't know what happened to their little boy. Here they came: Rhoda and Sam, the happiest young couple in the Village. She committed suicide, and he vanished into Spain. Here they came: two girls who worked in advertising and who lived together in fear and trembling, who told me all about their lives one drunken night. One of them found a psy-

chiatrist, married a very fat boy in advertising, and moved
to California and they are now very successful and vocal
Fascists. I don't know what happened to the other girl.
Here they came: the black man from Kentucky, who
called himself an African prince and had some ridiculous
name, like Omar, and his trembling Bryn Mawr girl-friend,
whose virginity he wore like a flag. Her family eventually
had him arrested, and the girl married somebody from
Yale. Here they came, the brilliant, aging Negro lawyer
who lived on whiskey and benzedrine and fat white women,
here they came, the bright-eyed boy from the South, who
was going to be a writer and who turned into a wino, here
they came, the boy who had just fled from his rich family
in Florida and who was going to live a different life than
theirs ("I don't need all that money, I just want to be
me") and who turned into a junkie, here they came, the
fagot painter and his Lesbian wife, who had an understanding with each other which made them brutally cruel
to all their playmates and which welded them, hatefully,
to each other. Here they came, the lost lonely man who
worked in the shipyards and lived with his mother, who
loved young boys and feared them and who jumped off a
roof, here they came, the nice, middle-aged couple everyone was always glad to see, the husband of which couple,
weeping and sweating, once threw me down among the
garbage cans and tried to blow me—"Don't tell Marcia.
Please don't tell my wife!"—here they came, the beautiful
girl who painted and who ended up in Bellevue, here
they came, the beautiful girl who was going to be a dancer
and who ended up in prison, here they came, the brilliant
Boston scion who liked to get fucked in the ass, and who
threw himself before a subway train—which chopped off
his head—here they came, my God, the wretched, the
beautiful, lost and lonely, trying to live, though death's
icy mark was on them, trying to speak, though they had
learned no language, trying to love although the flesh was
vile, hoping to find in all the cups they tasted that taste
which was joy, *their* joy, without which no life is worth
living. Yes, I learned a lot. They frightened me, but I
learned a lot. Here, one night, came Sally, with whom I
was to live for nearly two years, very cool and sleek and
distant, with two white, male NYU students. They were
talking sociology, I thought they were full of shit, and

eventually I said so, and Sally and I had a fight. Then, I
haunted the NYU campus until I found her again and I
made her speak to me again, like a person this time, and
not like a poor relation, the object of sociological research.
Here, one night, came Steve, from Pennsylvania, the
wayward son of a famous general, and he fell in love with
me. I have to put it that way because that's what happened,
although I know I didn't handle it very well. But he meant
a lot to me and he taught me something very valuable, a
certain humility before the brutal and mysterious facts of
life. Sally eventually married a Negro lawyer, a very nice
man, and we're still friendly—I guess we cost each other
enough for that. Steve went off to Tangiers, and I am told
that he is drinking himself to death there. Yes. My days of
anger.

By and by, around about midnight, the room would be
under control, the last couples sipping their coffee. The
room would be rather nice then. The candles made the
room seem warmer, and the people looked gentler than
they were. I ate my own meals at no particular time, it
depended on the traffic and on my own mood, and it
didn't matter, since I always closed the joint. Many times,
I ate my supper at about two in the morning, sitting in
the locked restaurant alone. Around midnight, Hilda
would come out of the kitchen and sit down at her table,
near the fireplace. She always brought knitting with her,
I remember her hands as always busy—I think it was
because she wanted most of the people who came in there
to stay far away from her. Sometimes, Barbara came to
pick me up, or other friends might be there. Steve spent a
lot of his time there for awhile, and so did Sally—I still
remember some moments, still remember Sally and Hilda,
sitting at that corner table, laughing. Sally and Hilda liked
each other very much, and Hilda was very disappointed
when I failed to marry Sally. She felt that Sally had real
class, and that I very much needed Sally's stability. I still
remember Steve, rawboned, curly-haired, slouching in, his
eyes coming always directly to rest on me. It's painful,
sometimes, to look back on a life and wonder if anything
you did could have made any difference. So much is lost;
and what's lost is lost forever. Was it destined to be lost, or
could we have saved it? People rather made fun of Steve
in those days, and I was more sensitive about this than I

should have been. He was certainly exceedingly forthright, and I found this awkward as well as frightening. I must say for Sally that, later on, when she realized that Steve and I had been lovers, and might become lovers again, she did everything she could to understand it, and to understand him. But he frightened her. He frightened her in much the same way I did, for, though Sally was bright and beautiful, she was, at bottom, thoroughly respectable. That was really the trouble between us, though we may not have realized it then, and I was far too young to realize that a lone, black girl, operating in the Village then, *had* to be respectable or risk being destroyed.

Anyway, some nights around midnight, if the atmosphere seemed right, I would take down my guitar from where it hung above the fireplace and sit down on the high stool near Hilda's table, and strum the guitar awhile. And the room would grow quiet and then I would sing a few songs. And the people liked it and they told their friends and sent their friends down. Hell, they should have liked it, it was all for free, and of course Hilda liked it because I was good for business. I don't suppose that the cops liked it, but Hilda and the cops appeared to have a working arrangement and they hardly ever gave us any trouble. One night, quite late, there were only about four or five people there, I was sitting on my stool, singing, and Caleb walked in. And when he walked in, I'll be damned if I wasn't singing "Sometimes I Feel Like A Motherless Child." I did, too. He was in the joint practically before I knew it. I saw this big, black man stooping through the doorway, and I thought, *Shit, I wonder where he comes from, fuck it, I am not serving anybody else tonight,* and then, so to speak, my vision cleared, and I found myself staring at Caleb.

Well, he looked wonderful—big and black and shining; safe and proud. I hadn't seen him for the longest while. I forced myself to finish my song, while he stared at me, smiling. Hilda looked at me, and I finished my song and I said to Hilda, "That's my brother. Caleb." And I walked over to him. I was really very glad to see him. I couldn't have imagined I'd be so glad.

He stood up, and he hugged me.

"Hello, little brother. You *are* a long way from home."

"Hello, yourself. What brings you down here?"

"Well, if you won't come to me, I have to come to you."

"How is everybody?"

"Everybody's fine. Only, they'd feel a whole lot better if they knew how *you* were. Yeah. Their faces would get bright, and they'd really perk up."

"You want a cup of coffee or something? Oh. Caleb, this is Hilda, my boss. She's the cook here, and she's very good. You hungry? Let me fix you something to eat."

"Now, don't you go to no trouble for me. You take care of your customers. Or keep on singing, it's a long time since I heard you sing. How do you do, ma'am. I'm glad to make your acquaintance."

He and Hilda shook hands. Hilda said, "Here I been thinking you was all alone in the world, and you got this fine-looking brother."

I said, "He got all the looks in the family, all right."

"Is that why you don't want people to see us together?" He laughed as he said this. I hung up my guitar.

"No kidding, you hungry? Come on, I bet you're hungry, you're *always* hungry."

He smiled at Hilda and she smiled at him. He *is,* it's true, a very nice-looking man.

"Well, all right. What have you got?"

"I made some cornbread tonight," said Hilda. "If you anything like your brother, I *know* you like cornbread."

"You must have known I was coming." And he laughed.

"Come on in the kitchen and tell me what you want. We got chicken and ribs, you know, a whole lot of stuff."

"Then, how come you stay so skinny? Don't you eat here, too?"

"That's right," said Hilda, *"you* get after him. I'm glad he's got *somebody* cares enough about him. Because I am not starving your brother. He does *not* take care of himself."

I looked at Caleb, who was watching me with a wry, amused affection. "Waiting on tables kind of takes your appetite away," I said. "You get to hate just about the entire human race, just because it eats. But I'll eat with you, now."

"You just about through? I don't want to be no trouble."

"Don't talk like that. What kind of trouble—how can you be trouble? I'm just about finished, anyway."

I remember, that night, I was very glad Barbara wasn't

there, that no one who meant anything to me was there. Hilda was very nice. She took over my duties, and even went about talking to a couple of the customers, and giving them their bills, while I loaded up Caleb's plate, and mine. I so wanted to ask Caleb to have a drink with me, but I knew he wouldn't drink. Then I wondered if I dared. But I'm grown now, I told myself, and I poured some ginger ale for him, and tumbler of Chianti for me.

We sat down.

"So," he said, "tell me about yourself."

"There's nothing to tell. I've just been working—you know—and studying."

"How's it going?" But this was a polite question. It wasn't the way he would have asked some time ago. He didn't believe that my studying meant anything. He was just being polite to his kid brother, waiting for the kid to come to his senses.

And you can't really answer a polite question, because actually no question has been asked. I felt myself squirming and I sipped my wine and I said, "It goes all right." But I wanted to say, I think I may be making some progress, but it's rough and I know it's going to get rougher, and I'm very lonely.

"You still living over on the east side?"

"Yeah."

He didn't mention Barbara, and I didn't either.

"What's happening with *you?* How are things uptown?"

"Well, between my boss"—Caleb worked as a chauffeur for some broker who lived on Long Island—"that unhappy creature, and my work in the church, I keep pretty busy. You look tired, Leo. Aren't you taking care of yourself?"

"Sure. But I've been kind of busy, too, between this job and trying to study."

He looked at my wine glass. "You're not drinking too much, are you? The grape has ruined many a fine man."

I was furious, wishing that I'd poured myself a double whiskey, and abjectly glad that I hadn't. "No."

He still knew my moods and tones. "Don't jump salty. I only ask because you're my brother, and I love you. You can't get mad at me for that."

"I'm not mad at you. I'm glad to see you."

"Well, if you're so glad to see me, why is it that you never *do* see me? You lose my address?" He paused. "You think it's right to have Mama and Daddy worrying about you the way they do?"

"There's nothing to worry about. I'm a big boy, I can take care of myself."

"You're a very young boy, Leo, in a terrible world. We're older than you are, and we know that. We *have* to worry about you, you're our flesh and blood, the youngest boy in the family. We love you. You think it's right to make us suffer?" He paused again. "Our mother and father won't be with us forever. You ought to try to be nice to them while they're still around. After all, they were pretty nice to you. Weren't they?"

By now, my food was tasteless, and my wine was sour.

"Caleb, I don't know if I can make you understand—"

"Try. I know you think I'm just an old-fashioned goody-goody, but try. What makes you treat your family like you do? You think it doesn't hurt us, you think we don't have any feelings?"

I certainly couldn't doubt, watching him, listening to him, that he had feelings. Try. Try to wake the dead, try to hold back the sea, try to talk to your brother. Try.

"Caleb, I'm not trying to hurt anybody. I'm just trying to live my life. But you all don't—you don't like my life."

"We don't want to see you destroying yourself, if that's what you mean. What's so unnatural about that?"

"I'm not destroying myself. I'm working and studying. What do you want from me?"

Naturally, at this point, a particularly ruined-looking girl came over to the table to say good-night, and to get a closer look at Caleb. She didn't know what Caleb was thinking as she stood there, smiling and simpering and trying to make an impression on him. She made an impression, all right. I watched Caleb's smile stiffen. His eyes filmed over with pity and scorn; he looked briefly at me. At last, she was gone.

"She's a friend of yours?"

"She's just a customer. She comes in sometimes. She's a nice girl," I said, and then wished I hadn't said it.

"She is a very sad, lost girl. You spend much of your time with them kind of people?"

"Look. Let's not talk about it. We'll just get into a fight."

"You won't get into a fight with me," he said, "be-

cause it takes two to quarrel, and *I* will never fight *you*.
But I *have* to keep on at you. It's a charge I have to keep.
You're young, and the world has got you so confused you
don't know if you're coming or going. You're a very unhappy boy, Leo, it sticks out all over you, and it hurts me
to see it. But you haven't *got* to be unhappy and the
light's going to come to you one day, just like it came to
me. You're going to see that you, and all your friends, are
going to *have* to be unhappy just as long as you fight the
love of God."

I suppose any real conviction brings with it a species
of beauty, and, as Caleb spoke, a stern and mighty beauty
entered his face. I had no weapons against him.

"You're fighting now. I know. I know how *I* fought.
You're going to have to learn how *not* to fight, not to
insist on *your* will but to surrender your will and find
yourself in the great will, the universal will, the will of
God, which created the heavens and earth and everything
that is, *and*"—he leaned forward and tapped me on the
brow—"created you." He smiled. "That's right, little
brother. You."

He smiled, and he made me smile. I didn't have any
great objections to being God's handiwork. But I felt that
He might possibly have supplied us with a manual which
would have given us some idea of how we worked.

"I'm not like you, Caleb."

He threw back his head, and laughed. "I know you're
not like me! Why should you be like me? You think that's
what I'm talking about?" He looked at me very affection-
ately, still smiling. "Oh, no, Leo. I want you to be like
you. That's why God made you *you*. But I want you to be
more like you than you are now. I want you to conquer
the kingdom of the spirit. Then, you'll be you."

The last customers were leaving, and Hilda snuffed
out their candles. We sat in the light of our candles, and
the faint light that came from the kitchen, behind us.
Hilda went into the bathroom.

I looked down, away from his blazing eyes, and I said,
"You want some more to eat? You have enough?"

"I'm fine, thanks. But you sure didn't eat very much."

"I don't have much appetite these days."

"You've got too much on your mind." He looked at
me gravely; it was not a question.

"What made you come by here, Caleb—so late, to-night? You're usually in bed by this time. Aren't you?"

"They kept me late on the job. They're having some kind of trouble—rich white people have more trouble than anybody else in the world. Then, when I got on the subway, something told me to make a run by here and see how you were. And I'm off tomorrow."

Hilda came out of the bathroom, and picked up her bags and things. She had put on her turban and her ear-rings, and was ready to go.

"I'm going to put these bones to bed," she said. "I didn't leave you too much to do in the kitchen, Leo. Just put the food away, and we'll clean up tomorrow." She put out her hand, and Caleb took it. "You better listen to your brother," she said, "he's got better sense than you got. A burnt child dreads the fire."

"That's true," said Caleb, and laughed. "Good-night, ma'am."

"Okay, Hilda," I said. "Good-night. Sleep well."

"Good-night."

She left, closing the door behind her, and we sat in silence for awhile. I was aware of the streets outside, of how much Caleb distrusted these streets, of all that had happened to him on these streets, and all that had happened to me. I watched his face, sculptured and melancholy in the candlelight, sculptured and proud, like a mask created at our beginning. It was an unspeaking face, obsessed forever by the fire which had formed it. Only in my own memory was it my brother's face. When others saw Caleb, they saw a closed, proud, distant man, a man who would never reach out to them, and whom they could never reach. And the other Caleb, the raging, laughing, seeking Caleb, the Caleb who moaned and wept, the Caleb who could be lonely—that other Caleb, my brother, had been put to death and would never be seen again. I wondered if he ever thought, now, of the Caleb he had been. I wondered if he missed him at all. *I* missed him and was still hoping to hear from him again. But Caleb had put away childish things—why couldn't I?

That was a useless question, but it was a real one all the same. The last time I had seen Caleb had not been so very long ago; he had not seen me. It had not been the first time I had peeked in, so to speak, on his life. I couldn't but wonder if he hadn't found some mighty secret, a secret which I needed. For he seemed not to despise himself anymore. Terrible things would not happen to him anymore, and he would no longer do terrible things. But I could not risk saying this to him. I could not risk seeing him. The last time I had seen him had been the day I drove the Workshop car from the town to the city. I wandered around the city. I was hungry, but I couldn't eat. I couldn't force myself to mingle with the people for that long. Watching Caleb's face, watching Caleb watching his little brother, I remembered that I ducked into one of the movies on 42nd Street and sat in the top row and I let a white boy grope me and stroke me and finally I forced his blond head down on me and I made him give me a blow job. Then I felt sicker than I had felt before and I felt like murdering the poor white fagot who, with my white hot sperm still in him, crept quietly down the stairs, away. I couldn't watch the movie, couldn't stand the voices, didn't know what they were saying, didn't care, couldn't stand the stink of people. I left the movie. I stopped and bought a hot dog and a soda. I watched the people. I walked back to the car, and I drove down to the Village. I went to a bar I knew and had a couple of beers. It was just about the cocktail hour, but no one I knew came in. I let another fagot pick me up and feed me. I asked him for money, too, and he gave me three dollars. I got away from him by about ten o'clock, and I drove uptown to Harlem. I wanted to see my mother and father; but I didn't want them to see me. So, I drove through our block and I looked at our house. Their lights were on.

I stopped, finally, as I had known all along, really, that I would, in front of a great stone building which, in Harlem's heyday, had been a theater. It was now The New Dispensation House of God. It seemed very lively, especially for a Monday night.

I walked inside and walked upstairs to the balcony. I was nearly all alone there, though, on Sunday nights, it was packed. A few idle men, a few lonely and bewildered women; but, downstairs, the faithful were rejoicing. Caleb could not see me, I sat far to the side, in the shadows, but I could see Caleb. He sat just below the pulpit. That meant that, tonight, he was in charge of the testimony service.

He still looked like my brother—big and black—the transforming power of the Holy Ghost leaves some elements untouched. There was a light in his face which I envied and despised: Caleb was at peace. He had told me so. He had told me so. Caleb was found, but I was lost.

Caleb had had the tambourine. A plain black girl was at the piano. Somebody was beating the drum. They were singing:

> *Down on my knees,*
> *When trouble rides!*
> *I talk to Jesus,*
> *He satisfies!*
> *He promised me*
> *He'd hear my plea,*
> *If I would serve Him,*
> *Down on my knees!*

I had sat in the darkness, cursing and crying, my tears falling like a curtain between my brother and myself. My head was bowed and I could scarcely see them, but I could hear:

> *If I would serve Him,*
> *Down on my knees!*

I watched his face now, wondering if he had ever spied on my life as I had spied on his.

"When are you coming up to the house?"

"Let's see—what's today? Caleb, I don't see how I can come until my day off. That's Thursday."

He accepted this with a tiny, wry smile. With a certain defiance, I sipped my wine. "This is a pretty good job for you, I guess."

"It suits me. The people don't bother me. You know."

"What do most of the people around here *do?*"

"Oh, I don't know. I don't know a lot of people. The people I know—well, they mainly all want to be artists of one kind or another."

"How do they go about it?"

"Well—they work at it. Some of them do."

"They're not just kidding themselves?"

I looked at him. "Some of them are. Naturally."

"Leo," he asked me, after a moment, "can you tell me what it is—an artist? What's it all about? What does an artist *really* do?"

I had never known Caleb to be cruel, and so I couldn't believe that he was baiting me. I stared at him. "What do you mean, what does an artist do? He—he creates—"

He stared at me with a little smile, saying nothing.

"You know," I said, "paintings, poems, books, plays. Music."

"These are all creations," he said, still with that smile.

"Well, yes. Not all of them are *good*."

"But those that are good—what do they do? Why are they good, when they're good?"

"They make you—feel more alive," I said. But I did not really trust this answer.

"That's what drunkards say about their whiskey," he said, and he nodded in the direction of my wine.

"Well. I don't mean that," I said.

He watched me for a long while with his little smile, and he made me very uneasy.

"Why are you asking me these questions?"

"Because I want to know. I'm not teasing you. I don't know anything about it. And you say you want to be an actor. That's a kind of artist. Isn't it? Well, I want to know."

"I think it—art—can make you less lonely." I didn't trust this answer, either.

"Less lonely." He smiled. "Little Leo." Then, "I don't know anything about it, but I've watched some people who claimed to be artists and they all seemed pretty lonely to me. The man I work for has a lot of friends like that. They're lonely"—he watched me earnestly now—"and they're half crazy and I've seen them do terrible things. Do you really think that people like that, who are really in hell themselves, Leo—do you really think that they can help anybody?"

"They *do*." I said it stoutly, but felt, nevertheless, that my faith was not as strong as Caleb's. And I realized that Caleb was far from stupid.

"They do? How do you know they do?"

"Sometimes," I said, "you read something—or you listen to some music—I don't know—and you find that this man, who may have been a very unhappy man—and —a man you've never seen—well, he tells you something about your life. And it doesn't seem as awful as it did before."

"As awful," said Caleb, "as it did before." And he watched me, his face in the candlelight yet more austere and distant than it had been, and, at the same time, somehow—it was as vivid and elusive as a half-heard, half-forgotten bit of music—more than ever the face of my brother. "Has it been as bad as all that, Leo?" But he didn't wait for me to answer this. "What I thought," he said, rising and walking up and down the room, with his hands in his pockets, "was that a lot of these people didn't think of anything but self. Maybe they had gifts, but they didn't think the gift was for others, for the glory of God. They thought it was just for self. And that's what made them like they were—that they just thought of self. And that offended God, and so they lost the gift." He looked at me. "We were put on earth to love each other and to praise God, Leo."

"All right. But can't we"—hoping for daylight, hoping for reconciliation—"each praise God in our own way?"

"Oh, but that's taken for granted," he said, with a simple, monumental conviction, "of course we all praise God in our own way. No two people praise God alike. But *not* to praise Him is a sin."

I sipped my wine, feeling beleaguered and lost. Yet— I loved him, this stranger returned from the dead. Something in his face, his voice, something in his attitude as he stood before the fireplace, made him seem, to me, almost helpless, vulnerable, sad, and it made me think of a most melancholy song. *I have had my fun, if I don't get well no more.* Really, for a moment, I heard it: he might have been singing it. *Don't send me no doctor, doctor can't do me no good.*

But he had found his doctor, the Saviour, who was Christ the Lord.

"Yes, we have to find our way out of the prison of the self," said Caleb, "we have to release ourselves from all our petty wants, our petty pride, and just see that the will of God is far beyond us—like King David said, 'Such knowledge is too wonderful for me'—and just surrender our will to His will." He smiled a ruined, radiant smile. "We know He'll always guide us right. He'll never let us be lost." And then his face became both tender and austere, at once old and young. "Until that day, Leo, the soul is a wanderer and it has no hope and can find no peace. I know. *I moaned and I moaned, I moaned all night long*—you remember that song, Leo?"

I said, watching him, "*I moaned and I moaned until I found the Lord.*"

He smiled. "Yes. *My soul could not rest contented. Until I found the Lord.*" And he shook his head. "The old folks knew what they were talking about."

"The old folks had a lot to bear," I said.

"But they bore it," said Caleb, "they bore it, and they gave us the keys to the kingdom. It comes to you, Leo, it comes to you when you're all alone in the valley, deep in the valley, and it looks like the deep water is dragging down your soul, something whispers to you. He that overcometh shall receive the crown of life. He that believeth on me, though he were dead, yet shall he live. What a promise that is! And it's for every man, Leo. For every man."

I said nothing. Perhaps I was thinking of what he had had to bear. I watched his face. It was very beautiful. He moved up and down the room.

"I guess the light comes differently to every man," he said, in a different tone. He stopped pacing. "Me, I had to almost kill a man. I really wanted to kill a man, Leo. Did I ever tell you that?"

"You must have killed a lot of men in the war," I said. I wanted to go to the bar and pour myself a drink, but I didn't.

"I don't mean that. If I killed anybody, I didn't know it, I didn't see it." He stopped. "I suppose I must have. My Lord, you know, men were dying all around you, dying in a second, dying worse than dogs. Lord, Leo, you'd be talking to a man one minute, and when you looked up again, his head would be over yonder and his body God knows where. I remember watching one guy ahead of me one time, running, and a mine caught him and he rose up in the air just as pretty as you please, like he was flying or dancing, and one leg went this way and the other leg went the other way and the rest of him come floating down and he landed on his back. I never saw his face, but I saw lots of other faces. They all looked surprised. They were young. A lot of them were no more than kids. I had hated some of them. But, you know, when you look down on this poor, helpless, stinking mess —death has an odor, Leo, nobody can describe it—well, you know, it all goes out of you. You realize that the poor creature just wanted to live, just like you, and you think about his mother or his wife or his kids or about whoever loved him. And it makes you wonder why you ever bothered to hate anybody. You know, the body just turns into garbage when the gift of life has left it. What a mystery. We have no right to kill. I know that. But I must have killed some people. I was in darkness then, I know my Lord's forgiven me. I was shooting because I was a soldier, and people were shooting at me. All over this beautiful land where we were fighting, this beautiful land that God had given the people so they could rejoice and be fruitful and multiply, this land He had given them so they could praise His name, there was nothing but bodies and pieces of bodies piled up like tinder, nothing but the bombs going off and howling and screaming and moaning and the fear of death and the shadow of death and death all around you, on the right hand, on the left. Leo, the sea was red, it was like something out of the Bible. And it just went on, it just went on, every morning, every day, every night. I just wanted to stay alive. I was surprised every morning and every night that I was still alive. I thought I'd like to go back one day to some of those places where we were, when the war was over, and the people was more themselves, because it *was* beautiful, Leo, and some of the people were beautiful." He was silent for a long time. "Our unit got all messed up, and I got sent to Sicily and then we had us a time, baby, *all* up and down Italy. I'll never forget it." He stopped again. He looked a little surprised. "I didn't want to kill nobody during all that time. But I *did* want to kill this man."

"I've wanted to kill, too," I said. I said it quickly, not in sympathy, but to establish myself as unrepentant; for I felt his presence stifling me.

"Have you, Leo? Do you *still* want to? That's too bad."

"Well," I said, after a moment, "I won't ever do it. I've just felt that way sometimes, and I guess I will again."

"I hope you won't," he said. "It's the worst feeling that there is. It's the most destructive feeling that there is. It fills you with darkness, Leo. It's the soul turning away from God."

How I longed to pour myself a drink! But I did not move. I dreaded hearing any more of his story: dreaded it. I felt myself retreating, moving backward before him. I felt him pursuing me, moving me, inexorably, into a place where I would have to cry out and fall on my knees. I watched him, and said nothing.

"This was a white man. You know how it is in this man's army, Leo, they keep the black and the white separated—you know—and, naturally, all my buddies was colored, until I got overseas. I mean, you know, the only white cats we ever talked to was our officers and we didn't *like* talking to *them*. But overseas it was a little different."

Now, his face was almost the face that I remembered, surprised, and full of grief.

"But, like I say, our unit got wiped out, most of my buddies, and, well, you know, the man couldn't afford to be so particular once we was over there in all this mess together. If you depending on a guy for your life, you don't really much care what color he is. And we had to depend on each other. We had to.

"Anyway, by the time we got ourselves out of Cassino, Lord, I was buddies with this white guy from Boston, Hopkins. Frederick Hopkins. He seemed like a nice kid, blond, kind of skinny, real good-natured. He didn't—he just *didn't*—seem like most white guys. That's what made it so hurtful later. He wasn't a good soldier, but he wasn't a bad soldier; but he was quick; something like me. And we'd been buddies all through that slaughter. And he was all right until we got to Rome. I'll never understand what happened to that kid, when we got to Rome. Well—maybe I *do* understand it." And he laughed.

I didn't go to the bar, but I lit a cigarette.

"Did you like Rome?" I asked. I knew it was a foolish

question, but I had never seen Rome, I rather envied him for having been there, and I was trying, although I knew I could not succeed, to deflect him.

"Yes," he said, after a moment, "I liked Rome. I was in darkness in Rome, but I liked it. I don't know if I'd like Rome *now*. I'm not the same now. In Rome, I lived my last days as a sinner." And now his face was very sad, sad, and, at the same time, proud.

"Well, you know, we got to Rome. And it *is* a beautiful city, especially if you've never seen it before, and especially after all we'd been through. And the people were very glad to see us, and they were starving. I realized I had never *seen* starvation until I got to Rome." He looked at me. "I didn't know how much I had to praise God for. There wasn't nothing you couldn't buy in Rome, you could buy anything or anybody and it wouldn't cost you no more than cigarettes, stuff like that. And you know soldiers. When you been cooped up with all these men for so many months, cooped up with the *smell* of all these men, well, then, you want a woman. And I was just like all the others. I wasn't no better. We hit that town"— he laughed—"like locusts. And, it's funny, you know, I might have thought at the very back of my mind that I might be kind of shy—because I knew I wasn't going to meet no *colored* women in Rome—but I wasn't shy a bit. Maybe I wasn't shy because they weren't shy. They not at all like the women here, Leo. Not a bit. They don't look at you like women here, like they scared to be in the same street with you. No, they didn't care, not as long as you had the currency, didn't nobody care what color you were. And with a lot of them, it wasn't just the currency. I have to give them that. I *got* to give them that. A lot of these women, they were really loyal, and it was, you know, it was nice." He looked very young as he said this. "I had never really seen that before, not between black and white, and I hadn't seen it *too* often between those of the same color. If a woman found herself a nice man, be he black, blue or yellow, well, she took care of him and there wasn't nothing she wouldn't do for him. Nothing."

He sat down at the table again.

"I forgot," I said, "to offer you a cup of coffee, Caleb. Would you like a cup of coffee?"

"If it's no trouble. Am I keeping you up?"

"I told you that sometimes I don't leave this place until four o'clock in the morning."

I went into the kitchen and put a light under the coffee and took out the cups, the sugar and cream; and had to face the fact that I simply did not have the courage, under Caleb's eyes, to pour myself a drink. This exasperated me, and made me very angry with Caleb. But I was afraid that if I poured myself a drink, I would be doing it only to hurt him.

He sat very quietly at the table until I came back. I poured the coffee and sat down and lit another cigarette. He watched me with a bright, disapproving smile, but only said, shaking his head, "Little Leo." Then, "We were in Rome for quite a long while, between you and me I don't believe that this war was very well managed at *all*, and by and by I found me a real nice little girl, her name was Pia."

Then he stopped—for quite a long while; and his face changed, unreadably; now, it was not merely a private face, but a personal face. He kept his eyes on the table. He sighed once, looked shamefacedly, just like Caleb, up at me, and smiled. He stirred his coffee and blew on it as he picked up the cup. "Ah," he said, "I have to tell you—I was different in those days. Well, you remember how I was." He paused again, and sipped his coffee. "And I have to tell you that most of the guys, well, they were still, you know, going from here to yonder. I mean, you know, maybe they had *lots* of girls, but me, I just had one. She was a pretty girl, she really was, and she was a *nice* girl. She really was a nice girl." He blew on his coffee again. "She was a blonde and I didn't know but that seems to mean something in Italy because there aren't many, I guess. And she came from a nice family except they'd lost all their money. They expected us to get married. Married! Can you imagine that?" And he looked up at me, with his eyes very big. I said nothing. "And when I look back," he said, "I guess I wasn't, you know, very truthful. I wasn't thinking. I was like a child. I was happy with Pia. I had never been so happy before. I thought maybe I would stay in Italy."

Then he was silent again. I felt that he wanted to cry. I sensed tears somewhere in him, dammed up, drying fast. I wished I could have reached out and stroked the place where the tears were hidden; stroked the place and probed it and let the blood-red, salty tears come out. *There is a fountain filled with blood.* His face would have changed then, and he would have become Caleb again. But he did not want to be Caleb anymore.

"I was so happy, I didn't see what was going on around me. Well, the colored guys and the white guys didn't really get along, not most of us. Frederick and me still hung out together, and he had other colored buddies, mainly because of me, I think, and we had some nice times, but most of the guys, you know, they just stayed away from each other. Most of the white guys, we tried to stay away from them and they sure stayed away from us." How careful his voice was now! "Well, we didn't need them, we weren't at home. They couldn't, you know, like in the States, tell you where to sit and when to stand and all that; they couldn't stop you from going out with a girl if you wanted to; if the girl didn't care, there wasn't much they could do. They couldn't stop you from making friends with the people. If the people wanted to make friends, well, you know, that was it. But they didn't like it. They gave a whole lot of guys a whole lot of trouble. And they told the people, oh, they told the people ridiculous things, Leo, like we had tails and back home we weren't allowed on the streets after dark and wouldn't nobody in the States never sell a black man no liquor because we got savage when we was drunk and started cutting up people just like savages, cannibals, and we was always raping white men's daughters and wives and mothers and sisters and—and—our—*member* was so huge that it just tore white people to pieces, you know, ridiculous and childish stuff like that. And a lot of the people believed it, and guys had trouble sometimes, especially with the women, on account of stuff like that. And we was there supposed to be fighting for freedom. Well, it was, you know, it was just ridiculous.

"But, you see, since I was spending all my time with Pia, I didn't go to the bars much, and I wasn't running after women, so what was going on around me didn't bother me. I just didn't see it. My free time, I'd go on over to Pia's house and talk to the folks for awhile. They were really nice old-fashioned people and they seemed to like me, we got on very well. I was really surprised. They treated me like a gentleman. Of course, they was too intelligent to believe any of that stuff the Americans was spreading around. We'd go out and eat dinner, Pia and me, or maybe we'd eat at the house, and we might go dancing someplace. But we wouldn't go where most of the Americans went. We might go out in the country. We rode out in the country many a night. And sometimes we'd just sit there, under that beautiful Italian sky."

His coffee cup was empty. He stared into it. "And she could make me moan. She really made me moan. Over and over and over. It was—it was mighty. I never shook like that. I wanted us to have a baby so bad. I knew it would be beautiful, it would have to be, it was so beautiful with us. And I really thought I could stay in Italy. I didn't see how I could ever leave. But I knew it was going to be hard for us to get married as long as I was in the service. They didn't like it, and they could make it mighty rough. So I hadn't figured out exactly what I was going to do. I guess I thought I'd wait until I got discharged. I guess I thought I'd do that and then maybe open up a club or a restaurant, you know, then it could have been done, a lot of guys did it. Well, I was just happy for awhile, I guess, putting it off. But I certainly didn't see how I could live without Pia. I used to wonder sometimes how come I had to come all the way to Italy. I used to pinch myself. It didn't seem possible. And sometimes I'd catch myself laughing, Leo, just like a kid."

He rose from the table and walked back to the fireplace. I heard his song again. *Won't somebody write my mother and tell her the shape I'm in.*

"I didn't—think—that Frederick Hopkins had any reason to be upset. We had been buddies, tight buddies. I never thought of him at all. I'd see him, naturally, and everything certainly seemed to be all right. If he seemed a little strange sometimes, well, that didn't bother me, white people are always a *little* strange. He was always talking about his women. I never talked about mine. I never have talked about women, I don't believe in that. But he knew I had this girl, because I'd told him. The other guys knew, too, naturally, that I had this girl somewhere, but they didn't mess with me because I had, you know, a bad reputation. They thought I was crazy, and that was just fine with me.

"One night I come in this bar where we used to go

sometimes, late, and I found Frederick there, all alone, crying. So I tried to find out what the matter was—you know. And he told me this sad story about how some girl he was going with had put him down, and what I realized, right quick, was that *all* his women put him down and I could see why, he wasn't nothing but a baby, really, and all that talk of his was just talk. Well, you know, if you got to talk it all the time, you can't be doing much. I didn't say any of that, what I was thinking, to him, naturally, but I tried, diplomatically, I *think,* to show him where he might be going wrong and to make him look at it in another light. I tried to cheer him up, you know, even though I had just suddenly realized that I didn't have no respect for this man. He was just a poor, sick, homesick baby, no wonder the women put him down. And he looked at me, I remember, with this funny look in his eyes, and he said, You don't have no troubles, do you? And I said, Sure, I have troubles. Everybody has troubles. He said, You don't have no troubles with women, and I don't know what I said, I turned it off, somehow, it was just too silly, and I wasn't about to start talking about me and my women and you *know* I wasn't going to start talking about me and Pia. *He* might be a child, but I wasn't. So we went on in, and I forgot all about it. The next day, when I was fixing to go, he asked me if he could come with me and like a chump I said Okay, because I was sorry for him, you know, and, bam, he met Pia, and, bam, baby, my troubles started. That boy, my buddy, a man I'd tried to help, and we'd looked on death together, he took one look at Pia and he decided to take her from me. To his mind, it was real simple. This poor, ignorant Italian girl—but she was much better educated than him, he didn't know that—was running with me because she didn't know any better. But she certainly wouldn't want to be bothered with me, once she realized what *he* had to offer. And what he had to offer was his house and his cars and his money, back in Boston. What he had to offer was his family's social position, and the fine future waiting for him, in Boston. And he hammered away at it. And it wasn't, you know, that he cared about the girl, or had any intention of marrying her. He just wanted to get her away from me. He was determined to give her a taste of what life would be like if she stayed with me, and so he caused her to start being harassed in all kinds of ways, like one time they wanted to make her register as a whore, things like that. Oh. I can't tell you. Or we'd go out someplace, we'd be walking down the street, and somebody would insult her and I'd get into a fight and my liberty would be canceled. And then *he* would go to see her. Stuff like that. And then she and *I* would fight about *me* getting into fights, and what was happening, though we didn't realize it right away, was that all the pressure was getting to us, and we weren't the same with each other. She didn't believe Frederick, but, just the same, he had planted a seed, I could see the doubt begin, I could see it in her eyes when she looked at me, I could see the fear begin, I could see her wondering if she could really make it, if anybody could ever love *anybody* enough to take what she was going to have to take. And I lay on my bunk one night—I was different then, I've changed, I've changed—and I hadn't seen her for two weeks because I hadn't had no liberty, and I thought, This is really something. I'm five thousand miles from home, in this man's uniform, protecting *him*, and he brings his poison all the way over here with him to spoil my girl and ruin my life. I lay on my bunk and I cried worse than Frederick had ever cried. But I cried because I was mad. I had whipped too many people, I was *tired* of whipping people, and it hadn't done me no good, here I was, lying on this bunk, and I might as well have been in chains.

"The next time I saw Frederick it was in a bar, I was by myself, he come in, and he was whistling. He didn't see me right away. He came along, slow, whistling, with his cap on the back of his head, and, I don't know, I never *decided* to kill him, just as he came closer that was all that was in my mind, and I knew I was *going* to kill him. I knew it. I had never noticed before how, when a guy whistles, there's a funny little trembling high up in his neck. I noticed it now. His neck wasn't going to be trembling long, he was whistling one of his last songs. I noticed the space between his eyebrows, that kind of little no-man's-land between the hairs, there's bone there when you touch it and if a bullet goes in there, you're dead. I watched his whole body as he moved toward me, and I saw him lying flat and still, on his back, forever. It takes less than a second to kill a man. I wanted him to look surprised, like I'd seen so many look.

"And I knew exactly how I was going to do it, and I would never be caught. I knew we were going to be moving out of Rome soon, going north. And I was just going to stay real close to him, like white on rice. I knew, we all knew, the fighting was going to be heavy, where we was going. And one night or one morning just as soon as I saw my opportunity, I was going to pull that trigger and blow his head off. I didn't have any reason to be fighting the people I was fighting. But I had every reason in the world to kill *him*. And I knew I was going to do it.

"He looked surprised when he saw me. He stopped whistling. He started to say something, and then he didn't. I just looked at him. I didn't say a word. He sat down at the bar. Then, he just suddenly got up and left.

"Well, we moved on out. I only saw Pia once before we left Rome, and she was as beautiful as ever, but it wasn't like before. It wasn't like before in *me*. And then I stuck close to Frederick, I kept him in sight. It happened one morning, very early, not like I'd planned. He was all alone, he was near a tree. We was away from the others, nobody could see us, and the valley where we were was full of snipers. I started running up on him and I called his name because I wanted him to know it was me who killed him. And he turned around. He looked surprised, all right. He raised his hands in front of him, like a baby, and he was trying to say something, and while he had his mouth open, his mouth opened wider, all of a sudden, and another look came over his face, another surprise, an awful agony, Leo, I'll never forget it, and he pitched forward on his face. I knew I hadn't yet pulled the trigger. I hadn't heard a sound. I just stood there. Leo, I started to tremble. He lay there with his arms stretched out in front of him on the ground. I looked down at him and I looked around. I could hear shouting and running and all; but it all seemed like in a dream. I turned him over. He wasn't dead, but he was dying, and he didn't look surprised anymore. He looked at me, just for a minute, right in my eyes, and he said, I don't blame you. I'm sorry. I couldn't help it. Then he died. In my arms. Like that, he sort of hiccuped and then he was still, with his eyes wide open. All of a sudden, he was mighty heavy. He'd gone into

eternity believing I'd killed him. I just sat there. There
was noise and flame all around me. Guys were running
and crying and ducking. Some guy pulled on me and
pulled and he was shouting something and just then the
earth blew up right at my feet and Frederick rolled out of
my arms. And I was on my face like he had been, and
then I started crawling and then I started running. We
was all running in the same direction, we must have been
running to some kind of shelter, but I didn't know what I
was doing, my legs was just carrying me, carrying me with
the others, wherever they were going. I kept thinking
how I should go back and close his eyes. I fell, and I heard
somebody right nearby scream. It sounded like Frederick, but I knew it couldn't be him, he was back there
where I'd left him, he was dead. When I fell, I didn't get
up, I just hugged the ground. I listened to the screaming
and tried to figure out where it was coming from and I
tried to inch my way in that direction but I couldn't see
ahead of me and the earth was shaking and turning over.
I wanted to help whoever it was, because I thought that
might make up for Frederick, but then, the screaming
stopped, and I knew. No. No life can be given back. And
that was the moment of my repentance, Leo. It was a pain
I had never felt before, a heartbreak I had never felt
before. I saw my whole life stretching ahead of me forever like this, in lust and hatred and darkness, and to end
like this, face down, hugging the earth, and you feel your
bowels moving for fear, Leo, and to be like that until the
earth covers you. I struggled up to my knees. I knew, I
knew for the first time that there was a God somewhere. I
knew that only God could save me, save *us*, not from
death but from that other death, that darkness and death
of the spirit which had created this hell. Which had sent
men here to die. I cried out, I cried out something, I
remember I was thinking, *Lord, send the angel down*,
and then I was struck. It didn't hurt. It knocked me flat
on my back, it knocked me out of my body, and I remember I thought of Frederick's eyes and I thought, Well,
now, I can tell him I didn't pull the trigger. And it
seemed to me God's great mercy that I hadn't, and I
praised Him for His mercy, that He'd held me back from
mortal sin, and was taking me home now, washed of my
sins, forgiven. I thought I was dying, but I wasn't afraid.

I understood for the first time the power and beauty of the love of God."

A silence fell when Caleb ceased speaking such as I had never known before, and have not known since. It was a silence loud enough to wake the dead. It was the silence that Jesus had in mind when he told the Pharisees that if his disciples held their peace, the stones would immediately cry out. It was a silence in which one seemed to hear the bloodstream move. One wondered at its cargo. In the awful light—the awful light—and in this silence, we now watched each other. How terrible it is to overhear a confession! He was more than ever my brother now, forever—and he was more than ever a stranger, forever and forever: because I had seen him for the first time. We listened to the sounds coming in from the streets. It was three o'clock in the morning.

I did not say anything. I rose and went into the kitchen and poured myself a glass of rum. I came back with it, and sat down at the table again.

He walked over to me, and put his hand on my shoulder.

"When you've been down in that valley, Leo," he said, "when you been wrestling with the angel, it changes you. It changes you. Everybody hits that valley, Leo, but don't everyone come up. Love lifted me. And I'm free at last."

Free at last, free at last, praise God Almighty, I'm free at last! These words rang in my mind. I sipped my rum. His hand was very heavy on my shoulder. I felt his weariness, and smelled his sweat—fleeting, like my memory of our past, and indescribable, inaccessible, like that. What did I feel? I cannot tell. I will never know. I felt, for the first time, and it must be rare, another human being occupying my flesh, walking up and down in me. And that is why I cannot tell, that is why I cannot remember. Oh. I remember the candle before me, burning low; I thought, I must put it out. I remember that I thought that the police would soon walk by, checking the lights. They might come in. I remember thinking, I promised Caleb that I would come home soon, to see my father and my mother. I remember the way the restaurant looked at that moment, the tables not cleared, coffee cups and dessert plates everywhere, and some tables needed new candles. I remember all that, and his hand on my shoulder, and the silence.

I was nineteen then, and Caleb was twenty-six. Years and years later, I grabbed Barbara back from her Sutton Place window ledge, eight stories up. Let us pretend that I was a man by that time. I remember that moment very well. I remember that Barbara and I had had what we both then considered to be our deadliest, irrevocable fight. I remember that I took my gray topcoat off her sofa, and put it on, and walked out of her living room, walked the long corridor to the door. I had left her on the floor, in her nightgown, crying. I walked out of the apartment, slamming the door, and buzzed for the elevator. I watched the indicator as the car moved up to eight. Eight. Somehow, that number began to scream in my mind. The indicator struck six, and, without knowing that I was going to do it, I turned away from the elevator, and took out my keys and opened Barbara's door and walked back into the apartment. It was silent. I slammed the door behind me—or, rather, the door slammed behind me, and, far off, I heard another door slam, the door to Barbara's bedroom. But both doors had been slammed by the wind. I ran to the bedroom, and opened the door— what guided me?—and saw Barbara, with her back to me, sitting on the window ledge, swinging her feet like a child, and about to drop. I pulled her back by the hair. I remember that moment, I remember it well, and I know that I have since used it in my work. But I have never consciously used that moment in the restaurant with Caleb. I remember it only in flashes, hot and cold. It may be that, by the time I dragged Barbara back from the ledge, I knew enough to know that she might be sitting there. But I did not know, when Caleb walked into The Island on that far-off night, how many ways there were to die, and how few to live.

"You'll see it, too, one day," he said—very carefully, very softly—"the light. I know you will. I know it. You don't know how hard I pray for you."

Well. I remember that he helped me wash the dishes. We talked of other things, and we laughed a lot. We were almost friends again. I remember that, at one point, he picked up my forgotten, unfinished glass of rum and poured it into the sink. "Soon, you won't be needing that, little brother." I remember the way the rum and the soapy water smelled. I remember how it looked—and we both laughed as it vanished down the drain, white soap and black sugar. We left the kitchen spotless. He helped me set up my tables. I turned out all the lights and locked up the joint and I walked him to his subway. I watched him run down the steps and he turned, one last time, at the bottom of the steps, to smile and wave. I realized again how glad I'd been to see him. Then, he disappeared. The morning light was rising now, as I walked home, walked toward the river, walked toward Barbara.

I kept my promise to go home on that Thursday, but of course that didn't really help. I had made—I had made it without knowing that I had—some enormous and unshakable resolution. I had arrived at an awful cunning, which was to be protected by silence. I knew that Caleb would never see the case as I saw it—no one would ever see my case, and so I would not waste breath presenting it. But I knew what I was going to do. I was alone all right; for God had taken my brother away from me; and I was never going to forgive Him for that. As far as the salvation of my own soul was concerned, Caleb was God's least promising missionary. God was not going to do to me what He had done to Caleb. Never. Not to me.

I walked home, that morning, as I say, and I stood over Barbara for a long time, and watched her sleeping in our bed. I remember the way she looked that morning, her hair curling over the pillow, one thin hand clutching the blanket, as though she sensed departure. She worked very hard, my poor little girl, at some bleakly piss-elegant establishment, like Longchamps. I sat at the window, and lit a cigarette. Our room faced what had once been a courtyard; directly facing me was the opposite wing of this decrepit complex. In some windows, the shades were down—those hideous kinds of paper shades, which leap out of your hand and curl round and round themselves and are as hard to reach, then, as a treed cat. In other windows, the shades were up. No one in Paradise Alley could really have anything to hide. The people slept. Everything was still. I can't stay here, I thought. And I looked back at Barbara. I closed the window and I pulled down the shade and I got undressed.

The proud and desperate years began. That winter ended, and the summer came again. Barbara got a job in summer stock, but I didn't. I didn't go away with the

Workshop, though they wanted me to come and play Crooks again and drive that goddamn car again. I stayed with The Island, and I found a voice teacher, and I studied that guitar. A few of the show business people who came in were nice to me, and they invited me here and there. I began to be seen around. It was accepted that I was talented —this came as something of a surprise, but it was a nice surprise. I sang at The Island almost every night, and more and more people came to hear me—so many that Hilda had to hire a helper for me; and we had trouble with the cops, which eventually ended those sessions. Hilda gave an Island ball at a big hall in Harlem, and she had got some very big show business names to perform, and I was on the bill, too. That was the very first time I ever saw my name on a poster and I carried it to my mother and father and they came to the ball—but Caleb didn't; now, he was in the world, but not of it—and my mother and father were very proud of me, and we had a very nice time that night. And, like all kids, with their first taste of the deeply desired approbation, I saw myself on the heights already. But, in fact, I wasn't being hired, and it was a very long time before I was.

Barbara and I split up, for the first of many times. We didn't see each other for a long time, not until I took Sally to see her in her first Broadway show. She played a very small part, but she was noticed, and she got offers from Hollywood which she had the good sense to turn down. I plodded on, and Sally and I split up, and I left The Island and started singing in a short-lived Village supper club. I got hired, as I've said, for bit parts here and there, odd parts here and there, but nothing led to anything and I was beginning to be more and more frightened. Steve and I split up, insofar as we had ever really been together, and, at the same time, Caleb got married, and I was the best man at his wedding. He married a woman named Louise, heavy and black and respectable, who would certainly take excellent care of him. I remember the wedding because I hated being there. By now, I was twenty-five, and I was terribly ashamed of the life I lived. Everyone had found the life that suited them; but I hadn't. Caleb looked safe and handsome that day, he had become a preacher and was now assistant pastor at The New Dispensation House of God. Now, he had a wife and a home and he'd have children, all according to God's plan. But, my life! It made me, I know, very defensive and difficult. I was a short-order cook, I was a waiter, I was a busboy, I was an elevator boy, I was a messenger, I was a shipping clerk—and that's when times were good. Otherwise, I was a bum, a funky, homeless bum, a grown man who slept in flophouses and movies, who often walked the streets without the price of subway fare, and who really knew no one because I didn't *want* to know the people in my condition—I didn't *like* my condition, I was *not* going to make peace with it. I was not going to enter the marihuana-drenched, cheap-beer-and-whiskey-soaked camaraderie of the doomed. I was going to change my condition, somehow, somehow—how? —and I was too proud to approach the affluent. My recollection of those years is not that I pounded the pavement, but crawled on my face over every inch of it. Breaks came and went, but terror and trouble stayed. The worst of it was, perhaps, that I most thoroughly avoided the people who loved me most. Barbara, for example, once spent a week in New York looking for me. She couldn't find me. I knew she was in town because I knew the show she was with was in town. But Barbara had a job, and I didn't. I knew I couldn't fool her the way I fooled others—I hoped—with my clean shirt and mattress-pressed pants and shiny shoes and clean fingernails. How I managed to keep clean the half dozen shirts which saw me through those years I'll never know. I knew—or I felt—that people were beginning to give me up. They felt, I was sure, that I was destined, simply, to become a part of the wreckage which lines every steep road. And, since I felt this way, I began to act this way—the most dangerous moment of all. I began to smell of defeat: that odor which seals your doom. I was drinking far too much, for people will always buy you a drink. And it was in a bar, in fact, that something happened which turned out, as we survivors love to put it, to be my first real break, the solid break, the break which made the others possible. It certainly didn't look like a break. It only looked like a job. I wasn't absolutely on my ass at this point. I was working as a short-order cook in Harlem. But, of course, I didn't want to spend my life as a short-order cook, and I was very low because I knew my mother wasn't well.

This man came over to me, a white man, very friendly, and said his name was Ray Fisher. He asked me how I was, and what I was doing. I didn't know the man, and I hated people to ask me questions like that, I was ashamed to tell people what I was doing. But I was also too proud to lie. This man had heard me sing, somewhere, and he had seen me on the stage; which caused me, I must say, enormously to respect his powers of observation. And he told me that a little theater group was going to do an experimental version of *The Corn Is Green*. This production would utilize Negroes, and they were looking for a Negro boy who could sing, to play the lead. He was a friend of the director's, which was how he knew about it, and he knew that the director had also seen me, and had a hunch about me. He said that it was only scheduled for seven performances, and the pay wasn't very much. But, on his own behalf, and on behalf of the director, his friend, he very much hoped that I'd think about it—it might, he said, with that innocent earnestness which characterizes so many Americans, be a kind of breakthrough. Anyway, it might be worth looking into, he thought, and he gave me the address of the theater. Which wasn't in the Village, but way down on the East Side, precisely the neighborhood where nobody would ever dream of going, especially not to see an experimental production, with a Negro in the male lead, of *The Corn Is Green*.

I remember looking at him, and saying, "The corn is *green?*" I was sure he was joking, or mad. You meet all kinds of people in bars. But he didn't seem to be joking, and he didn't seem to be mad. I'd never read the play, but I'd seen Ethel Barrymore play it. I didn't remember the boy's part at all. It all sounded, really, almost completely mad: I kept staring at Ray, whom I didn't yet recognize as the hand of God. But we had a few drinks; he was really very nice; I promised I'd go down, because he really seemed to mean it. But what decided me, really, was a telegram under my door, when I got home that night. I was living on 19th Street and Fourth Avenue. It was, you know, well—shit!—they really *have* been looking for me. So, in the morning, I called the barbecue joint, to say I'd be coming in late, and I went on down.

When things go wrong, the good Lord knows they go wrong; one can find oneself in trouble so deep and so bizarre that one *knows* one can never get out of it; and it doesn't help at all, as the years swagger brutally by, to recognize that much of one's trouble is produced by the really unreadable and unpredictable convolutions of one's own character. I've sat, sometimes, really helpless and terrified before my own, watching it spread danger and wonder all over my landscape—and not only my own. It is a terrible feeling. One learns, at such moments, not merely how little we know, but how little whatever we know is able to help us. But sometimes things go right. And these moments, humiliatingly enough, don't seem to have anything to do with one's character at all. I got to this tiny little theater, and I met the director, Konstantine Rafaeleto, a nice man, a heavy-set Greek about forty-odd, and I liked him right away, liked his handshake, liked his eyes. The first thing he said, after "Good morning, Mr. Proudhammer. I'm glad we found you—you're a hard man to find, do you know that?" was "Do you know the script?" I said, No, but I'd seen the play. He said, "Forget that," and handed me a script. I thought he wanted me to read, but he poured two cups of coffee and we sat down and he began to tell me what he had in mind.

He had not been in my country long, he said, only about eight years; he was part of the multitude driven here by the latest European debacle; thus, one of the lucky ones—but he said this with a sad and winning irony. Then he said, with a smile, that he did not pretend to understand my country, or the place of black people in this strange place. I was wondering what all this was leading up to, naturally, and I was already half convinced that he was just a nice intellectual nut, who probably couldn't direct me across the street. But I think he caught this in some expression on my face, for he smiled, and said, "I am *not* a lecturer. I *am* a director. I thought that I would try a little experiment." He paused, and looked at me, now, very narrowly indeed. He said, "I don't know if you agree with me, but I don't think that any of these problem books and plays and pictures *do* anything"—we were in the era of *Earth and High Heaven* and *Gentlemen's Agreement* and *Focus* and *Kingsblood Royal* and *Pinky*—"I don't think that they're even *intended* to do anything. They just keep the myths alive. They keep the vocabulary alive. Of course, we can all feel unhappy about the poor unhappy darkies—we can afford to, we've got so many happy ones. Why not feel sorry for the Jews, we've killed so many. But a gas oven is a gas oven, and isn't a darky still a darky?"

I sipped my coffee, and watched him.

"Now," he said, very attentive to the quality of my attention, "the experiment I have in mind is *just* an experiment. The principal element of this experiment, that is, the play, is far from ideal. I mean, I don't want you to think that I think it's a great play. But it's a relatively truthful play, and sometimes very touching, and there are elements in it which I think we can make very exciting."

I was watching him while he spoke—watching him more than I was listening to him, which is a habit of mine. I always think that you can tell a great deal from the way a man looks at you when he's talking. Konstantine—Connie—*was* a kind of nut, as it turned out, and he was to pay very heavily for this later, for the voice of Senator McCarthy was loud in the land. But he was *my* kind of nut. He had real convictions, and he'd thought some of them through, and he tried to live by his convictions. Not even later, when his reputation and his means of making a livelihood were on the block, and nearly all of those who could have helped him had turned away from him, did I ever hear him complain. He only said, "Well, I guess it's time to take a deep breath and hold your nose and go under. Thank God, I learned that long ago."

That morning, while he was talking to me, he looked me directly in the eye, and he was much too involved in what he was trying to say to me to have energy left over to hand me any shit. He wasn't trying to impress me, and he wasn't blackmailed by my color. He talked to me as one artisan to another, concerning a project which he hoped we would be able to execute together. This was a profound shock, he couldn't have known how profound, and it was a great relief. No one in the theater had ever talked to me like that. No, I had become accustomed to the smile which masked a guilty awareness. Americans are always lying to themselves about that kinsman they call the Negro, and they are always lying to him, and I had grown accustomed to the tone which sought your complicity in the unadmitted crime. The directors I had talked to had to suspect, though they couldn't admit, that the roles I was expected to play were an insult to my manhood, as well as to my craft. I might have a judgment on the clown or porter I was playing. They could not risk hearing it. Of course, I couldn't risk stating it, though there were also times when I couldn't resist stating it. But this tension, created by the common knowledge of an unspeakable and unspoken lie, was not present in Konstantine's office that morning. He was the first director I'd met with whom I really wanted to work. For that matter, he was the first director I'd met who talked to me as though I could.

He poured more coffee, and he said, "One of the things that's most impressed me in this country is the struggle of black people to get an education. I always think it's one of the great stories, and nobody knows anything about it. If there *were* a play on that subject, I'd probably do that. But I don't know of any, and so I thought I'd try this experiment with this play. I think you'll see what I mean when you read it. I certainly hope you do. Very few of the elements in the play are really alien to American life. You've got mining towns like that, for Christ's sake, *worse* than that, and people just like that, right on down to the squire. People don't really differ very much from one place to another, anyway."

By now, I had caught his drift, and was dying to get home and read the play. I didn't know yet whether he was crazy or not, but he was beginning to excite me.

"So I thought," he said, "I'd take this play, this mining town situation, with no comment, so to say, only making the miners and the servants, people like that, black. It's true that the play takes place in Wales, but I think we can make the audience forget that after the first few minutes, and hell, anyway, there *are* black people in Wales. And I figured we'd let the Negro kids improvise around the stretches of Welsh dialogue—dialect, really—and of course we've got tremendous musical opportunities with this play." He looked at me and smiled. "How does it strike you, son? Oh. Of course, Ray Fisher must have told you that I want you to play the boy—to play Morgan Evans. That could be a Negro name, couldn't it?"

"So could most white names," I said, and after a moment he laughed and I laughed with him.

"Can you read the script right away?" he asked. "And get back to me right away?"

"I'll read it today," I said, "and I'll call you as soon as I've read it."

"Call me this evening at home," he said, and scribbled his number on a piece of paper and handed it to me. "I hope you'll like it. That'd be the only reason for doing it. There's not much money in it, and no glory."

"Well," I said, a little embarrassed now, "I'll call you this evening."

"Right." He held out his hand. "People call me Connie. May I call you Leo?"

"Certainly," I said.

"Well, good-bye, Leo. I hope we can do something."

"Good-bye, Connie. I hope so, too."

And we shook hands, and I left.

I read the play, of course, on the subway, and had finished the first act by the time I got uptown. I didn't want to go to work until I'd finished reading the play and so I went into a bar and ordered a beer and read to the end. It was a mad idea, all right, and I kept telling myself that, but I couldn't help getting more and more excited. I could see what Connie had in mind; I could see that it might work. Perhaps I didn't altogether like the faintly missionary aspect of the white schoolteacher, black-promise business, but it really couldn't be helped and if we played it right, it wouldn't be stressed. It was only going to play for seven performances, I reminded myself, but anybody in my business has to approach any project as though it has the possibilities of shaking the world. I didn't know how I was going to handle the boy, Morgan, but I felt that I could understand him and felt that I could do it. And, obviously, Connie felt that I could do it or he wouldn't have been looking for me. He was so sure that I could do it that he hadn't even asked me to read. So, it looked all right. It looked very nice. And, no matter what happened now, my morale had once again been saved. And, after all, who knew what might come of it? Who could know? And I sailed out of the bar, with my script under my arm and sailed up the avenue to the barbecue joint in a beautiful gentle wind. I wasn't helpless anymore. Maybe I was going to live.

I called Connie that night from the barbecue joint. "This is Leo Proudhammer. I just wanted to say, thank you. You've made me very happy."

There was a pause. Then, "You've made me very happy, too, Leo. Can you make it at ten in the morning?"

"Right."

"Till then."

"Till then."

Well, this meant that I would be working nights in the barbecue joint, and rehearsing all day. But this was one of the greatest times in my life, and I'll never forget it. It was the very first time in my life, and after so long, that I was handled as an actor. Perhaps only actors can know what this means, but what it meant for me was that the track was cleared at last for work, I could concentrate on learning and working and finding out what was in me. I wasn't carrying that goddamn tray, and I wasn't at war with myself or the play or the cast. I didn't have the feeling, which I'd had so often, that I was simply hanging around, like part of the scenery, and was going to be used like that. It was the first time I was treated with that demanding respect which is due every artist, simply because of the nature of his effort, and without which he finds it almost impossible to function. I was being challenged and the very best was expected of me. And I was going to deliver my very best.

Connie worked me like a horse. Sometimes he'd say, "Now, you know you're not telling me the truth. Don't you? You're cheating the boy." So we'd do it again; I knew what he meant; I remembered everything he said. My first encounter with Miss Moffat I'm still not sure I ever really got right. It *is* a very tricky moment, deceptively cute—"Please, miss, can I have a kiss?" and she spanks me on the bottom, try being cute when you play it—and Morgan turned out to be the hardest role I'd ever been assigned. But it was also the best role, and I didn't at all mind being worked like a horse. He worked all of us like horses. I had trouble the first week or so with the actress who was playing Miss Moffat. She had been a fairly big star in the thirties, a sort of second-string Janet Gaynor or Sylvia Sidney, and she was saddled with one of those awful Wampus Baby star names. She was known professionally as Bunny Nash, and though she was now far on the far side of fifty, she couldn't change it. She was having a little trouble adjusting to work in a settlement house theater. She was more than a little troubled, though she couldn't have admitted this, by finding herself surrounded by so many Negroes. Outnumbered, really: for Connie had cast all the serving roles, Bessie, Mrs. Watty, all the mine boys, and Old Tom, as black people. This meant that of fifteen speaking roles, ten were black. This made it hard on Miss Moffat, for, in the play, Miss Moffat's relationship to her peers is quite perfunctory. Her only real relationship is to Morgan. And, as Connie was directing the play, this is also true of all the "black" people in the play, who look on Morgan as their hope. For the first week, Connie concentrated on these subsidiary and unspoken relationships, leaving the center of the play virtually untouched. And this worried Bunny Nash, who had looked on *The Corn Is Green* as a starring vehicle for herself. But Connie knew Bunny Nash, and it suited him to have her a little worried. He wanted a kind of tug of war between Miss Moffat and Morgan, in order to make vivid in the production what is only implicit in the script; that, whereas, clearly, Miss Moffat is a mystery for Morgan Evans, he is, equally, a mystery for her. And he wanted Bunny to play it not merely as the imperious, knowing, and rather noble spinster schoolteacher, but also as a woman more than a little frightened by what she has undertaken.

And, in fact, Bunny and I *were* frightened of each other in different ways, and for different reasons. Connie used this. Cruelly and painstakingly, he walked us, in our own personalities, over the ground we had to cover in the play. He never spoke of the tension between Bunny and Leo, but used this tension—or, rather, forced us to use it—to illuminate the tension between Morgan and Miss Moffat. It worked. He got what he wanted. It made our fight scene in the second act a really painful, tearing fight —Morgan, hateful, bewildered, weeping, striking out, and Miss Moffat, equally bewildered, terribly frightened and hurt, struggling for control. Having hit that peak, as it now seemed with no effort, and resolved that tension, our confidence mounted and we went to work in earnest. We had found our feet, and were able to play the difficult and, at bottom, quite improbable third act as friends whose friendship has cost them more than a little.

Connie used a lot of music in the play, and I had a solo, unseen. Before the curtain rose, I was to sing, accompanied by my guitar, an old mining song, "Dark As a Dungeon." On the lines,

> There's many a man I've known in my day,
> Who lived just to labor his poor life away.
> Like a fiend for his dope, a drunkard his wine,
> A man will have lust for the low, rugged mine . . .

I always thought of my father, and I sang the song for him. But I hadn't been home. And I hadn't really told anyone very much about the play, for by now I knew a whole lot about the best-laid plans of mice and men and I didn't want to risk having to explain that everything had fallen through. The guys at the barbecue joint knew, of course, and they'd all been very nice. If they hadn't been, it would have been very hard on me, because I didn't want to quit my job and then be on my ass again, after seven days. And they were all going to come down and see me, with their wives or their girl-friends or whatever, on different nights. But, though I worked in Harlem, so close to home, I hadn't been home. I said to myself that it was because of my hours. We often rehearsed from ten to ten, and then I worked in the barbecue joint till dawn. Then, I grabbed a little sleep and went back to the theater. It was a schedule which I probably couldn't hope to survive today, but then it was nothing unusual. And I'd done it before, by this time I'd done it many times. Just because it's so impossible a schedule, one crams, without ever being able to recount how, a great many things into it. So, I could have gone to see my mother, whom I knew to be ailing. I had managed, on tighter schedules, to do less important things. My parents had no phone, but there was a phone at The New Dispensation House of God and I could have called Caleb. Or, I could simply have explained it to the guys at the barbecue joint, and they would have understood and would never have given me a hard time about it. They were very nice guys and they liked me very much and they *did* very much hope I'd make it, even if it meant that I'd change and never talk to them again. So, there was really no reason for my not going home. Any psychiatrist will be glad to give you the reasons, of course, but I have always very keenly felt, in the psychiatric account, the absence of the two most important people, one of them being the psychiatrist and the other being me. Anyway: I didn't go home. Ten o'clock in the evening was too late, I said, and six in the morning was too early. And so, one night, after a particularly hard and rewarding day, I walked into the barbecue joint and found Caleb sitting at the counter, drinking a cup of coffee and waiting for me.

Now, the cats in the barbecue joint, unlike the people downtown at The Island, so many years ago, knew all about Caleb and me. He was Reverend Proudhammer: they all knew that. They treated him with that species of respect which masks despair. He was in his bag, as we now say; had found his niche, as the English say; nothing more could be expected from him and they expected nothing. Really, he was for them exactly what I might be in a few years, or a few months, a few weeks, a few days: beyond them, and useless. He had made his way—all right. They had not made theirs—all right. The fact that he was a Reverend and I was trying to become an actor made no difference at all, no difference whatever. They knew, without knowing that they knew it, simply by having watched it, by having paid for it, what nearly no one can afford to remember: that the theater began in the church. We were both performers, that was how they saw us, brothers, and at war. They may have expected more from me than they did from him simply because my pulpit was so much harder to reach, and they hadn't, after all, yet heard my sermon.

They knew it was going to be a bad night for me. I came in, breathless, carrying my book, bareheaded, and wiped the rain off my face and hair as I hurried through the restaurant. Red, my boss, signified something to me but I was full of the play and anxious about being late, and so I simply didn't react. I hung up my coat and ran into the bathroom. Red came in behind me.

"Your brother's out there," he said. "He's been here for more than an hour."

I was peeing and it suddenly splashed all over my hand and all over the floor.

"My brother?"

"Reverend Proudhammer," he said, "*your* brother."

I washed my hands, and dried them. I said, "Oh, shit."

"Well," he said, "he's here." He watched me in the mirror. "It might be some kind of trouble in your family, I reckon, so"—he watched me; he was a pale Negro, with a reddish skin, freckles all over his face; I liked Red very much, and he liked me—"if it is, you just go on with him and don't worry about nothing." He started out the door. "How's it going downtown?"

"It's going pretty well," I said. I turned and looked at him. He could see it in my face. He could hear it in my voice. He smiled—a smile I've seen only on the faces of black Americans. "Red. It's going very well." I couldn't help it. I said, "Red, you know, I'm going to be *very good!* You're going to be very proud of me."

He smiled again—that smile. "Well, all right," he said, and left me.

I combed my hair and stared at my face, my God, my so improbable face, *where did you get those eyes?* and walked out to meet Caleb. He was sitting at the counter, as I've said, and I sat down beside him.

He was stern, as always, beautiful, as always. I said, "Hello, Caleb."

He was drinking coffee. I had the feeling that he'd drunk quite a lot of coffee. He was pretty well dressed, with a hat and everything—certainly someone, somewhere, someday, should do a study of the American male's hat!—and I wasn't. It was winter, and I was wearing a turtleneck sweater and some old corduroys. I hadn't had a haircut and I hadn't shaved. He looked at me and that was what he saw. I knew it. I can't say I didn't care. I cared. But I knew that there was no longer anything I could do about what Caleb saw. And I knew this because there was no longer anything I could do about what *I* saw.

"Your mother wants to see you," he said, after he had completed his scrutiny. "She's sick and she wants to see you and she thought I could find you and that's why I'm here. Do you think you can take time off and come home and see your mother?"

We looked at each other. I didn't say anything. I walked to the coat rack and picked up my coat. I looked briefly at Red, and Red nodded. I walked back to Caleb. "I'm ready," I said.

Caleb stood up and put some money on the counter,

but Red shoved it back at him. "You're part of the family, Reverend Proudhammer," he said, and Caleb smiled, a stiff, lordly smile, and we walked out. The other cats had not said anything. They knew that there was nothing to say.

The rain was falling pretty hard. I had my book under my arm and my shoulders hunched and we walked down the avenue. I realized that we were going to have to pass The New Dispensation House of God, and this made me want to laugh. Laugh may not be the most exact word. I asked, "How's Louise? And the baby?"

"They're fine," he said. "I keep telling the kid that he's got an uncle, but he doesn't seem to believe me anymore."

I didn't like this. It smacked of a certain kind of blackmail. And I didn't like Louise very much, I thought she was a dumb, pretentious, black bitch. But, on the other hand: "I've been busy, Caleb," I said.

"How can a man get so busy," cried Caleb, "that he don't have time for his own flesh and blood!" I knew the tone. It fell on me like the rain fell on me. There was nothing I could do about it. We passed the church and heard the singing and I saw Caleb's name on the black-white board. "Don't tell me you've been *busy*. You ain't been as busy as I've been and I've been to see Mama every day. *Every* day. And every day she asks me if I've seen you."

Then, we walked in silence. Just before we turned off the avenue, we passed a bar and someone I knew was going in and he hailed me. Then he saw who I was with, and he just kept on, into the bar.

"You got some fine friends," Caleb said.

"Yes," I said deliberately, "I do."

"Do you realize you're going to be thirty pretty soon?" Caleb asked. "Now, what do you think is going to happen to you?"

"I know I'll soon be thirty. And whatever's going to happen to me is none of your goddamn business."

He stopped and turned and looked at me. We stood stock still in the rain. "I'm a man now, Caleb," I said, "you leave me the fuck alone, you hear?" and he slapped me, slapped me so hard that my book fell from beneath my arm, and I had to scramble like a child to rescue it from the torrent. All my notes were in it. I hoped they weren't all ruined. We were opening in a week. I stared at Caleb. "You bastard," I said. "You bastard. You no-good, black Holy Roller bastard." And he slapped me again, and we stood there.

"Once, I wanted to be like you," I said. "I would have given anything in the world to be like you." I was crying. I hoped he couldn't see it, because of the rain. "Now I'd rather die than be like you. I wouldn't be like you and tell all these lies to all these ignorant people, all these unhappy people, for anything in the world, Caleb, anything in the world! That God you talk about, that miserable white cock-sucker—look at His handiwork, look!" And I looked around the avenue, but he didn't. He looked at me. "I curse your God, Caleb, I curse Him, from the bottom of my heart I *curse* Him. And now let Him strike me down. Like you just tried to do." And I walked away and left him.

I ran up the stairs to our house. I wiped my face and hair as best I could, and I knocked on the door. My father opened it.

Perhaps it was the play. Perhaps it was the fight. Perhaps it was his face. I'll never know. I was not stunned to see that my father was old. I knew that he was old. I was not stunned by the fact that he was drunk. I knew that he was usually drunk—though Caleb still insisted that he would soon give up his sinful ways and come to the Lord. *Bring your burdens to the Lord and leave them there!* I thought, and I stared into the crater of my father's face. What had fallen on that face, to sink it so? What had happened to the eyes? the eyes of an animal peering out from a cave. I heard Caleb's footsteps, far below me, slow and certain, like the wrath of God. It took a second before my father recognized me. Then, he smiled, my God, how his face changed, what a light came into it, and he pulled me into the house with one hand and turned, crying, "Old lady, look who's here! Now, I *know* you going to be all right."

He pulled me into the living room, where my mother sat in the easy chair, covered with blankets. She was very still. Her hands were in her lap, and she had been looking into the streets. Now, at his voice, she turned. Her face was as yellow as a yolk, and her eyes were like two raisins.

Her hair was piled on the top of her head, held with a comb, as dry as stone, and as dull. And she smiled and held out her arms. She said, "My gracious, boy, I just been sitting here, thinking about you. Now, *where've* you been?"

I heard Caleb's footsteps in the outside hall, and I walked over to my mother and kissed her. She smelled old. She held me tight, and I was uneasy. I was able, at last, to look up into her face and I smiled into her face, just as Caleb came into the room. Whatever I had ever felt for my mother, my beautiful, almost white mother, came down on me, and I said, "Mama, sweetheart, why do you want to get everybody all worried and upset this way? Don't you know we love you?" And Caleb sat down on the sofa. I didn't look at him but I knew he'd leaned back and pushed his hat to the back of his head.

"Ain't nothing wrong with me, Leo," she said, "except age and weariness. But I sure have missed seeing you. Now, what have you been doing with yourself?"

I had to say it. I hoped she would understand me. My father stood behind me, and Caleb was watching. I said, "Mama, I'm doing a play." I watched her. "A very good play, Mama, I think I'm going to be very good and make all of you very proud of me." I said, "Mama, I've been rehearsing all day, every day, from ten in the morning until ten at night, and then I work all night in this bar-becue joint where I cook, you know, and serve the people, and that's why I haven't been to see you." I watched her. She didn't say anything for awhile. She smiled at me. It was a very secret smile, it was not meant for the other two men in the room at all, and I knew it. She said, "Leo, how old are you now?"

I said, "Mama, I'm just about to be twenty-six. Now, you ought to know that," and, after a moment, she laughed and I laughed and my father laughed.

"Twenty-six," she said, and looked at my father a moment and then looked out of the window, "it seems like a dream." I watched her face, which was bonier now, and very very handsome. Her eyes looked over the streets, as though she was waiting for someone. She looked at me again, and laughed like a girl. "When can I come and see this play, Leo?"

"We open—the play opens"—I picked up my book

from the floor and took out my rain-soaked notes, looking for the handbill advertising the play, I was suddenly very proud of it, my name was on it—I found it, it wasn't too ruined, and handed it to her—"you see, Mama? We open in a week."

She looked at it and my father came to read it over her shoulder. She giggled again, and handed it to him. "Read it," she said, "your eyes is better than mine. Read it out loud, so Caleb can hear it."

And so my father read, The Clay House Players present Miss Bunny Nash—"why I've heard of her," cried my mother, "you working with *her*?"—in *The Corn Is Green*, a play by Emlyn Williams, directed by Konstantine Rafaeleto, with so-and-so and so-and-so and so-and-so, and co-starring, all by itself at the bottom, in block print, Leo Proudhammer, *as Morgan Evans*. My father and my mother looked at me. "You see, Mama?" I said. "You see?"

My father folded the handbill. "You reckon we can make it down there, old lady?" He was smiling. I hadn't considered how much he loved my mother.

She sucked her teeth. "Make it *down* there? You *know* we going to make it down there." And she looked out of the window again.

"How about you, Caleb?" our father asked. "It *is* your brother. I don't think God can find no fault with that."

And I realized at that moment, though my father would never say it to me, and certainly never to Caleb, that he was very disappointed in my brother. And I knew my brother knew it. Caleb and I stared at each other. Caleb pushed his hat further back on his head, and he said, "Daddy, you know I don't go to the theater, and that's all there is to that. I've made my choice and Leo's made his choice. Now, I've got to be getting on home." And he stood up. My mother was watching him.

"But you haven't got to go right *yet*," she said.

He smiled. "Mama, I got to go to work in the morning and I got to preach tomorrow night. Now, you know I need a little rest. You need a little rest, too."

"Oh, I'm all right," she said, and shifted under the blankets, away from him, "I'm just tired. Ain't nothing wrong with me."

He watched her. Then he grinned, looking like Caleb

again—just for a moment. He put his hat on his head properly. "Well, all right. But I got to go. See you tomorrow." He patted me on the head. "Good-night, little brother. I'll always love you and I'll always pray for you."

I said, "Good-night, Caleb."

And he left. I stayed and had a couple of drinks with my father and mother. We had a rather nice time, but I didn't stay too long because I could see that my mother really needed rest, and my father had to get up to go to work in the morning. My mother held me very close, and kissed me. My father kissed me, too. I didn't go back to the barbecue joint, but went straight home and fell into bed. The alarm clock rang and I ran to the theater.

Konstantine's experiment, as it was known all over town, was causing something of a stir. People were very curious about it; curious about Bunny Nash, whom no one had seen for ages; curious about me, who had virtually never been seen—and my billing was Connie's idea; and curious about the future of Konstantine Rafaeleto, who would certainly, any day now, be hauled before The House Un-American Activities Committee. Connie was very calm—as calm as anyone can possibly be as an opening night approaches. We worked. Bunny Nash was also worried, because she might also be called. No one knew what was going to happen, we might indeed be closed before we opened, and so all we could do was work.

The morning of the day which will end in the opening night is a very strange moment. One wakes in a tremendous silence, the judgment morning silence. Something has gone terribly wrong somewhere in the world; one racks one's brains to remember what it is. And one doesn't wish to get up, because that will, somehow, compound whatever the disaster has been. One lies in bed very straight and still, and listens with great attention to the morning. I listened to my neighbors. They were apparently playing cards. Someone was joking with someone at the street door. I had a terrible melancholy hard-on, and I wanted to pee or jerk myself off, but didn't have the energy for either. I didn't want to get up. It was in this bed I had slept with Sally, and then with Steve. And this room had witnessed both departures. I looked at the clock. It was just nine. What was I to do until this evening? This evening: and I immediately ran to the bathroom. I was cold and shaking and sweating. But I couldn't stay in the bathroom forever; and what *was* I to do until this evening? All my other days, my whole life, it now seemed, had been spent at the theater. But there was no rehearsal today. Tonight was it.

And what I did that day, I really don't remember. It took me a long time to get dressed and get out of the house. Once out of the house, I had no idea what to do. I walked into a cafeteria and got breakfast. I remember carrying the tray to the table, looking at the breakfast, swallowing the milk, and walking away. The man sitting opposite me looked at me as though I were completely mad, and I certainly couldn't blame him. Recklessly—I rather felt that this was the very last day of my life—I took a cab to Broadway; to the theatrical section of New York, that is, not having the courage to go downtown to my own theater. I wandered around these sordid and frightening and beautiful streets—*Little Leo. On the great white way*—and made the very great mistake of walking into a movie called *My Son, John.* I have no idea why I did it, having never had any respect for Leo McCarey's work, and having always been totally impervious to the charms of Miss Helen Hayes. She's always impressed me as an aging, not very bright drama student, perfectly suited for Christmas pageants, preferably someplace in Vancouver. She always makes me think of football rallies and there was indeed a great deal of football talk, as I remember, in this exceedingly shameful and depressing film. It was just about the worst thing I could possibly have done that day. That movie made me ashamed of human beings and ashamed of my profession and I thought, *My God, if this is what is supposed to happen to me, I swear I'll go back to the post office.* It was more shameful than anything I'd ever had to do with my fucking menial tray. I walked out into the streets again, to find a cop beating up some poor man in the gutter. *My Son, John.* I walked into a bar, wondered if I dared have a drink, ordered a beer, sat there. It was only five in the afternoon. On any other day, it would have been seven. I sipped my beer and three or four hours later, it was only five-fifteen. I thought of going uptown to escort my father and mother to the theater, but I knew that such an effort was thoroughly beyond me. In fact, there was absolutely nothing I could do except stew on the back of the stove until showtime. Our curtain was at eight, and I was due at the theater at seven. I left the bar, and wandered around. I wished I'd had a friend to talk to, or some refuge where I could have hidden. It was awful to walk around these streets this way, all dressed up, and carrying my terrible secret, which was that I wasn't really Leo Proudhammer any more and hadn't yet become Morgan Evans.

At the stroke of seven, I arrived at the theater, over which was hanging the desperate chill of death. Konstantine *had* been called before the guardians of the American safety, and would be going to Washington in a few days. He told me this very quietly when he came into the dressing room. And it must be admitted that not even this dragged me any closer to the real world. I heard him, and I cared, but I heard him and cared from very far away.

Presently, we all stood on the tiny stage, the stage manager with his watch in his hand. There was an incredible silence. Bunny, holding on to Miss Moffat's bicycle, looked at me and smiled, very faintly. The Negro girl, Geneva Smart, who was playing Bessie, and who was very good, swallowed hard, once, and then stood perfectly still. The stage manager said, "Places, please," and we stood there. Then he gave me my cue for "Down in the Dungeon," and I began to sing in this silence, feeling, from beyond the curtain, something sweeping up to me, life sweeping up to me, and carrying me and my song. I finished my song, and got into the wings, and the stage manager, after a moment, said, "Curtain," and the curtain rose, and we were on. That is, *they* were. Morgan doesn't appear until the second scene.

I watched, and it seemed to be going well. There seemed to be a lot of Negroes in the audience, you can always tell if you know the way Negroes react and the kind of things they react to. They laughed a lot at Miss Moffat, and they liked her, and they applauded when she said "this part of the world was a disgrace to a Christian country." Bunny was very energetic and very good and the atmosphere was very alive and electric. They were carrying the play, the audience, I mean, and that's what you always pray will happen. Then, the scene was over, and I and four other "nigger boys" took our places and started to hum. The curtain rose.

I've done lots of plays since then, some of them far more successful, but I'll never forget this one. There is nothing like the first cold plunge, and any survivor will tell you that. When the curtain came up, I knew I was going to vomit, right here, in front of all these people. The moment I delivered my first line, "No, miss," I knew I was going to be all right. And you can tell, from the other actors and from the audience. Bunny and I were working very well together, and some very, very nice things happened in our scene at the end of the first act, when she has read Morgan's composition and invests him with a sense of his potential which he has never had before. I played that scene for all that was in it, for all that was in me, and for all the colored kids in the audience—who held their breath, they really did, it was the unmistakable silence in which you and the audience re-create each other—and for the vanished Little Leo, and for my mother and father, and all the hope and pain that were in me. For the very first time, the very first time, I realized the fabulous extent of my luck: I could, I *could*, if I kept the faith, transform my sorrow into life and joy. I might live in pain and sorrow forever, but, if I kept the faith, I would never be useless. If I kept the faith, I could do for others what I felt had not been done for me, and if I could do that, if I could give, I could live. Our scene ends the first act, and the curtain came down, and they gave us a mighty hand. We rose with the tide generated in the hall by Konstantine's experiment. Our last scene came, and I think we played it well. I know we played it well. The curtain fell, and we heard this tremendous roar from the people. Konstantine stood in the wings, with this smile on his face. He grabbed me and kissed me and pushed me away and the curtain rose for our curtain calls. We went out in the order which we'd been assigned, and I came out next to last. There is no baptism like the baptism in the theater, when you stand up there and bow your head and the roar of the people rolls over you. There is no moment like that, it is both beautiful and frightening —they might be screaming for your blood, and if they were, they would not sound very different. I bowed and bowed, while the colored kids in the audience stamped and cheered, and I turned to bring on Bunny. She came and we stood there together and bowed and the curtain fell and I went off, leaving Bunny there alone. The curtain rose and fell, and Bunny smiled and bowed. But Bunny was a pro, and a very nice woman, and she reached out her hand for me again and Connie put his knee in my behind and pushed me on. They were standing and cheering. Bunny and I bowed together and the curtain fell and Bunny went off and then the curtain rose again and I was out there by myself. And all the years of terror and trembling, all the nearly twenty-six years, were worth it at that moment. It was only then that I realized I hadn't seen my mother and father in the audience. I had been playing for them, oh, how I wanted them to be proud of me! But I hadn't thought about them at all. For awhile, it didn't seem that the audience would ever let us go, the curtain rose and fell, and, I don't know why, a certain fear began knocking in my heart. I tried to see if they were there. But they were not there. I would have known. Red was there, with his wife. I saw them standing and clapping.

The curtain fell at last, for the last time, and then we were in our dressing rooms, and the mob came pouring in. The colored kids came in, and I signed autographs for almost the first time in my life. *Variety* was there, and they said I'd been tremendous, and looked at me with wonder; that wonder with which one, eventually, must learn to live; it is the way the world will always look at you. Red came in, and his face was like a fountain. He kissed me, not saying anything, and his wife, laughing and crying, kissed me. It certainly looked like one more of our boys had made it. *Life* magazine was there, and they made an appointment to interview me. A star is born, they said—wow! *The East Side Explosion*, they called me. Hilda was there. I hadn't seen her for years. Sally was there, with the man who was going to be her husband. I had a telegram from Steve—how in the world had he known? And a telegram from Barbara, who was on the West Coast, making her second movie, the movie which won for her, in the supporting actress category, her first

Academy Award. Oh, yeah. We kids were going to make it, all right. But Caleb wasn't there, and my mother and my father weren't there.

By now, it was midnight, too late to go uptown and too late to call The New Dispensation House of God. So, I tried to throw everything out of my mind, and walked with Konstantine to the cast party, which was being held in Chinatown. I was exhausted, with the particular, peculiar, and exhilarating exhaustion only a performer feels. I knew I had been good. I had been very good. I could feel it in Konstantine's very quiet pride. I had not betrayed him. I had not betrayed the play. I had not betrayed myself and all those people whom I would always love, and I had not betrayed all that history which held me like a lover and which would hold me forever like that.

I hardly remember the party, except that Connie was grave and triumphant, and I got a little drunk and tried to make love to Geneva Smart, who had the good sense to laugh at me, but very nicely. We got some of the reviews, and the reviews were extraordinary. They said very nice things about me, "incandescent," "unforgettable," "an actor not merely seasoned, but highly spiced"—shit like that. A lot of it came out of pure embarrassment that Konstantine was being called to testify. But we certainly looked like a hit, and it was clear that we were going to run for longer than seven performances. As it turned out, we ran for over eight months, and were the talk of the town and I was sometimes the toast of the town. I did some television. I was signed for a movie. I began doing night clubs and records. When *The Corn Is Green* closed, I did my first movie and then I did a play in England and came home to do a revival of *Cabin in the Sky* on Broadway, which was a tremendous personal triumph for me. I had made it. I looked back and I wondered how I got over.

But I got a telegram the morning after the opening of *The Corn Is Green*, telling me that my mother had been carried to the hospital. While she was dressing to come to my opening, she had a stroke and fell into a coma from which she never recovered consciousness, and she died two days later. Caleb spoke at her funeral, and the choir sang, "Get Away, Jordan." My father just sat there. It was the first time I had seen him in a church. And I must say for the old man, in spite of the fact that he was so lonely now, and in spite of the way Caleb went on at him about his soul, he never relented. No, he went his own way, and sometimes stood on the avenue, listening to black nationalist speeches, and he was a faithful client of the black nationalist bookstore. After I met Christopher, he and Christopher would spend hours together, reconstructing the black empires of the past, and plotting the demolition of the white empires of the present. It was good for my father, who adored Christopher, and was good for Christopher to find someone that old whom he could trust and admire. I sang, alone, for my mother, a song she had sometimes sung to me: "Mary, Mary, what you going to name that pretty little baby?"

Pete left very soon after dinner, and Barbara and I sat before the fire, as calm, I thought suddenly, almost, as two old people.

They had sent the telegram and the money order to Christopher while I had been soaking in the tub.

"How do you feel?" Barbara asked.

"Fine. Sleepy. Like a cat."

"You look like one. Curled up there like that. A tired tomcat, finally come home."

"But not a *spayed* tomcat?"

She laughed. "Oh, no. I know that's been your fear, but it's never been your problem."

"But *I've* been a problem for you very often, Barbara, haven't I?"

"I don't doubt that you will be again, Leo," she said, and smiled. "I've also been a problem for you. But we've come through so far, and we will again." She paused. "It isn't, our story isn't—isn't a story anyone would have *chosen* to live. But, I had to ask myself, Barbara, would you change it if you could? *Would* you? And I had to realize that I wouldn't. So—that's all there is to that." She rose, and kissed me on the forehead. "And now, my dear invalid, I must put you to bed. You must sleep until you wake up—that is, no one's to wake you. I have a date for lunch, but Pete will be here in the morning, and the maid will be here, too."

"All right, princess," and I rose. I had to say it: "I

thought you might be a little afraid of seeing Christopher again."

Barbara laughed. "Good Lord, no. How could I be afraid of anything, Leo, after all those years of storm and strife with you?" Her face changed. "What happened between Christopher and me happened because of you. *We* both know that. *You* haven't got to know it. And we both love you. *We* both know that. Now, go to bed."

We kissed each other—like brother and sister. "Good-night," I said.

"Good-night, my dear."

I turned into my bedroom and undressed and got into bed. Barbara was right; I was very tired. I was very peaceful, after our long storm. Barbara had done something very hard and rare. As though she had known I would need it, and would always need it, she had arranged her life so that my place in it could never be jeopardized. This room in which I lay had cost her more in the way of refusals than she would ever tell; perhaps it had given her more in the way of affirmation than anyone would ever know. The incestuous brother and sister would now never have any children. But perhaps we had given one child to the world, or helped to open the world to one child. Luckier lovers hadn't managed so much. The sunlight filled the room. I heard voices, muted, laughing, in the big, wide room. My watch said ten to one. I went to my window and opened the blinds. It was a very bright day, and I suddenly wanted to be out in it. I went into my bathroom and stripped naked and stepped under the shower. For some reason, I thought of Paradise Alley. I laughed to myself, and I sang. I put on a sweater and slacks and walked out into the big room. Pete was sitting on the sofa, laughing, there was a suitcase near him, and Christopher, long and black, and dressed in a black suit, was talking on the phone.

"Look who's here!" Pete said.

Christopher looked over at me. "He just this minute stepped out of his room," said Christopher. "Yeah, just this minute. He looks all right, I can tell ain't nothing wrong with him that wasn't wrong with him before, you people are too much, I swear, got me all the way out here on a bullshit tip, you know how many affairs I had to cancel to make it out here? Shame on you! Shame, yeah, that's what I said. What?" He laughed. "Well, you want me to spell all that to you when I see you? No, you don't want me to do that, no, you don't. Yeah. Pete's got the address. We'll be there. What? Of course, he'll feel like coming, he ain't got nothing else to do, don't you know *I'm* here now? *I'm* his doctor, don't know why you didn't send for me before. Yeah, bye-bye, you have a nice lunch, you hear, and don't you let them people jive you, you too sweet and pretty. Now, why you want to say a thing like that? You hurting my feelings, Barbara. Yeah. Old brother Christopher is on the scene now, baby, bye-bye, see you later." He put down the receiver and smiled, and held out his arms. "Come here, Big Daddy. Look like you just can't do right. I ain't going to let you out of my sight no more. The minute you out of my sight, you got to go and fall flat on your face in front of umpteen million people. Shame on you!" He grabbed me and hugged me and kissed me. "I'm glad to see you, baby. I missed you."

"I missed you, too," I said. "How've you been?" And then, "You look all right."

"I've been fine. The people is pretty sick, but *I'm* all right."

"Black Christopher!" Pete said.

"Yeah, baby," Christopher said, "*black*—just like Kenyatta, and all them folks." He laughed again. "You better believe I'm black."

"It's hard to doubt it," I said, "when you put it with such force."

Christopher threw back his head, and laughed. "If anything was ever the matter with him, he's all right now. I know your little digs. You mean, if I didn't tell you I was black, you wouldn't know I was black. I heard you. All right."

It was good to see him, striding up and down this room, with his face so bright.

"What do you want, big man?" Pete asked me. "You want some coffee? You ready for lunch?"

"He shouldn't be drinking coffee," said Christopher, "that's bad for his heart. Let him have some orange juice, or something."

"I thought maybe he wanted something hot," Pete said humbly.

"Well, let him drink some *cocoa*. Or some Ovaltine. He ain't supposed to be drinking no coffee or tea."

"I think," said Pete to me, "that you may have a problem."

"Couldn't we compromise on coffee, with a *lot* of milk in it?" I asked.

"Now, it's *your* heart," said Christopher. Then he looked out of the window, and smiled and blushed. "Just make sure you put a *lot* of milk in it—hell, *I'll* do it, *you* won't do it right," and he suddenly walked out of the room.

"When did he *get* here?" I asked.

"A couple of hours ago. He must have packed his bags the minute he got the telegram. I *told* you he'd have been here already, if he'd had any bread."

"It's nice of him to come," I said.

"Yeah," said Pete, "especially considering how many other places he has to go."

"All right, Pete," I said.

"I mean, just don't go through your usual bullshit routine of thinking it was a great sacrifice or anything. It's no sacrifice for a kid to come to San Francisco for the first time to see some people who love him. If you'd get such details as *that* through your mind, *you* wouldn't be such a kid yourself, and Barbara and all of us would have a much easier time."

"Do I give you all such a hard time?"

Pete laughed. "Now, if I say yes, what are you going to do? Leap out of this window, or go off and have another heart attack?" He laughed again. Then, he sobered. "You give us a hard time, man, when we watch you giving yourself a hard time. That's all. You can't hide nothing from us, and you *damn* sure don't have anything to prove to us. *We* know you're Leo Proudhammer. *You* don't know it."

I watched him. He wasn't smiling now. I sat down on the sofa. Christopher came clattering in, carrying a bottle of milk in one hand, and balancing a cup and saucer in the other. He set them both down on the table before me, and said, standing over me, "Now, let's see what *you* think is a whole lot of milk—I put in two sugars, but I didn't stir."

Since the coffee cup held a little less than half a cup of

coffee, my only possible option was to fill the cup. I
stirred it a little, and I tasted it. Christopher watched me.
"Very good," I said gravely, "thank you."

He watched me with his deep and wry distrust. He sat
down on the sofa, and put one hand on my knee. "What's
happening in this town?" he asked Pete.

"Oh," said Pete, "a whole lot's happening in this
town, from broads to pot to civil rights to urban renewal.
Which scene do you want to dig first?"

"How do you tell them apart?" I asked.

Christopher punched my knee. "The broads and the
pot smokers tend to talk less," he said, "now, you'd remember that if you hadn't been so sick." He turned back
to Pete. "Well, we can't have Big Daddy here making
them scenes, so you can just kind of cool me and I'll make
it on my own."

"This town's not exactly as nice as it looks," I said.

"You trying to scare me?" Christopher asked. "You
tried that once before. Remember?" He smiled and
forced me to smile. "I thought you'd learned your lesson.
Ah. I might have to remind you again, bye and bye."

I watched him as he talked to Pete, watched his big
teeth, his big hands, listened to his laugh. He sounded so
free; a way I'd never sounded: a way I'd never been.

A double-minded man is never much of a match for
a single-minded boy. When Christopher first met me, he
decided that he needed me: that was that. He needed
human arms to hold him, he could see very well, no matter what I said, that mine were empty, and that was that.
If I was afraid of society's judgment, he was not: "Fuck
these sick people. I do what *I* like." Or, laughing: "You
afraid that people will call you a dirty old man? Well,
you *are* a dirty old man. You're *my* dirty old man, right? I
dig dirty old men." And, in another tone: "I just do not
want to be out here, all hungry and cold and alone. Let's
not sweat it, baby. Love me. Let's just be nice."

I first met Christopher at a party, briefly, when I had
been in rehearsal, and didn't see him anymore until after
the play had opened. When we had settled into our run,
his face leaped out at me again, the way a hungry dog in
the cellar leaps when you open the door.

We saw each other at another party, very late at night,
uptown, where I didn't live anymore. I very nearly didn't

get there. I was dead, because I had had a class in the morning, then the matinée, then the evening show. Then I had drinks in my dressing room with my agent, who wanted to talk to me about a guest appearance on a pretty lousy TV serial—he said that it might be a breakthrough. I finally fell into a taxi and realized, once it began to move, that I had absolutely no money on me. I asked the driver to take me to a bar near my apartment, where I could cash a check. Then the idea, tired as I was, and so close to home, of traveling to the party, seemed intolerable. I went into the bar, cashed the check, paid the driver, went back into the bar for a drink. The bar was absolutely hideous with gray, lightless people. I went into the phone booth to call up my host and ask him not to expect me.

But this was a friend from the evil days. He had been nice to me, and he was a Negro, and his life wasn't going too well. I sighed to myself as I heard the tone of his voice: "We're all waiting for you. Of course, it's not too late, are you kidding? There are people here who want to meet you, they've been waiting all night. Get in a cab and come on, you can pass out here."

Christopher told me later that he had been about to leave when the phone rang; and it was me; and he waited. They all waited, but from the moment I walked into the room I had eyes only for him. I was introduced to the people, who looked at me with the kind of wary respect with which I imagine they would greet a baboon or a lion who was free of his cage for the evening. Some people had seen me in the play, and they congratulated me on my performance. I was flattered, as always, chilled, as always. Someone remembered the small part I had done in that movie more than ten years before. I had been very young then, but this caused me to remember that I was not young anymore. And I was watching the boy, who was watching me.

People who achieve any eminence whatever are driven to do so; and there is always something terribly vulnerable about such people. They very soon discover that their eminence makes of them an incitement and a target—it does not cause them to be loved. They are trapped on their hill. They cannot come down. They cannot bear obscurity as some organisms cannot bear light—death is what awaits them when they come down from the hill.

"I met you before," said Christopher, "do you remember?" The hand with which he grasped my own was very large and dry; something in the nervous alertness of his stance, and the wary hopefulness in his eyes made him seem poised to run. The candor of his panic made me smile. I envied him.

"Of course," I said, "how've you been?"

"Oh," he said, with great cheerfulness, "I've been all right." He had a slight Southern accent. I had not noticed it before. "Oh! Congratulations. Your play's a big hit. Everybody's talking about it."

"Thanks," I said. "It looks like we may run for awhile." I wanted to ask him if he had seen the play, or if he wanted to, but for some reason I didn't.

"So," he said, after a moment, "I guess that's all you've been doing? Making it to the theater, and making it on home?"

"*And* crashing an occasional party."

He laughed, but looked at me quickly, speculatively. "You must be tired. Don't you have anybody to fight off the world for you, to protect you from jokers like this"—he indicated the room—"and jokers like me—don't you have anybody to make sure you come home nights?"

"No," I said sorrowfully, "not a soul," and we both laughed again.

"Shame on you. You shouldn't be wandering around alone, you're too valuable—I'm not joking, I mean it. This town is full of all kinds of sick people."

"Well, I think I've met most of them by now. So I'm safe."

"If you think *that*," he said, with a peculiarly aggressive distinctness, "you really *are* crazy." And then he added, almost as an afterthought, it seemed, and to himself, "You really *do* need somebody to take care of you—why don't you hire me as your bodyguard, man? That way, the future of the American theater will be a whole lot brighter." He said it with a smile, but also with a shrewd, calculating, coquettish look, as though he were saying, *That's right, mother. I'm bucking for the job.*

I was still impressed by his candor, but he was beginning to frighten me. We moved to the window. It was a high window, it was a blue-black night, we looked out on the cruel half-moon and the patient stars and fires of Manhattan.

"Look at that," he said, and put one great hand under my elbow, "look at that. Isn't that a gas? From so high up, it almost looks like a place where a human being could live." Then he looked down. He dropped my elbow. "But from down there, sweetheart, on that cold cement, you know you could howl and scream forever and not a living soul would hear you." Then he smiled. "But you don't know nothing about that, do you? You don't walk these streets, you just ride through them. You only see cats like me through glass."

"I come from the streets. It's true I ride now, but I used to walk. Don't pull rank on *me*. I *might* outrank you."

"Okay. Don't get mad. I was only putting you on. I can't help it. I always do that if I like somebody."

I knew what he was saying, I heard him; it was as though he had just smuggled a note to me; and he knew that I would not read it until I was alone. But he also knew that I would certainly read it. He did not look at me now, but stared out of the window. And, to bring us back from where we were, and also to carry us further, he now said (while I began to be aware that the rest of the party was watching us, and said to myself, I've got to circulate around this room once, and get out of here): "Someone once told me that if it wasn't for the lights from the earth reflected in the sky, nobody would ever be able to look into the sky. It would be too frightening. I've often thought about that. I wonder if it's true."

"I guess we'll never know," I said. "When all the lights on earth go out, we'll be gone, too."

"Well," he said, and laughed, "I certainly hope so. I sure don't want to be left alone down here, in the dark."

There was a note deliberately plaintive in that last statement, and I did not want to pursue it. "Where are you from?" I asked.

"Well, actually, I was born in New Jersey, but I grew up in New York—I grew up in Harlem."

"Where in Harlem? That's my hometown."

But I knew that his Harlem was not my Harlem.

"We used to live on 134th Street."

"We lived on 136th."

"Well, shit, you're one of the neighborhood boys, then—I wonder if I ever saw you—"

"No. You would have been a snot-nosed kid then."

"Yeah," he said, and looked at me quizzically, "I guess so. We wouldn't have had an awful lot in common—I was always in trouble." He gestured toward the room. "That's how I met Frank." Frank was our host, a social worker. "He knew my probation officer. He helped me out a lot."

I did not want to ask him why he had been on probation, both because I did not want to know and because I was certain that one day he would tell me.

"If you were born in New Jersey," I said, "and you were brought up in New York, how did you get that Southern accent?"

He grinned. "I haven't got a real accent." He looked at me. "I went to reform school in the South. And then, later on, I used to go with this broad from Miami and I sort of put it on, you know, for her—she went for it—and I guess it kind of stuck." He seemed a little embarrassed. He tapped on the glass with one astonishingly manicured fingernail. "Kid stuff," he said.

I laughed. "Maybe you should have been an actor."

"Not me," he said. "I don't have the nerves. Or the patience." He paused. "I'm fascinated," he said, "by space."

He was referring to those planets which were simply points of light to our eyes. They contained possibilities for him; and perhaps they really did, why not? The planet on which we stood was not extremely promising. But it had proved to be enough, and more than enough, for me.

"The only space which means anything to me," I said, "is the space between myself and other people. May it never diminish."

He looked as though I had hurt his feelings. "Ah," he said, with a really disarming and disconcerting gentleness, "you don't mean that." And when he said this everything about him seemed to shine, as though a light had been turned on from within. "Don't say things like that, it doesn't become you—and, anyway, I'll never believe you."

I was shocked—bewildered—by his vehement sincerity, and discomfited because he had caught me in a lie. Of course I had not meant what I had said; I had only, and far more cunningly than he would have been able to do for himself, wrenched his full attention around to me again. I had been putting him on.

"I guess what I mean," I said, then, guilty about having upstaged him and now, helplessly, feeding him his lines, "is the space between myself and *most* people."

He was a quick study. "But not all of them?" And after a moment, with a smile, "Not all of *us?*"

"No"—losing ground now every instant, and knowing it—"by no means all. I know some very nice people."

"I'll bet you do," he said, with tranquillity, "you're a very nice person yourself."

I felt a terrible fatigue. I watched his profile. He was looking with wonder into the sky. I watched his hands, pressed flat against the windowpane, like the hands of the orphan in the fable, the orphan trapped outside of warmth and light and love, hoping to be received, to be rescued from the night. His mouth was a little open, like the mouths of waifs and orphans. Not so very long ago, I had stood as he now stood and had hoped as he now hoped. What had my hope come to? It had led me to this moment, here. I heard his cry because it was my own. He did not know this—did not know, that is, that his cry was my own—but he knew that *his* cry had been heard. Therefore, he hummed a little and tapped with his fingers on the glass. He sensed that he had found the path that led home. But I was afraid. What, after all, could I do with him? Except, perhaps, set him on his path, the path that would lead him away from me. My honor, my intelligence, and my experience all informed me, that freedom, not happiness, was the precious stone. One could not cling to happiness—happiness, simply, submitted to no clinging; and it is criminal to use the unspoken and unrealized needs of another as a means of escorting him, elaborately, into the prison of those needs, and sealing him there. But, on the other hand, the stone I hoped to offer was, nevertheless, a stone: its edges drew blood, and its weight was tremendous.

Still, there he was, before me. And my fatigue increased.

"I've got to get out of here," I said.

"I know you do," said Christopher. "I wish you didn't.

We're all going to have to go soon. But I know you must be tired."

"I guess I better circulate just a little bit, anyway," I said, "then I'll split."

"I've kind of monopolized you, haven't I? Well, crazy. I'm not going to say I'm sorry because I'm not. I'm a real selfish monster."

"I outrank you again," I said. *"I'm* the monster here."

"You? You'll have to prove it to me."

"You'll just have to take my word," I said.

And I moved a little away from him. He followed me. We stood at the bar together, and he filled my drink. "I was born in the streets, baby, and I take nobody's word for *nothing*." He touched my glass. *"You* know I'm not going to take your word."

"You'd better."

"You trying to scare me?"

"Shit. I'm probably trying to make you."

He threw back his head, and laughed. "Tre*men*dous!" Then, "Do you like me? I like you, I think you're crazy."

Something rose in me, stronger than intelligence or experience. "Sure, I like you. I like you very much. You know that."

He gave me a smile of pure pleasure, and it cannot be denied that such a smile is rare. He touched my glass again. "Tremendous," he said. "We're going to get on just fine." He looked very grave. Then, irrepressibly, like a very small child, "You know something I was going to tell you before, but didn't have the nerve? You got your name written all over me. That's right. I got my name on you, too."

I smiled. "Okay. We'll see."

We walked back to the window. Everyone was leaving us alone, and yet everyone was watching us, too, waiting for their opportunity. An English girl sat on the sofa, talking to our host, but her eyes were on Christopher and me. Two drama students, both male, were loudly disputing some point about the Stanislavski method, concerning which, as far as I could tell, neither of them knew anything. They hoped that I would overhear and genially interrupt and even, perhaps, find one of them attractive. Not that either of them was "gay"—to use the incomprehensible vernacular; anybody mad enough to make such a suggestion would have been beaten within an inch of his life. But they were on the make, and what else, after all, did they have to give? Also, they were lonely.

"When can I come to see your play?" Christopher now murmured. "I don't think I've seen more than two plays in my whole life, and I didn't like them much. But I'd like to see you——"

"Anytime," I said. The English girl had screwed up her courage, and was approaching. One of the drama students had disappeared into the john. His friend, not knowing how to conquer the field, simply waited.

It was getting late.

"Well," said Christopher, with a curious, muffled urgency in his voice that I was to come to know, "as soon as possible, don't give me this anytime crap. Is it hard to get the tickets?—I mean, you know, I can scrape up the bread to pay."

"Don't be silly." We agreed on a night. "You can pick me up in my dressing room after the show and we can have a few drinks, maybe something to eat. Do you want to bring anyone with you?"

"No," he said.

During all these years, Barbara and I had seen each other with many people, always slightly envying and slightly pitying whoever was with the other. We had achieved our difficult equanimity, were reconciled to the way our cookie had crumbled, and very often, indeed, alone or together, made of these crumbs a rare and delicate feast. One can live a long time without living; and we were both to discover this now.

Pacing my dressing room some evenings before the curtain rose, glimpsing myself in the mirror, listening to the sounds, the voices, the life in the corridors, I found myself resisting, and wrestling with the fact that something had happened to me. I say something because I was reluctant indeed to use the word love—the word splashed over me like cold water, and made me catch my breath and shake myself. It certainly had not occurred to me that love would have had the effrontery to arrive in such a black, unwieldy, and dangerous package. Anyway, love was not exactly what it felt like. I don't know what it felt like. When something *does* happen to a person, it is

somewhat chilling to observe how the memory, so author-
itative till then, cops out, retreats, stammers out only the
most garbled and treacherous of messages. One couldn't
act on them, even if one was able to make any sense of
them. What floated up to me, like the sounds of some
infernal party on the dark ground floor of some dark
house, were echoes, images, moments—memories? But
they were too swift for memories. They came unreadably
into the light, and vanished. Was it memory, or was it a
dream? I could not know. My life was whispering something to me. Was it my life, or was it the whirring of the
wings of madness? I could not know. I could not even take
refuge in any fear of what the world might call me. The
world had already called me too many names, and while
I knew that my indifference was not as great or as deep as
Christopher's—was not the same quantity at all—the world
would never be able to intimidate me in that way anymore.
The world was not my problem. *I* was my problem. Something had happened to me. I was forced to suspect with
what relentless cunning I had always protected myself
against this. I was forced to suspect in myself some mighty
prohibition, of which sex might be the symbol, but wasn't
the key.

Barbara knew something had happened to me, knew
it at once, knew it before she met Christopher. I did not
tell her, but I knew she knew. I did not tell her because I
was ashamed—not of my liaison; but, in beginning to
thaw, I had to see how I had frozen myself; and, in freezing myself, had frozen Barbara. If I had merely been having an affair, I might have told her, without even thinking about it; for there would really have been nothing to
tell. But now—oh, yes, something had happened to me,
and now, for the very first time, really, Barbara was
threatened, and Barbara knew it.

Christopher sometimes picked me up after the show.
Sometimes he met me at home, sometimes he arrived the
next day, sometimes he'd merely telephone. I didn't
know much about his life then, except that most of it
took place in the streets, or in lofts, or in basements, or on
rooftops. I did not want to know. I gathered that I had an
interesting reputation in the streets. Some people considered me a fagot, for some I was a hero, for some I was a
whore, for some I was a devious cocks-man, for some I

was an Uncle Tom. My eminence hurt me sometimes, but I tried not to think too much about it. I certainly couldn't blame the people if they didn't trust me—why should they? They had no way of knowing whether or not I gave a shit about them, and all I could do to make them feel it—maybe—was to do what I could, and do my work.

Every once in a while, some of Christopher's friends came by the house. All of his friends were black. Sometimes, some of my friends might be there, and many of my friends were white. I knew that this made me suspect, but, then, everything about me was suspect, and always had been, and it was late in the day to start nursing an ulcer about it. I liked Christopher's friends very much, young, bright, eager, raggedy-assed, taking no shit from anyone; I had the feeling, hard to explain, that they found me very strange indeed; I had the feeling that the very strangest thing about me, for them, was that they rather liked me, too, but hadn't expected to and didn't trust the feeling. They were younger than they thought they were, much: they might arrive in their Castro berets, their Castro beards, their parkas and hoods and sweaters and thin jeans or corduroys and heavy boots, and with their beautiful black kinky hair spinning around their heads like fire and prophecy—this hair putting me in mind, somehow, of the extravagant beauty of rain-forests—and with Camus or Fanon or Mao on their person, or with *Muhammad Speaks* under their arms, but they were goggle-eyed just the same, and so far from being incapable of trusting, they had perpetually to fight the impulse to trust, overwhelmed, like all kids, by meeting a Great Man, and awkward like all kids, and, however they tried to dissemble it, shy. They were proud of Christopher for knowing me, and delighted by me for knowing Christopher. Christopher lived partly with me, partly with a sister I had yet to meet. He had his own key, he had the run of the house. I admit that, at first, I was a little frightened, but I don't really, anyway, have very much to steal, and I've just never managed to get very hung-up on possessions. I tend not to give a shit. This is a trait in me of which Christopher entirely disapproved, and I very shortly realized that with Christopher in the house, every tie, tie-clasp, cufflink, spoon, every plaque, trophy, ring, shoe, shirt, sock, watch, coat, was as safe as, if not indeed considerably safer than, the gold rumored to be in Fort Knox.

I usually left Christopher and his friends alone. I
didn't want to bug them. They had to be a part of my
concern, for I was their elder; but there was no real reason for me to be a part of their concern. I'd go to my
study, and read, or do nothing, look out of my window at
the Manhattan streets, wonder what had happened to me,
and begin—slowly, slowly—to be glad that it had happened. What I was going to do with it, or what it was
going to do to me, I didn't know. I was happy watching
Christopher's bright, black face, happy to know that I
had helped to make it so bright. He felt safe, he had a
friend, he was valued. He could say what he liked, he
could be what he was. It was, I must say, very beautiful,
and it made up for a lot: Christopher, lying flat on his
belly, reading all the long afternoon, Christopher keeping me awake all night with his sweeping statements and
halting questions, Christopher ruthlessly dominating his
friends, instructing them in everything from terrorism to
sex, or Christopher and his friends, boys and girls, dancing
to the hi-fi set. They were teaching me a great deal; made
me wonder where I'd been so long; made me wonder
what it would have been like to have had children. I
often eavesdropped on their funny, earnest, quite terrifying
conversations. They knew that they were slated for
slaughter, at the hands of their countrymen, willfully.
Beneath everything they said lay the question of how to
prevent or outwit or face that day. "We are not going to
walk to the gas ovens," Christopher said, "and we are not
going to march to the concentration camps. We have to
make the mothers know that."

I suppose that if their nominal representatives in
Washington, that virtuous band of men, could have
heard them—those brave descendants of cowboys, rob-
bers, rapists, pirates, and whores—everyone in the barbed-
wire business would have made a tremendous killing. I
liked them. If they had ever been represented, loved, by
the people who had kidnapped and used them, they would
not have had to spend so much of their youth evolving
dubious strategies for self-defense. When the shit hit the
fan, I wanted to be at the wire with them—not, being black
like them, that I flattered myself about having any choice.

Barbara met Christopher one night in my dressing

room. I was a little nervous about the encounter; but it was brief, because Barbara had a date. She looked quite marvelous that evening, and I could see that Christopher was very taken with her. Christopher was sitting in a corner. I had just finished dressing, and we were about to leave the theater. Christopher and I were merely going to grab a bite at Downey's, and then go home. "Why don't you grab a bite with us?"

"Thank you. I'd like to, but I can't. I have a *family* night. My mother and father and brother and sister-in-law are in town and they've always wanted to see '21' and so I've reserved a table there, like the dutiful daughter I am. They haven't yet been to see the play, you'll note, but they're coming next week—they didn't think that they could do it *justice* tonight, since they've only just got in. And you've never met my family and so I thought I'd corral you—they're dying to meet you." We both laughed. "That's progress," she said, "don't knock it." She looked at Christopher. "Hello. My name is Barbara King."

"I know," said Christopher. He rose, grinning, and held out his hand. "My name is Christopher Hall."

They shook hands. "Wouldn't *you* like to come to '21'?"

"I'd love it," said Christopher, "but it's up to Big Daddy here."

He put his hand on my back, briefly, and something flickered between them for a second.

Barbara looked at me with great, mocking amusement. "Well, Big Daddy?"

"We're not really dressed for it, Barbara. I think it would be too much of a hassle."

We left the dressing room, and started for the steps. "How long are they going to be in town?"

"Oh, another four or five days, I expect. I don't know."

We said good-night to the doorman, and we were in the streets.

"Well—is tomorrow Sunday? We can have brunch at my house tomorrow."

"Oh. That's even better. It makes a great story to tell in Kentucky." We laughed again. But, for the first time in my life, or, at least, the first time that I could remember it happening in this way, I wanted to get rid of her.

"Are you from Kentucky?" Christopher asked.

"Yes, Christopher," she said, "I'm from Kentucky. But I left it just as soon as I could. All right?"

He smiled, embarrassed. "You're certainly all right with me," he said.

"Any friend of Big Daddy's." She turned to me. "Do you want me to drop you? Or are you kids going to walk?"

"I think we'll walk. It's just a couple of blocks."

"Okay. See you tomorrow. Good-night, Christopher."

"Good-night. I'm glad to have met you."

"Likewise," she said, and she got into her car, blowing up a kiss. She leaned back, and was whirled away. I felt a little awkward.

"She seems nice," said Christopher. "Especially for a broad from Kentucky."

"She *is* very nice. She's probably my best friend."

"You've known each other a long time?"

"About half my life, I guess. Since I was younger than you are now."

He seemed to think about this as we walked, watching the people.

"How come you two never got married?"

"Our families objected," I said, and I laughed. Then, "No, that's not the reason. It would just have been a terrible marriage."

"Because she's white?"

"Partly. I don't mean that it's *her* fault."

"Oh," he said, slyly, "I know *you* would never mean *that*."

"You think we *should* have got married?"

"No. You too much of a Puritan. That would have fucked up *my* scene altogether, and a whole lot of other folks, too." He turned me into Downey's. "Now, you just remember who you come with, you hear? I don't want to have to start no shit."

We stayed out very late that Saturday night, and I had completely forgotten about the brunch. But suddenly I heard Christopher turn and curse and jump out of bed.

"What's the matter with you?"

"Move your ass, Leo, them people going to be here in about an hour."

Then I remembered. "Oh, Christ."

"Go get in the shower, I'll go to the store. Move your

ass now, Leo, I swear I don't know how the fuck you managed all these years without me." He got into his dungarees, ran into the bathroom, peed, and splashed his face in the sink, hurled himself into an old shirt, got into his sneakers, pulled the covers off me, pulled me to my feet, pushed me into the bathroom, grabbed my wallet, and dashed out the door. Bam. I felt shaky and short of breath, but I was more or less together by the time he got back. He put the groceries away—we had had almost nothing in the house—and went to take his shower and I started straightening up the place. The telephone rang. It was Barbara.

"I thought I ought to warn you that we're on our way. Are you up to it?"

"Oh, yeah, we're ready. Thanks to Christopher. He woke me up. I think I have a hangover, but I'm not conscious enough yet to be sure. How many are you again?"

"Mama and Daddy and brother Ken and his wife, and a friend of theirs, and me. I'm afraid it's not going to be *the* most exciting brunch you've ever had, but what the hell. You know. We pass this way but once, et cetera."

"Et cetera. Okay. We're ready. Maybe I can persuade Christopher to do his soft-shoe routine."

"Please don't—he'll be there?"

"Oh, yes. He'll be here."

"Here we come then. Later."

"Ciao."

Christopher went to the door when the bell rang—he didn't feel that I should answer my door; to please him, I stood in the living room, waiting. To be meeting Barbara's family, after all these years, suddenly seemed hilarious. It also seemed sad. I wondered what Barbara was thinking. I wondered what Christopher was thinking. I heard a confused, nervous gaggle of voices, and I walked into the foyer.

I was on.

"Hello. I'm Leo Proudhammer. I guess you've met Christopher—Mr. Christopher Hall. Hi, Barbara." We usually kissed each other, lightly, when we met but we didn't this time. "Come on in the house." I led the way into the living room. Christopher, indescribably, impeccably sardonic, brought up the rear. We seemed, as we entered the living room, to be taking up battle positions.

"You must be Mrs. King," I said, and took her hand in mine, as boyish and open and charming as I knew I could be, and she smiled dazedly up at me from behind her flashing spectacles, dazzled and floundering. "I've been wanting to meet you for years," I said. I turned to the father. "And you, too, sir," I said, and held out my hand. He took it, briefly, staring at me with a face as blank and as helpless and as treacherous as water. I could not resist dropping into this pond a hard, sharp pebble. "Barbara's told me so much about you," I said. "It's a pity we couldn't meet sooner."

"This is my brother, Ken," said Barbara, and we shook hands. He was older than Barbara, with a friendly face, a softening body, and thinning hair. "And his wife, Elena." Elena was dark, and rather pretty, very chunky. There was down on her upper lip. We shook hands. "And their friend," said Barbara, "Tyrone Bennett," and I turned to shake hands with a heavy-set, pale-eyed, albino-looking man, in his middle forties, perhaps, with loose, nervous lips. "Pleased to meet you," I said, "please, let's all sit down. Make yourselves comfortable." Mrs. King sat down on the sofa, still smiling, her gaze seeming to be helplessly riveted on me, and Mr. King sat beside her. Elena and Ken sat down, and Bennett strolled to the window and lit a cigarette. Christopher leaned on the bar, and Barbara went over to him.

"My," said Barbara's mother, "it's so nice of you to have us." She laughed, like a girl. I was worried about the effect of her accent on Christopher's nerves. I looked over at him. Barbara was talking, he was listening, with his same sardonic smile. "Why, I just can't get over it. Sitting in the house of a real famous movie star."

"Oh, stop it, Mrs. King. Your daughter's a famous movie star. You should be used to it by now."

"Oh, but that's different. Barbie's not a movie star for me. She's my own flesh and blood. Of course, we're proud of her, and all—but you—you're real special. It just makes me feel so *good* that a boy like you could make so much of himself. It really does. Why, I could cry." I kept smiling. Barbara and Christopher were still in conference at the bar. "Your mother must be real proud of you."

"Well, I hope my father is," I said, "but my mother's been dead for awhile."

"Oh! That *is* too bad. But your father? I hope he's enjoying good health?"

"Oh, yes"—and I almost said, "ma'am," I felt myself being strangled by her sincerity, and I felt abandoned by Christopher and Barbara, who were still leaning on the bar. "We see each other all the time. He's tough, my father. He was built to last at least a hundred years."

"Are you from New York?" Ken asked me. He had taken out his pipe, and was playing with it the way pipe smokers do.

"Yes. Born and bred."

"You an only child?"

"Oh, no. I have an older brother."

"He in show business too?"

"Oh, no." I paused. "He's a preacher."

"That's kind of interesting, isn't it?" said Bennett, turning and looking at me, "to have a preacher and an actor in the same family?" He chuckled. "Y'all get along?"

"Oh, I think it happens very often," said Elena, "especially—well, it's very common, anyway." She turned to her husband. "Who was it we saw, last time we was up here—that singer? The one I was so *crazy* about? Oh, you know who I mean! A *beautiful* girl."

"She has all *kinds* of enthusiasms," Ken said to me, smiling. "I don't know how she expects *me* to keep up with them." He turned back to Elena. "Lena Horne?"

"Oh! She *is* beautiful. And she is such a *lady,* don't care what she's doing, it just stands out all over her. I just adore her, don't you?"

"I do indeed," I said. "I really do."

"But she wasn't the one. No, this was another one—a whole lot *darker* than Lena Horne."

"You're thinking of Pearl Bailey," Barbara said.

"Yes. That is the one. With those hands, and all. She *is* a scream. Now, *she's* got a brother who's a preacher, at least that's what we was *told.*"

"Yes, she does," I said. "You're right, it *is* common. Most of us come out of the church, one way or another."

"Why is that?" asked Barbara's father. A slight flush on his face told me that he had almost said "boy."

"Well, that's a very loaded question," I said. "It could keep us here for several days—"

"Christopher and I are being bartenders," Barbara

said. "There are lots of Bloody Marys and there's just about anything else you want. Now, who wants what?"

"The reason that so many of us come out of the church," said Christopher, "is that the church is the only thing we had—the only thing the white man *let* us have."

They all stared at him. "I'll have a Bloody Mary," said Barbara's mother.

"Me, too," said Ken.

"Hell, might as well make it Bloody Marys all around," said Bennett. He watched Christopher. "Why do you say that?"

"I say it," said Christopher, "because it's true." He looked up at Bennett, then continued dropping ice in glasses. Barbara was putting the glasses on a tray. Her hair was down, she was wearing slacks and low heels and she was as silent as the waitress which she once had been. Christopher began to pour.

Bennett looked at me, but I said nothing. Christopher winked broadly at me, and I suppose they all saw it, but they didn't—nor did I—know how to react. Barbara began passing around the drinks. Ken looked at Barbara for a moment, shrewdly. Barbara brought a drink to me.

"Well, it just seems to me," said Ken, finally, "that that's maybe putting it too simply—like you're blaming the white man for everything."

"I'm not blaming you," Christopher said. "You had a good thing going for you. You'd done already killed off most of the Indians and you'd robbed them of their land and now you had all these blacks working for you for nothing and you didn't want no black cat from Walla Walla being able to talk to no black cat from Boola Boola. If they could have talked to each other, they might have figured out a way of chopping off *your* heads, and getting rid of *you*." He smiled. "Dig it." He took a swallow of his drink. "So you gave us Jesus. And told us it was the *Lord's* will that we should be toting the barges and lifting the bales while you all sat on your big, fat, white behinds and got rich." He took another sip of his drink, and squatted on his heels in the middle of the floor. "That's what happened, and you all is still the same. You ain't changed at all, except to get worse. You want to tell me different?"

"I don't think I want to tell you anything," said Bennett, and turned back to the window. "I don't think you can listen."

"Try me," Christopher said, and he winked at me again.

"My," said Barbara's mother, and patted her husband's knee, "you don't have to talk to *us* this way. You don't know how many colored friends we *have* down where we come from. If you ever get down that way, why we'd be happy to make you welcome. Why, Barbie can tell you. We don't care about the color of a person's skin—we never have done! My daddy would have skinned me alive had he ever heard of me mistreating a colored person, or calling them out of their name. And I never have. I loved my daddy too much. My daddy used to say, God made us *all*. We're *all* here for some reason. Barbie can tell you. Tell him, Barbie." She had been leaning forward, toward Christopher; now, she leaned back. "Why, Barbie grew up with colored folks. She'll tell you that herself." She looked at me and smiled and sipped her drink. "He'll learn," she assured me. "He's young." She looked at her husband, looked at Ken, glanced at Barbara, who was now in the kitchen, on the other side of the bar. "Now, let's just talk about something else. Mr. Proudhammer—where did you go to school?"

Christopher snorted, but delicately, and rose from the floor and joined Barbara in the kitchen. His laugh rang out across the room, then hers. Ken and Bennett and Barbara's father looked toward the kitchen; but they did not move.

"I went to high school," I said, "here in New York."

"You didn't go to college? My!"

"And you made it, all right, didn't you?" Bennett asked. "Why, I bet you make more money than I do—I *know* you make more money than I do," and he chuckled. "And I bet you didn't do it sitting around, feeling sorry for yourself, did you?"

"Hell, no," Ken said. "He just made his own way. And *anybody* can make his way in this country, no matter *what* color he is."

I thought, Great God, I'm not going to be able to take this much longer, even if it *is* Barbara's family. And, in a minute, Christopher's going to throw everything in the kitchen out here on these defenseless heads, and we're all going to end up in jail.

Barbara said, "That's pure bullshit, Ken, and you know it. None of those boys who work for you are going to make their own way, you've seen to that—you've *helped* to see to that—they can't even join a union. So, don't you sit here and talk to Leo as though you had something to do with the fact that Leo's still alive. You didn't have a damn thing to do with it. Leo's tough. That's all. And you're a no-good bastard. I've told you that before."

"And I've told *you* before," he said, turning red and wet, "to hold your tongue—to *mind* your tongue in front of your mother."

"The way," said Barbara, "that you've always minded yours in front of *me?* Don't give me any of your shit, Ken, I *know* you."

"Hush, children," said Mrs. King, "we didn't come here to fight. Why, we're embarrassing Mr. Proudhammer." And she finished her drink, and set it down; the old girl could drink. I rose to give her a refill. I said, "You're not embarrassing me. But there's no point in pretending that Negroes are treated like white people in this country because they're not, and we all know that."

"But look at you," said Ken. "I don't know what you make a year, but I can make a pretty shrewd guess. What have you got to complain about? It seems to me that this country's treated you pretty well. I know a whole lot of white people couldn't afford to live in this apartment, for example—"

"Of course you do," said Barbara dryly, "and they work for you, too."

He threw an exasperated look toward the kitchen, but held his peace, and looked at me. I realized that I was beginning to be angry, but I also realized that it was a perfectly futile anger. I had not been surprised by Christopher, nor had I been in the least surprised by this family. But I was a little surprised by Barbara, who seemed to be paying off old scores. I didn't care at all what these people felt, or thought. Talking to them was a total waste of time. I just wanted them to get loaded on their Bloody Marys and get out of my house. I was a little angry at Barbara for having brought them here at all. And yet, I was aware, with another part of my mind, that Barbara was showing me something—showing me, perhaps, part of the price she had had to pay for me?—and she was, at the same time, exhibiting her credentials to Christopher. This argued an uneasiness on Barbara's part which, again, after all these years, surprised me.

The question had been addressed to me, and so I was compelled to answer it, praying that, then, we could let the matter drop. I said, "You can't imagine my life, and I won't discuss it. I don't make as much money as you think I do, and I don't work as often as I would if I were white. Those are just facts. The point is that the Negroes of this country are treated as none of you would dream of treating a dog or a cat. What Christopher's trying to tell you is perfectly true. If you don't want to believe it, well, that's your problem. And I don't feel like talking about it anymore, and I won't." I looked at Ken. "This *is* my house."

They sat in silence, angry themselves now, uneasy, and trapped, and I put on a Billie Holiday record, "Strange Fruit." Yes, I was being vindictive. I poured myself a refill, and sat down. Mrs. King gave me a reproachful look, but I avoided her eye and lit a cigarette. Christopher, holding a carton of eggs in his hand, leaned over the bar and smiled and said, "What the man just told you is that you're stuck with your criminal record and he's not going to be an accomplice to it, or let you feel good about it. How do you all like your eggs?"

And yet, surprisingly enough, it turned out not to be such an awful afternoon, after all. Christopher's insolence had released him, and, in a curious way, it had released them. Bennett's pale, vindictive eyes and his busy wet lips conveyed but too vividly what he would have done with Christopher, had he encountered Christopher in his own bailiwick; this not being the case, and since he was now, morally at least, encircled, he relaxed and proceeded to enjoy the afternoon as though it were a species of vaudeville show and something he would not soon be doing again. Ken, no match for Barbara anyway, contributed anecdotes from their childhood, which Barbara took with wry good grace, and the old lady, knocking back Bloody Marys as though there were no tomorrow, told stories about presidents and governors who had visited her home when she was young. She confessed how upset she had been by Barbara's choice of a career, and said that Barbara got her stubbornness from her father—which transparent fiction seemed to delight the faceless old man. I watched Christopher watching them from the heights of an unassailable contempt, as they became more and more themselves, more and more human, and less and less attractive. They could not know how much they revealed, how pathetic and tawdry they were—this master race. But they were dangerous, too, unutterably so. They knew nothing about themselves at all. I wondered —but idly—how they had got that way; wondered, but from a great distance, as the sun grew paler in my living room; as Ken grew blander, more shapeless, and by now he was clenching a pipe between his teeth with the energy of the dying; his wife grew more flirtatious, though not with him, exactly; the old lady grew drunker and madder, her husband appeared to be waiting for God knows what dreadful event; and Bennett, licking his nervous lips each time he looked at Christopher, could not have realized that he was a study in lust and bloodlust. But they were not my concern. Christopher was my concern. The problem was how to prevent these Christians from once again destroying this pagan. Barbara sat among her kin, dry and cold, looking very young, and putting me in mind of a living sacrifice. When, at last, they rose to go, and bags and hats and various appurtenances were collected, and the last male left the "little boys' room," and we stood chatting in the foyer, I had a splitting headache. Barbara now kissed me on the cheek, and said, "Thanks, Leo. I'll talk to you later." Then, very deliberately, she thanked Christopher, and kissed him, too. I kissed the old lady, because she wanted me to, and shook hands with Elena and the men, said I would be happy to be their guest when I came to Kentucky—"Give us a chance!" the old lady cried. "You'll see we ain't nearly so bad down there as people up North *say* we are!"—and allowed Christopher to walk them to the elevator. I closed the door behind them, and walked back into the living room and stretched out on the floor.

Soon, the door slammed behind Christopher, and he came padding in. He stretched out on the floor beside me, and rubbed his hand over the back of my neck. "Wow! Baby, are they for *real?*" He sat up, clasping his knees. "Damn. They really fucked up. That old lady should be in an asylum some place." He laughed. "No wonder Barbara split—she took one look at *them* people and she started making it—she *hauled* ass, baby!" He laughed again, and stretched out on the floor again. "Wow!" Then, "Barbara's tough. I didn't know a white chick could be so tough."

I said, "She's tough, all right."

He said, "She's really for real. She's something." He looked over at me. "You must be tired, Big Daddy. You want to take a nap?"

"I don't know. What do you want to do?"

"If they hadn't stayed so long, I was thinking about maybe going to a movie. There's a couple of movies in town I wanted you to see. But, now, I don't think I feel up to it, and I *know* you don't."

"No," I said. "I guess I don't."

He put his head on my chest. I held it there.

"Christopher—something I've been meaning to ask you—what do you want to do?—with your life, I mean."

He laughed, his head bouncing up and down against my chest.

"I already told you. I want to be an astronaut."

"Come on. Be serious."

"I *am* serious. I think I might dig going to the moon—or Mars—you know—"

"Come on. You know that's not about to happen soon. You're going to be earth-bound for awhile. So, what do you want to do on earth while they're figuring out whether or not they're going to let you on the moon?"

"Well"—thoughtfully—"I guess I don't want to spend the rest of my life in that shoe store." He had a job in a shoe store in Spanish Harlem. "I don't know. I'm a high school dropout, Leo—*you've* heard of cats like me, who drop out of school? And I've got a record, baby. It's not so easy for me to tell you what I want to do."

"Well, I think we can fix all the legal shit. But what do you *think* you want to do?"

He was silent. "I could learn a lot just working for you."

"That's cool. But that's not enough."

Silence again. His breath came and went against my chest. "Why not? You don't want me to work for you?"

"Come on, now, don't be coy—"

He leaned up, smiling. "What does that word mean—coy?"

"It means that you know damn well that I'll be glad to have you with me all the time, and you just want to hear me say so. That's being coy."

He grinned. "Oh. Thanks." He put his head on my chest again. "I don't know, Leo, I want to learn—everything I can. That might sound funny, coming from me, but I really do. But"—he leaned up, looking at me very earnestly—"this is no cop-out, believe me, but—what I really want to learn—it doesn't look like it's being taught. I mean—I don't want to learn all that shit they teach you here. That's not where it's at. I don't want to be like these people. I know kids in the street who know a hell of a lot more than—all those people in school. I don't know—I always feel like they trying to cut my balls off. You know what I mean?"

"Yes," I said, "I do." I put my hand over my forehead.

"You got a headache?"

"A little. It'll go away."

"Should I get you some aspirin?"

"No. Finish what you were saying."

"Well. That's it. I like the people in the streets, there's a whole lot of beauty in the streets, Leo, and I'd like to help, I'd like to teach, but somebody's got to teach *me*."

I watched his face. His face made me want to smile. "Well. First things first. We'll try to make you ready."

He looked down, then looked into my eyes again. "You know something?"

"What?"

"I got a birthday coming soon."

I laughed. "And what do you want for your birthday?"

He laughed, too. "Would you get me a camera? Just a simple, ordinary camera. I thought I might fool around with that for awhile—you know, maybe I can at least make a kind of record of what's happening. And I can go a whole lot of places where no camera's ever been."

I said, watching him, "I'm hip."

"So it wouldn't really be a waste of your money."

I pulled his head onto my chest again. "Don't sweat it, baby. Everything's going to be nice."

"I believe you," he said, after a moment, and then we lay quietly on the floor, until the sun was long gone, and night filled the room. The street lights pressed against my window. It was very silent. Christopher had fallen fast asleep, snoring and whistling. I lay there, and stroked his kinky hair and thought of my father and mother, and my brother, and of Christopher, and a line suddenly came flying back at me, out of my past, from *The Corn Is Green*. It made me laugh, and almost made me cry. It was Bunny's curtain line: *Moffat, my girl, you mustn't be clumsy this time. You mustn't be clumsy.* Ah. So! I laughed to myself, and stroked Christopher's hair, laughed perhaps a little sadly and ironically but without grief. This little light of mine.

"I *can* explain it, in a way, and, in another way, I can't," Barbara said. She stood very straight, walking up and down my living room. It was about three o'clock in the morning. Christopher was God knew where. "If I could have explained it before it happened, then, obviously, it wouldn't have happened."

I said, "Barbara, I don't need any explanations. I really don't. I don't feel—whatever you're supposed to feel when something like this happens. I just don't. I don't feel—*wronged*." I watched her. Her face hurt me. It was true that I did not feel wronged: what *did* I feel? An immense fatigue, a sense of going down beneath a burden; of barely holding on. "Don't you see what I mean? Old Princess?"

She turned away from me, and walked back to my bar and poured herself another drink. I joined her at the bar. My living room was lit by one dim light, and my record player was playing Dinah Washington, very low.

I poured myself a drink, and touched her face. She smiled, and we touched glasses. She sat down on one of the barstools, and lit a cigarette.

"He reminded me of you," she said, "when we were young. I was reaching backward for you—and for me—I think—reaching backward, over twenty years." She sipped her drink, and smiled, threw back her head, and sighed. "He was you before our choices had been made. Before we'd become—what we've become." She looked at me, seemed to try to look into me, her eyes were enormous. "Do you know what I mean?"

"I think I do." Then, "Do you think what we've become is so awful, Barbara?"

"No. Oh, I don't mean that. But it isn't—is it?—
exactly what we had in mind. I didn't," she said at last,
"expect to become so lonely."

"Neither did I," I said. Then, for a moment, Dinah's
voice was the only sound in the room.

"I think *he* wanted"—she stopped—"I think *he* wanted
to find out—if love was possible. If it was really possible.
I think he had to find *out* what I thought of *his* body, by
taking mine." She paused. "It wasn't like that," she said,
"with you and me."

"No. It wasn't like that with you and me."

"I'm glad for one thing," she said. "I was afraid that
I'd—seduced Christopher, or allowed Christopher to seduce
me, only in order to hurt you. I was terribly afraid that I
was only acting out of bitterness. And that would have
had to mean that I'd been bitter all this time. But it wasn't
that. It was just—*you*. That's terrible, in its way, but it's
true. I wasn't trying to hurt you. I was trying to get back
to you. And he realized that, oh, very quickly. *Then*, he
realized that love was possible. I shouldn't be surprised if
that didn't frighten him."

"He'll be back," I said. "He'll be back, or I'll go into
the streets to find him. He's not lost, don't sweat it. I
won't let him be lost." She said nothing. "Look. That's
all that matters now, isn't it—that the kid not be lost?"

"I hope I haven't wrecked everything," she said.

"I don't think you have. But if you have, then we'll have
to face that, too. And if you have, well, I don't know how
I'll feel then. But I don't think you have. And now you
ought to go home. We've both had it."

"I suppose so," she said, and rose. She was still very
straight and steady. "When he left me—he said he was
coming here."

"It's only been three days. He's probably at his sister's
house. He'll be along."

"I must tell you," she said, "it has not been easy for
me. It has not been easy at all to have lived all these years
the life I've lived and to know, no matter who I was with,
no matter how much I loved them or hoped to love them
and no matter what they offered me, it has not been easy

to know that if you whistled, called, sang, belched, picked up the telephone, sent a wire, I'd be there. I'd have no choice, I wouldn't be able to help myself. I've not been free—not all these years. And with time flying—and time's worse for a woman than it is for a man. No, it's not been easy. And sometimes I hated you and hated myself and hated my life and wanted to die, to die!"

Her words and her voice rang in my ears, they always will, and her face burns in my mind.

I said, from the depths of my terrible fatigue, "I couldn't have done otherwise. I couldn't have done otherwise—*then!* And once we'd made that turning—could we have done otherwise later, Barbara? *Could* we?"

"I know," said Barbara. "I know." She sat down on the barstool again. She picked up her glass and raised it in a sorrowful, gallant, mocking toast. "Let us drink to the new Jerusalem."

She left, and I went to sleep, wearier than I'd ever been in all my life. Sometime that morning, Christopher came crawling into bed beside me. He was as cold as sweating metal, almost that dangerous to touch, as funky as a fishstall. God knows where he had been. I never asked him. He crawled into my arms, sighing like a mother, found a place for his head, and then lay still. And then we slept.

On our last night but one in San Francisco, I was allowed to go out. It was to be a very quiet evening; the idea was for me to be bothered as little as possible by people who might recognize my face. We were to pick up Pete and Barbara at the theater, after the show. Pete loaned Christopher his car, and we drove to a Chinese restaurant, crowded and fashionable, but very good. It was strange to be out. I felt, well, *rested* is perhaps the only word, and for the very first time in my whole life. I was not, so to speak, running, but was learning how to walk. At the door to the restaurant, my notoriety suddenly hit me, like a glove—a not unpleasant tap, but a definite one. I had been exulting in the glory of having had my sight returned to me, I was going to be able to see the world again, for awhile. I hadn't thought about the world seeing *me.* Yet, here the world was, in the headwaiter's face, in the faces turning toward us, in the hum, the buzz, the *rustle*, which marked our passage through the room. Christopher marched before me, stern, elegant, and tall like a chieftain or a prince, taking very seriously his role of lieutenant and bodyguard. We found our table, and sat down, and people smiled at us, and it was a rather nice feeling, that evening, to feel oneself recalled to life. We ordered two dry martinis, and our menus came, bigger than the most thorough map of the world, and Christopher grinned, and said, "This is certainly not the moment to start thinking of the starving Chinese. You know what some of my friends would say if they saw me in a place like this?"

"Well, then, order your usual bowl of rice, baby, and eat it in the kitchen. The starving peasants will rejoice, believe me, to have you swell their ranks."

"Later for the kitchen. I know that I can *always* make it in the kitchen. But let me see what I can do out here with—let's see now—some sweet and sour pork, how does that strike you? You know, we mustn't forget our roots, they ain't hardly got no grits, but how about some egg foo *young?*" And he went on like this, until mercifully, our waiter suggested that we put ourselves in his hands and allow him to order our meal. So we did that, and he didn't let us down. Perhaps it was because I'd been away so long, but everything tasted wonderful, and the room, the people, the rise and fall, the steady turning, as of a wheel, of many voices, the laughter, the clink of glass and silver, the shining hair, the shining dresses, the rings and earrings and necklaces and spangles and bangles and bracelets of the women, the tie clasps and watches and rings of the men, all created an astounding illusion of safety and order and civilization. Evil did not seem to exist here, or sorrow, or intolerable pain, and here we were, a part of it. I was a celebrity, with a bank account, and a future, and I had it in my power to make Christopher's life secure. We were the only colored people there. I had worked in the kitchen, not a hundred years ago; outside were the millions of starving—Chinese. *I'm going to feast at the welcome table,* my mother used to sing—was *this* the table? This groaning board was a heavy weight on the backs of many millions, whose groaning was not heard. Beneath this table, deep in the bowels of the earth, as far away as China, as close as the streets outside, an energy moved and gathered and it would, one day, overturn this table just as surely as the earth turned and the sun rose and set. And: where will you be, when that first trumpet sounds? I watched Christopher, making out with the chopsticks, smiling, calm, and proud. Well. I want to be with Jesus, when that first trumpet sounds. I want to be with Jesus, when it sounds so loud.

I signed the restaurant's golden book, and I signed a couple of autographs—but the people were nice, they remembered I'd been sick—and we walked out to the car. It was a beautiful, dark-blue, chilly night. We were on a height, and San Francisco unfurled beneath us, at our feet, like a many-colored scroll. I was leaving soon. I wished it were possible to stay. I had worked hard, hard, it certainly should have been possible by now for me to have a safe, quiet, comfortable life, a life I could devote to my work and to those I loved, without being bugged to death. But I knew it wasn't possible. There was a sense in which it certainly could be said that my endeavor had been for nothing. Indeed, I had conquered the city: but the city was stricken with the plague. Not in my lifetime would this plague end, and, now, all that I most treasured, wine, talk, laughter, love, the embrace of a friend, the light in the eyes of a lover, the touch of a lover, that smell, that contest, that beautiful torment, and the mighty joy of a good day's work, would have to be stolen, each moment lived as though it were the last, for my own mortality was not more certain than the storm that was rising to engulf us all.

I put my hand on Christopher's neck. We stood for a moment in silence. We got into the car.

We drove through the streets of San Francisco, though I wanted to walk. "You can't," said Christopher flatly, "you'll be mobbed on every streetcorner. I promised Barbara and Pete to take real good care of you, so stop giving me a hard time, all right? Be nice."

"I really would like," I said, "to know more than I do about what's going on in the streets."

He looked at me. "You *do* know. You want to know if they still love you in the streets—you want to know what they think of you." He sighed. He was driving very slowly. "Look. A whole lot of cats dig you, and some of them love you. But, Leo—you a fat cat now. That's the way a whole lot of people see you, and you can't blame them, how *else* can they see you? And we in a situation where we have to know which people we can trust, which people we can *use*—that's the nitty-gritty. Well, these cats are out here getting their ass whipped all the time, Leo. You get *your* ass whipped, at least it gets into the papers. But don't nobody care what happens to these kids— nobody! And all these laws and speeches don't mean shit. They do not mean *shit*. It's the spirit of the people, baby, the *spirit* of the people, they don't want us and they don't like us, and you see that spirit in the face of every cop. Them laws they keep passing, shit, they just like the treaties they signed with the Indians. Nothing but lies, they never even *meant* to keep those treaties, baby, they wanted the land and they got it and now they mean to keep it, even if they have to put every black mother- fucker in this country behind barbed wire, or shoot him down like a dog. It's the truth I'm telling you. And you better believe it, unless you want to be like your brother and believe all that okey-doke about Jesus changing peo- ple's hearts. Fuck Jesus, we ain't about to wait on him, and him the first one they got rid of so they could get their shit together? They didn't want him to change their hearts, they just used him to change the *map*." Then he stopped. He said, in another tone, "I'm just trying to tell it to you like it is. We can't afford to trust the white people in this country—we'd have to be crazy if we did. But, naturally, a whole lot of black cats think you might be one of them, and, in a way, you know, you stand to lose just as much as white people stand to lose." He paused again, and he looked at me again. "You see what I mean?" he asked me very gently. I nodded. He put one hand on my knee. "You're a beautiful cat, Leo, and I love you. You believe me?"

"Yes. I believe you."

"Then don't let this other shit get you down. That's just the way it is, and that's the way it's going to be for awhile." He looked at his watch. "Hey. I know a place I'll take you."

He stopped the car on a very crowded street, a street crowded with young people, black and white. They seemed to me to be very, very young; no doubt I seemed to them to be very, very old. There was something oddly attractive about them. Perhaps they reminded me, distantly, of myself, long ago. Perhaps they reminded me, dimly, of something we had lost. I had never worn such costumes, surely, beads, robes, sandals, and earrings, or walked quite so slowly, or dared to embrace another in the sight of all the world, or been so oblivious to the presence of the cops, who patrolled the streets in twos, or stood in doorways, holding their clubs motionless, with their eyes fixed on something straight ahead, and their lips recollecting a sour taste. It was late, but store windows were lighted, with very strange things in the windows, and the stores seemed to be open—but I was not allowed to investigate, for Christopher was walking fast, one hand under my elbow. A couple stopped, looking at me, and Christopher turned me into the entrance of what had once been a movie theater. Unavoidably, he had to stop to get tickets, and I could feel a crowd gathering behind us. I felt terribly uneasy. I turned, once, to look behind me, and I smiled. A colored cat called my name, and laughed, and said, "Be careful, man. You're under surveillance!"

"I know," I said, and Christopher and I walked into the theater. I wondered if the boy had meant to tell me that I was under surveillance by the cops, or under surveillance by the people.

Whatever he had meant, I was under surveillance by both.

We entered a dark and noisy barn. All of the seats had been removed from the orchestra of this theater, and hundreds and hundreds of boys and girls filled this space. Some were standing, some were lounging against the walls, some were sitting on the floor, some were embracing, some were dancing. The stage held four or five of the loudest musicians in the world's history. It was impossible to tell whether they were any good or not, their sound was too high. But it did not really matter whether their sound was any good or not, this sound was, literally, not meant for my ears, and it existed entirely outside my capacity for judgment. It was a rite that I was witnessing—witnessing, not sharing. It made me think of rites I had seen in Caleb's church, in many churches; of black feet stomping in the mud of the levee; of rites older than that, in forests irrecoverable. The music drove and drove, into the past—into the future. It sounded like an attempt to make a great hole in the world, and bring up what was buried. And the dancers seemed, nearly, in the flickering, violent light, with their beads flashing, their long hair flying, their robes whirling—or their tight skirts, tight pants signifying—and with the music assaulting them like the last, last trumpet, to be dancing in their grave-clothes, raised from the dead. On the wall were four screens, and, on these screens, ectoplasmic figures and faces endlessly writhed, moving in and out of each other, in a tremendous sexual rhythm which made me think of nameless creatures blindly coupling in all the slime of the world, and at the bottom of the sea, and in the air we breathed, and in one's very body. From time to time, on this screen, one recognized a face. I saw Yul Brynner's face, for example, and, for a moment, I thought I saw my own. Christopher touched me on the shoulder.

"I came here a couple of times with Pete. It's a gas and there are some real people here and they're making some very nice things happen. I just wanted you to see it. But we have to flee in a minute. The people are starting to recognize you, and, anyway, it's almost curtain time."

"Okay."

But I stood there a few moments longer, and tried to understand what was happening.

"Guns," said Christopher. "We need guns."

It was the next day, we were driving down from Hunter's Point.

I said nothing.

We drove across the Golden Gate. We had no particular destination in mind. It was a bright, windy day, and I liked watching Christopher handle the car. Christopher liked cars—I don't; possibly because of the Work-shop days. The bridge rushed at us, and the sky seemed to descend, and the water was at our feet. Christopher laughed, and looked at me, then looked around him. "This could be so beautiful," he said, "for all of us."

"Yes," I said. Then, "But all I want is for you to live."

"Alone?" he asked.

I did not know what he meant.

"Alone?" he repeated. "Walking over the bodies of the dead? Is that what you want for me, Leo? Is that what you mean when you say you want me to live?" He looked out over the bay again. "Look. I'm a young cat. I've already been under the feet of horses, and I've already been beaten by chains. Well. You want me to keep on going under the feet of horses?"

"No," I said.

He looked at me. We swung off the bridge, and ended up in some fishing town, the name of which I don't remember. We entered the town, very slowly: "If you don't want me to keep going under the feet of horses," Christopher said, now with his dreadful distinctness, his muffled urgency, "and *I* know that you love me and you don't want no blood on my hands—dig—but if you don't want me to keep on going under the feet of horses, then I think you got to agree that we need us some guns. Right?"

"Yes," I said. "I see that." He parked the car. I looked out over the water. There was a terrible weight on my heart—for a moment I was afraid that I was about to collapse again. I watched his black, proud profile. "But we're outnumbered, you know."

He laughed, and turned off the motor. "Shit. So were the early Christians."

That evening, Barbara and Pete put us on the plane to New York. Caleb met us at the plane, with Louise, and one of the children, growing up now, a perfectly respectable, black family—and respectable, mainly, because their name was mine. As we say in America, nothing succeeds like success—so much for the black or white, the related respectability. Christopher and my father and I spent a day together, walking through Harlem. They looked very much like each other, both big, both black, both laughing. Then, I went away to Europe, alone. Then, I came back. I first did the movie, *Big Deal,* not a very good movie, really, and then I did a new play, and so found myself, presently, standing in the wings again, waiting for my cue.

NEW YORK, ISTANBUL, SAN FRANCISCO, *1965–1967*

About The Author

JAMES BALDWIN was born in New York City on August 2, 1924. He was the first of nine children and grew up in Harlem where his father was a minister. For six years, after his graduation from high school in 1942, he found work in a variety of minor jobs. When he was twenty-four he left for Europe and lived there almost ten years. During this time, he wrote his first three books: *GO TELL IT ON THE MOUNTAIN, NOTES OF A NATIVE SON*, and *GIOVANNI'S ROOM*. They firmly established him as one of America's outstanding young writers. In 1957, he returned to New York, where he now lives when he is not on one of his frequent trips abroad.

In 1961, Mr. Baldwin's fourth book, the collection of brilliant essays entitled *NOBODY KNOWS MY NAME*, brought him broad public recognition as well as distinguished critical attention. Perhaps the most meaningful book ever to discuss being Negro in America, *NOBODY KNOWS MY NAME* was the recipient of numerous awards. The following year brought similar acclaim for his best-selling novel, *ANOTHER COUNTRY*. In 1963, the prophetic *THE FIRE NEXT TIME* jolted both the critical world and the book-buying public. Instantly acclaimed, as Granville Hicks said, as "a great document of our times, in literary power as well as in strength of feeling and clarity of insight," the book rushed to the top of all the best-seller lists. Mr. Baldwin's magnificent first collection of short stories, *GOING TO MEET THE MAN*, appeared in 1966.

James Baldwin is also the author of three plays. The first, *THE AMEN CORNER*, was originally produced at Howard University. It had a long and successful run in Los Angeles, later opened on Broadway in 1965; another production toured the world under the auspices of the State Department. A dramatization of *GIOVANNI'S ROOM* was staged by the Actor's Studio workshop. In 1964, his *BLUES FOR MR. CHARLIE* opened off Broadway and was published simultaneously in book form. Like *THE AMEN CORNER*, it has been produced throughout this country and Europe.